Books by Blanche d'Alpuget

Mediator: A Biography of Sir Richard Kirby

Monkeys in the Dark (fiction)

Turtle Beach (fiction)

Robert J. Hawke: A Biography

Winter in Jerusalem (fiction)

Blanche d'Alpuget

White Eye

A Novel

SIMON &

SCHUSTER

New York

London

Toronto

Sydney

Tokyo

Singapore

SIMON & SCHUSTER
Rockefeller Center
1230 Avenue of the Americas
New York, New York 10020

Originally published by Viking Penguin Books Australia
First U.S. Edition 1994

SIMON & SCHUSTER and colophon are registered
trademarks of Simon & Schuster Inc.
Designed by Pei Loi Koay
Manufactured in the United States of America

1 2 3 4 5 6 7 8 9 10

Library of Congress Cataloging in Publication Data
D'Alpuget, Blanche
White eye: a novel/Blanche d'Alpuget—1st U. S. ed.
p.   cm.
1. Man-woman relationships—Australia—Fiction.
2. Murder—Australia—Fiction.
3. Women—Australia—Fiction. I. Title.
PR9619.3.D24W48   1994   94-4037
823—dc20   CIP
ISBN: 0-671- 62005-3

*For Mario and
My Dear Fraters and Sorors,
with Love*

F rom the sky above Mount Kalunga the landscape stretched in an autumn plaid of stubbled fields and sheep pasture. A lake, like a long splash of quicksilver, washed the base of the mountain and continued north for another ten kilometers, its eastern shore dotted with islands of lignum, where waterbirds nested. At this time of day, birds would swim on the lake: little flotillas of pelicans and swans; ducks dabbling in the bulrushes around the foreshores; and flocks of coot, water hen, and darters. But there was no life on the surface of the water this afternoon. Duck-shooting season had opened, and for two days the quietness of mountain and lake had been a rumpus of explosions. Before lunch on Sunday, the shooters had packed up their tents and four-wheel-drives and left, their route marked by a fading trail of dust. The waterfowl, however, were still too nervous to venture out into the eerie stillness.

On the southern foreshore of Lake Kalunga, the land looked green in comparison with the surrounding brown and yellow paddocks. This patch of ground, enclosed by a Cyclone-wire fence, had once been the heart of an old wheat and sheep farm but was now a scientific research station. The original homestead had been the largest structure for forty kilometers; these days, its green iron roof seemed quaint and unimportant beside the station's big new buildings with their telecommunication dishes and antennae. A tar road ran north from the homestead to the laboratory complex, then continued in a straight line past a small house before curving west and ending at the airstrip. Beyond the strip was the wire fence, and beyond that a narrow stretch of no-man's-land from which rose the dark, pine-covered flank of the mountain.

The body of a woman lay in the grass of this common ground. Swarms of flies and other insects had already laid thousands of eggs in the mouth, nostrils, and eyes. In another few hours the eggs would hatch, and the second stage of the cleanup would begin. The corpse was stiff, for the woman had been dead since early morning.

From first light, a female wedgetail eagle had been observing the foreshore of the lake, and the body. As Sunday wore on, she watched the men with guns drive away and followed their vehicles with her eyes for a hundred kilometers.

When the bird was sure there were no men hiding in the bulrushes, she descended. She was hungry. She knew from the great swarm of flies and the tense, cawing ravens that the body was food.

The eagle circled lower. On the Cyclone-wire fence the ravens moaned excitedly; they needed the eagle to cut the belly for them before they could feed.

She relaxed her shoulders, so her wings rose from the horizontal, and let herself slide slowly down the air. It slipped under and over her dark, layered plumage like water slipping over a fish. As she descended, she steadied herself by flexing and easing her shoulder muscles, employing her underwing feathers as brakes. She sculpted her element, now using her long, broad tail, now with subtle movements of the primary feathers on her wing tips, fingering the air into the contour she wanted for landing.

In the heat of the day, when eagles soar highest, Diana Pembridge drove to the camping ground near the lake. All summer she had observed a family of wedgetails hunting over the wheat fields and the mountain, and sometimes seizing ducks from the bulrushes. A huge, dark-phase female eagle had claimed this district as her territory more than twenty years ago, when the Pembridges grew wheat on the flat land south of the highway and ran sheep on ground that was now the Exotic Feral Species and Microbiology Research Centre. During January and February, the female, her young mate, and their newest offspring had sailed together through the tall blue days, but now two had vanished. Which two Diana did not yet know, for on the autumn thermals the wedgetails rose to amazing heights, too far from the ground to identify.

As she looked toward Mount Kalunga, she saw the one remaining eagle coming down. From the way it was flying, in slow spirals, she could tell it was curious about something it could see on the ground on the other side of the airfield, but from where she was standing she could not work out if the eagle would alight outside or inside the Cyclone-wire fence. Beyond the fence, near the base of the mountain, was the land where Diana exercised her falcons.

She focused her binoculars on the bird, holding her breath with excitement: it was the wily resident hen eagle, and Diana had never seen it so close. The huge wings measured, she estimated, three meters across.

The eagle hovered lower and lower, her big pale feet extending like airplane wheels. Suddenly there was a shot. The bird jolted, then cartwheeled to the ground.

The road between the shore of the lake and the Cyclone-wire fence ran due west for half a kilometer, then petered out on no-man's-land. Diana looked for the injured eagle as she drove, but the ground was uneven. When her van rounded the edge of the fence she could see no one, only a bit of bright-red clothing hanging on the wire. Maybe there's a rabbit tied to it, she thought: the lure that tempted the eagle down.

Up ahead, the big bird floundered along the ground, its right wing broken and flopping out, unfoldable. Diana jerked on the handbrake and reached into the back of the van. She grasped a slide-action rifle and her fowling net.

As soon as the eagle saw her, it made a desperate effort to fly, jumping away on its big, black-feathered legs, left wing pumping, right wing trailing over the grass. Diana dropped the rifle and sprinted after it.

She netted it on her first try, only to realize she was a fool to have forgotten her gloves; as she pulled the net tight, tipping the eagle onto its side, the bird's taloned feet thrashed free. It was like a panicking horse. She grabbed at the legs and, with her face averted, held on, her arms jerking in their sockets from the eagle's kicks. It curved its body up and, through the net, struck her leg with its beak—but suddenly the fight went out of it and it collapsed in a heap of loose feathers. Diana held tightly to its legs, then turned to look at what she had caught.

The eagle was lying on its back, glaring at her from beneath pale, almost white, eyebrows. For a moment she was bewitched by the power of this mysterious, other life, then a movement at the edge of the tree line caught her attention.

She squinted at the spot. The figure stepped forward a pace so she could see him, then vanished again among the Aleppo pines.

"Morrie!" she yelled.

There was no answer and no movement from the trees. Had he forgotten how to speak?

"Why did you shoot the eagle?" she shouted. Her words fell into the silence of the afternoon.

The eagle kicked, jerking her attention back to her task.

One-handed, she unbuckled the belt of her jeans and dragged it through the loops. She folded the eagle's broken wing flat against its side. The bird was lying still again, and she was able to slide the belt around its body and wings and secure them. With both hands around its legs, she lugged the bird, upside down, to her van. She needed to drive to the vet's—an hour away, in town—before the eagle had a stress fit.

Instead of seats, the van had poles in the back for birds to perch on, but they were all too small for the wedgetail's feet. With her pocketknife Diana cut a strip off an old blanket and wrapped it securely around the largest pole. When, wearing gloves this time, she picked up the eagle and stood it on the perch, its massive feet gripped with ease. With eyes bright as suns, it stared past her as if she were invisible, fixing its attention on something far in the distance. It was still terrified—Diana knew from the way it flattened its feathers—but she was almost certain it had no injuries apart from the broken wing. She pulled the black curtains that encircled the rear section of the van and quietly closed the door. In the dark, the eagle would probably go to sleep.

As she walked around to the driver's seat she glanced toward the mountain.

He was back again.

He had moved farther forward and was standing near the gray fence post that had once marked the western boundary of the Pembridges' property. Morrie looked as sinewy as dried meat, his only clothing a string tied around his waist, with a bit of rag hiding his genitals. A rifle rested across his shoulder. Diana turned to see what he was pointing at, over near the fence, but there was only the piece of red cloth she had glimpsed earlier.

She looked back at him, her hands raised in inquiry. He gave an emphatic, almost impatient, jerk of his chin, then motioned for her to follow him.

Diana did not try to get too close but let him walk past her, and when he was about two meters in front, she fell in behind his easy loose-kneed stride. The land closer to the fence dipped and rose from the erosion of water running off the mountain, but when Diana saw the cloud of flies, she knew what was there.

The body lay on its side in the creekbed, facing the fence, hands tied behind its back, bare buttocks a pale blue-gray, the legs a slightly darker color from suntan. Diana's heart jumped: it was Carolyn Williams. Carolyn had unhinged her jaw, screaming at whatever had been done to her.

Diana flinched away. "Morrie . . .?"

"I never kill anyone! They tell lies. They shut me up wrong." He was quivering with agitation. "Last night. Lights comin' here. Then, goin' again. This mornin', early, it was there."

Diana interjected, "For God's sake! She was shouting for help! When you heard her, why didn't you—"

He shook his head. "No noise. She make no noise."

His mind had lost the power to dissemble, she realized, leaving his face a mirror of his thoughts.

"The police will have to question you."

"No! No!" he wailed. "No policemen!"

Diana took a step back to the corpse. Now that the first shock had worn off, she realized she was seeing details she had missed before: a mole on Carolyn's back she remembered from childhood; brown roots showing through her scarlet-tinted hair; the scuff marks of a row of toes inside a gold sandal. Again and again her glance was drawn to the mouth, silently screaming out flies. One for every time I wished you dead, she suddenly thought. In the next moment she realized she must be very careful of everything she said and did from now on.

"Morrie, you must . . ."

But when she turned to look at him he had vanished again. She squinted at the trees and saw him standing between two pines; he was invisible unless you knew he was there.

She ran back to her van and climbed into the cabin, where a faint alkaline stench of bird mutings was ever present.

With the lake behind her, the road ran south, still parallel with the fence, past an outlying house, the laboratory complex, and the administrative and residential buildings of the research facility. It had been a private road when this land belonged to the Pembridges, but now it was public, like the paddock on its other side, which was used as a campsite by duck shooters. As she drove past the camp she noted the forty-four-gallon drums brimming with rubbish and the crates of empty bottles and cans in unstable towers. There were piles of duck feathers around spots where plucking machines had been set up. Just twenty minutes ago she had been walking around here, checking that fires were properly smothered, picking up bits and pieces—more cans, a dirty sock, a digital watch, a condom. She'd found a stick, carried the thing to the garbage, and flipped it in, feeling a twinge of loneliness.

The memory of the condom made her brake sharply. There had been an ornamental pink hair comb nearby, she recalled, the sort of junk Carolyn loved. Diana had thrown the comb into the garbage too. As the van slowed, she realized she had been driving at ninety kilometers an hour along the rutted dirt road.

Had Carolyn been shot? Or was she stabbed?

She could not remember seeing any blood.

Maybe it wasn't murder. Maybe she committed suicide. The moment this idea was out of her head, Diana knew it was ridiculous. *Carolyn's hands were tied behind her back, as if she had been a prisoner.*

She was already passing the lab complex where Carolyn used to work. BIOHAZARD signs were attached to the doors of its low, white buildings and fixed to the Cyclone wire every hundred meters. The signs had red broken circles with skull-and-crossbones painted above them.

Up ahead was the T-junction where the unpaved road to the lake met the highway. She could turn right, drive to the main gates of the research facility, and report to one of the guards that Carolyn Williams's corpse was lying over near the mountain. Or she could turn left and drive straight to the vet in Kalunga—and have time to think of an explanation about how and where she had found the eagle and who might have shot it. She stopped as a truck thundered toward her. When it had passed, she idled for a while, then shoved the van into gear and turned left, following the truck into town.

Chapter **Two**

Diana thought that Jason Nichols might be catching up on some sleep after having spent much of the weekend attending to injured birds and the neglected animals from a scruffy little circus on the outskirts of town. She was relieved to see, when she pulled up at his clinic, that the front door was ajar.

The eagle lashed at her—first with its beak, catching her on the face, then with its foot—when she tried to lift it off its perch, so in the end she threw the torn blanket over its head and dragged it out of the van. As she barged into the vet's clinic she almost trod on his receptionist and another woman, both huddled over a spread of tarot cards. Jason was looking on, bemused.

"Go straight through," he said, and after a glance of apology to the women, who stared at Diana and her extraordinary bundle, he followed her into the examining room.

"It's a wedgie," Diana said. "She's been shot. She needs a general anesthetic while we X-ray the wing, then something for pain when she comes to."

"Okay, boss."

There seemed to be nothing damaged except a couple of tail feathers and the wing, but it was too soon to be sure. While the eagle was still unconscious, Diana braced both wings flat to its sides with thin leather thongs and Jason injected the bird with a painkiller. They carried her out to the laundry, where he had a big cardboard box in which his computer had been delivered. Diana held the eagle upright until she regained consciousness and could stand on her own. As soon as the bird woke, however, she showed signs of distress again. She twirled her head around and flared her long, blade-shaped hackles until they stood out from her neck.

"Turn off the washing machine," Diana whispered.

When the noise stopped, the eagle relaxed, and they tiptoed out.

"Let me put some cream on that lovely cheek of yours to prevent its bruising," Jason said. He gave his mild, shy grin.

"It's my leg that really hurts." Her thigh was hot where the wedge-tail had struck her when she captured it.

"Where did you find the eagle?" he asked suddenly.

"On the flying ground." The instant she spoke, she felt color rise from her neck to her hair roots. She turned to hide her face, coughing. Jason gave her back a tentative pat.

"I hope you're not getting the bug I had," he said. "Those new flus are killers."

When she stopped gasping, her cheeks felt even redder, and there were tears in her eyes.

"You look exhausted," he added. "What a weekend!"

He walked with her back through the waiting room, where she paused to apologize to the receptionist and her friend, a small, sharp-faced woman whom Diana had seen driving around in a Land Cruiser. "Did those duck-killing drongos shoot the eagle?" the woman wanted to know.

"Not sure," Diana muttered.

The receptionist said huffily, "I don't imagine it was one of your animal liberationist friends."

Back in the van, Diana rested her head on the steering wheel. In her mind she was on the veranda of the old homestead with her mother, welcoming their guests to the weekend of duck shooting in 1973. Louise and Jack Williams had driven over from their property for the Friday night barbecue. Beautiful Louise. "Diana's very tall for twelve, but so quiet," she said. "Carolyn, the little wretch, thinks of nothing but boys!" Someone standing nearby quipped, "Like mother, like daughter." Everyone laughed, even small, dour, wealthy Mr. Williams. Joan Pembridge smiled gently.

Diana started the engine and five minutes later was back at her house in Fig Tree Gully Road.

Grace Larnach bent and straightened slowly as she tidied the wreckage left by the anti-shooting campaigners who had slept on the floor downstairs that weekend. Downstairs was Grace's part of the house, set up as an art gallery. She ran it with occasional help from Diana; when Diana was away, Grace looked after the birds and the animal hospital in the back garden.

Diana kissed her on both cheeks and went through to the kitchen to make tea. When she returned with the pot and two mugs, she said, "Any phone calls?"

Grace took a long slurp. "I wrote 'em down."

Diana went to the desk and looked at the list: most of them were radio stations wanting interviews about the anti-shooting campaign.

Grace watched her curiously. "You expecting someone particular to ring?"

Diana shrugged. "The big wedgie was shot, down near the lake. I took it straight in to Jason, so I haven't had a proper look round yet. I better get going." She left her tea steaming on the desk.

There were three hours of daylight left, she calculated, enough to drive to the flying ground, check the corpse again, and call the security guards from the research facility. As she drove, she tried to remember details of the body, but her mind was stuck on Carolyn's unhinged mouth. She must have been yelling loud enough to burst her lungs. *Why did nobody hear her?* In the stillness of night, someone must have heard her shouting.

Diana looked across the wide fields of burned-off wheat stubble beside the highway. If you knew this country well, you knew where all the houses were, tucked away behind trees—and there were hectares upon hectares of uninhabited land where a woman could scream her head off without being heard.

She drove past the campsite again and along the marshy foreshore of the lake. When she rounded the curve she saw that Morrie was waiting for her. He was now wearing blue jeans and an unbuttoned shirt: clothes she had left for him by the fence post last Christmas. The shirt still had folds in it from its box. Diana remembered how Louise Williams had shocked everyone at that long ago barbecue by ruffling his dark curls. "He's a sweetie, that rouseabout of yours," she had said to Diana's father, who answered in a jocular tone, "Not too sweet when he's got a skinful."

Diana jumped down from the van and once more allowed Morrie

to lead with his silent, thin-legged stride, making for the place where the body had been.

It was still there. The hands, tied at the back, were contorted like a falcon's feet when it seizes prey. Diana wondered, Where's her ring? Carolyn had worn a gold ring on her middle finger. One day in the street a few years ago, when a bearded man—someone from the research facility—had walked past, Carolyn leered at him, rubbing the ring on her middle finger. "Lost it up his bum once," she said. He hurried on, head down, while Carolyn pealed with laughter.

Diana turned to Morrie. "Did you see a gold ring?"

He shook his head. "Look." He pointed to the fence. About fifty meters from where they were standing, there was a gate. Diana followed him to it. In very wet years this stretch of ground, known as Top Paddock in the old days, had a stream running through it, although mostly the watercourse was dry. But gilgais flourished, making it a good sheep paddock. When they reached the gate, Morrie pointed at a gilgai. Diana thought she could just make out in the dry ground beside it the outline of a tire. The dark-green stems of grass were damaged. "Drive along here." He began to walk backward from the gate toward the corpse, pointing all the time at the ground, murmuring, "Look, look: fox. And little fox. You see: lotsa feet." Bending over, he touched the ground, showing the marks left by foxes. "I throw stones. Make them go." Foxes would have been pleased to feed on the body, Diana knew. Morrie halted, pointing urgently at the grass. "Look. Shoe. You see shoe. Nother shoe. Two people. You look: two walk." Diana shook her head in frustration. He ran to one of Carolyn's gold sandals, picked it up, and placed it over a footprint he could discern.

"Don't touch things!" Diana said. She glanced across her shoulder, at the house on the ridge, then pulled her shirt out of her jeans and wiped Carolyn's sandal where Morrie had held it. "I'll have to get the police now."

In a moment Morrie had reached the old fence. He hurdled its sagging barbed wire and was gone, up the slope, into the trees.

She stared after him. Can I risk it? she wondered. Can I risk lying about Morrie? It had been this time of day, twenty years ago, when police dogs had found him in the Pembridges' barn. When he was led out, his eyes were white with terror. A detective returned to the homestead that night to say Morrie had confessed. "Seems he was infatuated with Mrs. Williams. Got jealous," the detective said.

Diana looked back at the corpse once more. There were some

long, dark hairs on Carolyn's T-shirt, which she had noticed earlier.
Now, paying attention to their length and texture, she felt the fine
hairs on her arms rise, like the fur on the back of a cat. She picked
off a few; there were still plenty left for the police.

A gray-uniformed guard, weary with boredom, came out of the
gatehouse beside the sign that said EXOTIC FERAL SPECIES AND MICROBI-
OLOGY RESEARCH CENTRE. PRIVATE PROPERTY. TRESPASSERS PROSECUTED.
"Name?" he asked.

"Can I use your telephone?" Diana said.

"Name?" he repeated irritably.

"Diana Pembridge. I need to ring the police. There's been an
accident."

He yawned and jerked his head to indicate she could use the telephone in his box.

C h a p t e r **T h r e e**

Sonja Olfson was one of the civil servants who had survived the privatization mania of the late 1980s, when the government downsized the Exotic Feral Species and Microbiology Research Centre. All scientific staff were now on industrial payrolls, while a handful of government employees—directors of administration, finance, housing, science liaison, security, and personnel (the Gang of Six)—saw to the day-to-day running of the place. Sonja was director of personnel.

When her husband was away, she often spent time in Kalunga with Margaret McLeod, who worked for Jason Nichols, the vet. Sonja had taught Margaret decoupage and was helping with a cuff-link box that Margaret was decorating for Jason's thirty-first birthday. Margaret had been a general science teacher in an inner Sydney school, but after a stress breakdown she moved to the country "to hang loose." In High Street, Kalunga, townsfolk in wide hats nudged elbows against freckled arms when Sonja and Margaret appeared, the one so small, alert, and tailored, the other large and given to wearing alarming colors. Ms. McLeod, people said, also liked a drink. Through Margaret, Sonja had got to know Jason socially.

After Diana had left his clinic on Sunday, Sonja said, "I watch her from my veranda every morning, training those hunting birds. What's she like?"

He grinned and glanced at Margaret, who snorted. "Grazier's daughter. Typical country attitude: if you haven't lived here for three generations, you're a tourist."

"That's a bit harsh, Margie," Jason objected. "I find Kalunga people quite friendly."

"You're the vet!" She turned to Sonja. "You know what they call you directors?"

"What?" Sonja's small, pointy face under its thatch of carrot-colored hair made her look, sometimes, like a fox.

"Cruisers," Margaret said.

Sonja seemed hurt by the gibe. Jason patted her shoulder. "You're missing John, aren't you?"

She nodded. "He's in South Australia. Then he's going to Sydney to give some lectures. . . ." She sighed so deeply, the others stared. John Parker would not be an easy man to be married to, they were thinking, and Sonja was hardly the type to brush aside difficulties. She was often unwell; if somebody sneezed on the other side of town, Sonja caught a cold. Jason and Margaret marveled that she could be Senator Hilary Olfson's sister. "Somebody scrambled the genetic code," Jason once quipped.

Sonja did not live in the staff condominiums at the Research but in a pretty wooden bungalow, raised on pylons, out near the lake. It had its own little oasis of native trees and a guest pavilion. When she arrived home that afternoon, she stood on her veranda, gazing at the silver-blue water, feeling profoundly peaceful. From the back of her house it was only fifty meters to the fence, and beyond it lay the campsite where the duck shooters had cursed and caroused for two nights. Now the guns had stopped, the shooters had left, and the world seemed clean again. Sonja gave a sigh of contentment. A vase full of apple-gum leaves scented her big front room, while from the kitchen came the aroma of vegetable soup simmering in the Crock-Pot. She grew beans, spinach, sorrel, carrots, zucchinis, lettuce, and herbs in her garden. On her roof there were solar panels. "What's the use of whining about environmental degradation?" she would demand. "You have to *do* something."

It was almost sundown. This was the hour when she and John would sit together on the veranda for a drink, while above them the sky turned from the color of washed denim to gold, then orange, and swans honked on the lake. "Oh, my darling, I miss you!" she said aloud, raising her glass of mineral water to the canvas chair where his long legs should have been stretched out toward her.

It was her first marriage but his third, and this fact sometimes overwhelmed Sonja with a sense of injustice. She felt the other wives had stolen something from him, cheating her of what she should have enjoyed.

She was still sitting there, sipping her drink, wondering what he might be doing at this minute in Bangkok—shopping for silk, she hoped—when three white Land Cruisers went tearing along the road toward the airfield. In the second vehicle she recognized Joe Miller, the director of security.

The vehicles went past the airstrip and bumped onto open land, heading for the perimeter fence.

At various points in the fence there were gates big enough for a water tanker, in case of bush fires. The Land Cruisers drove toward a gate that was up to the left and behind a hillock. They disappeared behind the hill, reappearing a few minutes later on the other side of the fence. They lurched from side to side as they crossed the dry watercourse. Sonja went inside and dialed Joe's car phone. From her living room she could see the convoy slowing down.

"Miller," he answered. The Land Cruisers had stopped about twenty meters from the lake.

"What are you doing over there?" she asked.

"Talk to you later, dear."

"Joe, please don't condescend—" He had cut her off.

Sonja fumed. Is it because you can't bear the thought of having a woman as your equal? Is it because I won't agree to your ridiculous security surveys of the staff? She felt breathless with irritation. It was the second time people had been nasty to her that afternoon. First, Diana Pembridge had given her the brush-off when they met in Jason's clinic; now her colleague was being rude. She felt tearful, but tears did not come. Instead, an unbearable restlessness and curiosity about what they were doing over there took hold of her.

Her bicycle was downstairs, on a concrete area underneath the house. The white Land Cruiser that came as a director's perquisite was parked there too, but Sonja tried to use it as little as possible, biking to and from the administration building, except on rainy days. It would be impossible, she realized, to pedal through the long, dry grass to the spot where they were gathered, over near the mountain; she decided to drive.

When Joe Miller saw the small, determined figure of Sonja Olfson coming toward them, waving to get his attention, he hurried to cut her off. The fewer people on the site, the better for the investigation.

He put a confidential, fatherly arm around her shoulders. "Did you see or hear anything unusual out here last night?" he asked.

She shook her head. "You're going to be nice to me now, are you?" she answered reproachfully.

"I'm always nice to you." He began walking her away from the spot where his young officers, a constable from the Kalunga police, and Diana Pembridge were gathered. Then he told her.

Sonja looked at him blankly. "Oh, my God! And John's away!" she blurted, and stared back toward the house, perched on its own, a kilometer from the nearest habitation. She clapped a hand over her mouth, remembering something.

"You know what Carolyn told me?" she asked in a small voice. "I gave her a lift into town last night. She said she was going for a drink at the Arms *to check out the duck-shooting jocks*." Her little pointed face turned pale. "I think I'm going to . . ."

Joe waited, eyes averted, until the heaving noises stopped. Then he led her back to her Land Cruiser and sent one of the young blokes to sit with her while he returned to the group around the corpse.

What Sonja had just told him was exactly what he would have guessed was the background to Carolyn's death. He tried to re-member the expression she used if anyone asked, "How're you go-ing, Cas?" She'd toss her scarlet hair and answer, "Whoa!" then add something like: "I put human cells into a pig brain this morning." She wanted you to agree that life was a game and you could do what you liked. All out of whack, poor kid. He walked thoughtfully around the site; there was nothing he could explain yet, except perhaps that the clothes were too obviously strewn wildly about.

The light was fading, and there was no point searching any longer for a murder weapon. The constable from the Kalunga police had spoken by radio to Homicide in Sydney. They agreed it was best to get the body into a morgue as soon as possible.

Two of the guards laid a stretcher on the ground.

One of them had been taking photographs, the other, under Joe's direction, making drawings. "Seen enough, boss?" he asked. Joe de-tected a faint sneer.

"Load her up," he said. He dragged Carolyn's red cotton pullover from the fence.

"Goodbye, darling." The guard smirked, his small eyes flicking at Joe.

. . .

In her study that evening, Diana Pembridge sat staring at the hairs she had taken from Carolyn's T-shirt, wondering if she was mistaken, if they were ordinary hairs, from a human.

Now that the horror of seeing the corpse had subsided, an aftershock of weariness gripped her, and she wanted desperately to go to bed. She had been at her desk for an hour already, puzzling about how to get into the Research. Not just inside its fence—that was easy; she could do that with wire cutters—but inside the animal houses. The security system had alarms and cameras, and armed guards patrolled the lab complex.

On the screen in front of her she had keyed in: "Dear Senator Olfson, I have had no acknowledgment that you have received my letter of 28 January. In it I applied to be appointed for 1993/4 to the Ethics Committee of the Exotic Feral Species and Microbiology Research Centre, Kalunga, New South Wales. Please let me know as soon as possible if my application did not reach your office and I will send a duplicate, plus copies of the names and addresses of my references." She read through what she had written, thinking ruefully that if she had been cunning she would have sucked up to people at the Research, as her cousin, Kerry Larnach, had done, and would not now be trying to wheedle her way inside. She printed the letter and signed it, then dialed the senator's fax. As the paper slid through, Diana glanced at the hairs again. They were laid out on the tissue in which she had wrapped them for safekeeping. Each was about ten centimeters long and very dark, almost black. She fingered her scalp and then jerked out a hair. Beside the others, the texture of hers was different, even to the naked eye.

At six o'clock next morning, the Kalunga Shire garbage men drove to the campsite by the lake, collected the contents of the forty-four-gallon drums, and took them to the industrial incinerator at the Research, where all Kalunga's garbage was burned.

Diana remembered the condom and the hair comb later that morning while she was being interviewed by the two Homicide detectives—one jokey, one serious—who had arrived from Sydney on Kalair's first flight.

"And you put them in the garbage?" the jokey one said. "I'm going to charge you with public mischief. Do you know what it's like, sorting through three-day-old garbage?"

They were seated in a cream-painted room in the Kalunga police station; telephones kept ringing, and men and women in white overalls came and went.

The serious one telephoned the Research to ask that the incinerator not be turned on, but he put down the receiver shaking his head.

"See what you've done?" the smart aleck said. He found Diana very attractive. Her skin was the color of fine sand when a wave sweeps back, and her blood came and went beneath it like light playing through a cloud. Emotional, he decided, despite the drop-dead gray eyes. Her cheeks turned into a sunset when she spoke about the deceased coming to see her the week before. Was Miss Pembridge Dr. Williams's dyke friend? he wondered. From what he had learned already, it seemed that Williams was the sort who liked it every which way, but he could not tell with this girl. She was stately and aloof and tried to give nothing away—but he knew she was lying about how she came to find the corpse. She was also stressed out: people often were after seeing a stiff. "Hey, I'm sorry. Joke? It was a joke," he said.

"But not funny," Diana muttered. She felt feverish with exhaustion. After the autumnal heat of the weekend, a southerly change had come through around midnight, making her windows creak like a ship in a gale. She had been asleep only an hour when the wind woke her, and could not settle down again. She had lain awake listening to it, feeling as if the whole world rocked and she was back in that terrible autumn of 1973, when she and Carolyn became, as it were, blood sisters. She, Kerry, and Carolyn wanted to go onto the lake in the punt, while their fathers and the other men shot from the bulrushes around the foreshore. Her father had called out, "Hey, you kids! Help Carolyn load her gun." Diana and Kerry both used twelve-gauge Winchesters, but Carolyn had a child's gun. She sat looking bored while they were shooting. As soon as they took a break, she asked, "Would you like to see my tits, Kerry?" His blunt, freckled face turned red. "You're a moll," he muttered. She joined her thumb and forefinger and made quick thrusts through the circle with her middle finger. "I bet you'd like that!" She giggled. Kerry grabbed her by the throat, and she started to cry. "Stop fighting!" Diana yelled. Suddenly the guns on the foreshore were silent, and Carolyn's screech sounded across the lake. Above, the sky was a vivid, cloudless blue, and a wedgetail eagle soared through it. The wedgie's watching us, Diana thought.

The beeping of the fax machine jerked her attention back to the present. A page of transmission slid out. After a few seconds the serious detective held up his hand, signaling Diana not to leave yet. Both men stood at the machine, reading and nodding. When transmission stopped, they took the fax and left the room.

From the foyer of the police station Diana could hear the voices of people who had gathered, avid for gossip. Kalunga would talk about this for another twenty years, she knew—as the town still talked about what had happened at the lake in 1973, as if it were only last week that Doug Pembridge and Louise Williams had been murdered. The gossiping outside reminded Diana of her father's funeral, when people who had never set eyes on him drove four hundred kilometers just to stand in the back of the church and stare. She decided to ask to leave by the rear door.

When the detectives returned, she realized there was something in the fax that had changed their attitude toward her. The jokey one went to the kitchenette to make coffee, while the other one came and sat beside her.

"What's in the fax?" she asked.

"I'd like to tell you, but I can't," he said. He cocked an eyebrow at her. "You would not, by any chance, have taken something from the site, would you?"

The hairs on her T-shirt, Diana thought. Surely three hairs can't count. "No."

"You're positive about that?"

"Yes."

An envelope of the photographs the security guards had taken the previous day was on the table. The detective shuffled through the eight-by-ten black-and-white prints, until he found the one he wanted. "I wonder if you would mind looking at this and explaining something to me and Goofy over there. . . ."

It was a photograph of Carolyn from behind. "You said in your statement that when you saw the body the hands were tied and they resembled, you said, raptors' feet. Would you mind, for a couple of non-ornithologists, saying a little more about raptors?"

She almost smiled with relief. "I meant hunting birds." She tensed her fingers into talons.

"Is 'raptor' a veterinary term? Would only specialist people use that word?"

"No."

He became thoughtful. "Does anyone else around here share your interest in rehabilitating these birds?"

"Maybe Jason Nichols, the vet."

"He's a local, like you?"

She shook her head.

W hen the detectives returned to the interview room, they sipped their coffee in silence for a while.

"D'you reckon she knows a lot more?"

"Dunno. But she's taken something from the site. Did you watch her eyes?"

"Yep, Lying about that too."

"Well, we needn't have worried about the condom in the garbage. Poor bitch."

The preliminary postmortem that had come through on the fax reported that ten milliliters of seminal fluid had been found in the deceased's vagina. DNA prints would not be ready for several days. The injuries and method of killing were something else again.

"Bloody animals."

He picked up the fax and read aloud: " 'Death from myocardial infarction, caused by myocardial ischemia, caused by air embolism. Air in the cerebral and coronary vessels. An air embolism from an injection in the cubital fossa vein. . . .' And she knew what was happening, because she struggled like hell to get her hands free, producing the cadaveric spasm."

"What do you reckon?"

"I think we ask the vet where he was on Saturday night. Then we go through the list of everyone in New South Wales and Victoria who applied for a duck-shooting license this year, and we see if any of them are vets or have worked for vets."

When they arrived at Nichols's house, Diana Pembridge's van was parked outside. The receptionist said, "Jason's fixing an eagle. You'll have to wait." They decided to check him out first and question him later. But by noon that day, the Homicide team working at the Research had discovered in Carolyn's flat the letter that had been posted to her a week earlier. And then, in the Monday afternoon post, three more letters turned up, all threatening young women who were employed at the Research.

"It's what I thought when I saw the body yesterday," Joe Miller told his daughter, Susan, on the telephone that evening. Susan was a sergeant in the Surveillance Squad of the Feds. "It had that look of an obsession. Know what I mean?"

"Yuck."

"Two lasses gave notice an hour after opening their mail this afternoon," he continued. "The director of personnel is tearing out her hair. It's not easy to get staff to move to the bush, even during a recession."

He sounded animated. Normally, murder made him quiet. "What's wrong, Dad?" she asked.

"Nothing's wrong, sweetheart. Girl been murdered, that's all. Happens every day."

"C'mon," she said. "You know what I mean." The silence was so lengthy, she thought the line had been cut.

J ohn Parker had just checked into his hotel room when Sonja rang. His flight out of Sydney at nine o'clock that Sunday morning had landed at Bangkok airport at 3:00 P.M. local time, but he had not reached the city until almost five. By this time it was late evening in Australia.

"*What's happened?*" he asked in alarm.

The telephone system at the Research, they suspected, recorded the number of every call, incoming and outgoing, and the time at which it was made; their arrangement was that only in an emergency would she ring him in Thailand, when he was supposedly somewhere else. Sonja had biked to the staff canteen, where there was a pay phone, to ring John. While dialing, she considered the tone to adopt in breaking the news about Carolyn Williams: "My love, I have something horrible . . ." No. "Darling, do you remember Carolyn Williams from the rabbit fertility control program . . ." "Last night, darling, something distressing . . ." That was smoother. It sounded more serene. John once said, "The loveliest quality in a female is *serenity.*" They were in a restaurant in Sydney, where fast-talking women made calls on their mobiles. "Hens trying to be roosters," he remarked.

"What's distressing?" he demanded.

"While you were on the train to Sydney last night, Carolyn Williams, the girl from the rabbit fertility control program, was murdered."

He felt a bolt of adrenaline.

"I was here on my own," she added in a plaintive voice.

"Good God! Who did it?"

"They don't know. But I'm concerned about . . ."

"Yes. Of course."

"Unless they catch the person quickly, this place will be turned inside out."

He was silent.

"Considering that, do you think you should go ahead with the new contract? Would it be better to wait until things settle down?" she said.

Parker plunged his fingers into his long, thick hair. It had been chestnut-colored when he was young. Now it was streaked with gray. "Damn it! Silly bitch."

"*John.*"

"She *was* a silly bitch. Wiggling her arse at everyone."

"I thought you liked her."

"I didn't like her. I didn't dislike her." It never failed to irritate him that his wife judged the world and everything in it according to whether it pleased her or not. "Well—horrible news, but thanks for tracking me down and telling me," he said. "This is bad publicity for the Research. I'll tell the people here about it and . . ." He was distracted, suddenly, by the memory of Carolyn asking him one night, "Would you like to beat me?"

"I can't hear you!" Sonja yelled.

"We'll come to a decision," he mumbled.

After they had said goodbye, he stood at the window of his fifth-floor room, looking down into Rama IV Boulevard, feeling agitated but blank. The air outside was gray with exhaust gases from the motorcars and samlors that jammed the roadway, while along the pavements flowed a river of small, neat people. Bangkok was getting more overcrowded, like everywhere else. Except for the food and Patpong, he thought the whole place should be incinerated. "Go home!" he shouted at the people. "Home to your burrows!"

At five-fifteen, a car arrived to take him to the Siam Enterprises estate, north of the capital, where on Monday morning he would choose a new chimpanzee.

Siam Enterprises was the largest breeder of laboratory animals in Asia. It already dominated the fast-growing East and Southeast Asian scientific market and was moving to challenge the huge American firm Charles River with a promotional campaign on the West Coast of the United States. Siam was producing hundreds of thousands of mice, rabbits, dogs, and cats each year, and scores of modified species, but quality control was not yet as high as it should be. After a male chimpanzee arrived at the Research with his canine teeth still in, Parker had insisted on inspecting animals before they were dispatched to him—without clearance, to circumvent the nine-month quarantine period in Australia. He did not enjoy breaking the law. Nor did he enjoy paying the exorbitant sums that Kerry Larnach required to fly a chimp from Karatha to Kalunga. "But as they say in Boston, bad laws must be broken," he liked to say. And anyway, he and his team were on the side of the chimps. The couple of dozen they had to sacrifice would help save the whole species.

As a precaution, however, he did not reveal to people from other labs at the Research how often he went to Thailand, and he never mentioned the breeding farm.

"If the worst comes to the worst and they discover we're working on chimps," he told Sonja, "your sister will do everything she can to hush it up. Not to save me. Not to save you. But because no politician can tolerate a family scandal." Sonja's sister, whom political cartoonists sometimes depicted as a rottweiler wearing a wig, was the minister for science, technology, and the environment.

The managing director of Siam Enterprises had sent his own Mercedes and his after-hours chauffeur to drive Parker to the breeding farm in Saraburi that evening. The after-hours chauffeur was a different species from the day-shift driver, who twittered while he steered and embarrassed Parker with flattery and questions, even remarking on his passenger's physical appearance. "Tall man!" he would say. "So taaall." Parker was six feet three and carried himself high. He had remarkable cornflower-blue eyes and in youth had been considered an Apollo, but these days there was something dried out about him, an air of pessimism, as if from years of fruitless struggle. His eyes, their color fading now that he was approaching fifty, yearned out to other people, only to withdraw hurriedly when they met an answering glance.

It amused him that these days Otto Grossmann sent him to Saraburi in the Mercedes and insisted that he stay at Siam's expense in Bangkok in the Dusit Thani or some other opulent hotel. In earlier years, Grossmann had been happy for him to stay in the Golden Elephants Guesthouse in Banglampoo, where the tariff was twelve dollars a night, including breakfast. He could have slept on the pavement, for all Grossmann cared.

Now there was always someone to welcome him at the airport, flowers in his room, a car at his disposal, and whatever he required in the way of physical relief. At first he regarded these luxuries with distrust. He accepted them, he told himself, so as not to offend his employer-host, and his treatment of the prostitutes Grossmann sent to his hotel—"Just a hand job, thank you"—was scrupulous. But one day a girl arrived who was so frightened, ugly, and stupid, he suddenly wanted her with a pigsty lust. It was a revelation, this predator within. A revelation. And a liberation. "My testicles seem to be connected to my frontal lobes," he told Grossmann, who said, "Good. A man needs to relax." In Thailand, Parker found himself distracted by thoughts he had not known it was possible for someone of his upbringing and education to have. To be a complete human, he told himself, one must be a complete animal first.

One had to learn to think like the animals. That's all they were—animals escaped from the prison of Nature, now turning Nature upside down. Parker had brooded long on the chaos of the world, the nightmare of history, and the looming cataclysm of ecological collapse. There was no future, he realized. Day by day his mind roamed the wasteland. By now he was working on a disease that, in twelve hours in 1985, had killed sixty apes and monkeys at Siam Enterprises. Next day, two keepers and a vet died, and in the evening, the company's senior molecular biologist, driving back to Bangkok from Saraburi, ran his car into a klong and drowned. The deaths of neither the humans nor the primates were reported in the press, nor did news of the disaster escape into the scientific world. Had it done so, the company would have been ruined. Parker himself knew nothing of what had really happened when, late one night in 1985, he was offered, via telephone, thirty thousand dollars if he would come immediately to Thailand on a confidential basis to advise on an outbreak of influenza among laboratory apes. Grossmann said later they had chosen him because he had worked at the Center for Disease Control in Atlanta before going to Australia. "We knew you were familiar with unusual bugs." Parker was stunned. "We do our research," Grossmann added.

On the drive north on Sunday evening, Parker thought about Carolyn Williams and wished he had been able to ask Sonja for more details: who found the body, for example, and when? But his wife had a million antennae. Sometimes the mad idea occurred to him that she had hidden a tracking device in the heel of his shoe and could discover his whereabouts anytime she liked. He stared through the black-glass windows that made the vivid green world outside turn gray, and felt enveloped by a sense of ease. He would no longer have to suffer Carolyn's smirks in the canteen at lunchtime. I've got the last laugh, he thought—on her and all the other bitches. He gave a broad grin. I've got the last laugh on Grossmann too.

He liked thinking things through in an orderly way, and he now turned his mind to the problem Sonja had raised. A murder investigation could mean police everywhere at the Research. They might want to examine his high-containment laboratory, U-1. How could Lucy, the chimp in U-1, be concealed?

He imagined the situation, step by step. U-1 could not be entered without prior arrangement with the staff. That would give time to remove Lucy. They could anesthetize her, put her in the Land Cruiser, and drive around until the police had gone. But how to explain the large cages in the chimp room? We'll say they're for foxes, he decided.

The second problem he foresaw was that the police would mount observation on people coming and going at the Research. At the front gate there were security guards. But the airstrip might be put under surveillance too. In that case the police would see Kerry flying in the new chimp. That is, they would see *something* being delivered at night to U-1. Kerry would have to land the chimp at the Kalunga airfield, and a couple of the boys would collect it in Sonja's Land Cruiser. There would be no difficulty in taking it past the guards at the front gate if cardboard was stuck over the crate to make it look like boxes of wine. Even if the guards looked inside the Land Cruiser, which they never did, they would see nothing unusual. Then he remembered the stench of a chimp that has been crated up for five days, and how fearful and horror-struck they became—like humans—when they got feces on their skin. The boys will have to pull up somewhere, he thought, sluice out its crate, and shampoo it. In the forty kilometers of empty road from Kalunga to the Research there were dozens of spots where they could stop to give the animal a wash. Twenty liters of water would be plenty.

He gave a sigh of pleasure. Now that he had got into the habit of clandestine activities, he found he was never at a loss for inventive solutions, and it struck him as tragic that for so many years he had believed himself to be a second-rater, one of those men who started with great promise—he was considered a budding genius at grammar school—but never lived up to early expectations. He had been in the wrong society, he knew. That English lower-middle-class restraint had been a straitjacket not only on his emotions but on his intellect and ambition. "Nothing in excess" was the dreary motto of his dreary childhood, crowded with a nag of women: widowed mother, pious maiden aunts. A tyrant invented the taboo on excess. Excess was all! From excess came vision. From excess he had learned to soar! Up there, he could look down upon the battered planet and understand it. But that sort of vision one could reach only by a passage through the extreme.

Outside, night had fallen. The traffic was lighter than usual, and after another few minutes the car turned off the northern highway onto the leafy country road that led to the Siam breeding station. They swept under the arch of the gate, with its logo of an orchid, passed the animal houses, and drew up on the gravel outside the reception building. Behind it there was an artificial island made by a moat and an electric fence around an area of jungle. The chauffeur had telephoned from the car to announce Parker's imminent arrival, and Grossmann was waiting to greet him. He advanced, arms outstretched, as Parker unfolded and straightened himself from the back of the car.

Otto Grossmann was a glossy, physically compact man who always looked triumphant. He was freshly showered and cologned. His cream safari suit was made from silk.

"John! Good to see you!" he cried. He was almost a head shorter than his visitor. Taking Parker by the arm, he led him inside. "We've got some other people here this evening." He was pushing his guest toward a bedroom. "I need you to explain White Eye to them."

Parker stopped so abruptly, Grossmann collided with him.

"To explain the work you are doing on a vaccine against it," Grossmann said. "And the other business."

Parker said, "Are they scientists?"

Grossmann was never quite sure when Parker was making a joke or when he was just being naive. "*Scientists?*" He laughed. "They're financiers."

They entered a bedroom full of bright-colored cotton cushions. Grossmann closed the door and jerked Parker's arm, making him bend down to hear. "These men want to put up capital for my new biotech company. Trouble is they don't understand biotechnology. They've read about genetic engineering, but they don't know what it is or how it's done. They don't know what gene shears are. They don't know we can inhibit a bit here and add a bit there and . . . voilà! You see the problem I have? They'll lose face if they have to ask me questions. But if *you* tell them . . ."

"What *will* I tell them?" Parker said.

"You say what you have said to me many times: that with a vaccine against White Eye, Siam Enterprises is poised to become the most successful breeding house *in the world*. You won't, of course, tell them that White Eye is recombinant. How did you describe it to me that day? 'A Legionella bacterium to which genetic material from gonorrhea has been added so that it attacks the mucous membranes. In addition it has the deregulated gene for botulism poison. These additions make it highly infectious plus extremely virulent.' One of the most dangerous organisms you'd ever seen, you said." Grossmann chuckled at the memory of how excited Parker was with his discovery. "I suppose you could tell them how dangerous it is," he added.

A thin smile moved across Parker's mouth. "Should I point out that Siam's success will depend upon the primates in other breeding houses—unvaccinated, poor things—somehow contracting White Eye?"

"John! John! Your English sense of humor!" Grossmann's drum-tight belly strained the buttons of his fine silk jacket. When his laughter was over, he said, "These are grownups. They don't need you to tell them how to do pee-pee."

Parker was pleased to find himself outraged by the idea of industrial sabotage. If my sense of wrongdoing were dead, how would I be so excited by what I am involved in now? he asked himself. In order to break the moral code, one had first to know it, and without that scandalized Methodist inside his brain, Parker knew he would not have half the thrill he did in recognizing that Otto Grossmann was an evil man.

His guests that night were a Thai general, a casino operator from Hong Kong, a man from Indonesia whom Grossmann introduced as being "in cement," and two men from Bangkok, whose interests were left unspecified. One of them, Parker noticed, was wearing a gun. He took his cue. English wit and English high-mindedness inspired him. That great scientific demand *Simplify!* was at his beck and call. By the time the mangoes and sticky rice were served, the men around the table felt they could stride into a laboratory as confidently as they would stride into a boardroom or a bordello.

Next morning, Parker woke to soft, tropical air and cries of the jungle coming from beyond the bamboo blind on his window. Chimpanzees on the artificial island were hooting and barking in trees just ten meters behind the guesthouse. He got up and looked out onto a lawn bordered by a vermilion cascade of bougainvillea. Smaller primates, lanky-armed monkeys and gibbons, were loping on the buffalo grass. The noise level was appalling, for added to the boisterousness of the apes, at first light thousands of invisible creatures applauded the appearance of the sun with shrill, buzzing, whirring, screeching voices. The trees drummed and roared as if a Lilliputian football crowd were hidden in the branches.

Parker whistled a few bars of "The Battle Hymn of the Republic" as he went outside.

All the keepers wore khaki uniforms nipped in at the ankles with tightly laced army boots, to protect them against leeches. The head keeper, a man in his sixties who used to train elephants, had the logo of a white orchid embroidered on his shirt. He listened impassively to Parker's instructions as to the type of chimp required: a sexually intact male with a high tolerance for close confinement, familiar with and friendly toward Lucy, the female who had already been in U-1 for three months. Lucy was rather passive, but with estrogen injections she would become more assertive, so it would be helpful if her new boyfriend was a former sex partner, even better if he had already sired offspring on her. Sometimes, in confinement, the males wimped out.

The head keeper returned with two chimps on leashes and went off to fetch one more from the island. The farm had two main categories of primates: caged and free, but even the caged chimps were allowed to spend some months each year roaming wild on the island. All three animals the keeper brought to Parker had spent their first years of life in cages and remained both tame and hardy for close confinement. They squatted on the floor beside their tethers and observed Parker like little old men, but after a few moments their concentration lapsed and they fell to fingering their hair and staring into space. Parker tested their lungs, blood pressure, hearing, sight, muscle reflexes, ejaculatory power, and playfulness. Japanese researchers had developed a good standard test for playfulness in chimps. Most laboratories preferred playful animals, for they recovered more quickly after a general anesthetic and their morale when in close captivity, which was how his animal would be living for the rest of its life, remained higher than in specimens of more phlegmatic temperament.

By late morning Parker had found the chimp he liked, an exuberant young adult called Sailor, Lucy's first cousin, who, according to the head keeper, had copulated with her at every opportunity when she still lived at the farm. Sailor had a long, droll face and a lively eye. He sat quietly, his gaze reaching out toward Parker as if he were yearning for something he couldn't touch. He made soft, friendly noises while he was being examined, yelling only once. Parker suspected that as he got older, Sailor would become unmanageable unless castrated, but if things went well he would be sacrificed before then. "Knock his teeth out, will you?" he said. The keeper gave a slight bow.

"And fix his noise box too."

The buildings at the breeding farm were long and low, like those at the Research, but only half were fully enclosed and air-conditioned. These were either for temperate-climate animals or they were for the acclimatization of tropical species that would be living in air-conditioned labs. The fifty chimpanzees and ten gibbons that had died in the epidemic of 1985 had been in an acclimitization house for the night. Had they been in one of the other buildings, there would have been a worse disaster—maybe a national disaster, maybe an international disaster. Parker had long since stopped wondering about what might have been. By the time he arrived with Grossmann that dark night when he first came to the breeding farm, the building with the dead primates had already been isolated and the air-conditioning system throughout the complex shut down. In the weeks that followed, the keepers dismantled and sterilized every air-conditioner. They scalded the water tanks and rinsed them out with strong disinfectant. Parker never asked what happened to the bodies of the people who died. The apes, after he had taken tissue samples, were cooked in an industrial autoclave that Grossmann had flown in from Germany. They were buried in sealed drums.

But these precautions were not necessary, as Parker now knew. White Eye was phenomenally virulent, but it died within hours of its host's death. As the tissues of the infected animal became saturated with toxin from millions of rapidly reproducing bacteria, the White Eye bacteria themselves began to disintegrate in their own poisonous soup. He had watched two cigar-shaped creatures on a slide swim toward each other, hesitate, back off, and fall to pieces. There, illuminated by the light and mirrors of a microscope, he had witnessed the death of a life form more vigorous and reproductive than any other on earth. He had had to wipe the tears of a strange excitement from his eyes.

As he left the primate house, a mud-spattered four-wheel-drive pulled up outside the reception building.

Grossmann was waiting on the veranda to greet the visitor, his weight shifting from foot to foot until the passenger in the muddy vehicle jumped down, then he rushed to embrace him. The young man was dressed in paratrooper's camouflage gear, and he had dark, wind-ruffled hair, like the hair on a statue. Parker could only see him from behind, but he felt intimidated. Two small, hair-covered arms encircled the man's neck and clung with tiny pinkish hands to his thick, dark hair. The driver of the vehicle, a Thai, began unloading aluminum cases, a tripod, and other bags.

Grossmann introduced the newcomer: "Michael Romanus—Dr. Parker."

He was a Latin, slightly above average height, with a bar of black brows across his forehead and a straight Mediterranean nose. "G'day," he said. The accent was Australian.

Parker wanted to cut and run, but before he had a chance to do more than mumble "Howdoyoudo?" a fracas broke out.

Grossmann's after-hours chauffeur had come slip-slopping on plastic sandals around the side of the house and looked on as the bags were being unloaded. Grossmann gestured to him to lend a hand, but when he did so, Romanus spun away from Parker and grabbed the case. "Let go of that!" he said vehemently.

The chauffeur replied, "Fuck you," and dropped it.

"Hey!" Grossmann yelled. He said something in Thai, and the chauffeur sloped away, giving a toss of his shoulder-length hair. "He's hot-tempered," Grossmann said. Turning to Michael Romanus, he added, "You young men!"

The photographer looked sullen and made kissing noises to the baby orangutan hanging on his neck.

They went inside. The orangutan continued to cling to Romanus, and Grossmann tried to coax it to come to him, all the while questioning his visitor about where and how he had acquired it. Parker's agitation was growing. He found Romanus's presence as unsettling as Grossmann found it energizing, and was reminded of a horrible experience from his childhood, when his uncle had taken him to a stud form to watch a stallion service a mare. His uncle and the other men were excited by the gleaming, quivering stallion, the way Grossmann was now, but Parker had wanted to flee.

He had the weird feeling that he recognized Romanus.

Grossmann said suddenly, "John, Michael is like a son to me. Siam is financing him and another photographer to take pictures of Thailand's national parks. It's good for them, it's good advertising for us, and it's good for the country. Eh, Mike?"

"Sure," Romanus said, as if he couldn't care less.

"What's your specialty?" Parker asked. He knew these wildlife photographers often specialized. Sometimes they had science degrees. They usually knew a good deal of zoology.

"Mostly primates. A few birds."

"Birds!" Parker said with relief. "I've seen your picture inside the jacket of a book of bird photographs. I live near a lake where there are thousands—tens of thousands—of waterfowl. I've used your book to identify them."

"Which country?" asked Romanus.

Parker hesitated, but Grossmann gave him an encouraging nod. "Australia. Western New South Wales."

"Lake Kalunga," Romanus said. "Raoul Sabea did those shots. I've never been there, but I'd love to see it."

"You must come and stay," Parker said. "My wife has a house close to the lake, and there's a guest room."

Romanus grinned. "You're on."

T he southerly had died away before sunrise on Monday, leaving a chill in the air and a sky that glittered with energy. Diana was alone at the back of the police station. She gazed at the sky to try to calm herself, sensing that the detectives knew she was lying, but she couldn't tell them about Morrie. Whatever promises they made, in the end they would pull him off the mountain—with dogs again, if necessary—and he would go completely mad. They're suspicious of me already—and someone is sure to tell them about Carolyn and Raoul, she thought. On certain days she remembered the exact smell of Raoul's skin, how she had sniffed him in as if he were newly mown grass. It was here, on High Street, Kalunga, a bit farther along the road, that she first saw him—a tripod on his shoulder, a metal camera bag in one hand, and a red bandanna around his forehead. She had stared at his narrow, eagle nose. "Lady, please showing me where is the bird lake," he'd said, his face pushed into the window of her van. "Are you Raoul Sabea?" she asked in wonderment. She owned all his books of bird photographs and had even ordered from London the expensive volume on primates to which he had contributed some transparencies. Other people took pictures of birds. Raoul's birds were gods in a raiment of bright feathers.

For the six months he lived in her house, she convinced herself every morning that *today* she would discover the beautiful man who took the miraculous photographs. But every day the man was just as he was: macho, vain, selfish. And the photographs were as they were: inspired. At night they made love, yet it was more a furious disappointment they shared. In daylight she shuddered at the memory of it: not love, she thought, but something dark that hid behind love.

Finding him in bed with Carolyn could have happened yesterday: his curved nose lifting from her belly as an eagle lifts its head from prey—and she, Diana, standing in the doorway, just back from shooting foxes, with the slide-action rifle under her arm. "Diana! Don't!" he had whispered.

Kalunga was laid out like the vascular system of a narrow leaf. High Street ran down the middle, with branch veins to the Kalunga River and, on the lower edge, the railway line. Beyond the railway tracks were flat paddocks where mobs of merino sheep fled at a pernickety gallop each time a train went past. High Street and the north part of town had big, untidy peppercorn trees planted for shade along streets of sober wooden houses standing in half-acre blocks. The south side, where Jason Nichols and Kerry Larnach lived, was known as the "professional" part of town. Its houses were newer, built of brick rather than weatherboard, with small, neat gardens and pavements planted with jacarandas because, the Shire Council said, they gave a "more cosmopolitan" look to the town. Kalunga's population was 1,100. Diana parked in the thin shade of a jacaranda.

Now that she was at the vet's place, she paused and reasoned with herself about the eagle. To expect such a bird to hunt after a broken wing was like asking an athlete to win a medal at the Olympics after a broken leg. Learning to fly at all was an enormous effort for any wing-broken bird—and hunting required the most powerful and agile flight. There were two possibilities: one was to find a nature park where the eagle would be left in the open and fed—but the parks were already overloaded with injured wedgetails, she knew, and there was nowhere on the eastern side of the continent with room for another cripple. The sensible course was to ask Jason to inject the eagle with Lethobarb. I should have shot her yesterday, Diana thought.

The veterinary clinic was in a street of large, cream-brick bungalows. It was one of twins—Jason's residence was the other—with a novelty letter box in the shape of Donald Duck. "Protected species, isn't it?" he said when people remarked on it. Besides his remarkable letter box, Jason had a red Porsche, in which he raced to and from Sydney on weekends. In all other respects he was neat and ordinary. When he arrived in Kalunga three years earlier, Diana had tried to recruit him to the anti-duck-shooting campaign. "I don't think I should be political," he said. Only this year, when he was sure that public opinion was swinging in favor of the ducks, did he agree to help: he treated injured waterfowl from dawn to midday on Saturday and Sunday in a first-aid tent; and when the circus, en route from Adelaide to Brisbane, had arrived on Saturday morning at the camping ground on the outskirts of Kalunga, Jason inspected *all* the animals—the thin-hipped lion, the ostrich with a grubby frill around its neck, the chimpanzees, even the dogs—and reported them as suffering from malnutrition. The television news crews who were covering the opening of the duck-shooting season and the simultaneous anti-shooting campaign ditched their assignment and instead reported on the evening news that the campaigners had not only defended ducks, they had uncovered a circus full of starving beasts.

Margaret, the receptionist, greeted Diana with exaggerated friendliness. "Love the new feather," she said, staring up at Diana's hat.

"Black cockatoo."

"*Love it*," Margaret repeated with an envious smile. She stood up but sat down again suddenly, grabbing the side of her desk. "Heavy night," she murmured.

Inside the consulting room, Jason was on the telephone.

"Have you heard?" he asked after he rang off. "That nympho from the Research was drinking with some men in the Kalunga Arms on Saturday night. She left with a couple of them. She's been found strangled down by the lake."

"Who were the men?" Diana asked.

"Out-of-towners. Probably duck shooters." He tried to look grave, but his face suddenly lit up with glee. "*Murdered!* Makes you realize, doesn't it?"

"Realize what?" she asked. Two X rays of the broken wing were clamped on his light box.

"The times we live in—everything out of control." His eyes flashed with a flea market of cheap ideas: The Total Breakdown of Society, The End of Life on Earth, The Destruction of the Planet. "Africa's had it. So has South America. The United States is falling to pieces. But

I reckon you and I will be all right, out here in the bush. It's the cities that will be destroyed. And city people."

Diana went to the light box.

"It's a clean break," she murmured. "Let's go and see her."

When they opened the laundry door, the eagle flared her mane until her hackles stood erect, and she glared at her visitors from beneath jutting brows. Then she did something very few animals can do: she stared defiantly into human eyes.

Diana had the extraordinary experience of knowing that those sherry-colored lamps were seeing right through her own pupils, to the retinas at the back of her eyes. She withdrew a step and observed the bird carefully. The eagle was, as she had guessed yesterday, almost a meter tall, and her wings fully extended would approach three meters. Her wide-spaced legs were two black pillars beneath her heavy body. Apart from a retrice that had broken during capture, which Diana knew she could imp, the feathers were undamaged, glossy and dark. No lice, she thought. A dull-feathered bird could turn white overnight from thousands of hatched mallophaga. The eagle's trousers were thick and fluffy, the feet looked sound, and each toe ended in a perfect small blue dagger. The beak was unblemished, and there was not too great an overhang—the sign of plenty of bones in her diet. The bird was at least twenty, maybe thirty years old. She could live to forty-five in the right conditions.

Diana looked at the feet again to convince herself they were sound. Flying at eighty kilometers an hour, the eagle would strike with two tons of pressure in her feet. Prey heard for a moment the *whoomp! whoomp!* of majestic wings, then a blow smashed out of the air.

The eagle had been preening—another good sign, for it meant that although she was captive and helpless, her spirit was strong. Diana had never seen such a dark bird, or such a glossy one. She felt suddenly that the black feathers had turned into a reflecting surface, like the lid of a black piano, and as one can sometimes see one's face wavering in a piano lid, she caught a glimpse of herself in the glossy plumage.

Jason was standing close behind her.

"Is the wing too badly broken to be pinned?" she asked.

"No. You saw that it's only the ulna. But . . ."

"I'll train her to fly."

He gave a loud sigh. "Sheer madness. What's more, I was hoping to be able to use my laundry again to wash clothes."

"It'll be only a couple of days, then I'll take her home."

"Okay, okay. Let's get scrubbed up, then, shall we?" Jason was fanatical about correct preparation for surgery, but if the operation to be done was just a matter of cutting out lead shot or a bit of wire or glass, he often invited Diana to make the incisions and put in the sutures. Pinning bones he did himself, while she stood to his left, acting as surgical nurse. When he was writing he looked clumsy, but with a scalpel in his left hand, he was an artist.

His incision was so skillful, there was almost no blood. When she congratulated him, he reddened with pleasure. Suddenly he turned to her. "Come on, you do the pin."

He was holding the edges of the broken bones together, ready for the metal pin to be inserted. It slid in easily, extending a couple of centimeters beyond the feathers. There would be a horrible moment three weeks hence when the bone had healed and they had to remove the pin. Meanwhile, it was essential to have the wings positioned exactly, or the eagle would never fly again. Diana trembled with nervous tension as she secured the leather thongs.

She and Jason stood side by side at the stainless-steel trough, washing their hands. "How about dinner tonight?" he asked. He was scrubbing his nails with small, fierce movements.

"A drink," she said. "I'm too tired for a late night."

"A late night." He sighed. "Long time since I've had one of those. A drink, then. Do you still have that gorgeous black dress that slides off your shoulders?"

She flushed. Raoul had taken photographs of her in that dress, and she had kept one, framed, in her bedroom. Jason had seen it once when he followed her into her room while she was fetching an umbrella for him.

T he previous night, after speaking to her husband, Sonja had tried to contact her sister. She knew that if Hilary first learned of the murder from newspaper reports, she would be furious and would look for a scapegoat, preferably someone at the Research. She could imagine her sister's white, meaty hand reaching for a telephone, the impressive bosom heaving. She'll accuse me of deliberately keeping her in the dark, Sonja thought.

Her sister regarded Sonja as an embarrassment. With parents medical and legal and their brother one of the state's highest paid QCs, Sonja was a letdown to Olfson family glamour. "Why are you buried out there in the bush in that fifty-million-dollar white elephant?" Hilary asked sometimes. "Get a job in Sydney! There are plenty of biotech companies where John could find work." Hilary herself was always dashing to conferences or drafting legislation in the early hours of the morning. In between, she had lunch with Nobel Prize winners.

Sonja knew her sister did not think much of John either, although she was coquettish in a heavy sort of way when she met him at social gatherings. She liked to introduce him as "My brilliant brother-in-law—you should ask him about gene shears." But the first time she saw him, she'd said to Sonja, "He's a bit gloomy isn't he? And two wives *already*." Her eye appraised his old corduroy trousers and the tweed jacket with patches on the elbows. For a terrible moment, Sonja thought Hilary would say what she was thinking. But suddenly Senator Olfson flashed her politician's grin of triumph. "Well—he's got lots of possibilities," she said, as if she were a real estate agent and John a derelict house she wanted to off-load.

"She despises us," Sonja complained to John.

"She's vain and stupid," he replied.

"She would like to close down the Research."

He snorted. "Her bureaucrats won't let her. The government has squandered a fortune on this place in the past ten years, so it can't stop now. We're safe for another decade."

Sonja's phone call on Sunday evening was answered by her sister's voice on a machine. She left a message saying, "Something important to tell you—ring me back as late as you like." That will make her sit up, Sonja thought. Hilary had once remarked, "I know you're always tucked into bed with a mug of Ovaltine by nine o'clock."

Sonja decided to soothe her nerves by doing some work on the plywood wastepaper basket she was decorating. She put a Mozart concerto on the CD machine, cleared a space on the dining table, and laid out her tools. Then she examined her piece. She had sandpapered it already and sealed it with six coats of gesso, until her basket felt as smooth as porcelain. All she had had to do then was paint on two coats of sealer and allow them to dry. Now she could begin applying the decorative motif she had chosen. It was a scattering of bows she had seen on some gift wrap. She laid out the paper bows on greaseproof paper, ready to glue on. She rubbed glue onto the back of the first one, pressed it against the side of the basket—and disaster! the bow crinkled. As she tried to pat it straight with a sponge, it tore. She plucked it off with gritted teeth.

Her hands were shaking.

I've got an infection! she thought. Her hands never shook. John once remarked, "You could do brain surgery with those hands." She went to the bathroom mirror to examine herself: her nose looked pointy, the way it did when she was upset, and she was as pale as chalk. Under the fluorescent glare, her hair had turned an insipid shade of orange. I'm starving hungry, she thought. For a moment she struggled against thoughts of the coconut fudge in the biscuit tin in the fridge.

In the kitchen, still shaking, she crammed the coconut fudge into her mouth. The sugar was piercing, but after a moment the fierce sweetness vanished and she felt much better.

The phone woke her at 1:00 A.M.

"Mus' be important if you wan' me t' ring you *anytime*. Doan tell me you're freggo—I mean preggo!" Hilary chortled. She was in a cheerful mood, but that changed quickly.

"*Duck shooters?*" she said. "They think it's *duck shooters* who murdered her? Fuck! I okay the ducking fuck-shooting licenses."

Sonja, still trembling from the shock of smashed sleep, said, "I'm sorry, Hilary. I didn't know that."

"Of course you did. The attorney general gets advice from the minister for the environment about what fauna to shoot. Thanks anyway." She rang off.

On Monday morning, Senator Olfson put her staff straight onto the case.

The early-morning ABC radio news bulletins and many of the commercial stations reported the murder of a female scientist on the weekend. Some described the victim as "considered brilliant by her colleagues"; one added "and popular." Most claimed that Dr. Williams's body had been discovered on the Research itself.

Hilary telephoned the director of security, Joe Miller.

When she discovered that the corpse had not been found on government land at all, she issued a ministerial press release, which thundered at "irresponsible reporting." By 10:00 A.M., the nation's most popular current affairs/entertainment television show had invited the minister for science, technology, and the environment to appear on its lunchtime segment. The show's producer promised Hilary's principal private secretary that the murder would be merely a peg. On it the minister could hang a discussion of the work being done under her aegis to eliminate feral pests. "We'll show footage of the 1950s rabbit plague," the producer said.

"As long as they ask no questions about duck-shooting licenses," Hilary cautioned. Her private secretary rang the producer back.

"The minister cannot touch on anything to do with duck shooting, because in this murder case it may well be sub judice."

The producer laughed sarcastically. "There will be Greens in the audience. I can't guarantee what they'll ask."

"Lying bastards!" Hilary shouted when she heard this. "They've primed the Greens to ask me about duck shooting." Her office moved from Damage Control to Crisis mode.

"I'll make an environmental statement," the minister announced. Balefully, her gaze rested one by one on the faces of her staff. None of them could immediately think of anything she might announce one hour from now that would divert the attention of environmentalists from the recreational slaughter of waterfowl. Hilary pressed a large white hand to her brow. "Lucky I'm here to think of solutions." She knew she was a martyr to public duty and not really appreciated. "I'll foreshadow legislation to reform the ethics committees," she announced. "From now on, there will be *two* animal welfare representatives on every committee in scientific institutions where animals are used."

"Brilliant, boss," said her PPS.

Hilary told him to get her the file on the Ethics Committee at the Research, then to get Sonja on the telephone. While he was engaged on the second chore, she flicked through the file, her big face creasing with annoyance. "Did I sign this?" she called out.

The PPS returned to her office.

"This letter to Dr. Parker, appointing him as animal welfare representative on the Ethics Committee at the Research . . . *Did I sign this?*"

He wore a hangdog look.

"*Why did you let me do that?* Parker is my brother-in-law!"

"That was 1990, Minister. He wasn't your brother-in-law then."

She grunted. "But he works in the organization. The ethics committees are meant to have people from outside to review their use of animals. He shouldn't have been appointed—even if it was before my neurotic sister married him."

The principal private secretary stood behind her and read the letter quickly. He had written it. He knew the appointment had seemed all right at the time. "Oh, but look, boss. Dr. Parker *is* an outsider. He's freelance. He's got a lab there, but he's got nothing to do with the rabbit and fox fertility-control program—and that's where they're using thousands of animals."

Hilary flung herself back in her chair. "Peter. Do you want to see me stand up in Parliament and explain all that?"

He did not.

"Do you realize what a meal of it the Opposition will make?"

He did.

"I suppose the recommendation to appoint Parker came from the Gang of Six, among them my sister?"

"Yes."

"And did she absent herself from the meeting at which Parker's appointment was recommended? No! And why bloody not?" The hand came down hard on her desk. "He was her lover then!" The senator glared.

Peter judged that silence was the best response.

"You know as well as I do that Sonja finagled a job at the Research during that long streak of pessimism, back in 1984. *She* recommended Dr. Parker should be brought to Australia from America and appointed senior research scientist—and the minute he had an excuse, he resigned. He didn't repay a cent of his establishment expenses! But *abracadabra!* He suddenly has hundreds of thousands of dollars for industrial research from a bunch of crooks in Thailand."

"Oh, Minister, Siam Enterprises is one of the most—"

"Peter," she said wearily, "I've had dinner at the house of the managing director of Siam Enterprises in Bangkok. The other guests were three generals and a heroin billionaire. We ate off gold plates." She glanced at her watch. "I've got to go. Bring my briefcase."

She took the file to read in the car, thinking that the other guest at that dinner in Bangkok had been a totally gorgeous young man, Michael something—a photographer.

By the time she arrived at the television studio, Senator Olfson had discovered the correspondence from Diana Pembridge: year after year, this person had put her name forward for the Ethics Committee at the Research. There were copies of letters from the Australasian Ornithological Association, from headmasters of schools, from the National Parks and Wildlife Service, and from the radicals, Animal Action, all recommending Miss Pembridge as animal welfare representative on the committee.

"Why don't we like Diana Pembridge?" she asked Peter, who promised to find out.

When she emerged from the lights of the studio, rouged and pancaked, her head high with victory, he had the answer.

"She's a radical, boss. Not a wet radical. Some members of Animal Liberation object to her because she kills rabbits and foxes."

"*Thank you*," Hilary said. She settled herself into the velvety upholstery of her government limousine and turned to him with an affectionate smile. "I *like* people who kill rabbits," she said. "When I described the rabbit fertility-control program in there, the audience cheered."

That afternoon, Diana got a phone call from a man who claimed to work for the minister for science. Did Diana own shares in any company that contracted work to the Research? he asked. Was she prepared to make a sworn statement to that effect? A few minutes later, her fax began jerking out a letter inviting her to accept appointment to the Ethics Committee at the Exotic Feral Species and Microbiology Research Centre.

Hilary had spoken to Sonja by then. "Where's John?" she said. "Your switchboard told my secretary that he was in South Australia, but they don't know where to contact him there."

"He's doing fieldwork," Sonja replied.

"Wish *I* could just go incommunicado," Hilary said. "Leave my mobile phone under a rock somewhere. Well, too bad. This is an emergency. Sonja, you have to persuade John to step down from the Ethics Committee."

"Why?"

"I'm sorry to have to tell you," Hilary said, "but my office has received complaints about the nature of his appointment. Nothing personal, merely—"

"*What?*"

"Sonja, please just do as I say. I'll explain the situation to John *at length* when I see him. Meanwhile, darling, take my word for it. How are you, by the way?"

"If John goes, there'll be no animal representative on the committee," Sonja blurted.

"Yes there will. There's a local girl who's ideal. That's my other phone ringing. Talk to you later."

For a few moments Sonja was too stunned to think. Her office in the administration building was on the senior executive floor, at the top, and from the window behind her desk she had a view of the lake. She swiveled her chair and stood, her gaze reaching across the white oyster bed of laboratory buildings, to the glossy black blisters on the roof of her own house and beyond that to the silvery water. Who has complained about John? she wondered. Somebody has betrayed us. Somebody has told Hilary about the chimps! And the "ideal local girl": that could only be Diana Pembridge. Over my dead body, Sonja thought.

Diana shook out the black dress and pulled it over her head. The neckline left her shoulders bare—"For me to bite you," Raoul had said. She felt hot, remembering his teeth running across her skin. "Damn you, Jason," she said, as she clipped on a pair of gold earrings—but he had been so helpful over the weekend, she felt obliged to humor him. For a shy man, Jason Nichols was strangely intrusive. "You shouldn't wear red," he had said one day. "I like you in cold colors."

He was seated at the bar, dressed in his usual conservative gray trousers and navy jacket. She felt suddenly tired and irritated.

"Anything wrong?" he asked, then smiled dryly. "Anything *else* wrong, I should say."

Diana shook her head. The image of that open mouth, the iridescent flies rushing out of it like sparks, would not go away.

"I'd heard you and Carolyn Williams were, ah, related."

Diana gave a weary smile. People said that Carolyn was her half-sister, not Jack Williams's daughter at all but sired by Doug Pembridge in his long on-again-off-again affair with Louise. "You must have seen her at the Research rabbit house. Do you think we look alike?"

"I don't believe I ever met her."

The only man in the world Carolyn neglected to seduce, Diana thought, reaching for the gin and tonic Jason had ordered for her.

On Tuesday afternoon, in Bangkok, John Parker packed his overnight bag, ready to catch an evening flight to Sydney. By not washing his hair since he arrived in Thailand, he had managed to save three miniature bottles of hotel shampoo, plus five little soaps. They would be Sonja's gift from Thailand. She didn't smoke, so there was no point in taking an ashtray, but on the writing table there was a brass elephant paperweight that would appeal to her, he thought. She loved decorating small, pretty things. The elephant smiled and held aloft in its trunk an advertisement for "Tours You Will Never Forget." He wrapped it in a pair of socks and shoved it in his bag.

At 5:00 P.M., there was a knock on the door. It was the night chauffeur, whose long hair partly hid a missing ear—bitten off by a dog, Parker had been told.

"You're early," he said.

Somchai held out a stainless-steel box.

"No!" Parker said. "Why wasn't it done up at the farm?"

Somchai shrugged. "Forgot."

"What about his teeth?"

"Teeth fixed. We go now, you fix throat."

The airfreight storage area was close to the airport, north of the city, on the way to Saraburi. It was dark by the time they arrived at the Siam Enterprises warehouse. Parker stepped out of the air-conditioned car into the wet heat of the Bangkok night and from there into a cool, icily lit space that seemed at first to be a vast garden. Under halogen lights, thousands of orchids, palms, and ferns stood in still rows, ready for export to Japan and Europe. Siam was not only the biggest animal breeder in the region; it had the most advanced plant nurseries as well. The driver led the way through the vegetation, carrying the stainless-steel box. In the far end of the warehouse, barbarous noises erupted from a cluster of wooden crates.

Arriving there, Somchai pointed to a crate with SAILOR stenciled on it. Black fingers moved like slow, thick tentacles through its slats.

"Let me see," Parker muttered. He did not trust Somchai to know which chimpanzee was which. Hunkering down in front of the box, he looked in. Two brown eyes full of intelligence and feeling looked back at him out of a long, mischievous face. A yellowish, thick-skinned palm pushed its way out of the cage, and from the creature inside there came a low pant-hoot. Sailor's gums were still slightly bloody from the operation to remove his canine teeth. Animals in other boxes, excited by the sight of visitors, began to pant-hoot for attention. Then all at once the air filled with the ear-splitting noise of chimpanzees *wraa*-barking. They drummed their fists on the floor of their crates and yelled. The big young male in front of Parker was the most boisterous of all. Somchai handed Parker the stainless-steel box and went to fetch a wheeled cart.

They trundled the crate to the far side of the warehouse, where some men wearing gum boots were hosing the floor. There was a branch of ripe bananas on the wall. The chimp saw it and pressed the back of his hand against his mouth eagerly. Somchai opened the door of the crate and held out a banana. Sailor loped forward on his knuckles, glancing at the humans with a nervous, open-lipped grin.

The driver groomed him, while Parker, busy with the stainless-steel box, prepared a syringe of Pentothal. And then, when the chimp's attention was settled on eating the banana, Parker jabbed him in the shoulder. They stretched him out, head tilted back and mouth open.

Parker had a drip of Scoline ready, which he injected. Almost immediately the limp body began to twitch wildly, making the men in gum boots titter. After a few seconds fasciculation stopped. "Quick!" Parker said. Somchai handed him an Oxy Viva pump and mask. Parker put the mask over Sailor's face and pumped. He had almost a minute now to cut the vocal cords. He took the laryngoscope from the box, put it into the huge mouth, and pushed the tongue aside. From the light on the laryngoscope he could see the two pale, glistening strings. Somchai handed him long-handled scissors. The strings sprang apart like severed elastic, only a bead of blood appearing at the cut ends.

Parker gave the chimp another slug of oxygen, then stood up and waited for him to regain consciousness.

Everyone watched intently to see if the animal registered that something was wrong, but he only blinked and held out his hand for the new banana that Somchai offered him. "Boo!" Somchai said. "Boo!"

Sailor gazed at the chauffeur, grinning fearfully.

"Boo! Boo! Boo!" Somchai yelled. He began to laugh.

Brown rubber lips formed into the shape that made a hoot, but there was no sound. The men in gum boots turned away.

"Good now," Somchai said. "Make no trouble."

Although in the budget a sum was set aside for travel to and from Bangkok based on the business-class fare, Parker chose to fly economy, for in the economy section there was no need to be polite to fellow passengers. Usually he was seated in the non-smoking section, but again something had gone wrong with arrangements, and he found himself sitting between two women who lit up as soon as the No Smoking sign went off.

"D'you mind?" one asked.

"Not at all. Smoking helps reduce the population," he replied in a friendly tone.

The one in the window seat needed to make frequent visits to the lavatory. "All that nicotine has to get out of your system somehow," he remarked when she asked him for the third time if he would mind leaving his seat so she could get past his long legs. When she returned, she invited him to take her place by the window. He dozed and around 5:00 A.M. Australian time was woken by deep-pink morning light pressing around the edges of the plastic shutter. During the night they had flown over the Gulf of Thailand, Malaysia, Indonesia, and the Arafura Sea, and crossed the Australian coastline. He could now gaze at the great dry continent down below.

Parker felt communicative and turned to the women smoking next to him. "Thousands of years ago, when humans first set foot on this land, its forests swarmed with giant marsupials—kangaroos as tall as elephants, wombats the size of hippos, a marsupial lion—but they were no match for the new arrivals. The huge animals and their forests vanished, replaced by hectares of parched terrain."

One of the women squinted at him. "Are you David Attenborough?"

Parker grinned at her, his long, fine lips pressed together. Then he looked out of the window again. It had taken millennia to create the wilderness below; in mere decades now, the same sterility was being achieved in other landscapes. The whole planet was facing environmental holocaust, as everyone knew, for man was now a plague on his own house—and everywhere there was self-disgust. You saw it in the epidemic of graffiti, in drugs, on T-shirts announcing

LIFE'S A BITCH AND THEN YOU DIE, in the black tide of religious fanaticism. "We will be living like rats," Jacques Cousteau warned—he and a thousand others. But nobody would act. Nobody would do the deed. Every six months the population of France was added to the world. Every decade there was another China. And these seething masses were added to the poorest parts of the world—to India, Brazil, Africa, Bangladesh. In the space of a long weekend there were an extra million humans to feed. This monster with five billion mouths killed off, every hour of every day, seven species of other living things. By the middle of the twenty-first century, the ogre would have destroyed half of all the species of life on earth. With air, water, and soil poisoned, nations would collapse into fighting over resources; human flesh would be the most abundant source of protein, and the only question left unanswered was whether environmental holocaust would strike the next generation, or the one after. Parker smiled to himself.

For some unfathomable reason, he still liked humans. He felt sometimes a cry arise within him: *Make me indifferent to them! They deserve no pity and no respect!* He closed his eyes again so he could visualize the bronze statue that would be erected in his honor one day not too far into the twenty-first century. He would look as he did now, craggy, a little worn around the edges, and he would hold in one hand a globe etched with the continents, the oceans and archipelagos, and in the other a twist of DNA. Around the base of the statue would be inscribed the basic method, the thirteen steps, that had led to White Eye Vaccine II.

"Good joke?" the woman next to him said, having another stab at conversation. Parker turned away to hide his smile. Once he began thinking of the surprise he was going to give Grossmann, he could not keep the grin off his face. He recalled the day he had made an emergency trip to Bangkok, demanding that Otto see him immediately, in private. "Mr. Grossman," he said, "I was running an ELISA to test cell supernatants for the presence of a recombinant secretory protein I've been working on, and I used White Eye–infected chimp serum as a negative control. I thought I was going barking mad when I saw that a protein in the chimp serum carried the ß galactosidase flag that I'd used in my own recombinant protein. Naturally, I wanted to investigate this unexpected event, so I compared the mode of action of White Eye with a range of bacterial and viral proteins capable of generating similar responses. I selected several antibodies for serology testing. The tests came back positive for gonorrhea, botulin toxin, and Legionnaires' disease."

Otto yawned and took a sip of jasmine tea. "I assume you'll trans-
late that into English or German for me."

"Yes! Yes, Mr. Grossmann. Simply that people put flags on proteins they have *made*. What I'm saying is White Eye is recombinant.
Somebody *created* this bacteria."

Grossmann nodded.

"It's got an LD ratio of two. An LD ratio means—"

"I know what a lethal dose ratio is," Grossmann interrupted.

Why isn't he outraged that it's recombinant? Parker wondered. He
was still in a whirl of self-important excitement from his discovery.
"I'm writing a paper on it for *Nature*," he blurted. The silence
stretched around the teak-paneled room.

Grossmann gave a faint smile. "I don't think writing a paper for
Nature is such a good idea."

Parker felt a moment's pain as he realized that up to this moment
he had understood nothing. A desire to flee overwhelmed him, and
he rose from his chair, but across the desk, Grossmann's eyes pinned
him.

"I'll shred my notes," Parker said. A warm, strong palm cupped his
pale, sweaty hand.

"That's my man," Grossmann murmured.

Since then, Parker had discovered that Otto had a colony of White
Eye in the Siam laboratory in Bangkok, ready for the day when he
would order it to be bred up and let loose in the animal breeding
houses of his competitors. When their primates began dying like
flies (and taking their keepers with them), healthy chimps that sold
for five thousand dollars would be worth twenty thousand dollars
overnight. A fifty-million-dollar company would become a two-bil-
lion-dollar company.

But back in 1985, things had gone awry. The vaccine to protect
Siam's animals had not worked, and they had died, along with two
keepers and the vet. The biochemist who drowned had produced
the faulty vaccine. This same scientist, Parker suspected, had developed White Eye for Grossmann—and the man's fate made him
wonder what was planned for him, once he had achieved the vaccine Grossmann needed. He had no intention of disappearing into
a klong. Parker guessed that once Grossmann had an effective vaccine, he would arrange for an outbreak of White Eye in some obscure but respectable institution: a university monkey house in
Canada would be the right sort of place. The disease would probably be hushed up so as not to jeopardize government funding. A few
months later, another outbreak would occur, somewhere else, and

Grossmann would leak news of this disaster to the media. There would be denials. When finally one of the major newspapers reported the existence of a virulent new disease, Grossmann would pounce: Siam Enterprises, he would announce, had been working since the 1980s on a disease of primates that sounded identical to the infection. . . .

Siam would make a fortune from Vaccine I. Parker himself stood to earn two million dollars in bonuses. All his basic work had been done for him by the man who drowned, whose lab books on the vaccine had been handed on. It was still so crude that side effects ranged from fever to vomiting and headaches. They had tested it on rat, rabbit, and chimp, and finally on a couple of the keepers at Saraburi. When they survived, suffering nothing worse than fever and loss of appetite, Parker infected them with White Eye. They were symptom-free. Since then, all staff at the breeding farm and in U-1 had shots every six months.

"But it's a sledgehammer," Parker complained to Grossmann.

"It works," Otto said.

"Give me *time*," Parker pleaded. "I can make a *better* vaccine. I can make a vaccine that will *sterilize* animals."

"*Are you crazy?* I want my animals to breed!"

"Otto," Parker answered quietly, "not *your* animals. Only theirs."

Grossmann gave a bellow of laughter, roaring until the buttons on his safari suit threatened to fly off. "You've started to think the way I do!"

"I got the idea from a biological-control program in Australia," Parker said. "I'd like to explain—"

Grossmann stopped smiling. "John, explain nothing. To tell you the truth, I don't like this sterilizing-vaccine idea. People might ask, How come Siam's primates are all breeding, but nobody else's? Hey? That raises problems, I think. You have two more years to improve what we've got. I need two years to build the facilities we'll need when we begin rapid expansion."

Already the two years were up. "Another twelve months," Parker begged Grossmann. "Otto, *please* let me explain the process to you. . . ."

He had made this request only yesterday, when they were standing on the lawn behind the reception building, in the steamy heat of midmorning. Gray monkeys ran free across the grass, rushing forward a few meters, then squatting on their haunches, brilliant eyes jittering, before leaping up and running on. The photographer, Michael Romanus, was near the house, taking pictures with a camera covered in a plastic helmet that silenced the noise of its shutter. He was able to stand extraordinarily still, Parker noticed. With the silent camera and his camouflage clothing, he would be invisible in a forest.

A gibbon that had been feeding near Romanus loped away, then noticed Grossmann and came rushing forward as he held his arms open in welcome. The gibbon leaped into them and lay back, a slender coal-black hand pressed to its brow to shade its eyes from the sun. Otto made kissing faces and asked, "Do you want to listen to a scientific rigmarole, Kitty?" It stretched out a long black arm and grabbed hold of the buckle of Parker's belt. "Naughty," Grossmann said. It yanked the buckle. "Kitty!"

Stop playing with that ape! Parker wanted to shout. *Make the wretched thing let go of my pants!* He felt desperate. Of course Grossmann wanted to be able to deny knowledge of any unethical aspect of his product. "There could be a fortune in this process if you use it in other areas," Parker said. He needed to arouse Otto's enthusiasm for a commercial application of Vaccine II. "A fortune," he repeated.

"Let go!" Grossmann said, and slapped the gibbon's face. It leaped from his arms with a scream, bounded across the lawn, and disappeared up a mango tree. "I'm listening," he said.

"In the domestic pet market," Parker blurted. "You see, Otto, I am linking two proteins to Vaccine I—"

"What do you mean, *Vaccine I?*"

Parker babbled on. "The vaccine we have against White Eye. I link to Vaccine I two proteins. One of these affects the zona pellucida of chimpanzee ova, the other affects the acrosomal membrane of chimp sperm. The sperm cannot get into the egg. The egg is locked, so there is no fertilization. But the hormonal system remains untouched; the sex drive in both male and female animals is normal. There will be no change in behavior. Animals will copulate as usual, *but they will never reproduce.*"

Grossmann became thoughtful. "I can see that could have some application."

"We could send out mixed batches. Some Vaccine I, some Vaccine II, but nothing to discriminate between them. It would be impossible to prove that the animals were not breeding because of the vaccine, because some would be."

"You're developing a head for business," Grossmann remarked. "I need a good commercial product ready to go into production by the end of 1993. I have a lot of capital invested—you have no idea. . . ."

No, *you* have no idea, Parker thought. The majesty of his vision filled him with excitement.

At the royal-blue customs desk in Sydney, he handed over his British passport to a snub-nosed person, who remarked, "Y'like staying there?" as he examined the immigration card.

Parker, who from habit had been checking out the air-conditioning vents, gave him a puzzled look.

"The Regent, sir."

He had forgotten that on his immigration card he had written that while in Sydney this time he would be staying at the Regent Hotel. Sometimes he invented penthouse apartments in Vaucluse. On forms that asked his brand of motorcar, Parker liked to print with his left hand in an illiterate script, "Daimler."

"That's where you're stopping while you're in Sydney, isn't it, sir?"

"It is."

"How long do you expect to be in Australia this time?"

"Depends on my fiancée."

"Then back to Thailand?"

"Or Antarctica."

The immigration clerk had orders to identify frequent travelers between Thailand and Australia. Parker was a borderline case; he had arrived from Bangkok four times in the past twelve months. He hardly seemed the type to be a heroin courier—tall and vague, like a tatty English aristocrat. But as the training manual warned: "Be Safe. Obey Instructions. Leave Interpretation to Others." The clerk pressed a button under his desk. A light came on behind him, invisible to Parker, who took his passport and customs declaration card with a gracious word of thanks.

Sergeant Susan Miller, dressed to resemble a ground hostess, was loitering with a junior male colleague behind the row of immigration booths. She was playing the role of someone available to help travelers who did not know where to go next when they had passed through Immigration. Her colleague, wearing gray trousers and a blue shirt, looked like some sort of airport attendant. When the light went on, Susan murmured to him, "Gawd! What d'you reckon *he'd* be carrying?"

"Dandruff?"

"Check him out."

"Right, Sergeant," he muttered.

When all the passengers from the Bangkok flight had left the airport, the Surveillance Squad people joined Immigration and Customs officers who were already gathered in the Operations Room.

"What happened with the tall geezer with the dirty hair?" Susan Miller asked.

"He had a brass elephant hidden in a sock. And some soap and shampoo."

I n Kalunga, people talked about the murder morning, noon, and night, making a day seem as eventful as a year. The tractor dealer advertised burglar alarms for sale, and the woman who bred bull terriers sold a whole litter of pups in one afternoon. Grilles were placed over the doors of houses that had not been locked in twenty years. Townsfolk told each other, "Now it's a waiting game."

The Golden West Motel was completely booked with detectives and "forensic experts," who went to the Kalunga Arms in the evening after spending the day at the Research and, when questioned about the investigation, answered, "It's going okay" or "Wooden know about that."

On Tuesday, news leaked back to town that threatening anony-mous letters had been sent to the Research. It was said that two women had resigned on Monday after reading their mail.

When the detectives sauntered into the Arms on Tuesday evening, men sidled up to them to ask, casually, about the letters. The postal clerk said he felt guilty because he had placed the letters in the mailbag that went out to the Research. He had a vital clue: all the letters had been posted in Sydney. "They'll want to take my fingerprints," he said, which irritated the barmaid who had pulled beers for Carolyn and her male companions on Saturday night. Before the postal clerk's fingers, her beer-pulling arm had been the most envied body part in town.

But on Wednesday morning, before anything was resolved, the whole murder team departed on Kalair's seven o'clock flight to Sydney, carrying away witness statements, things in paper bags, and plaster casts of prints they had found at the scene of the crime. The town seemed to collapse like a punctured balloon. People took each other aside on High Street to say, "If you hear anything . . ."

At nine-fifteen Wednesday morning, Diana left her house in Fig Tree Gully Road and drove three blocks to the post office. Months ago, she had ordered a new book on the world's eagles, and it had just arrived, according to the postal clerk who rang her to say the detectives were making a big mistake in not taking his fingerprints, and by the way, there was a newsletter for her, and a parcel from London.

The post office was opposite the Kalunga Arms and next door to the courthouse and police station. It was built of stone and had "1873" engraved on its entablature. Diana drove up in a hurry; she was on her way to Canberra, where she would be briefed on the responsibilities and rights of the Ethics Committee by someone from Senator Olfson's department.

She had requested a briefing because she wanted to find out how far she could go in asking for information about experiments on animals at the Research. Senator Olfson's principal private secretary had said, "The committee chairman will tell you that." When Diana asked who was the chairman, the secretary put his hand over the telephone briefly, then came back on the line and said, "He's stepping down. Perhaps you should have a briefing—but we can't pay your traveling expenses."

She had a few minutes to collect her mail before leaving for Canberra, where her appointment was for 2:30 P.M.

With the eagle book under her arm, she went to her mailbox, where she found a few bills, what looked like a check for a central desert painting Grace had sold last week, and an envelope addressed in childish printing. Kids wrote to her from all over the district with questions about animals. Others sent her photographs of the birds in their gardens, asking which foods to give them. From the bulk of this envelope, there was a picture inside it.

The letter contained a neatly folded sheet of paper. She spread it out, and her heart pounded. At the top was her own face, cut from last week's *Kalunga Shire Chronicle*. Her head had been snipped off at the neck and joined to the naked golden torso of a *Playboy* beauty, who, in place of legs, had an eagle's feet stuck onto her hips. Above the collage was printed in the same childish hand. "CW =." Next to the equal sign was another colored picture cut from a glossy. It was of a mallard drake pasted onto the sheet upside down, so that its legs stuck stiffly into the air. It meant, presumably, "dead duck." Next to the mallard was another equal sign. And next to that, the letters DP: "CW = a dead duck = DP."

Diana walked to the police station, where the junior constable was eating a doughnut and reading yesterday's *Telegraph Mirror*. "Break-fast," he mumbled, and took a final bite. "What's up, Diana? Some villain been shooting ducks again?"

She placed the letter on the counter. "I'll ring Sydney," he said.

"I can't wait. I've got a meeting in Canberra. I'll be back this evening."

The constable rang Homicide and described the letter.

"Grab her!" a detective told him. But when he ran out to the pavement, Diana's yellow van had already disappeared.

In Joe Miller's office, on the top floor of the Research's adminis-tration building, there was a bookshelf where sporting trophies cel-ebrated two phases of his life now gone forever: agility and marriage. Surrounded by football cups, Sandra's thin face smiled diffidently from a photograph. It was four years since she had died, and peo-ple said it would take him five to get over it.

Out above the lake he saw an eye wink in the sky. He locked his office and galloped downstairs. His was the only Land Cruiser still in the car park, because all the other directors were already at the weekly meeting. He had telephoned the chairman, the director of administration, to say he would be late. "The murder?" Administra-tion asked. "Maybe." Admin was on the suspect list. So was Finance. Both had confessed to affairs with Carolyn, and both had been around the Research on Saturday night. Admin said he was reading, and his wife backed him up. Finance had told detectives he spent until 2:00 A.M. doing cryptic crossword puzzles. Since Finance had grown up on a farm, he might know how to handle a big hypodermic. The murder weapon, which had not yet been found, was believed to be a 50-ml syringe with an 18-gauge needle. Vets had hypodermics that size to aspirate blood from horses, but for human use they were rare. "You might find one in an intensive care ward for injecting dextrose into a diabetic who's OD'd on insulin," one of the forensic team said.

The junior constable from Kalunga to whom Diana had given her dead-duck letter that morning had permission to go by air taxi to the Research to show the letter to Joe Miller, who had copies of the other threat letters on file. As head of security, and a former Homicide man, Joe had certain privileges.

The constable had never seen the lake from the air, and his first view of it was so astonishing that for a while he forgot why he was flying. The world below was a patchwork of gold and brown autumn paddocks, thirsty for rain. Set on this dry background was a long, pale opal of water, its colors shifting between silver, sky blue, and pale green as the aircraft's altering course shifted his perspective. He had never known that within the lake there was an archipelago of green islands, where thousands of birds lived. He could see them diving, swimming, and flying about. He peered out the window, wonder-struck like a kid at the zoo. The pilot gave him a nudge.

"I said, d'you want me to wait?" Kerry Larnach bellowed over the noise of the engine.

"No," he shouted back.

"Something interesting?"

The constable shook his head. "Routine."

Like hell, Kerry thought. "Joe Miller's come out to meet you," he yelled.

The Land Cruiser was already parked at the airstrip, and Joe was standing beside it, looking up at the sky.

"I do appreciate this," Miller said as they shook hands. He grasped the constable's elbow lightly, an old trick for gaining the confidence of the person he was meeting. On the drive back, Joe pointed out to his visitor some features of the Research. "See the solar panels?" he asked as they passed Sonja's house. The constable nodded politely. "There's a laboratory under the house, Underground One. It used to be a dam."

The road went on for almost a kilometer through dry, weedy paddocks that had been allowed to return to bush and were already dotted with saplings growing from seed. The laboratory complex was farther on. "We had a lot of pilfering before I put the booms in," Joe said.

At the administration building, there was a small courtyard coffee shop, with bleached canvas umbrellas over the tables. A couple of typists were drinking cappuccino and smoking, which was not allowed indoors.

"Morning, Champions," Joe greeted them.

"Morning, Coach," they replied.

"My basketball team," Joe said to the constable. "Twelve-thirty sharp on the court, right?" he called over his shoulder to the women.

Upstairs, he pulled on thin rubber gloves and handed a pair to the constable. When Diana's letter was smoothed out on his desk, he sat nodding at it. "Similar writing," he said. "Same sort of idea." His chair was on casters. With a push, he was away from the desk and at his filing cabinet. Another push brought him back with colored photocopies of the death-threat letters. They, too, were made from bits and pieces of people and animals cut from newspapers and magazines. In place of heads they had a circle, a square, or a triangle, and the young woman's name was in letters clipped from a magazine. Underneath, one had a fox's body, another a rabbit's, the third a pair of scissors.

"This is the Williams billet-doux," Joe said. "I had to go through about fifty *Penthouse*s to find the original picture."

"Tough," the constable murmured.

Carolyn's letter, found by the detectives in her apartment on Monday, had a rabbit's head in profile. Joined to that was the naked body of a woman viewed from behind, on elbows and knees, her backside raised in the air. The message said: "You root like a rabbit, you deserve to get myxo." In the letter to a lab technician, in place of a body there was a pair of open scissors with small, high-heeled shoes stuck on as feet. Its message was: "Scissor Woman: You think you can cut up life and stick it back together again? See how you like it when it happens to you."

"What's that about?" the constable said.

"This lass works with enzymes called gene shears. What she does is inhibit the function of genetic material. We think it's a reference to that."

The constable nodded as if he understood. The pictures were fierce and unrelieved, as if the person who made them had felt things too dark to express openly.

"These days, they can take, say, human genes and put them into a pig, and the pig will grow faster," Joe said. "Or firefly genes in to-bacco plants will improve the tobacco. People here are altering the myxo virus so it'll make rabbits sterile."

They contemplated the weird composites in silence. Then Joe cocked an eyebrow. "Spotted the difference yet?" He pointed to the message on Diana's letter and the messages on the others. Diana's was hand-printed. "And look at the difference in the cutting," Joe said.

When the constable paid attention, he realized that the cutting out in the Research letters was skillfully done, while in Diana's letter it was rough.

"I'd reckon it's a local copycat," Joe said. The whole of Kalunga knew about the death-threat letters. Trying to keep things quiet in a country town was like trying to tell birds not to sing. "Posted locally," Joe added, turning over the envelope. "The originals were all posted in Sydney."

The constable did not look convinced about the copycat idea.

"Definitely by a different person," Joe said.

"By a different hand," the younger man objected. "Not necessarily a different person." His frank gaze appraised Joe Miller. It was the look of a younger man realizing that he has the measure of a master who, suddenly, seems to him a has-been.

After half an hour's earnest description of "the legislation" and "the department's view," the mandarin with giant shoulder pads who was briefing Diana grinned suddenly and said, "Just go for it. That's what the minister wants." She flicked her fine, straight hair off her forehead. It was career woman's hair, the sort that did not lose its cool.

"You mean . . .?" Diana hesitated.

The mandarin gave the impression of an IQ of 140 and no time in her schedule for fools. "The minister's hot to stop government funding to the Research. Any ammunition will be welcome. If I were you and I wanted to get duck-shooting licenses restricted, I'd go at it . . . sideways." She waited a beat. "That's only a personal opinion."

"Of course," Diana agreed, straight-faced.

Across the desk, the young woman suddenly leaned forward. "This government is in deep doo-doo with the Greens. My department'll do anything to appear friendly to the environment, as long as it doesn't cause unemployment in marginal seats. *Now's your chance.*"

Diana frowned. "I've been wondering why I—"

"It's got nothing to do with you. You're just a dice they can roll." The woman gave another flick of her shiny, quick-witted hair. She was very young to be so high on the public service ladder, and she liked to think of herself as having balls. "The fuckers," she added with a grin.

Four hundred kilometers away in the old homestead at the Research, the directors' meeting had just reached Item 7 on the agenda.

The homestead, with its green iron roof, its wooden verandas on three sides, and its hushed, dark interior, was a relic of the convictions of an earlier age. Its slender veranda columns and wooden walls made it seem frail and out of place beside the rugged brick condominiums, and admin buildings.

Five white Land Cruisers and a bicycle were drawn up on the gravel drive in front of it. Inside, in what had been the living room when Diana was growing up, the directors were seated at a long, polished table littered with papers and coffee cups. Four of the men wore beards and spectacles; Joe was clean-shaven. Sonja was seated halfway down the table and was hitting it with the flat of her hand, like her sister, but Sonja's hand was small and freckled, and the gesture was shrill rather than authoritative. Some of the men exchanged covert glances. Administration, at the head of the table, had fixed a bleak smile on his lips, which, partly hidden by his beard, looked like a little pink boat in a brown sea.

"Diana Pembridge is not a 'highly regarded local conservationist,' as the minister claims," Sonja said. "She's a ratbag! She's a radical animal activist! She's totally wrong for the Ethics Committee, and we, as a board, should refuse to rubber-stamp this ministerial inanity. We must refuse!" She slapped the table again.

The chairman said in a plaintive tone, "But, Sonja, I heard you say last week that the anti-duck-shooting campaign she started was a terrific idea."

"That's wild animals!" Sonja shouted. "We're talking about laboratory animals. We need someone who understands *lab* animals!"

The director of finance rolled his eyes. He had a woolly red beard and was notorious for running onto his front lawn early in the morning to shout at the sulphur-crested cockatoos. "Monsters! Flying dogs! Stop that barking!" he would yell. He enjoyed stirring Sonja up. "Surely animals are animals," he said.

"They are not!" she answered fiercely. Laboratory animals were merely equipment, as everyone around the table knew. But she could not make that point, in case it was recorded in the minutes and then dug out by some troublemaker using the Freedom of Information Act. "I warn you, if Pembridge gets on the Ethics Committee, she will turn this place *upside down*." She gave a final slap to her papers and jumped up, muttering, "I need a cup of tea."

The others sat in attitudes of thunderous silence. They had much serious business to consider before 5:00 P.M., but it looked as if the director of personnel would stall the whole meeting on this footling issue of the Ethics Committee. The thing that irritated them all was that she was such a mouse socially, yet in meetings Sonja became unyielding. "Can't handle power," they said among themselves. "Or grog." There were jokes about how she had bullied John Parker into marriage. Speculation on their sexual practices remained a favorite pastime, for among the junior female staff John was known as a lecher. No one was surprised that he had kept his apartment in the residential area and stayed only a couple of nights a week with his wife.

"What'll we do?" Administration whispered to Finance.

"Let her rave on for a bit," Finance whispered back. "God knows what's really upsetting her."

At the sideboard, Sonja was making herself a cup of raspberry leaf tea and taking deep breaths to calm down. She had noticed a little rash in the fold under her breasts that morning and feared she would have another outbreak of boils. The fact was, she was terrified about everything at the moment. If Diana's appointment to the Ethics Committee went through, how long would it be before she demanded an inspection of U-1? Under existing legislation, committee members were entitled to visit laboratories and animal houses unannounced. That morning, Sonja had rung John, who was still in Sydney, and in veiled terms had described to him this latest threat to his research.

"If that happens I'll move to Thailand," he said brusquely.

"And what'll I do?" she gasped.

"Come too, of course."

"But what will I *do*?" Her package at the Research was worth ninety thousand dollars a year, plus a fabulous pension if she stayed in the public service until she was fifty-five. She would not get *that* in Thailand.

"You can discover your inner shopper," he said, and laughed at his wit.

He was due at Sydney University to give a lecture on immuno-sterilization to vet-science students and was not interested in her news. *He leaves everything to me,* Sonja thought. John's reliance on her used to be a thrill, but this morning she had felt strangely let down—especially when he was evasive about what he had bought for her in Bangkok. Animal, vegetable, or mineral? she'd asked, hoping the answer was "vegetable," which would mean Thai silk. "Animal and mineral," he said in a bored voice. "Women always want more from men than they can get," he'd once remarked. Sonja felt he was accusing *her* of being demanding. *It's because I love him that I'm so concerned for his welfare,* she told herself. While this turmoil was disturbing the surface of her mind, on another level she was steadily calculating her next move at the meeting. She lifted the dripping tea bag from her cup with care, dropped it onto a saucer beside other sopping bags—their strings made them look like drowned mice, she thought—and returned to the table.

"I explained myself very poorly, Mr. Chairman, and I now realize I must go back a step and say *why,* from the point of view of personnel, we must not agree to Pembridge," she said.

She had their attention. "I've had two resignations already this week over the appalling Williams business. Morale among the women is, I can tell you, at a critical point. There has been a stream of females through my office in the past two days, all of them wanting to know their entitlements if they resign. I think I've persuaded most of them that our new security arrangements will safeguard them and that they should stay on, but I expect another half-dozen clerical and typing-pool resignations in the next few weeks. That will have a carryover effect on the morale of the scientific staff."

A tight silence enclosed the table. If the scientific people began to leave, the Research was in real trouble.

"That's half the background," Sonja continued. "The other half is this: Diana Pembridge is obviously a political appointment by a minister who has never been supportive of this place. We all know, I think, my sister's view of the Research. Well, if Hilary places her *agente provocateuse* on the Ethics Committee, what sort of signal will that send to an already demoralized staff?" She looked from face to face, her eyebrows raised in query.

"Not a bad point," the chairman murmured. He eyed Finance, hoping for a bright suggestion, but Finance was stumped.

Sonja said, "May I propose, Mr. Chairman, that this board inform the department that in view of the state of uncertainty here, it declines for the moment to endorse an appointment that is likely to be controversial? We should point out that we don't want compensation claims for mental anguish and the like, which could result from a further decline in morale."

"We certainly don't!" Finance exploded. "Did you see that postman in Melbourne who got half a million dollars compensation because he was worried he'd get the sack?" He snatched handfuls of his hair with stubby fingers. "Mad! Everything's gone mad!" he cried. "We've turned into a nation of infants! *Who'll change my nappy? Waaaah!*"

"Yes. Well," the chairman said. "Other thoughts? Anyone?"

There were somber looks along the table. "Right," he said. "I think that settles it. Thank you, Sonja, for your contribution. I must say that none of us—well, that is, I, anyway, have not yet come to terms with all the difficulties we face since the dreadful event on the weekend. I suppose it will be weeks or months before we know its full effect, and in the meantime . . ."

Sonja had on her small, serious face and nodded rhythmically as the chairman spoke. She was mentally constructing a triumphant report to John about how she had turned the meeting around.

The words " . . . so I'll hand over to Joe to tell us what happened" startled her.

"Yes," Miller said. "It happened around 3:00 A.M., we estimate, and I can't guarantee that it won't happen again. This place is easily penetrated. The reason we've had no trouble until now is that we've had no trouble until now. It's one of those flukey things: a house can go for decades without being burgled, but once it's been knocked off, it'll be knocked off again. That's now the situation here, I'm afraid."

"What situation?" Sonja whispered.

"The labs were burgled last night," Housing whispered back.

"What!"

"Someone got in through the northwest gate, went past the airfield and your place, and burgled the labs. Nothing much taken, but . . ."

"I'm replacing the lock on the gate," Joe continued. "But a pair of bolt cutters can bugger it again."

"My God," Sonja said. "You mean our millions of dollars' worth of equipment is up for grabs for anyone with *bolt cutters?*"

Joe nodded. "This place is like the whole country: we rely on distance for security. Since Sunday night, I've had my staff concentrated around the residential area. I don't have the manpower to patrol the labs as well." He looked at Sonja. "I've had extra people at your place for the past three nights—don't know if you noticed them."

"I didn't. Thank you, Joe." She sounded contrite.

When the meeting broke for afternoon tea, Sonja went to the women's room and leaned against the door while she rummaged in her handbag for her private telephone book. It had burrowed down to the bottom, beneath some hard candies, sunscreen, a *Teach Yourself Spanish* tape, and the waterproof bag containing the little Mediterranean sponges that she used as tampons. She found Kerry Larnach's office number and dialed him from a phone in the corridor outside the loo. "Can you come by?" she asked. They had a code. "After dark is okay." "Dark" meant: It's about the chimpanzees.

Larnach was in his office in High Street, Kalunga, staring at Kalair's balance sheet on his computer screen. He could pay wages for five more weeks. After that he would default on the next round of interest on the three million he owed for aircraft. Maybe the bailiffs would move in even before then. There was nothing from the air fleet he would be able to hang on to, not even the crop dusters. They would repossess his flat up at the Gold Coast. Probably even his house. It was almost funny that the one surefire area of profit these past few years had been his flights for Parker. This chimp delivery, however, would have to be his last, because soon every move Kalair made would be scrutinized by accountants.

"I'll be there before seven," he said. He needed to do a bit of work in his toolshed before going to the Research.

At the breeding farm in Saraburi, Michael Romanus needed to do a bit of work in his own toolshed, the darkroom he had set up inside the suite Otto provided for him at the Siam Enterprises guesthouse. He had fastened black cloth over the second lavatory's window and door and turned the vanity table into a bench to hold chemicals; in there he was able to process the black-and-white photographs he took of the farm's primates. These pictures—portraits, really—were kept on file to help the company identify animals in case of insurance claims from customers. Romanus was required to leave his negatives with Grossmann's personal assistant and to make three prints of each photograph: one for the customer and two for the company. Each evening, in the darkroom, he made a fourth print, for himself.

Diana had filled her van with petrol on Tuesday, and the next morning she had not given fuel for her trip to Canberra another thought. On the outskirts of the city, starting for home, she glanced at the gauge and saw the needle already pointing to empty. The closest garage was five kilometers away, but the engine stopped before she reached it, and she had to walk.

On the road that afternoon she had been bird-watching. She had already seen flocks of crimson rosellas, ganggangs, galahs, and sulphur-crested cockatoos, both on the wing and feeding in paddocks beside the road. In a farmhouse garden, about twenty king parrots swung, beak over feet, from branch to branch in a berry tree, agile as pirates climbing rigging. Farther west she saw apostlebirds, a pair of yellow-tailed black cockatoos, and, on the edge of a pine plantation, white-wing choughs, whistling to each other with mellow, mournful voices. Diamond firetails bounced along the roadside border before swooping away in undulating flight, their scarlet rumps flashing. The best bird of the day, however, had been a brilliant blue forest kingfisher that should have left already on the migration north. He gave a dry, hard, high-pitched rattle, then flew fast and straight, a sapphire arrow.

With her hand loose on the wheel and her eye roaming the landscape, she tried to keep her mind off the letter she had received that morning, and the disappearance of her petrol, focusing instead on getting inside the animal houses, but her attention kept returning to the letter. She remembered that the postal clerk had said, "By the way, there's a newsletter for you, and a parcel from London." Yet there had been no newsletter in her mailbox that morning. She decided to check once more when she reached Kalunga.

After a while she began thinking of the eagle, and the battle ahead. *To hold her on my forearm, when she weighs seven kilos, not to flinch, to keep as still as rock* . . . I'll have to start lifting weights, Diana realized. And I'll need the cantilever. Raoul had made it for her. He had welded the rods, cut the belt for her waist, shaped the support for her arm. The contraption was to help her while she trained a young wedgetail with gold still in its plumage, captive-reared and needing months of daily exercise before he could hunt well enough to live in the wild. The morning she had released him, Raoul took photographs, for which a German magazine had paid twenty-five thousand dollars. I should have demanded a percentage, she thought bitterly.

The afternoon was warm and still, with a special clarity, a glassiness, that filled the air with a vibrating, invisible presence. There was so little breeze, the landscape seemed immobile; trees and paddocks appeared to be bright paintings of themselves. Only when she looked steadily could she see that every leaf of the thousands on each tree made tiny glittering movements; the whole countryside was dancing in minute steps. *That wasn't dog hair on Carolyn's T-shirt*, she told herself again. Her mind drifted back to the landscape. At this time of year, her parents had always looked anxiously for the first rains to bring up the barley grass, because it was good sheep feed and broke the summer dry. But March was also the month for saffron thistles, Paterson's curse, and wild oats. This was a drought year. Scrawny stock wandered across dun-colored paddocks, searching for green pick, and the kurrajong trees were flat underneath, where they had been eaten by sheep.

Toward dusk, she saw the silver flash of eyes not far from the highway and slowed down. When she'd found a place to stop, she took her small rifle, the .22, ran to the fence, and climbed through the wire. In three shots she got two rabbits. The eagle would need plenty of meat when she brought it home from Jason's in a day or so. Meanwhile, the owl, the frogmouth, and the peregrine would not refuse fresh coney.

Back at the van, she skinned and gutted the soft, hot corpses, then rinsed her hands with water from the thermos and tossed the guts into the grass. Ravens were ramming their beaks into them before she drove away.

It was growing dark by the time she entered the broad wheat country, and night had fallen long before she reached the outskirts of town. She drove slowly along High Street, hoping to see a light inside the police station, but it was in darkness. At the post office, she stopped and went to her box. There *was* something else in there, after all: the Primate Rescue Organization newsletter. How did I miss that this morning? she wondered. As she drove down Fig Tree Gully Road toward her house, she peered forward, wanting lights to be on inside, meaning Grace was still there. They could sit in the kitchen over a pot of tea and exchange the news of the day. But the house was empty.

Sonja had left the directors' meeting at four forty-five, changed into Reeboks, and mounted her bicycle. It had a basket on the back for her files, her handbag, and whatever else she needed to carry home. She pedaled at a leisurely rate, taking a few minutes to ride around the lanes of the laboratory complex to see what damage had been done in last night's burglary. One door showed the ghost of a stolen biohazard sign, and nearby there was a broken window. A box of autoclave bags had been reported missing, and a couple of vending machines inside had been robbed.

When she reached her house, Sonja leaned the bicycle against a pylon and went to the clothesline. All her washing, including a terry-cloth robe, was stiff dry, and it was with a sense of virtue that she lugged the laundry basket upstairs. She enjoyed the many small environmentally aware practices she observed each day—such as hanging out the clothes instead of flinging them into a dryer, as they did up at the condos. That morning, before leaving home, she had turned down the thermostat on the hot-water system and sorted the organic from the inorganic garbage. "You don't drink. You don't smoke. The trouble with you, Sonja, is you have no redeeming vices," Hilary once said. Sonja was still thinking about that remark when she took the kitchen scraps to the compost and saw scattered across the wilted lettuce leaves and cucumber peelings traces of the sorrel soup she had given Lek, the Thai animal keeper, a week earlier. "That's the last time," Sonja said to herself. "You cook your own food in future, you ungrateful slut."

It was too chilly to sit on the veranda now, but from the western window of her house Sonja could keep her eye on the airfield and be ready to jump into the Land Cruiser and drive across to meet Kerry. As she sat down, her backbone seemed to collapse, and she closed her eyes for a moment. The meeting had taken its toll. She often told John, "Don't think it's easy for me to get the things through meetings which I do—for you!" She felt as if she would never be able to get out of the chair again, although she now remembered she wanted to check on U-1 before the staff left at six. But she was too tired.

A Walkman lay on the wicker table beside her chair. She fiddled with the black sponges on the headset until they felt comfortable against her ears, then leaned back to be soothed by the Largo from *Xerxes*. After a few bars, the warm voice of the teacher announced: "Lesson Six. Vocabulary. A Spanish grocery store." She ate a pear as she listened, her jaws stopping now and then as she practiced the tongue gymnastics of a Spanish noun. Come Christmas, she and John would be in Chile on their long-delayed honeymoon. The thought of traveling with him, having him all to herself, away from the lab and other people, acted on her nervous system like a balm. She imagined the miracles she would achieve with his grooming and personal hygiene when he could forget the tension and worry of work for six weeks. After ten minutes she stopped the tape.

A pair of daytime binoculars lay on a ledge inside the front door, handy in case something interesting happened on the lake. (John had identified a royal spoonbill with them recently.) She took them to the western window and, working from a spot on the side of Mount Kalunga, moved across the sky in what she knew to be the flight path of the air taxi. Sure enough, there it was, its wheels already down. Noise from incoming aircraft reached her house only a few seconds before they were to land, and even then some quirk of topography and prevailing winds muffled the sound.

She crossed the living room to the kitchen, where an internal television monitor was fitted between the work counter and the serving shelf above it. She flicked on the screen and saw that everything in the main lab looked normal. Although it was now nearly 6:00 P.M., the technicians were still working. One was writing in his lab book, another was seated at a microscope, and the third young man was manipulating an image on one of the computer screens. Sonja pressed the Animal Room switch, thinking, Lek will have left already—but when she looked into the Animal Room, there was Lek, lying on a pile of cushions beside Lucy, watching CNN. The chimpanzee was meant to be in her sleeping cage by now. Instead, Lek was feeding her Cheezels out of a box, and a rabbit was on the loose. John had told Lek a hundred times that the rabbits were to stay in their cages, especially after they had been bled. This rabbit had been bled recently: Sonja could see the sutures in its ear. The rabbit was cantilevering itself slowly across the floor, following a trail of carrot rings laid out like sweets at a children's treasure hunt. Lek had kicked off her shoes, and both she and the chimpanzee were playing with some mice with their feet while their hands and mouths were busy with the Cheezels. As Sonja watched, the girl stretched toward a mouse and, giving a quick nip of prehensile toes, picked it up, bent her knee with that extraordinary double-jointed suppleness they all seemed to have, and dropped the mouse in her lap. The chimp watched, then did it too. "A bloody circus!" Sonja said aloud.

W hen she pulled up in the Land Cruiser, Kerry was waiting, his hands on his hips. From thickset boy he had grown into a heavy-featured man, whose face broke easily into smiles but just as quickly became saturnine again. This shift from sunshine to storm gave a certain power to his personality, an undertow of aggression that unsettled people. "Been asleep?" he said with a grin.

"I was practicing my Spanish vocab."

He grunted. "Well? What's up?" Kerry hated to waste time. He had surrendered himself body and soul to drudgery to get the airline flying again after it went bust in '82 and killed his father with worry. Now, at the age of thirty-three, he was so hardened to work that he was unable to appreciate anything unrelated to it.

Sonja told him about the extra patrols around her house at night.

Two days ago, Kerry's little brother, his best pilot, had left for Karatha in northwest Australia to collect the new chimp. He was due back with it on Friday night. "Instead of landing it here, land at Kalunga, and we'll drive in and pick it up. It'll be safer," she said.

"*Safer!* At the airfield it will be *safer?*" Kerry gave an exaggerated shake of his head. He had known from the moment he met Sonja eight years ago that he could bully her. "Do you have any idea what would happen to me if we were discovered flying an unquarantined chimpanzee?" It was a rhetorical question. "I wouldn't just lose m'license to operate, but me and m'brother'd go to jail. Are you *aware* of that?"

"Yes, Kerry. Of course. We know—"

"The fine is twenty thousand dollars. Sometimes I think you don't give a stuff about the risks I take for you."

He wants more money, she thought. Her instinct was to try to assuage him. "Would you like to come to the house for a beer?"

"Yeah. I've got something I need to show you. Better to do it up there."

While she was in the kitchen, he wandered around her main room, occasionally touching the small decorated objects on display. There was a low bookshelf running the length of one wall, and on it were boxes, plates on stands, canisters, a wooden hat block, and shoe lasts, all of them decorated with colorful pictures of fruit, flowers, cherubs, gods and goddesses, insects, and birds.

"Where d'you find the time to do all this?" he asked.

"I come home and start cutting out, and I forget everything."

He fingered the gleaming surface of a vase, his expression conveying the vague contempt of someone whose ethics do not allow time to be wasted on the arts.

When he was seated at the table near the window, he took a magazine from his attaché case and opened it carefully. "Take a look at this," he said.

Inside was a photocopy of the Primate Rescue Organization newsletter. On the cover was a picture of someone in a balaclava, looking like the IRA and holding two baby chimpanzees. The caption read: WE RESCUE BABIES! STORY PAGE 3.

"Have a read." He sat back with an expression of contented disgust.

She read quickly. It was an account of a raid by PRO, as the organization liked to call itself, on a commercial laboratory in southern California where "dozens of chimpanzees are kept in appalling conditions while scientists infect them with AIDS." The story went on to explain that chimps were the test animal of choice for AIDS research, and that PRO activists had decided "to liberate these medical science slaves." They had stormed the laboratory, breaking down a door with a sledgehammer, but in the event had been able to free only two very young chimpanzees. A legal battle for the return of the apes had now begun. Members were asked to send donations urgently and to turn to the editorial on the next page for background.

The editorial, headlined PRO ADOPTS RADICAL ACTION, explained the new policy of direct intervention to save the lives of captive primates. "We will try to avoid injury to humans," it said, "but if in the course of saving the lives of primates injury to their captors does occur, so be it." The organization's logo, a pale, long-thumbed human hand clasping an ape's dark paw, was printed above and below.

"Now look at the contact list," Kerry said. He turned over to the back page. There were the names, addresses, phone and fax numbers of PRO representatives in various parts of the United States, and beneath them a short list of "Other Countries." Australia's spokesperson was "Diana Pembridge, 8 Fig Tree Gully Road, Kalunga, NSW."

Sonja's hands tightened on the pages. "When did she join them?"

"No idea." He tapped the side of his nose. "A few weeks ago, I got the feeling I should keep an eye on my cousin's mail—amazing what you can open with a bit of wire—and there it was. Found it this morning."

"You never told us she was your cousin!"

Kerry shrugged. "Didn't I? Must've forgotten. The Larnachs were the workers. The Pembridges, they were the squatters." He grinned, but Sonja was not paying attention.

"God almighty! These activists have all sorts of tricks," she muttered. "They check the animal food suppliers to find out what type of food is being ordered—"

"Yeah, I told you that," he said. "And it's Muggins here who flies in your forty-kilo bags of monkey chow, isn't it? I bet the people who work in animal food supplies wonder what a country airline does with chimpanzee biscuits. Feeds 'em to the—"

Sonja interjected, "All sorts of animals can eat monkey chow!"

"Yeah." He finished his beer and stood up. "I reckon this'll have to be our last run to Karatha for you. It's getting too dangerous. What with . . ." He waved in the direction of the mountain.

Sonja seized his arm. "How much do you want?" she asked.

Kerry shook off her hand. "For what?" he asked.

Sonja stared at him. "For collecting John's chimps."

He grinned slowly. "Aw—that. Not going to do that anymore. I thought y'might be worried about something else."

"What?"

"Those letters."

She looked blank.

"You're the cutter-outer, aren't you?" He touched the vase again. "This stuff you do. Everything cut out."

She clapped a hand over her mouth. "You think I sent those letters!"

Kerry shrugged. "See ya." He clattered down the front steps.

She stood in the center of her living room, almost unable to breathe. If Kerry suspected her of sending the collage letters, so

could others. Everyone knew her hobby was decoupage. The police thought the murderer had sent the letters: so they must suspect
her of being involved, somehow, in Carolyn's demise. And if Joe
Miller started sniffing around the house and U-1 . . . My blood sugar
is low, Sonja thought. I must eat.

She decided to call on Joe first thing next morning, put the accu-
sation before him, and protest her innocence.

Joe's secretary said he was in Kalunga and would be unavailable
until the afternoon.

"I've got to go into town for a haircut," Sonja said. "I'm sure to run
into him."

Joe had left early to talk to Diana Pembridge, ostensibly about the
letter she had received, in fact to ask her where she had been two
nights ago, when the laboratories were burgled. He had not mentioned at the directors' meeting that one of the security guards had
seen a vehicle that night which looked identical to Diana's van. Meanwhile, information on the murder had come in on the fax, sending
several early theories out the window. The animal forensic experts
had discovered that the hairs on Williams's T-shirt were not human,
not rodent, not canine, equine, or bovine, but from some other animal. Perhaps chimpanzee.

Joe rang Sydney immediately to say that a circus had camped on
the outskirts of town on the weekend, but in College Street they
knew that already and an all-stations alert for the circus had gone
out. "It's a great lead," the detective said. But there was a gap of five
hours, from seven o'clock, when Carolyn had left the pub with two
duck shooters (so far unidentified), to the hour of her death, which
was estimated between midnight and 3:00 A.M. The latest theory was
that after leaving the Kalunga Arms, Carolyn and the duck shooters
had either visited the circus or teamed up with someone who worked
in the circus, or with someone who had visited it that day. . . . They're
groping, Joe thought.

"We're getting good cooperation from the shooting club," the detective added. "But they can't work out who got back after midnight.
They reckon everyone was tucked into sleeping bags by then, because the whole camp was getting up at five. We're thinking maybe
it was circus people she went off with. That could explain the method
of killing. And the other injuries. Animal handlers would be familiar with what the perpetrator did to her."

"What about the vet?"

"Plenty on him. He bought the Porsche in 1991; paid cash. Told the salesman he'd won some money in the lottery."

"Did you talk to him before you left?"

"Yep. His alibi is sound. He had guests for dinner on Saturday night. They watched a video and left around eleven. We cross-checked. The guests confirmed what he said."

"Anything on the letters?"

"About a million fingerprints. Probably none of them belonging to the person who made them. But there are traces of stuff for gas chromatography and spectrometry."

He said that he wanted to talk to Joe anyway, because since discovering that the hair on the body was not human, dog, horse, cow, or rabbit, the murder team had decided to check all the vehicles at the Research for signs of other animals. "Can you give us access to the fleet, so we can vacuum the vehicles in the next day or so?" he asked.

The road to Kalunga was empty. There had been some good rain overnight, and the morning was fresh and bright, with a wide, pale-blue sky. Farmers were out on tractors, scarifying their paddocks while the earth was still damp. Joe tooled along, puzzling over the burglary of two nights earlier. Looked at from one angle, there was a tenuous link between it and the letters: both were protests of a sort against the work of the Research. The letters seemed hostile to genetic engineering; the burglars had pinched a biohazard sign and the bags used for sterilizing biological waste. They were amateurs. There were fingerprints everywhere, made by small, female-size hands. The question Joe asked himself was: What was the Pembridge girl up to? A biohazard sign and autoclave bags might be the things she would want as "evidence" against experiments at the Research. According to the police, she was lying about how she found the body. And then one came back to the letters again. It could seem a smart move to send a letter to herself, because "logically" that would rule her out as their originator. People got "logical" ideas when they were in the grip of an obsession. "The devil is a great reasoner," his mother used to say.

Joe found Diana's house at the river end of Fig Tree Gully Road. It was an old stone place, two-storied, with a sign on the front gate announcing there was an Aboriginal art gallery inside. A bus with OUTBACK EXPLORER painted on its flanks was parked outside, and a group of loudly talking, white-haired men and women were gath-

ered beside the picket fence. Joe noted the side entrance and decided to use that.

Behind the house there was a huge, unkempt garden and a patio
shaded by a wisteria vine, still holding the last of its summer leaves.
He knocked on the back door and, after no answer, opened it and
stepped into a big country kitchen with a gray slate floor and wood-
topped counters so worn from years of chopping that they undu-
lated like sand dunes. There was a cage of white mice on the floor
in one corner. "Yoo-hoo!" he called. From the front of the house he
could hear the raised, excited voices of the elderly explorers.

He returned to the patio and made his way through the dappled
shade of trees toward the end of the garden. An old, gray doe kangaroo that had lost some of her tail levered her body slowly forward,
then stood as still as a post, watching him with long-lashed eyes. In
a dog kennel he saw the rear end of a sleeping wombat, and else-
where in the garden, sudden movements revealed the presence of
other animals hurrying to hide themselves. The trees ended in a ti-
tree fence, beyond which nothing was visible.

"Miss Pembridge! You there, Miss Pembridge?" he called.

From behind the fence came a volley of quacks. A gate in the fence
opened, and Diana beckoned him inside with her free hand.

Ducks crowded around his feet, weaving their long, smooth heads.
All of them were crippled in some way. One drake was missing half
his foot, another had lost an eye, and here and there wings drooped
limply. "War wounded," Diana said. Standing on her fist was a peregrine falcon, a gorgeous creature, that crouched and glared, then
began to scream.

"Falco!" Diana said.

The bird screamed more loudly.

"What's wrong with it?" Joe asked.

"He's jealous because I have a visitor. Excuse me."

Joe stayed where he was, surrounded by excited ducks. The aviary
was ten meters square, lightly roofed with chicken wire, with a pond
at one end and some bushes. Beside the open area there was a
wooden mews for birds of prey. It was divided by a narrow space
with a tiled roof, rather like a bus shelter. The mews and the shelter had concrete floors and wooden perches for the raptors. The
birds could perch in the open or in the small, dark rooms behind.
In one enclosure, an owl and a frogmouth, each leashed to jesses
on their legs, were asleep on bow perches. Diana put the peregrine
on a small block perch in the other enclosure.

"We'll have to leave," she said. "That bloody falcon . . . " It was screeching again. "The owner brought it to me because its screaming was sending him deaf."

"What are you going to do with it?"

The falcon was bating from its perch. "Go on! Break your neck!" she roared at it. "I've been training it for five months. . . ."

Inside the house again, they went past the back of the gallery and up a flight of stairs to her workroom. It was set up with a word processor, a fax, and filing cabinets. There were paintings and photographs of animals and birds on the walls. Joe laid out a colored photostat copy of her dead-duck letter, placing a clear sheet of plastic on top of it.

"I need to ask you one or two questions," he said.

He left an hour later, carrying a set of her fingerprints on the plastic sheet.

Since he was in town, he decided to have a look around. Country towns never seemed to change: the same old-fashioned shops, the same old-fashioned shopkeepers, the same dogs lying on the pavements, snapping at flies. He parked in Church Street, near the empty cathedral, and wandered along High Street, past the Kalair office, the news agency, the saddlery shop, the tractor franchise, and the place that sold agricultural poisons, until he reached the white-curtained window of the Sit 'n' Chat coffee lounge. A sign said CAP-PUCCINO. He had a pang of homesickness for Riley Street, and although he knew the cappuccino would be Nescafé with fluffed-up milk on top, he went in.

Sonja Olfson was engrossed in a magazine at a table at the far end of the room. Joe, who was light on his feet, stepped outside again. He continued down the road to the hardware store, where he needed to find out if anyone had bought bolt cutters recently.

Inside the Sit 'n' Chat, Sonja turned the page and cursed. Her magazine had a hole cut in the right-hand page, destroying the rest of the article she was reading. Its title was "Keeping Your Man Happy—Dos and Dont's," and she had just come to a most interesting section on sex. She flipped the pages. There was another hole. And, further on, another. Something drew her eye to the advertising copy that remained beneath the missing illustration. It referred to scissors. She laid the magazine on the white Formica tabletop and stared unseeing at Van Gogh's sunflowers on the opposite wall.

John Parker had been away for five days, and despite being eager to return to his lab, he boarded the Kalair flight from Sydney to Kalunga on Thursday morning in an ambivalent frame of mind.

These days, he found Sydney as obscene as every other big city: a bedlam of shops, cars, and swarms of people. People. People. Cities reminded him of the London flea plague in the fifties. His bedsheets had been peppered with fleas; on Sundays the minister held aloft the Bible and cried, "Every swarming thing! Every swarming thing is an abomination unto the Lord!" Parishioners were urged to cleanse their houses, literally and metaphorically. Ha! Look at what forty years of progress have achieved, Parker thought. Look at the insects now! Tokyo: educated professionals sitting three hours a day in their motorcars in traffic jams. Jakarta: a nightmare. Bangkok: ditto. London: a joke. Los Angeles: a time bomb. In Bogotá, children had turned into cockroaches, living in the sewers. Africa was starving and swarming. In Paris, the level of sulfur dioxide in the atmosphere was so high that women with dyed hair who lingered at sidewalk cafés could suffer a change of color in the space of an hour. And so on and on—a murrain of humans on every continent. Self-extermination had now joined art and spoken language as a hallmark of the human being.

Once, the great empty spaces of the Australian bush had appalled him: the dry air, the huge skies, the glittering leather-leafed trees. Now he longed for the stillness and the absence of shops. And he longed for his work, dull and uneventful as it was most of the time. He wanted to get back to work, and he wanted desperately to escape the crowds and pollution of the city—but return to work meant return to Sonja. Parker felt a chill in the pit of his stomach when he thought of his wife. *Why did I get involved with her in the first place?* he sometimes wondered. There had been plenty of other women eager to oblige him—but she'd been the most persistent; the one who telephoned him and sent him presents. He found it difficult now to remember all the reasons he had used to convince himself two years ago that he should marry her. *If we're married she can't give evidence against me in case something goes wrong with the chimpanzees.* That, as he recalled it, was the most cogent argument he had when it became obvious she was obsessed with matrimony.

"For God's sake, what difference will it make if we're married?" he'd asked.

"I just want to be able to say, My husband. . . ." She had that pleading look she put on when she was determined. At the back of her Poor Innocent Me eyes, he had seen millennia of females squinting at him.

Since his return from Bangkok, they had spoken daily, conscious that eavesdroppers could be on the line, constraining themselves to pallid banalities and obscure references to work in U-1, Kerry Larnach, and the security patrols around Sonja's house. "How are the animals?" he asked each day. A month before leaving for Bangkok, he had injected three buck rabbits and Lucy, the chimpanzee, with the ultimate version of Vaccine II. By the time he got back, they would have raised antibodies and be ready for testing with White Eye. Assuming that went smoothly, the next step would be to mate them with unvaccinated fertile partners. (Sailor would have to do his duty as soon as he arrived.) If conception did not occur, Hallelujah! Hallelujah! Praise the Lord!

Sometimes he risked asking, in an offhand voice, "And Lek is okay? Not bothering you?"

To his inquiry about the animals each morning, Sonja answered, "The zoo is doing fine." She wanted to talk about the murder and the latest gossip on leads. She had already had grilles put on the side windows of her house and was thinking of getting an electronic watchdog—a machine that made barking noises when a beam of light was interrupted. "What in hell use is that?" he muttered. "Everybody knows we're not allowed to keep dogs at the Research." In a hurt voice, she answered, "If you weren't away three or four or even five nights a week, I wouldn't have to think of ways of trying to protect myself."

I should've seen that one coming, he thought. On Wednesday night she had telephoned in a state of dudgeon over a remark Larnach had made.

"Well, *did* you send the letters?" John asked. He meant it to be jocular, but the moment the words were out, a voice said, *You'll pay for that.*

There was silence.

He could not help himself. "Is that No?"

"I'll see you at the airfield," she replied.

"No, no—wait!" he interjected. "You must give Steve a message. Tell him that tomorrow morning he should go into Level 2, remove the frozen aliquot—"

"The *what?*"

She had heard him use this term a thousand times. "A-l-i-q-u-o-t. Aliquot. He knows what it is. He's to take it out of the freezer, defrost some, and grow it up in broth in the rotary shaker."

He heard her mumbling "broth" and "rotary shaker" as if they were words from a foreign tongue, yet when they stayed at Hilary's house in Sydney, terms like "ribosome" and "RNA" would trip from her lips.

The Kalunga air terminal was a wooden shed with a weighing machine, old posters of Mediterranean holiday resorts, and, on the linoleum floor, in corners and near walls, the desiccated corpses of blowflies. Near the fence outside, crop-dusting planes were clustered, looking like the larvae of the larger aircraft, itself only a nine-seater, that had just arrived from Sydney. As Parker came down the stairs to the tarmac, Sonja stepped through the terminal's glass door to greet him.

He had an impression that she looked different, and he knew he should remark on this, but for the life of him he could not work out what it was that had changed. Of the many things he found offensive in women, one of the most annoying was the endless alterations they made to their hair, their clothes, and their face paint. They expected men to be as fascinated by these vanities as they were: his first wife became hysterical one day when he failed to acknowledge that she had had all her hair cut off. Stupid bitch, he thought. He was glad she was dead. And her Labrador. He would come home and find its muzzle covered in ice cream it had found on the street, or bloody from old meat it rooted out of garbage bins. One day his wife brought the dog into his lab, and while their backs were turned it licked up the contents of a petri dish. He realized what had happened when he noticed the dog wagging its tail slowly, looking pleased with itself and guilty, the hair on its chops strawberry-colored, which was the color of the gel in the dish. There was something sly and tail-wagging about Sonja right now, he thought. He tried to smile, racking his brains as he walked across the tarmac for something to say about her appearance. His opening remark would set the tone of the relationship for the rest of the day and, come evening, for his erection test. There would be storms before bedtime if he couldn't get it up. Sometimes he wanted to shout, "No! I don't find you desirable. I used to, for some reason, but I don't anymore. I have fantasies about that chemist in the rabbit fertility-control program, and the typists who play basketball, and crotch shots in magazines. Leave me alone until morning, and I'll be able to screw you then." Sometimes he wanted to howl like a wolf and run up the wall on all fours.

Her small face turned up for his kiss. Pressing his lips to her forehead, he murmured, "You look utterly delicious—I'm going to rape you this evening."

As soon as they were inside the Land Cruiser, she told him about Kerry's threat to bring in no more chimps and that Diana Pembridge was the Australian representative of PRO. "What will we do?"

"Kill her," he said.

Sonja did not think that was funny.

"We'll do nothing," he added. "Kerry wants more money. I'll haggle with him. As for the bird woman: what can she do? She can't get inside—"

"But she can! If she's appointed to the Ethics Committee, she'll have access to the laboratories."

"Well, then, I'll carry you away to the East," he replied. "You'll have to live on lotus blossoms and have your feet massaged with perfumed oils."

On the drive home she kept taking her eyes off the road to turn and smile at him. Suddenly he realized she would be angry that all he'd brought her was some shampoo and soap and the brass elephant. His gut turned uneasily.

"What's wrong, darling?" she asked.

"Nothing."

"You look as if you have a pain."

"I was pretty sick in Thailand this time. I didn't want to worry you. . . ."

"Oh, my poor love . . ."

"I'm almost better." He gave a brave smile, flushed with relief now that his escape had magically appeared, the twin problems of inadequate gift and flaccid member solved at a stroke.

They went to his condo first. Sonja always remained standing when she visited her husband's apartment. She had a special expression that said, I shall say nothing about the way John chooses to live in his private space. It's no business of mine that it looks like a pigsty and the pot plants are all dead.

When he pulled the elephant out of his sock, she said, "It's sweet." She stood staring at it lying in her palm, as if somehow she could make it turn into an elephant of diamonds and gold. She had intended to tell him what she had discovered about the collage letters and to ask his advice, but she was too upset.

At her house, she gave him a blue cashmere pullover she had ordered from David Jones as a homecoming present. Parker closed his eyes, which the sweater accentuated handsomely, and kissed her again, while a voice inside him shouted at her, "Stop looking like a dog pleading for a biscuit!" Fortunately, she had to get back to work.

What she called work was as different from what he called work as marching in place was different from dancing. Parker found it impossible to convey to Sonja the excitement of science—not because she could not understand if she wanted to, but because if she did she would want to degrade it somehow. If he was still at his bench in U-1 at 7:00 P.M., she telephoned every fifteen minutes, asking when he would be coming upstairs for dinner. "You're not getting overtime for all those extra hours," she said, sighing. "I don't do it for *money*," he told her between gritted teeth. Sometimes, on summer evenings when they sat on the veranda, having a drink, she asked, "Penny for your thoughts, my love." Almost always he was thinking about DNA. He had a dream in which he traveled over a curving strand of it, looking for a particular sequence. Sometimes the search was leisurely, almost erotic, like moving his hand up a woman's thigh. Other times it was astonishing. It became like the scene in *2001* when travelers clamber up over the dark side of the moon to encounter: a monolith! He dreamed of antibodies in images like that: suddenly what he needed to know stood before him, as eloquent as an idol on the moon.

It had taken him three years to modify Vaccine I so that it would both protect against White Eye and render a range of species—rabbit, chimp, and (therefore) human—sterile. Vaccine II now had such a complex structure, it resembled a huge jigsaw puzzle in which, when one piece was changed, all the other pieces tried to rearrange themselves. But developing it to this stage had been via a junkyard of disappointments. Two early versions had worked against White Eye but were unreliable as sterilizing agents. Another version had worked in rat and rabbit but not chimpanzee. A third had snookered chimp zona pellucida but not the acrosomal membrane of chimp sperm. That was his best version so far.

His challenge now was to simplify: he had to imagine the vaccine as merely Piece A (for the acrosomal membrane) and Piece B (for the zona pellucida and White Eye), and among the hundreds of thousands of pieces, he must touch only Piece A. He had spent months thinking about where he might find Piece A and, having found it, how to mutate it in a way that would not stimulate half a dozen other amino acids to mutate too.

Then, a month before Christmas, at Sonja's house, he had had a dream. It was the sort of hot, fertile summer morning when white butterflies danced around her garden, and the sunshine, dragging water from the lake, made the air tropical. In the distance was the rising and falling shrill of cicadas, their song like the sound of a jungle at dawn. Just before waking, he dreamed he was floating above a tropical forest through which flowed a river. Suddenly he realized that the pulsing, myriad lives of the forest represented the millions of possible combinations of genes. The river was a ribbon of DNA. Below him the orange-brown water abruptly flashed bright blue in one section—and that was the spot! That was the region on which he had to work. As he drifted on above the river, he noted landmarks on the bank on either side—then he sat bolt upright, awake, and shot his long white shinbones out of bed.

By seven that morning, Parker had been seated at his computer with MacVector up and running. By eight, he had constructed the sequences of synthetic oligonucleotides he would need. He was so excited, he had to go upstairs and walk around Sonja's bottle brushes and grevilleas for a few minutes, forcing himself to slow down, not to rush ahead but to check the oligo design and make certain it would modify specifically where he wanted it to. *What I'm doing will change the course of history*, he repeated to himself. *I will be as revered as Alexander and Saint Paul and Pasteur.* At the moment when, five years earlier, the idea of politically painless mass sterilization had occurred to him, Parker had felt his inner being vibrate like a harp string. But right now he had to concentrate on the annealing temperature. With a change in temperature, one could have the sequences go somewhere else as well, and the whole thing could mutate, like a piece of music suddenly switched from a major to a minor key.

Verification of the design took another few minutes. The technicians had arrived by the time he was finished, but he was too excited even to say hello.

The oligonucleotide synthesis machine was in a separate, smaller room that smelled of organic solvent and oil from machinery run by vacuum pumps. With the letters of the sequences jotted in his lab book, Parker went in, closed the door, and dialed in the codes. By the time he was finished, his shirt was wet. He closed his eyes for a moment and saw a huge stage bathed in lights, and beyond it an enormous crowd roaring applause. He was alone in the center of the stage. The day Inspiration had plucked the strings of his soul, it whispered, "John, your vaccine against White Eye can be used to stop the human race from breeding itself to death." "*How?*" he had demanded. Even now, to remember that answer made his legs quake.

It would be twelve hours before the machine had done its work. Then he would have to put the oligos through the HPLC machine to purify overnight.

At eight the next morning, Parker began the preparation of his target DNA for the polymerase chain reaction machine.

In the fridge in the Big Lab in an Eppendorf tube was the DNA from his last attempt at Vaccine II, the version that had not acted on the acrosomal membrane. He took it out and put it on the bench, then gathered the buffers, the oligos, and the enzyme he needed for the PCR machine. The next step was to put the purified oligos, the inadequate Vaccine II DNA, buffers, enzyme, and other oligos in a tube and to mix them with AmpliTaq enzyme. He had decided on AmpliTaq because, coming as it did from a bacterium of sulfur pits— "bacteria from hell" it was called—AmpliTaq would work at temperatures of up to 100 degrees Celsius. He pipetted the mixture into small tubes and placed them in the machine. What he proposed to do was so simple: what the Australians wanted to do to their rabbits, he would do to the human race. After preliminary PCR, he set up the final reaction, would which result in the designed mutation.

By noon, Parker had the DNA for perfect Vaccine II. He was halfway there.

Next he had a lot of cloning to do.

He was fast at cloning. "*Con brio,*" the technicians said. "A blind man could do it," Parker told them. "It's just pipetting and shaking." (Fifteen years ago, when he had first tried to isolate DNA, he could not do it at all. He had tried twenty times, and nothing happened. One day a doctoral student came and sat at the bench beside him with a Pipetman and a set of Eppendorf tubes. They used the same solutions, the same conditions, running every step at the same time. The student's worked. His did not. As a scientist, that still defeated him: he often found himself brooding about what it could mean, but although many possibilities occurred to him, none seemed satisfactory.)

The next step was to ligate the new DNA into a vector. That night, Parker transferred his new, cloned DNA into bacteria cells, and by the third morning he had colonies of bacteria dotted across a plate.

He spent a long while looking at them before choosing twelve. "Twelve," he murmured. His mind was making connections that fascinated him by their magical simplicity. Twelve disciples, he thought. Twelve tribes of Israel. Twelve months of the year. Twelve signs of the zodiac. Twelve inches to the foot. Twelve pennies to the shilling. The list jingled through his head as he inoculated each colony he wanted into a separate test tube of liquid broth growth medium. He would let it grow up for five hours in a cupboard set at 37 degrees Celsius. By the afternoon, he was ready to isolate and verify the DNA, which he did in an hour, at the bench.

Cleaving came next. If people were not so selfish, cruel, and irrational, all this would not have been necessary, he thought as he worked. In a test tube, he cleaved the isolated DNA with restriction enzymes, then ran the fragments out on a gel to confirm that the DNA had the right general pattern.

It was already dusk outside when he put on a mask and took the new DNA for Vaccine II to the UV light box. As he stooped over the box, he saw in his imagination the blue stretch of river once more, but now it ran between straight banks, tamed. Fluorescent bands of deoxyribonucleic acid glowed against an orange-red background. "I've done it!" he said. He had mutated the gene that caused the acrosomal membrane to pop off the top of a sperm so it could fertilize an egg. Now the membrane could not pop off. The sperm—all the millions of sperms—would remain sealed and useless. It occurred to Parker that he had just succeeded in doing what every man, secretly, would like to do: he had created a vaccine that could sterilize all the other men on earth.

For a moment he wondered if he should check the new sequences to make sure no additional mutation had crept in, but he decided not to. He was bone weary. In the past seventy-two hours he had managed to sleep only three hours a night, his mind churning in the dark even more vigorously than when he was fully awake.

The next step was rote, and starting it could wait until tomorrow: it was to transfer the DNA into mammalian cells in a flask, where they would produce large quantities of the protein. He would then isolate this protein and give it to the lab boys for hybridoma technology.

The protein isolation took a week, and on the second Sunday of Advent, the boys began their hybridoma work. They labored through Christmas and New Year, all of January, and half of February. On Saint Valentine's Day, there was a ceremony in U-1. Steve, wearing his swimming trunks, lipstick, and someone's high heels, handed Parker a heart-shaped card and a rack of Eppendorf tubes of purified monoclonal antibodies. The timing was exquisite: in four weeks Parker was leaving for Bangkok. He could inject test animals—some buck rabbits and the female chimp—with the antibodies that afternoon. In five weeks, when he returned to U-1, their immune reaction would have developed to a point where they would be fully immune to the disease, plus totally sterile. As soon as he returned from Bangkok, he could inject them with White Eye.

The first test for Vaccine II had now arrived. He hurried down the wooden steps from Sonja's veranda that afternoon, snapping his fingers with excitement.

The original architectural plans for the Research had the old stock dam near the lake converted into an underground area for housing a generator, a water-treatment plant, and other facilities. The first task of the engineering team had been drainage, excavation, and extension of the dam site, and installation of a concrete shell. Then a directive came from Canberra, saying that the whole complex must be moved farther from the lake to protect the birds. All the plans had to be redrawn, and the underground generator and water-treatment room was left without a purpose, until somebody realized that its concrete construction was ideal for the advanced air-filtering system that creates a high-containment lab. High-containment air-conditioning/filtering was installed, plus electricity and plumbing. But when it was finished, nobody wanted the inconvenience of working out there. There was a small, well-equipped high-containment laboratory in the main complex. When Parker offered to use U-1 on contract for his work for Siam Enterprises, it was a godsend to the Accounts Department, for although Parker was paying the equivalent of a peppercorn rent, at least U-1 was generating some income, and that allowed it to be moved to the cash flow side of the balance sheet.

Despite jokes in the staff canteen, there was no danger of contamination to occupants of the house perched above U-1, or to people who stayed in the garden flat.

The entrance to the laboratory was an ordinary plywood door next to Sonja's laundry. An Inclin-ator for carrying heavy pieces of equipment ran beside the stairs. At the bottom, there was a staff room with table and chairs, a fridge, a microwave oven, and a television/video unit. The staff room led through two sets of doors into the Big Lab, which smelled of ethanol and *E. coli.* From the Big Lab there were three doors: one led to the Animal Room, one to the room for the sequencing, HPLC, and other machines, and one to the Biohazard Containment Room, known as Level 2. Outside Level 2 was a corridor for changing into gowns, masks, booties, and gloves before entering. Inside Level 2, in a liquid-nitrogen tank, there was a frozen aliquot of White Eye bacteria.

The room was not much used, because most work was done in the Big Lab, which also was equipped with negative-airflow cabinets. Parker, who entered Level 2 most, never bothered with more than a gown and gloves, unless he had to dissect a cadaver infected with White Eye. He and Sonja, like everyone in U-1, were protected against the disease by Vaccine I, but he took no chances. He had a dissection bench set up with the tools he needed, including a mechanized bone saw, inside a clear plastic biohazard tent.

The door to the Animal Room had one-way glass so that, from the Big Lab, staff could check on the chimpanzees without being seen by them. Inside, a concertina door divided the animal room in two. It was extended at night to separate the chimpanzees from the rabbits and mice, and pushed shut during the day to make space for the chimps to play. Its equipment included brightly colored kindergarten-size furniture, a television/video, soft toys, building blocks, climbing ropes on one wall, and an exercise bicycle specially shortened for chimp-length legs. At first the chimps had been left caged all day, but they died from inactivity. Parker suggested it would be cheaper in the long run to pay for a keeper to play with them, and Grossmann had reluctantly agreed. Every six months, he sent down a boy from the breeding farm, flying him into Australia on the same route used for the chimps: Bangkok, Kuching, Ujung Pandang, Kupang, then Karatha. Siam's dispatch department always managed to send other freight on these flights, which then doubled back to Darwin and landed legally, thus making the whole arrangement economically viable. Meanwhile, for six months' work underground the keepers earned a one-hundred-fifty-dollar bonus. Even so, by the end of

1992, staff at the breeding farm in Saraburi were unwilling to apply for service in Australia, having been discouraged by tales of isolation, tasteless food, and evil spirits. Lek was not a keeper but a servant in the Saraburi guesthouse who had shown an interest in animals. She was a pug-faced militant vegetarian and had the famous Siamese temper. Meat products had to be banned from the staff room refrigerator soon after her arrival. Parker found her deliciously funny and encouraged her to tell stories about demons at morning tea.

When he went downstairs that afternoon, he found her holding a rabbit up against her shoulder, like an infant being held for a burp.

"Put that animal back in its cage immediately," he said. He went swiftly forward and gave her a light, sharp smack on the backside.

I n Bangkok, just before lunchtime, Michael Romanus collected a suit the color of vanilla ice cream from the tailor in Silom Road who made Otto's clothes. Romanus could not afford the suit himself; Grossmann was buying it. "There'll be a lot of rich people at my reception, Mikey. I don't want you to be embarrassed," he said. I wouldn't be, Romanus thought. But when he saw himself in the suit, he had to admit he felt good. From the tailor's shop he caught a cab to Grossmann's house. The heavy iron grille rolled back, and the cab crunched to a stop on white gravel outside the teak double doors. Romanus gave a hasty smile to the servant who let him in and made straight for Otto's study, as if late for an appointment. When he reached the door, he opened it and went into the room where Grossmann's personal assistant, Miss Bochang, guarded the inner sanctum that lay beyond. Miss Bochang, was not at her desk, as Romanus knew she would not be. She was on the other side of town, waiting to meet an animal dealer who would never turn up. Romanus locked the outer door and went to the desk, where the documents he needed were just where she had left them an hour ago. He laid them out in a row, took a camera from his pocket, and photographed them. Then he shuffled them back together, the way they had been when he found them, and grabbed the manila envelope marked "Michael Romanus, To Be Collected," in Miss Bochang's curly script.

He poked his head into Otto's room and waved the envelope. "See you at the party."

"Hey!" Grossmann called. "Show me the suit." Romanus sauntered into the room and strolled across the Persian rug. "I tell you, it looks great." Otto was beaming with pleasure. "After the reception, you and I will need some female company, that's for sure!"

"Whatever you say. I gotta run, Otto."

Grossmann returned his attention to the balance sheet he was studying, still smiling although the figures were not wonderful. He was thinking about going to La Parisienne with Michael: It was so amusing, the way the Australian always kidded the girls as if he had no idea they were whores.

Since Sunday, Diana had visited Jason's place once or twice a day to see the eagle, each time bringing it small meals. The bird still detested her, but it was now willing to eat in her presence, whereas at first it had refused to take food while she or any other human was in sight. The trick had been to starve it for twenty-four hours, then offer fresh rabbit the next morning. On her Tuesday visit, Diana had discovered that Margaret the receptionist, with Jason's compliance, had been inviting people into the laundry to look at the bird. Diana insisted on moving the eagle to the back garden, out of earshot of the clinic. Jason tried to make light of it. "At least I'll be able to get my washing done," he said. Margaret was deeply insulted.

On Thursday afternoon, Diana took from a cupboard in the storage area of the aviary her long leather glove and gauntlet. The gauntlet was a green-hide sleeve that fitted from her wrist to her elbow, reinforced longitudinally with strips of steel to protect her arm from the eagle's grip. In the storage area, which separated the two mews, there was a horizontal pole, like a ballet school bar, where the hunting birds perched while she hooded them. Diana kept all her falconing tools in this narrow room: a set of scales, lures in the shape of rabbits and pigeons, jesses, creances, her falconer's bag, and a variety of hoods, some as small as a walnut shell, others like half a cricket ball. She pulled on the gauntlet, then a glove, and tried her arm for strength by whacking it against the pole. There was only a dull thud. She removed the leathers and set out for Jason's clinic, stopping at the butcher's shop, where she collected a rooster's head. Cockscomb contained something that eagles relished. When she walked in, holding the head by its neck feathers, Margaret yelled, "Get that thing out of here!"

Diana went on through to the back garden. She had tethered the eagle to a liquidambar tree, but all she could see when she went out was a pair of large, cream-scaled feet, jessed, with a leash attached, underneath a nearby nandina bush. She hunkered down, holding her hands behind her back, and gave a two-note whistle. She was careful to keep her eyes lowered as she approached, since eagles regarded eye contact as a threat.

It was just visible as something denser behind the bush. Diana whistled again, then held at arm's length the rooster head. The leaves of the nandina bush vibrated, and next moment the eagle jumped from behind it. Diana tossed the food. A massive foot pinned it to the ground, the black neck arched, there was a ripping noise, throat muscles bulged. As the glossy head bent to eat the rest of the meal, Diana dropped the fowling net.

She drove around Kalunga until it was dark, giving the bird time to calm down.

When headlights appeared at the top of Fig Tree Gully Road, Grace, who had been on the lookout, hurried to the side of the house and opened the gate. As the van pulled up she whispered, "You got her?"

"Yes," Diana answered.

By now the evening star was shining and there was so little day-light left the eagle could see no better than the humans. Diana was hoping this would quiet the bird, but it did not. When she tried to take her from her perch in the back of the van, the wedgetail flat-tened her contour feathers close to her body and struck out with her foot.

In the end, Diana had to use the net again. Her captive struggled and kicked while she was being carried down through the garden.

Grace's wide, soft form moved on ahead with the flashlight, her face and limbs invisible in the dark. When they reached the ti-tree fence, she gave a whistle. A loud, rasping "cush-cush-sh-sh" an-swered. They entered, and Grace switched on the light, slowly in-creasing illumination. The owl shook its head at the light, while the frogmouth stood erect on its bow perch and made its huge eyes into yellow slits. The ducks set up a commotion, and the peregrine screeched.

Finally the eagle was installed, alone, in the second mews, while outside, the falcon, placed on a small block perch for the night, jumped in the air in a temper. Grace shuffled about, sighing. When she closed her eyes for a moment and looked at the light around Di-ana, she could see that Diana was tired and disturbed. She had warned her, "You be careful, or you'll have an accident." Instead of slowing down, however, Diana had taken on extra work. In just over a fortnight, when the eagle's wing had healed, she would have a full-time job training it. In the meantime, the falcon and the two night birds had to be prepared for release. The falcon was still a hopeless case, Grace knew.

She adjusted the dimmer switch so that later, when the owl and the frogmouth were fed, they would not be alarmed by sudden bright light.

Late in the afternoon, Kerry Larnach drove from the airfield to Kalunga and kept going until he was on the other side of town, on a potholed street that dwindled into dirt road and, finally, long, dry grass. Halfway down the street, there was a phone box with an out-of-order telephone. On either side, Paterson's curse and thistles grew on vacant blocks where car bodies rusted and old plastic bags, caught on bushes, flapped in the breeze. Toward the end of the street, before it became a dirt road, stood four small, shabby houses and one neat one, which was where Grace Larnach lived with her grandsons, Tom and Billy, aged eleven and thirteen. The boys had been sent out from Sydney a year earlier, when their father was jailed. Their mother, Grace's daughter, had her hands full with three younger children. "My relations," Kerry said, grinning scornfully at the miserable houses. His great-grandfather (and Diana Pembridge's) was Old Mister Larnach, a gold prospector and landowner who had found time to sire a legitimate tribe of his own, plus a bunch of half-castes to whom he gave his name. Grace was the granddaughter of Old Mister, as the town still called him. In boyhood, Kerry had hated having black relatives, but since he had become a big noise in the shire, his sense of shame had relaxed. These days he greeted Grace as "Auntie" when he passed her in the street.

Earlier that afternoon, he had telephoned the gallery and chatted with Auntie, pretending he had rung to talk to Diana. In fact he wanted to find out when Tom and Billy would be home alone; they had a set of keys to his cousin's place.

He walked up the cracked concrete path to the porch, where plants flourished in pots and the dusty, savage-looking cattle dog from next door strolled around on stiff legs, alert for enemies.

"G'arn!" Kerry said. The dog ducked, ran toward a hole in the wire fence, and shimmied through.

The boys were lying on a balding sofa in the front room, watching a video. Kerry had a football with him. As he pushed open the door, he said, "Hey!" and tossed the ball. Billy caught it.

Kerry sat on the sofa. "Whatcha watching?" he asked.

For a few minutes they all concentrated on Mel Gibson killing someone. Tom announced. "There'll be a slow bit now. We can stop it."

Kerry said he had come to offer them a car-washing job. They went outside to look at his Land Cruiser. "Twenty dollars for washing and polishing it every week. How much do you get for cleaning Auntie Diana's birdhouse?" he asked. Fifteen, they said.

Kerry guffawed. "She's robbing you."

The boys gazed at him with lustrous dark eyes. They were at an age that trembles on the edge of magic, bravado, and fear of adults.

"You got the key to it?" he said.

Half an hour later, he left, jingling in his pocket Diana's aviary key, front and back door keys, and the key to her van. "Ten-thirty tomorrow morning I'll come by the playground and give 'em back to you," he promised.

"*And* the new set," Billy said.

"*And the new set.*"

The kids watched him drive away, still as solemn as they had been throughout his visit. When the Land Cruiser reached the end of the road, they turned to each other and squealed.

"I thought we'd had it!" Billy yelled.

"Me too!"

"When he walked in I thought, Oh, no! We're dead!"

They had to run up and down the street and chuck gravel at a telegraph pole before they calmed down.

Kerry, meanwhile, was disappointed that Diana's office key was not among those he got from the kids by offering to make them a duplicate set they could keep. He wanted to have a look through Diana's filing system and figured it would be easier if he had the key to the door of her workroom.

The new chimp was due to arrive in twenty-four hours. In the worst case, if it seemed too dangerous to land the animal at either the airfield or the Research, Kerry had decided to have it ditched. He and his little brother had agreed on the signal: "Nice weather here—still warm enough to swim" meant "Throw the chimpanzee into the lake." Lake Kalunga was three meters deep, more than fifteen kilometers long, and four kilometers wide. It had a maze of submerged hazards—drowned trees, sunken duck boats, and old fence posts, from years when the water receded and the lakebed was used as grazing land. The location of these snags was known only to people like Diana Pembridge and the Larnachs, who had grown up near the lake. Another crate would be just one more submerged object. It would be well covered with water, probably never discovered.

Kerry drove home slowly, wondering what to do if Diana suspected chimpanzees were being brought into Australia unquarantined. He and John Parker had not worked out how Carolyn Williams had got wind of the chimps—yet she did not seem to know the animals were coming to the Research. Or if she did know, her questions to the animal food companies had been even subtler than they seemed. She had pretended to be conducting a "survey on commercial foodstuffs supplied to apes and monkeys in Australia" for CITES, the Convention on International Endangered Species.

Kerry's left leg jigged as he remembered the conversation he had had three weeks ago with the sales manager of Animal Food Supplies. "We've had a request for information from a Dr. Carolyn Williams about institutions ordering primate food, but before giving out the names of our customers, we are checking with them. . . ." Since yesterday, when he had read the Primate Rescue Organization newsletter, Kerry had been asking himself, Was it really Carolyn who rang? The person said she was Carolyn Williams and claimed she worked at the Research. That gave credibility to her survey story. But what if it had been Diana? Diana would not ring and say, "Hi, I'm an animal rights radical. I once threw red paint on thousands of dollars' worth of furs, but I was young and stupid then. Now I'm older and smarter, and I'd just like to ask . . ."

He was worried about Jason Nichols too. He had warned Parker that they must keep to a minimum the number of people involved: the lab staff, Sonja, him, his baby brother. When Parker needed veterinary assistance he brought in Nichols. "Jason'll do anything for cash," John said. But in Kerry's view, Nichols was not money-minded so much as eager for little adventures, a bit of lawbreaking to spice up his life. He had a face like an angel—and I wouldn't trust him as far as I could kick him, Kerry thought.

"Nichols is a weirdo," he warned Parker.

"No weirder than most other people," Parker had replied. "Our age is psychically disturbed. The church failed, and we put politics in its place. Now politics has failed. We believed in money, but money is failing. People don't know what to trust, so they trust anything. Look at the flood of ignorance and superstition everywhere, the anti-science sentiment among Western youth, the belief in magic and witchcraft."

Kerry drove past Nichols's house. The Porsche was not in the drive, but Margaret McLeod's bicycle was leaning against a side wall.

His own house was only two doors past the veterinary clinic.

Kalair staff joked that their boss ran the airline as a cover operation for his secret depravity: tools. In the back garden, Kerry had converted a double garage into a toolshed, its walls lined with shelves on which, in alphabetical order, were arranged gadgets from awls to vises. He had six weights of hammers, twenty screwdrivers, pliers tiny enough to pluck eyebrow hairs, ranging to implements that needed both hands and could yank an iron pin from a railway sleeper. People were always dropping in, wanting to borrow something. Just yesterday, Joe Miller from the Research had called by the office, wondering if he could borrow a small chisel.

After microwaving and eating dinner, Kerry went to his shed and cut a set of keys. At eight o'clock, he set his alarm for 1:00 A.M. and went to sleep.

In Bangkok, Michael Romanus spent two thousand baht on photocopying the prints he had made of the documents found earlier that day in Miss Bochang's room. From a business office near Lumpini Park, he faxed the photocopies to Raoul Sabea in Chiang Mai. They were the correspondence, airfreight bills, and receipts for sale of the "young red bird" he had brought to Grossmann in Saraburi. Otto had said he would have the baby orangutan flown to the orangutan rehabilitation center in Kalimantan; instead, he had sold it to a Swiss industrialist.

Diana fed the night birds at around nine each evening. Feeding every forty-eight hours would have been enough, but she wanted them a little overweight so when she released them they could tolerate a couple of hungry nights without becoming distressed. Neither bird had flight problems, but after weeks in captivity, they were out of hunting practice.

The frogmouth had been caught by children who found it asleep in a hollow tree. They had kept it in a cage, where it developed an ulcer on one of its small, weak feet, and it could barely stand when Diana first took charge of it. A farmer had found the other bird, a female masked owl, in his barn, half dead from rat poison. Diana had looked after these birds for only a fortnight but already had grown fond of them, the owl especially. She was tall and chestnut-colored, her face a lovely split-apple shape, outlined in black. She had long legs, rufous feather trousers, and the dramatic habit of suddenly turning her head 180 degrees when she detected an interesting sound. At first she was utterly silent, but after a few days she began responding to Grace's calls, and now she was almost chatty, crying "cush-cush" or "quair-sh-sh-sh" whenever she had company.

Diana cut the saddle off a rabbit and defrosted two mice. She stood in front of the perches and turned off the light, while the birds watched her, able to see in the dark by the mysterious illumination within themselves. There was utter silence, then a cool breath caressed Diana's cheek and ghostly fingers snatched the rabbit meat. From the far side of the mews came crunching noises. Diana held out a slightly warm mouse. The strong, silent wings of the frogmouth brushed past her, and the mouse vanished from her hand.

The town was asleep and silent when Kerry left his house just after one o'clock the next morning. The only sound, beside the noise of his Land Cruiser, came from a truck far in the distance, whose lights he saw from time to time as it plowed down the highway toward Victoria. He drove to Church Street, which ran parallel to Fig Tree Gully Road, and parked in the grounds of the cathedral. His footsteps sounded loud, but their noise vanished as soon as he reached the riverbank. It was cool down there, in the long, slippery grass. There was less than half a moon, leaving the black sky foaming with stars.

A dog barked at him but stopped when he left its territory. Three hundred meters along the riverbank, he arrived at the ti-tree fence of his cousin's aviary. Above him were the hack boxes, where birds could be fed without seeing their keeper. Kerry scribbled his flashlight over the tightly packed gray twigs until he found the gate, then juggled clumsily, trying to find the right key to the padlock.

Inside, he glanced at the weird paraphernalia: the jesses, creances, hoods, and lures. Seeing these tools of his cousin's passion was like seeing her naked. This was her little temple, with its ritual objects and pavilioned gods.

The back door, into the kitchen, was unlocked. He went quietly across the flagstone floor into the hallway and mounted the steps to her office. Her bedroom was upstairs at the other end of the house, a big room with a cedar four-poster bed and an old cedar wardrobe that had belonged to Grandma Larnach. I should've got that furniture, he thought. A floorboard creaked. He froze. There was no other sound, and after a moment he continued.

The office door was open.

Kerry closed it behind him, went to Diana's desk, and turned on the lamp. Can I risk the beep from booting up the computer? he wondered. He decided to look at the hard-copy files first.

There were four tall metal filing cabinets, two on either side of the desk, and it took him a while to work out that the system was divided into Birds, Marsupials, Mammals, and Reptiles. He began looking through Mammals. Under *C* there was no file on Chimpanzees. He tried *M* for Monkey, and went back to *A* for Ape. Then he thought of trying *P* for Primate Rescue Organization, but there was no file of the newsletters either. He was about to give up when, still in *P*, he saw PAN TROGLODYTES and remembered that Parker sometimes referred to "the troglodytes" when he was talking about chimpanzees. And there it was in the PAN TROGLODYTES file: legislation about chimpanzees, international protocols, the whole legal rigmarole. Pages of computer printout listed the names of laboratories, zoos, and circuses all over the world where chimpanzees were in use. Each animal's registration number, age, and sex was recorded, according to country. He flicked quickly to "Australia." State by state, there were lists of chimps in zoos and circuses; under "Scientific Institutions" there was an entry: "Use restricted in 1984 following implementation of the Wildlife Protection Act. As of February 1993, no record of chimps in use in scientific institutions." At the foot of each page was the legend "Prepared by the Primate Rescue Organization with assistance from Charles River Laboratories, U.S. Fish and Wildlife Service, World Conservation Union, TRAFFIC, and CITES." He knew that TRAFFIC monitored international trade in wildlife and wildlife products and worked hand in glove with CITES.

Kerry exhaled with relief. This was what Diana—or Carolyn, if it really had been Carolyn who telephoned the food company—was doing: updating the database. This made sense of the questions that had been put to the food supply company.

After the pages of printout in the PAN TROGLODYTES file, there was a note: "See Hylobates, Pongo, Gorilla." He flipped to *H* and found HYLOBATES AGILIS, MOLOCH, AND LAR—*Gibbons,* with a printout on the world's captive gibbons. He took a quick look at the PONGO file, which was about orangutans.

He was almost ready to leave, when a noise outside alarmed him. Downstairs, an engine started.

The office was at the end of the house closest to the driveway. Kerry tiptoed to the window and looked down. Diana's yellow van was backing out the drive. Where in hell is she going? Has she seen me? He ran to the desk, snatched the papers on it, and galloped down the stairs, out the back door, and through the garden toward the aviary.

The noise of his footsteps woke Diana, who thought that the kitchen door must have opened, allowing the wombat, which was missing most of one front paw, to blunder into the house.

She got out of bed and went downstairs, where the kitchen door was indeed open. But although she walked from room to room, calling "Archie! Where are you?" there was no sign of him. She locked the door and went back upstairs.

By eight o'clock on Friday morning, Kerry was airborne. Twelve hours later, he helped unload and install the new chimp. It was 11:00 P.M. before he got home again and noticed, on his bedside table, the letters he had taken from Diana's desk the night before. There were two bills, a check made out to Aboriginal Paintings and Carvings, and a postcard from Fiji from his aunt, Diana's mother. Underneath these items were paper-clipped faxes and copies of outgoing letters. Kerry leafed through them with one hand as he pulled off his shoes. Diana had written a letter on Monday to the director of the National Fish and Wildlife Forensic Laboratory, Southern Oregon State College, Ashland. She introduced herself as a member of the International TRAFFIC Network and asked the laboratory to identify "the enclosed material."

He was about to roll into bed, when he saw the word "chimpanzee." "It looks to me like chimpanzee hair. I found it in extraordinary circumstances and suspect it may be connected with the illegal importation of chimps into Australia. I would be grateful if you would let me know all you can about it as soon as possible."

He let his head fall with a thump onto the pillow. Where had she found the hair? he wondered. In the Cessna? She'd flown to Orange a few weeks ago on some bird business. Had she examined the interior of the aircraft then? He'd have to tell Parker.

When Joe Miller returned to the Research after his interview with Diana, he sent her fingerprints on the plastic sheet off to the forensic lab in Sydney by special delivery mail. Then he took out a ruler and a pair of calipers and compared the estimated size of the bolt cutters used to cut the lock on the northwest gate with the size of the bolt cutters missing from Kerry Larnach's toolshed. It could be a coincidence, but the sizes seemed identical.

He gave a push to the edge of his desk, sending his chair trundling back to the window, where he swiveled the seat and looked out toward the broken gate. It was still and peaceful out there now: sky, mountain, lake. House. With a push, he was back at his desk, where he typed into his computer the code word that would give him access to the list of outgoing calls from telephones in the residential quarters. He had already checked hundreds of calls from the condos but somehow had forgotten the house, out there on its own. He scrolled down the list of private numbers until he reached Sonja's, then hit the Load key.

• • •

To enter the corridor outside Level 2, one had to push hard. The door itself was of normal weight, but negative air pressure made it as heavy as the door to a vault. The corridor had shelves of blue cotton gowns, masks, and booties, and a big box of latex gloves in many sizes. Its only other equipment was an autoclave, where the bodies of all animals, including those infected with White Eye, were pressure-cooked until sterile. There was no difficulty in disposing of rat and rabbit remains, since every biological lab at the Research used rodents. Chimps were the problem. Parker had to cut down a chimp cadaver with the bone saw inside the high-containment room, then bag the pieces up, cook them in the autoclave, and send off the bags to the industrial incinerator up at the lab complex. Autoclave bags were of tough plastic and were carefully handled: it was a million-to-one chance that a bag containing chimp bits would be torn open and the species recognized. Except, of course, for the teeth: anyone who had taken Zoology I would recognize those teeth. Parker distributed the teeth through the bags he used for rodent cadavers. Like everyone else, he reasoned, biologists saw only the things that interested them, and nobody outside U-1 gave a damn about chimps, so in the improbable event of a tooth being seen, it was unlikely that it would be identified. Even the three technicians who worked right next door to the chimpanzee room seemed to forget the animals' existence. Each technician had been asked to sign a Commercial Confidentiality contract, agreeing to keep secret the details of work done for Siam Enterprises. None had bridled. In fact, Parker noted grimly, they accepted as natural that commercial interest should override the free flow of scientific ideas. "It's the decadent attitude one must expect these days," he told Sonja. Ever since the United States Supreme Court had ruled in 1980 that new life forms could be patented, ethics in molecular biology was doomed, according to him. "The path from Mendel was transformed to gold and now leads straight to Otto Grossmann," he said. He was sure the technicians knew that the chimps in U-1 were unquarantined, for they were explicitly forbidden to mention the presence of the animals. But they were paid better than any other gel jocks this side of the United States to keep their mouths shut.

Lek's small eyes had flashed with anger when Parker smacked her for playing with the rabbit. Her defiant expression made him want to spank her properly, but right now he had more urgent matters.

"I need the three vaccinated bucks," he said. "And Lucy. I'm taking them all in to Level 2."

Lek gave a sullen shrug and, standing on tiptoe, began to haul a rabbit from the fixed cages against the walls. These rabbits, which were supplied by the breeding house up at the lab complex, were not the timid creatures of the field but whopping big animals, unafraid of humans. They were pure white, with ruby-colored eyes. When irritated, they thumped, crashing their hind legs on the cage to make a sound like a gong. Parker watched as Lek, whose head reached only to his chest, struggled to pull a buck from its cage. The willpower of animals intrigued him. "If you want to study determination, just watch a donkey, or a hungry dog, or a cat in heat," he would say. The enormous, blind, unreasoning willpower of animals lived on in humans, obscured a little by intellect but in no way defeated. Sex and staying alive were the two great levers of animal will—and he alone could manipulate both of them, anywhere on earth.

After a few moments it became clear that Lek was not tall enough to catch the second rabbit, which was crouched in the back of the cage, hanging on with its claws. Parker caught it and a third one, lifting them over her head and lowering their kicking bodies into a carrying cage.

In the Big Lab, he paused for a moment to take a long sniff of its air. The ethanol and bacteria pong of the place always delighted him. "The smell of science," he liked to say. "I'm going to bang some bacteria into the bunnies," he called to the technicians.

Steve had been in the high-containment room that morning to take the frozen aliquot of White Eye from its tank of liquid nitrogen, defrost a tiny bit, and put it in a tube of broth in the shaker, to grow. Now, six hours later, the bacteria would be ready to use.

Lek traipsed after Parker as far as the changing corridor outside Level 2.

"Go back and get Lucy," he said. "Put her in the crush cage and wheel her in here. I'll be out to collect her in a few minutes."

It took another heavy push against the negative air pressure to open the door into the high-containment lab itself. Once inside, Parker turned on the warning light in the corridor outside, then he approached the rotary shaker where his White Eye was growing.

He took extreme care whenever he handled the unfrozen bacteria, always working with it inside a negative-airflow cabinet. An eye splash, he suspected, even for someone with his immunity, could be blinding. After drawing some of it into a syringe, which he laid at one end of the cabinet, he took the first rabbit he could grab from the carrying cage. His intention was to hold the rabbit inside the cabinet, give it a jab, then push it down the ramp at the side of the cabinet to a negative-airflow pen, where vaccinated animals had to stay until their antibodies had killed the bacteria. Or until they were dead. These rabbits (and Lucy) would, of course, show no effects of White Eye. In forty-eight hours they could be mated with fertile partners. If conception did not occur, Vaccine II would be ready for testing on humans.

Parker realized that the rabbit he was holding was so frisky he would either need an extra pair of hands to hold it down or have to knock it out. He dropped it back into the cage and went to the other side of the room to make up enough anesthetic for all three.

When the rabbits were lying asleep inside the cabinet, he pricked each one inside a nostril, administering a minute dose of White Eye, and while they were still unconscious lowered the soft, limp bodies into the infection pen. There were two negative-airflow pens in the Level 2 lab. The second one was for a chimpanzee, but the chimps hated it. To get a chimp into the pen, the crush cage was a necessary first step. The crush cage pinned its occupant against a wall, where it was easy to put to sleep. It was then transferred to the pen and infected while it was still unconscious.

None of the equipment in Level 2 was left running when not in use, and Parker had only just turned on the negative-airflow cabinet. When he switched on the chimp infection pen, there was a bump and a flash.

"Blast!" he muttered. Electrical Maintenance would take a day to fix it.

In the corridor, he degowned, demasked, and debootied, and strode back into the Big Lab. "Okay, who knows something about wiring?" he asked the boys.

Two of them nodded.

"Right," he said. "I've got a job for you. And Lek—let Lucy out to play again for a while."

It took the three men almost an hour to dismantle the metal casing around the pen so they could look for the location of the electrical fault. Then it was another hour of fiddling, trying to push a pair of pliers up into a space made for a small hand, before one of the boys could pull out the damaged wires. The working day was over by the time they had the pen fixed and reassembled. Lek entered diffidently to say that Lucy wanted to go to bed.

"Let her sleep, then," Parker said. "I'm too jiggered to do any-thing else tonight." He and the boys were hunkered down, switch-ing the chimp pen on and off to reassure themselves it was working properly.

Lek, meanwhile, was peering at the rabbits.

"*Off you go,*" Parker added over his shoulder. He hated the way she stared and fingered things. But she ignored him and continued squinting through the glass of the rabbit pen. In her own good time, she left. "Disobedient bitch," he murmured, and straightened up. For some reason he glanced at the spot where Lek had stood a moment ago. What he saw made the hair stand up on the back of his head.

In the negative-airflow pen, the bodies of the dying rabbits made feeble twitching movements. Their ruby eyeballs had turned a creamy white from the purulent discharge that was the eponymous symp-tom of White Eye. One was already dead. The others, gasping for breath, took only a few minutes longer. In small animals, the bac-teria killed in two or three hours; in larger ones it took half a day.

For a moment Parker thought he would burst into tears. "*That fucking PCR machine!*" he bellowed.

The technicians glanced at each other. "I'd say we got a mutation we didn't want," Steve murmured.

"Gremlins in the PCR again," Phil replied. The Polymerase Chain Reaction machine, housed out in the Big Lab, did continuing cy-cles of amplification and in the course of two hours would gener-ate a new gene. But PCR could create unprogrammed mutations: every four hundred nucleotides, on average, the AmpliTaq made a mistake.

Parker's mind raced. As soon as he saw the rabbits, he realized Vaccine II was junk. But why? The river of his dream appeared be-fore him: there had been an upstream and a downstream to it. Downstream was the White Eye section, Piece B. He had not touched that. The front of the protein, upstream, was the only area he had manipulated.

"There is Piece A, for sterility, and Piece B for White Eye," he said aloud. "I changed Piece A—and I lost Piece B. Fucking machine!"

He had only guessed that the PCR machine had let him down, but now that he had visualized the ribbon of DNA, he could grasp ex-actly what had gone wrong. The Polymerase Chain Reaction ma-chine must have introduced a stop codon, a triplet of bases, probably just after his mutated acrosomal membrane gene or maybe even within the gene for the acrosomal membrane. The stop had told the translational machinery to go no further. Since all of this was at the front of the piece of protein—upstream in the river—what he had made was a tiddly little bit of protein that would probably cause infertile sperm, and that was all. The raison d'être of the vaccine, its ability to combat White Eye, had never been translated.

"I didn't sequence the amplified material," he muttered. He stared down into the pen, where the disgusting final phase of White Eye was playing itself out. Because of negative airflow, no odor escaped, but seeing it was bad enough. He would now have to go through the loathsome procedure of removing the bodies, putting them in autoclave bags, and cleaning the pen. "I'd better put on a moon suit, and you two had better leave," he said. It was sheer luck the chimp pen had broken down. Had it been working properly, Lucy would be dying from White Eye by now.

The technicians looked at each other in embarrassment.

"Doc," Phil said quietly, "you don't have to lose all your design work, you know. All the other clones are in the fridge outside."

Parker's mind seemed jammed on his own stupidity, and he stared as if what the boy said was gibberish. Then a smile spread across his lips, and with a clumsy hand he ruffled Phil's hair. "Of course!" he said. "Of course they are! I used only one. I've got eleven more!"

"We could sequence them now," Steve ventured. "It'll only take three hours."

After dinner that evening, Parker returned to U-1 to leave the gels exposing to film overnight. Next morning, he read the sequences: the stop codon was just where he expected to find it on the clone he had used. He went quickly to the other clones and after a couple of hours found one that had only his desired mutation. "We're back on the road!" he announced at morning tea.

In nine weeks, with no more mix-ups, he would have made Perfect Vaccine II. Three months later, he would tell Grossmann, "Otto, get ready to become a billionaire." By Christmas, Parker would be ready to give the planet the best present it had had since Homo sapiens sprang out of a tree half a million years ago.

Romanus, in his elegant new suit, had taken photographs of the guests at Otto Grossmann's reception in Bangkok. He shot in color and next day gave Miss Bochang a few sets of prints to be posted out as mementos of the evening to those who featured in them. He had another set of prints, onto which he had stuck names and a line of description—"Siam Enterprises board of directors," "logging contractor," "primate dealer"—and these he tossed into a cardboard box he kept in his room.

It was a week now since Diana had taken a bird to the flying ground, and five days since she had visited her territory at all. She was anxious about Morrie and about damage caused by the Homicide team that had searched the area. Why on my land? she asked herself for the hundredth time. The dead-duck letter she had received on Wednesday morning seemed to say that it meant *something*.

When she pulled up at the lake's edge on Friday afternoon, the land near the fence looked as if an army had marched across it. Inside a boundary marked with pegs and red nylon rope, every centimeter had been trampled. Gilgais were flattened. The sandy bed of the creek had been dug up. But a couple of good rains would bring up the gilgais and reshape the creekbed. The desecration was not so bad as she had first thought.

Farther along the fence, something shiny caught the sunshine.

There was a new padlock on the gate, which on close inspection turned out to be already useless, for the hasp had been cut and all that held the gate closed was its stump. On the hard, bare ground below, minute chips of metal glinted. She jiggled the lock, pushed gingerly, then stepped through the gate.

It was a weird feeling to be standing once more on a place known so well but barred to her these past ten years. Ahead of her, the ground rose in a granite outcrop that concealed all the buildings of the Research beyond it. She imagined that at any moment her father could appear, arms held wide, grasping the handlebars of the Harley-Davidson he rode to check the fences.

In the weeks that had followed his murder, people tried to push her and Carolyn together. "The two poor little girls," they said. One day Carolyn announced, "I really hated my mother. I'm glad your rouseabout killed them." Diana remained silent, swinging her legs. "Did you like your father?" Carolyn asked. Diana nodded. Then she stood up and punched Carolyn in the stomach.

After a while Diana returned to her side of the fence, replacing the useless bolt and lock so that from the other side the gate would look secure. I mustn't blow it, she said to herself. It was only a matter of days now before she would be able to flash a pass at the guards and walk right into the Research. Standing with her back to it, she stared up at Mount Kalunga. The sun had moved, turning the mountain dark.

"Morrie!" she called.

The branches of the Aleppo pines swayed almost imperceptibly in the warm air currents of late afternoon.

"Morrie!"

She waited a few minutes for him to make some sign, then returned to her van. The owl was in there, ready for release.

The ebbing day colored the lake red-gold, like Japanese silk, and birds of all sorts called from their roosts in the lignum islands. A kangaroo herd of buck, does, and juveniles bounded past.

Inside the van, the owl waited with perfect alertness. Hooded birds would ride in the back of her van, crooning to themselves and leaning into the curves like men on motorbikes, but there was no such thing as a hood for an owl. Diana had put thongs on the owl's wings to prevent its flying around while she was driving, and at first it was huffy with her for embarrassing it. At the height of sunset, she carried it to the old fence post where Morrie left messages. She removed the thongs. The owl looked so beautiful that for a moment she wished Raoul were there to photograph it.

It stood still, facing the dark pyramid of mountain where it would hunt later. Its mysterious eyes surveyed the disappearing landscape, then it turned a little to stare out at the sky above the lake. Suddenly its satellite-dish face spun right around until its head pointed backward, at the airfield.

All Diana could see was a Land Cruiser. The people down there were invisible and inaudible to her—but not to the owl, which, from a kilometer away, was hearing their conversation.

After a minute, the twinkling red, green, and white lights of an airplane appeared, lights the bird had seen already. They distracted Diana's attention, and in that moment the night hunter, as if sensing the bond between them loosen, rose on silent wings.

Diana turned up her face just in time to see a denser piece of sky move above her, then vanish into the darkening air.

The aircraft was now only two hundred meters above the lake.

She returned to her van, thinking about Raoul's kisses of congratulation when she released a bird. These days, Grace and the boys sometimes came to the flying ground to watch her. The joy in their eyes gave her pleasure and eased her memories of Raoul. He had never contacted her. She didn't even know in which country he now lived. But he'd stayed in touch with Carolyn.

On a hot afternoon a month ago, Carolyn had appeared on the terrace at Fig Tree Gully Road. She was got up in a red pleated skirt that just covered her backside, with a pair of sunglasses perched on top of her head. Diana was standing on a ladder, cutting back the wisteria. She called out, "Grace, is the side gate open? Someone's got in from the street." She concentrated on secateuring a woody stem.

Carolyn called, "Diana, I've got to talk to you about something. I spoke to Raoul this morning. Please don't . . ." Her face creased with anxiety. Then she lisped, "I know you're very particular, miss, and I should have filled in a request in triplicate, but—"

"Get out!" Diana shouted. She had always been able to intimidate Carolyn. She was taller, she was stronger, she rode better, and she ran faster. When it came to shooting, there was no comparison at all. From her vantage point on the ladder, she could see the brown roots of Carolyn's hennaed hair. She made another savage cut.

"You've got to hear—"

"No I don't. Piss off." Diana jerked the secateur blades together.

"*Listen, Bozo!*" Carolyn yelled. "You want a better world, don't you? Well, it's about the illegal wildlife trade."

Diana came slowly down the ladder. Just then the door opened and Grace ambled onto the terrace. "You like a cuppa, love?" she asked Carolyn. "I'll put the kettle on."

"Die for one, Gracie." Carolyn smiled.

They went inside. The air was cooler in the kitchen, and on the table a basket of garden tomatoes gave out a spicy smell that mingled with the fragrance of Grace's corn bread, just out of the oven. Carolyn fiddled with her hair, twirling a strand around her long, gold-ringed middle finger. Hands like her mother's, Diana thought. "Well?" she said.

"Well. Raoul is in Thailand—"

"You said wildlife trade," Diana interjected. A vein beat rhythmically in Carolyn's neck. Diana stared at it, not listening properly, then with an effort she tuned in.

It sounded mad: Asia's biggest breeder of laboratory primates had sent between fifteen and thirty chimpanzees to Australia in the past five or six years, none of them with proper clearances. "We should try to find out who is buying them. As they're not being listed, they're probably being sacrificed."

"Since when have you cared about that?"

For the first time, Carolyn's nerve seemed to fail. "I know I was a bit slow off the mark, but for the past two years . . ."

Since your affair with my lover. "So how are these chimpanzees being sent to Australia?" Diana asked.

"I don't know. But there's a lot of illegal immigration from Thailand to Australia, so maybe—this is just a guess—the same method that's used to bring in people. Whatever that is."

Diana snorted. "Does it make sense to you that someone with enough money to spend on a scam like that would bother? Why not do the research somewhere else?"

"I know it sounds improbable. But these days . . ."

"So what do you expect me to do? Telephone the primate food supply companies and start asking questions? They'll expect a bomb."

Carolyn leaned across the table. "Say you're me!" Her face was so close, Diana could see the yellow flecks in her irises. She drew back.

"Do it yourself."

But Carolyn pressed on recklessly, her breath coming in short gasps. "I can't do it! You know what the Research is like. It's a boarding school! We don't have private phones in the labs. Everybody watches everybody else. The telephone system monitors incoming and outgoing calls. If I start making inquiries about chimpanzees, the whole place will know about it by lunchtime. Talk will go all round the country and back again in a week. People will think it's to do with AIDS. You've got no idea how much money there is in AIDS. It's a wonder the Mafia isn't funding vaccine research."

"Maybe it is," Diana muttered.

Carolyn paid no attention. "You'll have to—or I'll have to come over here and do it one day during the week. You can pretend you're doing a survey. There's an organization called TRAFFIC that monitors trade in wildlife and has links with the U.N."

"You are well briefed," Diana said dryly.

"I could use the phone in the gallery." Carolyn said. "That is, if Grace didn't mind. I wouldn't come upstairs and bother you."

Damn right you won't come upstairs, Diana thought. Her gray eyes glinted coldly.

"I'd better be going." Carolyn plucked in a vain, self-conscious way at her skirt. "I obviously haven't convinced you."

"You've convinced me," Diana blurted. But she could not force her pride to surrender. Abruptly she stood up and strode along the kitchen, the heels of her riding boots ringing on the slate. At the counter where the warm bread was cooling, she stopped, took a knife, and cut off a slice, which she crammed into her mouth. Then she turned and came toward Carolyn, the knife still in her hand. Her eyes fixed on Carolyn's neck, as if something about it hypnotized her.

Carolyn sat paralyzed. She wondered why she had thought it would be safe to come into this house again—but then two large, strong hands pushed down on her shoulders, and her head was suddenly cushioned against the soft warmth of Grace's breasts.

Diana laid the knife on the table. Her cheeks flushed, and the fury drained from her eyes.

"How 'bout I butter us all a bit a bread?" Grace said. "Stead a you eatin' it like that."

When Carolyn left, half an hour later, Diana flung herself into Grace's arms. "I hate her so much!" she wailed.

"There, there," Grace murmured. Diana was an idealist: it was herself she hated, for hating Carolyn.

Over on the airfield, the plane had landed and was taxiing toward the Land Cruiser. Diana drove along, distracted by the bitterness of her memories, passing within half a kilometer of Jason Nichols, Kerry, his baby brother, and Sailor, who lay limp and silent in the crate after traveling for four days sedated with Lorazepam.

At U-1, Parker and Lek came running up the stairs and scrambled into Sonja's Land Cruiser. Two minutes later, they pulled up near the wind sock beside Kerry's Cruiser, joining Jason and the Larnach boys. Sonja was on the veranda, keeping watch.

Since John's return she had assured Joe Miller there was no need for patrols around her place, and he had readily agreed, but neither she nor John believed this meant Joe would remove surveillance from the area.

Sonja had watched Diana put an owl on the fence and seen the owl fly away. She now followed the yellow van with her night-sight binoculars to make sure that as it drove close to the airfield it did not slow down. It didn't, and she returned her attention to the group now standing beside the two Land Cruisers. A sudden tingle of nausea spread through her. She refocused the binoculars to observe her husband's hand caressing Lek's bottom. She felt poisoned! Her system was toxic with adrenaline. . . . He bent down and kissed Lek while the others weren't looking!

Sonja slumped into a canvas chair. She pushed aside a bracelet and tried to count her pulse.

It seemed like hours, although it must have been only minutes, before headlights appeared up to the left near the lab complex. Sonja darted inside, her fingers trembling as she pushed the buttons on the phone. "Cruiser up at the labs," she said.

"Right. We won't be a tick," Kerry answered.

"Coming this way," she added.

Down at the airfield, her Land Cruiser was already moving. Young Brian Larnach returned to the plane and climbed on board, followed by Jason.

"Hurry, hurry," Sonja said.

John had to drive back under the house and get the crate out of the Land Cruiser and downstairs—or at least inside the U-1 door—before the security guards arrived for the evening surveillance check of the fence. The guards' vehicle was belting along the road. Sonja gripped the balcony railing, gasping for breath. On the airfield, the airplane was rushing down the runway. Her Land Cruiser sped toward the house, on a collision course with the guards, but it reached the turnoff first and a moment later was driving through her garden and vanishing underneath the house.

The guards continued on, leaving the road and lurching toward the Cyclone-wire fence. Sonja saw a flashlight beam aimed at the wire; the patrol was examining it for damage. Her intercostal muscles loosened, but the shock of what she had seen at the airfield returned, and as she descended the stairs she felt so disoriented that for a moment she forgot who she was.

John and Lek, with Kerry looking on, were washing Sailor in the staff bathroom. Lek was inside the shower recess with the chimpanzee, making splashing noises and squealing. Her wet brown arm shot out through the shower curtain, and Parker put a towel in her hand. The arm withdrew. A few minutes later, the whole woman appeared, blouse sticking to her breasts. She held the ape by the hand, and both of them stepped carefully out onto a cotton bath mat Parker had laid for their feet. Sailor was still groggy and hung on to the bath mat with his toes. Sonja stared at the two pairs of broad, strong feet.

"Why isn't Jason here?" she asked.

"He has to go to Sydney," Parker said. "He checked Sailor out at the airfield. We'll be finished soon, darling." He was hoping Sonja would leave. The more people, the greater the stress on the chimp and the longer it would take him to recover. Parker disliked visitors in the lab at any time, and tonight, after the fun he had had at the airfield, he was keen to be alone with Lek. Things had developed so fast after he had given her that smack on the bottom yesterday. Bench work! he thought. It was years since he'd had sex on a lab bench—but down in U-1 there was the problem of dodging the security cameras that watched from the ceiling. The Animal Room, the Big Lab, and the Machine Room each had a camera connected to the monitor in Sonja's kitchen, upstairs. The few blind spots were too small to allow him to embrace Lek without some parts of their bodies being seen. But there was no camera in Level 2.

"This is just routine," he added to Sonja, and gave her a light push.

"I don't want to miss anything." She stared at Lek.

The girl was now cuddling the clean-smelling ape, grooming him and making kissing faces, while he gazed at her sleepily and toyed with her ear. Sonja could not take her eyes off Lek: the movements of her limbs, the way her pig cheeks squeezed her eyes shut when she smiled, her big, square teeth and mauve gums, her black hair lying flat on her scalp, the movements of her small, bright eyes. What's she got that I haven't? she asked herself. Why does he kiss her, when he's always too tired to make love to me? I'll never get pregnant, she thought.

She stayed until Sailor was locked in his sleeping cage for the night and they had turned out the lights and all gone upstairs. There, on the dank-smelling concrete, Sonja turned to Lek. "Mr. Larnach is having dinner with us. There are plenty of vegetables. Would you like to eat with us too?" she asked.

The girl glanced at Parker for guidance. "No, sank you, Miss Sonja. Sank you very much. I have food."

"But it's too late for you to start cooking. Everything is ready upstairs."

"No, excuse me, please. I go to my own room now." Her eyes met Parker's again.

"Night, Lek," he said in an offhand voice.

"Good night Dr. John. Good night Mr. Kerry. Excuse me."

On the balcony, Parker said, "You mustn't ask her to eat with us, darling. She's a chambermaid, for God's sake."

When Sonja went to the kitchen, Kerry found the opportunity he had been waiting for all evening. "Mate," he said, "something to tell you about Jason Nichols." He glanced indoors to make sure Sonja was not listening. "You know I'm friendly with Kev from the police station? Kev and I went to primary school together. Anyway . . ." He peered inside again. Sonja's torso was visible through the serving hatch in the kitchen. "Kev reckons they're ready to finger Nichols for those letters. They've identified some of the pictures as coming from veterinarian magazines. That means he's a top suspect for the murder."

"Christ almighty!"

"They need to hassle him with something—misusing the post—so they can ask him for a blood sample. They'll claim there's blood on a letter. But actually they'll be wanting the blood to match with semen they got from Carolyn. If Jason refuses . . ." Kerry gave a shrug. "It needn't affect us, of course. But if he falls to pieces and tells 'em what a bad boy he's been . . ."

Parker gripped the balcony rail and stared into the sky. The inland air was so clear one could see stars by the million out here. Night after night he had gazed at them when he was puzzling about the disease that had killed Siam's primates. He would allow thoughts to flow into his mind unhindered while he wandered through constellations. There were billions of stars. There were billions of people. It was out here one night that the idea had come to him that if one wanted to reduce human population quickly and suddenly (there was now no time to do it slowly and gently), an efficient vector would be the air-conditioning systems of the world's cities. Those antheaps seething with people, all of them breathing the same recycled air! And suddenly he had realized what the White Eye bacteria could be made to do. In a leap so immense it terrified him, he had seen what *he* could do to change the course of history.

Later, when he calmed down and came back to earth, he realized he was being naive. One would not have the manpower to use air-conditioning systems to broadcast White Eye to more than a few skyscrapers in a few cities of the world. Take two giant buildings in each of three giant cities—say, New York, Beijing, and Bombay. If each building had three thousand people working in it, one could reduce the population by nearly twenty thousand. Ten thousand eight hundred humans are born every hour. In less than two hours the twenty thousand would be replaced. And such considerations aside, one would be committing mass murder. Mass murder was Nature's way, of course: famine, flood, disease. The Great Mother kept her wheel spinning, spewing out life and annihilating it in the next half-turn. She cared nothing for individuals. Now this abysmal creation Homo was murdering all others, but unlike Nature, it could not bring to life new forms. *Except for men like me! We are the new gods!* He had contemplated the glittering black sky so long that night, he became giddy from the strange vertigo caused by the pull of the stars.

None of the people he worked with, not Grossmann, not the technicians, not Sonja, and certainly not the Larnach boys or Nichols, had any idea of the grand design to which they were contributing.

"Don't say anything about Nichols in front of Sonja," Parker ordered Kerry.

• • •

At College Street in Sydney, a detective on the Williams case tried not to yawn into the telephone. It was past his teatime. Hunger had made him tired, and boredom made him want to yawn. "Yep, yep," he murmured. The caller, at last, seemed satisfied. "Okay, mate. Thanks again for all your help."

He hung up and opened his mouth as wide as a hippo, making a roaring sound. A couple of people at desks nearby looked up. "Miller on the blower again," he said. "Now he reckons, after examining the phone records, that there's an unholy alliance between John Parker and that arsehole who runs the airline. He says Parker is on the phone to Larnach more often than anyone else at the Research, including the girl who books travel."

"Where's Parker on the suspect list?" asked the woman at the next desk.

"About number . . . Wait on. I'll get it on my screen. He's near the bottom. His wife told us he was on a train going to Adelaide night of the murder. There was a ticket booked for him, via Melbourne."

"Have we checked that? Whether he was on the train?"

The detective yawned again. "Not yet, Sweetlips. Why don't you? Why don't you ring Joe Pain-in-the-Arse Miller while you're at it and tell him you're the person he should be pestering fifteen times a day? Why don't you—"

"You're cranky," she interrupted, "because he collected a set of Pembridge's fingerprints that we should've got ourselves. *You* should've got yourself. So don't take out your bad temper on me."

"I'm not bad-tempered!" the detective shouted. "I'm just sick to death of that old fart trying to take over my investigation!"

C h a p t e r **E l e v e n**

While Parker and Kerry Larnach discussed Jason Nichols on the balcony, and Sonja, in the kitchen, put the finishing touches to a tureen of gazpacho, Morrie was in the laundry of her house, sorting through a basket of clothes. He was looking for cloth to carry home the food he hoped to find that night. At the bottom of the basket he found a couple of pillowcases, which he pushed inside the string around his waist. Earlier he had discovered the electric light switch and had turned it on and off twenty times, chuckling with delight. Before leaving the laundry he gave the switch a few extra flicks, remembering the old days when he had rewired the stands in the shearing shed.

From the laundry he went to look in the window of the small house in the garden. A brown-skinned woman was in there, eating something that gave off a sweet smell and made him hungry. He decided to go back to the door he had seen beside the laundry, hoping it would lead to a storeroom, but the door was locked, so he set off for the homestead. Against the soles of his feet the road was smooth and faintly warm from the day's heat.

Sonja was in an odd mood that evening, Parker noticed. "You're knocking it back like your sister," he remarked when, before they'd got to the salad, she demanded a third glass of wine. One was her limit.

"Wine not?" she answered, waving her empty glass at him. "Drink! Drink! Drink!" she sang in a grasshopper voice. "Drinking doesn't hurt Hilary. She gets what she wants. Money, clothes, men. White limousines." She turned to Kerry. "She roots like a rabbit."

"That a fact?" Kerry said.

"Yairs!" Sonja continued loudly. "The minister for everything has a toy boy. Hasn't she, John? Hasn't Hilary got a man on her staff?"

"Sonja, I don't think we should—"

"Oh, why not! I'm sick of always obeying the rules. I go without things, but other people don't. Look at how they live up at the condos! They don't bother with solar power. They don't save fossil fuel. They burn it! Look at all the food wrap they use. And their garbage. They don't have a compost pit. Not one of them has a compost pit— did y'know that, Kerry?" She did not wait for his answer. "They use disposable wooden chopsticks when they cook teriyaki! Can you imagine that?"

The men stared at her.

"Let's go out and burn down a few hectares of rain forest!" she cried. "We could toast marshmallows on the fire!"

Parker said, "Darling, would you like me to make you a cup of peppermint tea?"

"No, but I'd love a fuck." She covered her mouth with her hand, giggling. Kerry and Parker guffawed, as if she had said something witty.

Parker pulled her against him and whispered, "Keep it hot for me." Then he gave her a slight shove. "Be a beautiful woman and make some coffee." She went off to the kitchen with an air of smug obedience.

Parker paid his Kalair bills with funds drawn from a special Siam Enterprises "Scientific Research" account in Bangkok. "To keep things simple," as Kerry put it—that is, to avoid Australian tax—they had established a system of electronic payment, which they could do themselves by punching the buttons on the telephone. Joe Miller might record that Parker had telephoned a bank in Thailand, but he could not take the next step and discover that this phone call was actually a money transfer to Kalair.

Parker and Larnach took their coffee to Sonja's study and settled up for the transport of the new chimp.

"I'll drive you to the airfield to pick up your Cruiser," Parker said. He was anxious to have another few minutes alone with Larnach, out of earshot of his wife, to discuss the Nichols problem.

"Sorry about Sonja. She's been semi-hysterical all week," he remarked as they got into her Land Cruiser.

"The murder's had a big effect on everyone."

"What are we going to do about Jason?" Parker had reversed and turned and was now driving out from under the house.

"Funny you should ask me that."

Parker squinted into the dark, peering past the thick undergrowth of Sonja's garden toward an outdoor lamp that marked the turnoff to the airfield. For a moment light shone into the cabin, revealing Kerry's coarse features, red-gold hair, and thick neck.

"I reckon he's got to be a worried man."

"Can you find out when the police are going to question him?"

"One thing about runnin' an airline is y' get to see who your passengers are," Larnach answered. "The agent who handles travel for the New South Wales police service happened to book three seats on our first flight out of Sydney on Monday morning. Names like Fred Nerk and John Smith. Open return."

"Let me know when Jason gets back from Sydney."

If he gets back, Kerry thought.

On Sunday evening, Margaret McLeod needed to reassure herself that Jason Nichols was coming to dinner—just the two of them. At seven-fifteen, when he had not arrived, she wondered if she should ring him. Her telephone was an ancient black contraption with holes for dialing and letters as well as numbers. Margaret stared at it, willing it to ring, and when it didn't she wandered back to the kitchen and took another sip of chardonnay. She had baked a peach pie for dessert, using the last of the fruit from a woody old tree in her garden. From the kitchen she went to the living room, where there were red candles on the dining table.

She moved around, straightening cushions she had already straightened, imagining the thrill of seeing Jason's sweet face smile at her tomorrow morning. They would look out her window at the peach tree, where she had hung a wind chime on Saturday afternoon.

Unaccountably, she found herself in the dark hallway beside the telephone again.

A machine answered at his end. "Hi, this is Jason Nichols. I would love to speak to you, but I'm afraid I can't right now. . . ." His voice made her so nervous she decided to have just one more glass of wine and wait a bit longer.

She waited five minutes, which was all he would need to lock up the surgery and drive to her cottage on the south side.

Outside her gate she hesitated, hoping the red Porsche would appear, but except for the bossy little fox terrier on the corner, strutting about, waiting for something to bark at, the street was as empty as usual. Margaret heaved herself onto the hard leather seat of her bicycle and set off, her violet culottes fluttering against her calves, her graying fringe lifting in the breeze, her earrings dancing rock 'n' roll.

Jason's car was parked in the driveway. There were no lights on inside the house.

A concrete path with hydrangea bushes on either side ran between the house and the clinic. She was surprised to see how wilted their leaves were, as if they had not been watered all day. Jason liked to garden on Sunday afternoons. "It gives me energy," he would say. One day he had taken her by the wrist. Her worn, coarsened palm resting in his slim hand embarrassed her. "Look at that!" he'd said admiringly. "That's a hand that's made things grow." At that moment she had known they must become lovers—and when she did the tarot later, the Empress jumped at her. The Empress! That was the True Love card.

Margaret had a key to the back door of the clinic. She knocked and called "Jason!" in her most musical voice, but when there was no answer, she crossed the path to the back of the house. The door was unlocked. The kitchen was spotless as usual, without a crumb on the linoleum. It had a pleasant, very clean smell, like a health food shop, which was not surprising, for inside the cupboards there were scores of neatly labeled jars of vitamins, minerals, and tissue salts, bottles of garlic concentrate, beetroot extract, Swedish bitters, wheat grass, and essential oils. The rest of the house had a thick-pile apricot-colored carpet that muffled her steps as she went from room to room, calling, "Jason—it's me, Margie." He had converted the third bedroom into a study. As she walked down the hall she heard the faint hiss of his Apple Macintosh.

"Jason!" she said sharply. The person sitting in the swivel chair did not move.

• • •

Margaret McLeod, of Church Street, Kalunga, told the police that Jason Nichols had seemed depressed on the afternoon before he left for Sydney. "But I can't believe he'd kill himself," she said. "And . . . and . . ." She appealed to Joe Miller, who had just arrived and was mopping perspiration from his brow, although by now night had fallen and it was growing chilly outside. "He wouldn't hurt a fly!" She sank her face into her hands and burst into tears.

Joe led her through the apricot-colored living room, where painted china animals and photographs of Jason's parents in chrome frames rested on gleaming shelves. They went to the kitchen. "How well did you know him?" he asked.

She felt frightened.

"Why did he go to Sydney, for example? What did he do there?"

She could feel her bones shortening. She was only a meter tall. "I don't know."

"Where did he stay?"

"With his—I don't know."

The junior constable said her bicycle would fit in the trunk of the police car and he would drive her home. Joe returned to look at the body.

The right hand was hanging loose, and the torso had slumped to the left side, the left arm still on the armrest. A 20-ml syringe with an 18-gauge needle lay on the carpet beneath the limp right hand. In the crook of the left arm there was a trickle of blood where the needle had punctured the cephalic vein. On the desk were two broken ampoules, a bottle of Water for Injection, and discarded wrapping from the syringe. There was some pale-yellow powder on the desk near the ampoules. Probably Thiobarbital, Joe thought. Medicos favored Thiobarbital for suicide. Usually they reduced the water, doubled the dose, and added potassium, to be certain of the effect. He crouched down to see the labels, careful not to touch anything. The corpse was blue-gray and peaceful-looking, its long eyelashes drooping over almost-closed eyes that had immense black pupils. The postmortem would report another myocardial infarction.

Joe levered himself upright and again read the message on the screen: MY LIFE IS OVER. I CAN'T GO ON.

The senior constable, who had telephoned College Street, returned. "We're to leave everything as it is and lock up for the night," he said. "The Homicide blokes will arrive at eight tomorrow morning." He hooked his fingers onto his hipbones and stared at the corpse with disgust. "Bastard!"

Joe nodded thoughtfully. "There's some cider in the fridge. Don't know if it's alcoholic or not, but I'd drink anything."

They found a couple of glasses and a bottle opener. "When I was a kid we had a yappy little dog," Joe said slowly. "Its barking drove my father mad, especially on Sunday afternoons when he wanted to have a nap. One day he told Mother he was taking it to obedience school to teach it not to bark."

"Yeah?"

"He took it to the vet and had its vocal cords cut. Mother never realized. She thought the dog was a genius. But I used to look at that mutt moving its jaws and think, Poor little blighter."

"Gives you the willies," the constable agreed. "Mate, what sort of a bastard would cut a woman's vocal cords so she can't scream for help, then kill her within earshot of fifty blokes?"

Joe shook his head.

The murder case against Nichols rested on four pieces of evidence. First was Carolyn Williams's severed vocal cords. Immediately that pointed to someone with veterinary knowledge. Second was the size of the syringe used. Third was the animal hair found on Carolyn Williams's clothing: it came from a chimpanzee. On the day of the murder, Nichols had handled a chimpanzee from the circus. The fourth fact was weaker but supported the possibility that the vet could have been in contact with Williams that night: She had been seen outside the post office in High Street, Kalunga, at about 11:00 P.M. on Saturday, several hours after she left the pub with two duck shooters. She went into a telephone box and appeared to be making a call. Nichols had guests until almost eleven. He could have had a tryst after they left. And there was more circumstantial evidence: Two of the collage letters sent to women at the Research had cat dander on them. No cats were allowed at the Research. Nichols knew the women who had received letters and a month earlier had sent all three of them humorous Valentine's Day cards.

"If he hadn't offed himself, that crazy Margaret might have been next," the constable added.

Joe grunted. He carried his glass of cider to the study to contemplate the scene once more. "There are two things that worry me," he said after a while. "What was his motive for murdering Carolyn Williams?"

"Dunno. But they'll probably find it when they read the computer files. What's your other problem?"

"He's left a suicide note but made no reference to the murder investigation. If he thought he was going to be charged with murder, why hasn't he complained about it? Murderers usually whinge about being hounded to the grave." And the third thing, Joe thought to himself, is that Nichols was a southpaw, so how did he inject himself in the left cubital fossa?

That night, Diana woke suddenly from deep sleep. She knew a noise inside the house had disturbed her, but now she could hear only the wind outside and the soughing of her curtains as they billowed out from the window and fell back again. She lay still, listening for the noise to be repeated. After a moment a floorboard creaked. Her heart pounded with fright, but her mind was clear. She rolled to the other side of the bed, near the wall, and reached down, feeling around until her fingers brushed against cool steel. She seized the rifle and hauled it to the bed. Then she slid her feet onto the floor and, with the gun to her shoulder, yelled, "I'm armed and loaded. Get out or I'll shoot." There was a wild flamenco on the stairs. Diana ran to the doorway and switched on the corridor light, but the intruder had escaped. When she went to the stairway, a stink as sharp as needles was in the air. She was so panicky herself, now the threat had passed, that her limbs began to quiver and she had to sit down for a moment. She looked through the gallery, the kitchen, and the ground-floor bathroom and laundry, but there was no sign of disturbance. She locked the kitchen door and climbed the stairs to her private quarters; only then did she notice a low hiss coming from the study. As she entered the room a floorboard creaked. There was a second groan of wood as she approached the computer, which she had turned off that afternoon but was now running, with her file on the Primate Rescue Organization up on the screen.

The chimp hair! she thought. They want to know if I know about the chimp hair on Carolyn's T-shirt.

It was still only Sunday morning on the west coast of America, but perhaps somebody would be at work at the National Fish and Wildlife Forensic Lab in Oregon.

The telephone was answered after a few rings by a cheerful woman. Diana introduced herself. "Has a letter from me with some hair in it, suspected chimpanzee, arrived?" she asked. It had, the woman said, and they were already examining it with a scanning electron microscope. They could confirm it was from a chimpanzee and in a few days would be able to tell her the animal's sex, approximate age, whether it was wild or captive-bred, and, if captive, its likely provenance.

"We'll fax you," the woman said.

Diana removed the PRO file and transferred to the screen her notes on the chimpanzees in the circus that had stopped in Kalunga ten days earlier. There had been three of them, all castrated males. The hair I sent to Oregon must be from a gelding, she thought, or else . . . A spasm shook her from her feet to her head. Or else, Diana thought, Carolyn found another chimp the night they murdered her.

Around dawn, she finally went back to sleep.

Billy and Tom were the first to bring news of Jason's death to the Aboriginal end of town. Early on Monday morning, after their aviary maintenance job at Diana's house, they came pedaling wildly across the potholes of their street and ran in at the front door, shouting, "Grandma! Somebody else is dead!"

When Grace was tired, her hearing diminished. "Why aren't you at school?" she demanded. She was weary this morning and had not quite heard what they said.

"The vet's dead!" Tom shouted. "He killed that lady! He left a suicide note on his computer. Can we have a computer?"

Grace subsided onto the mangy brown velveteen of the settee. Two days ago, Saturday afternoon, she had given Jason tea and hot scones in the kitchen at Fig Tree Gully Road. He had just returned from Sydney and had come to see how the eagle was getting on. When she urged him to take home some tomato soup for his supper, he said, "I'm meant to avoid acid foods—but what the hell? And I *will* have butter on my scone." His face was flushed, as if he were excited about something, but his colors were turning gray. It gave her an ache in her heart to see such a young man dying.

He had a present for Diana, a CD he had bought in Sydney. "Sorry I've been so uptight," he said. Diana read the card he had written and kissed his cheek. Then they went down to the aviary together.

At five o'clock, a tourist bus had unloaded its Japanese passengers, and Grace was run off her feet until almost six, when they left, carrying away seven hundred dollars' worth of small items—dilly bags, boomerangs, hunting sticks, and greeting cards. She had been delighted. Diana, however, was subdued. Grace thought Jason might have discovered something wrong with the eagle, but Diana said, "No, she's perfect. Another fortnight and I can start work with her."

"So what's wrong?"

"He's in trouble," Diana muttered. "He admitted he's told me and everyone else dozens of lies . . . ." Her expression was bewildered and angry. "*He apologized,*" she said. "He said, 'I've done something for which you'll never forgive me, and I apologize. But it's all finished now. I'm going to put it right.' "

Grace caught hold of Billy, who was not so quick as his younger brother, and pulled him to sit beside her on the settee.

"Who told you about the vet?" she asked.

"Everybody! There are policemen at his house, and nobody is allowed inside." He shook himself like a hooked fish. "Let go!"

"Where were you last night?" she growled.

"Let go! You're hurting me."

"You tell me where you two were last night." She had hold of his arm the way she held a goanna and was pressing a nerve in his hand. "I woke up last night and went into your bedroom to see you two were properly covered up. But you weren't there. *Where were you?*"

"Nowhere! Let go." The slightest movement shot fire through his wrist.

"I don't let go until you tell me."

Tears sprang to Billy's eyes, and he turned desperately to his younger brother. Tom was shifting from foot to foot, inventing something.

"Grandma, Grandma—don't be cross," Tom burst out. "We were looking for bush tucker. Real black-fella stuff." *Black-fella stuff?* Every time she mentioned initiation to them, they jeered, "We don't want black-fella stuff!" The thought of them growing up uninitiated filled her with weariness. I'm old and tired, she thought.

"Bush tucker? At night? What bush tucker?" she said.

Tom began bravely. "There's a big tree over near the railway station, with special ants in it, and at night . . . ," but his courage failed under his grandmother's gaze. She knew every tree within fifty kilometers. "We were just mucking about," he added lamely.

"Where?"

"Just . . . about."

She had waited for hours for them to come home, but she must have dozed off, for at some stage they had crept back into the house and, finding her lying on Billy's bed, had gone to sleep in her room.

Billy felt her grip on his wrist loosen slightly, and with a sudden jerk he freed himself. He rubbed his arm resentfully.

"You know there is a murderer on the loose?" Grace said. "If he murdered a woman, he won't mind murdering a couple of kids."

"But, Grandma," they cried. "He's dead! He confessed, and then he killed himself."

"You're not to go wandering around at night," she grumbled. "Now off you go to school."

Grace kept some Rhode Island Red hens and a long-legged rooster in an enclosure in the backyard. When she appeared later that morning with the kitchen scraps in a plastic pail, crooning, "Here, chooky-chooky," the hens came running. The rooster paced forward with a stately gait, each foot lifted high, pecking the hens out of his way. While they ate, Grace went to the nesting boxes. There was an egg in each one. She gathered them up and was about to leave, when she noticed that a square of corrugated iron she had fixed over a hole in the wire at one end had been shifted sideways. Those kids! she thought. She had placed the iron so its corrugations ran horizontally. If a black snake or a big lizard got through the hole, it would be unable to wriggle past the corrugations and get at the eggs. But now the iron was standing with its lines running vertically. A snake could slide straight up a corrugation and, scratching its belly a bit, slide over the top into the henhouse.

She put down the pail holding the eggs and with both hands yanked the square of iron away from the wire fence. As it lifted she gave a cry of pain. A piece of metal hidden behind the iron had fallen on the instep of her foot. Grace lifted it off and saw it was a sign, like a metal road sign, but printed with red interlocking broken circles on a white background. The word BIOHAZARD was underneath. On the dusty ground outside the chookhouse wire, in a spot that was normally hidden by the corrugated iron, she saw a metal cash box. She squatted down and counted the dollar, two-dollar, and twenty-cent coins. It came to thirty-five dollars and twenty cents. For some moments she stared at it, her heart jumping with fright. Thieves! She had let them become thieves. The police would take them away to reform school. Then it would be juvenile detention . . . .

She was still in a daze when Diana arrived, wheeling a suitcase over the uneven concrete path from the front gate, calling, "Yoo-hoo! Gracie! Are you home, Grace?"

"Thank God!" Diana said as she heaved the suitcase in the front door. She was unusually agitated and distracted. "I thought I'd missed you," she added.

She hasn't heard about Jason, Grace realized.

"Somebody got into the house last night," Diana rushed on. "You remember a few days ago when I thought Archie had wandered in? Now I'm sure it wasn't Archie. Anyway, they've been in my study, so

I've put all the confidential files in here, and backup disks. Can they go in your big trunk? Nobody will think of—" Suddenly she stopped. "What's wrong?"

When Diana drove home that morning after calling by Jason's house, she thought of all the strange, feverish things he had said to her in the three years she had known him. She had always discounted them, and now she wondered why. His fetish about cleanliness and hygiene during surgery had seemed funny. A nick with a scalpel turned into a drama. He would almost faint at the sight of his own blood. One day when they were out bird-watching, his nose began to bleed and he rushed back to his car, calling, "I'm going to get ice! I need ice!" Wimp, she'd thought.

The question of why she had never treated him seriously niggled at her. Suddenly she realized that part of the answer was that she had never found him threatening, the way that at some obscure level a woman recognizes a threat in men, as a bird, seeing tapered wings, hears a voice cry "Falcon!" How can they accuse *him* of raping Carolyn? she asked herself. She felt the skin on the back of her neck prickle.

T he detectives who searched Jason Nichols's computer on Monday morning found that the word processing program on which he had typed his last sentence had been cleared out.

In a drawer in the clinic, several large hypodermic syringes, of the type used to murder Carolyn Williams, were discovered. There was an Oxy Viva pump and mask, Mettzenbaum scissors, and a laryngoscope, all the tools necessary to cut vocal cords. There was, of course, a large supply of Pentothal and the short-term muscle relaxant Scoline (traces of both had been found in Williams's body) and dozens of pairs of disposable latex gloves.

Everything in the clinic was in its proper place and perfectly clean. The forensic team vacuumed the house and the car, hoping to gather fibers from the clothes Carolyn had been wearing the night she died, for there was little chance of finding her blood or skin on any of the surgical instruments. A search of the Porsche, the house, and the clinic failed to uncover Carolyn's gold ring.

On Monday morning, in the Kalunga police station, Margaret McLeod had a nervous breakdown.

• • •

Rumor reached the Research by lunchtime that the murder was solved. By late afternoon it was known that when detectives began questioning Nichols's receptionist, she blurted, "It's my fault! I made the collage letters!" and burst into tears, becoming so distraught the doctor had to be called. When she had calmed down she told police that she had been jealous when Jason sent Valentine's Day cards to some girls who worked in the rabbit house. "I wanted them to leave him alone," she said.

That night at the Research, there was a party beside the swimming pool. The director of finance, dressed in suit and tie, dived in and managed to swim a few strokes before younger men came to his rescue. Administration wore a pointed green hat and ran around pinching girls' bottoms. John Parker took the opportunity to kiss Lek in the Big Lab, in front of the boys. She staggered back, dazed, with a glance behind her. Steve, Phil, and Freddie pretended to have seen nothing. Meanwhile, Sonja was distraught. She had never found the right moment to tell John that, long before the police knew, she had worked out that Margaret had sent the collage letters. At the staff party, after a gin and tonic, she confided to her secretary and some other young women that Margaret had tricked her. "She *begged* me to teach her decoupage," Sonja said. "It never occurred to me she'd use what I taught her . . ." She swallowed a sob. "Everybody I trust . . .," she murmured, and turned away.

In town, rumors about Jason Nichols began to circulate. People remembered that certain animals had disappeared in the past few years, including the dry cleaner's goat. There was the death of the news agent's cat following a visit to Nichols's clinic. "But I was never given Sox's body, was I?" the news agent's wife said. Someone vandalized Jason's Donald Duck letter box on Wednesday night.

Joe Miller called a special directors' meeting for a confidential briefing. At the end of his description of how police believed Carolyn Williams's murder had taken place, the director of finance rolled his eyes. "Christ, man! You've talked for an hour and told us nothing!"

Miller gave an affable smile.

"You've not informed us what Carolyn died of, or where, or why. We don't know if she was strangled, or suffocated, or why you're so sure Nichols is the swine who did it."

"That's right," Sonja interjected. "What *did* she die of? All you've told us is that she left the duck shooters, rang Jason, and asked him to drive her home. Then, you say, he killed her somehow, drove into the Research using her card to open the front gate, went on past the airfield, opened the northwest gate with her keys, and dumped her body near the mountain." She looked along the table. "There's nothing reassuring about any of that as far as the female staff are concerned. If anything, it makes a girl feel she's in more danger out here, where nobody can hear a cry for help, than in the city."

Along the table, the directors' expressions said they expected better than what Miller had given them.

"Why didn't anybody hear her calling for help from Jason's house?" Sonja persisted. "Kerry Larnach lives only two doors away. Was he home that Saturday night? Why didn't he hear anything?"

"I'm sorry," Joe replied. "Until the coronor's inquest I can't tell you anything more. Even if I knew more."

"Of course he knows more," Sonja muttered to Administration beside the tea urn. Her face was pointy with irritation. "I don't believe poor Jason did it. Do *you?*" Her eyes fixed accusingly on the vulnerable pink leaf of lips inside Administration's beard.

"Well—hard to say." He stroked the beard thoughtfully, a habitual gesture that set Sonja's teeth on edge. "You had dinner with him that night. Did he seem to have murder in mind?"

"Of course not! There are a lot of men here with more reason to murder Carolyn Williams than Jason ever had." She jigged her tea bag, then moved her gaze onto the director of finance.

Administration gave a pained smile. A week earlier, he had courageously gone along the top-floor corridor to Joe Miller's office to admit that he had had an affair with Williams, which had ended some months ago when he arrived at her condo one night and found Finance's plump white body stretched on the living room floor while Carolyn played with his feet. Joe happened to know this already. "I was furious, but I didn't kill her! You've got to believe me!" Administration said. Momentarily his legs bent, as if he were about to go down on his knees before the director of security.

"They're accusing Jason because he's dead," Sonja added. "It's the easy way out."

Her colleague gave a melancholy nod. In fact he was delighted to hear that Nichols was the murderer. Incautiously, he added, "But it makes life simpler for us to be able to assure the staff that the crime's been solved."

"It has not been solved!" Sonja objected. "Whoever did this murder is much too smart for Joe Miller and the Homicide Squad. I don't find that a relief, and I don't think other people will either."

But most people did accept that the vet had murdered Carolyn Williams. In Kalunga, neighbors who had feuded for thirty years were speaking again; grudges had vanished over beers in the Arms; at the Research, the backbiting was less savage. But as tension relaxed, kindness ebbed too, and soon people returned to their cheerful habits of scorn and self-righteousness. When Margaret McLeod left the hospital, a contingent of women called on her to suggest that she sell her cottage and return to Sydney. "You're really a city person," said the leader, who spoke from the pulpit of the Kalunga Uniting Church on Sunday mornings and had, as she pointed out, the good of the whole community in mind. Margaret rang Sonja, whom she had not spoken to in more than a week, but the director of personnel was in meetings all day, her secretary said.

An urge to erase the town's shame took hold of the Shire Council, which decided to hold a "Kalunga Pride Week" in March 1994. Kerry Larnach, who was preparing to go to Saigon for a holiday, found time to arrange for two return airfares to Cairns as first prize in the Kalunga Week lottery. Diana agreed to contribute by leading ornithological tours of the lake.

Her anxiety over what had really happened to Carolyn and Jason Nichols increased. When she told the Homicide Squad detective that she was sure Jason had been gay, he looked polite but bored and went on supervising the packing of the clinic. One of the boxes he labeled JASON NICHOLS: APPLE MACINTOSH COMPUTER, PLUS CONTAINER OF 15 BACKUP DISKS.

"He had no motive to kill Carolyn—or himself!" Diana reiterated, but even as she spoke, doubts assailed her: what was the unforgivable thing Jason had done?

The detective bit off a piece of tape with his teeth. "A motive depends on a secret, and Nichols had a secret. He was a closet queen, eh?"

She nodded.

"And Carolyn was just the sort of girl to find out—and she'd tell the world, wouldn't she? She made people admit things about themselves they didn't want to admit. She wouldn't allow anybody any decency. If you told her you had a corn, she'd stamp on it, right? She was a bitch." Diana nodded but knew that somewhere there was a trick in what the detective was saying.

"The fact that a week after Williams's murder Nichols shows remorse, tells you he's got things to put straight"—he grinned, and this time he lifted his eyebrows at her, asking, Yes? Follow?—"strengthens our case," he finished.

On Tuesday, a letter came by special delivery from the minister for science, technology, and the environment, saying that Diana had been appointed to the Ethics Committee of the Research, "but due to a delay in the ratification of appointments, you will be restricted to observer status for several weeks." "*What?*" she shouted. "What's going on?" She was so angry, it was several minutes before she read the next sentence, which said that in the meantime, she was welcome to attend meetings, and a security pass to the Research was available at the administration building, to be collected as soon as she liked.

Diana had set aside the whole week for flying the peregrine falcon, to have him ready for release before the eagle's training began. Each morning when she drove him out to the flying ground, she paused beside the eastern fence, at the back of the lab complex, and with binoculars examined the buildings. She was memorizing the shape of each building, where its windows were placed, and how many there were. Chimpanzees, she reasoned, would need to be kept in a section that was walled off from the rest of the lab complex. When, at last, she could tour the Research, she intended to walk the length of every building, counting the windows.

The falcon, meanwhile, had stopped tearing out his breast feathers and was flying more dynamically, but he was still an unstable bird. His high-pitched, staccato "chak-chak-chak-chak" was so insistent that after an hour in close company with him, her ears rang. Out at the flying ground, he missed his prey time and again or, if he struck it, failed to bind it with his talons. He often dived after the food he had dropped, plummeting into bushes and sometimes getting stuck. Once, he almost flew into the Cyclone-wire fence. On Wednesday, in a fit of megalomania, he tried to fell a swan. The swan flew to water, as the falcon should have realized it would. Diana watched from the shore, blasting on the whistle she wore round her neck, shouting "Falco!," warning him to let go. He ignored her, and the swan dragged him into the lake and tried to drown him. Somehow, he shook free, mounting from the water with lashing wing strokes. The next day, Diana noticed, his hunting improved.

All week she had been careful not to let the falcon see the eagle, because she feared that the sight of the larger bird might send him into a jealous decline. On Friday morning, she thought, This is ridiculous, and with the unhooded peregrine standing on her fist, she strolled to the eagle's mews. The eagle was standing in majestic profile, her gaze fixed on the sky. After a while she shook her mane feathers, like a woman loosening her hair. The hooked face turned abruptly, and she glanced insolently at her visitors. Immediately, the peregrine went into a frenzy of bating and screaming, but all at once the eagle pinned him with her eyes. The falcon froze.

He had traveled so well on the drive out to the flying ground that morning, Diana decided as she got close to the Research that she could safely leave him in the van for a few minutes while she collected her security pass.

It was a bright, hot day, with a sky the color of laundry bluing. There would be no rain for a few days, from the look of the weather, but there had been more than twelve millimeters in the past fortnight, and already the barley grass was coming up. On the drive out she had seen farmers sowing oats in some paddocks and in others spraying against earth mites. The spray everyone used, Le-Mat, killed foxes and rabbits and other small animals. For the next month she would have to be on the lookout for poisoned hunting birds. Meanwhile, the oats would sprout in a yellow-green fuzz across the wide, flat fields, drawing flocks of hundreds of galahs. They uprooted the sprouting oats to eat the seeds underneath. Years ago, when she was a child, she and Morrie had sat on adjoining fence posts and shot at them, laughing maniacally. As a shot rang out, the flock would explode into the air like a pink firework.

She wondered again about Morrie: all week there had been no sign from him—although he must be needing supplies by now, she thought. His method of asking for things was to leave an empty container of whatever he wanted next to the old fence. Normally, he required a bag of flour a month, and it was five weeks since she had brought him any.

When she reached the gatehouse at the front entrance, she was directed to the top floor of the administration building, to Joe Miller's office. His secretary was a soft, middle-aged woman who came to the gallery sometimes to buy small gifts for her grandchildren. Once, Diana had taken her out to the aviary to see a beautiful blue-gray harrier that had flown into telegraph wires. He could never fly free again, but there was a breeder in West Australia who would care for him and had a harrier hen with whom he might be happy in captivity. The woman's expression had become childlike as she gazed at the bird. "Look at the white spots on his wings!" she whispered.

She had ready in an envelope Diana's electronic key, plus an ordinary one for a padlock, both welded to a tag saying they were issued to Diana Pembridge exclusively, and unauthorized use would be prosecuted. The electronic key opened the red-and-white boom at the main entrance and another at the entrance to the laboratory complex, she explained. "And this is for the gates in the perimeter fence. We'll be changing to an electronic system for them, too, in a few weeks. Meanwhile, this key opens all of them."

As Diana took them, the woman added, "I shouldn't tell you this, but now you're allowed to go wherever you like, you know—so you don't have to detour around the outside to get to the lake. You can drive straight through."

"*Are you sure?*"

"It was agreed to at a debate about the freedom of movement of Ethics Committee members. It's in the minutes."

Diana pocketed the keys and galloped downstairs to her van. To be able to drive straight through the Research would cut ten minutes off every trip, saving her forty minutes a day—not to mention how useful it would be for checking the lab complex from the front.

But when she set off down the long, smooth road, the familiar terrain of home with its violation of unfamiliar buildings made her mentally queasy. For years after this land had ceased to belong to her, she had yearned for it with an almost animal force; now she felt her passionate attachment had loosened, while her love for it had grown. Her grandfather had begun the desecration, ring-barking the forest and introducing hard-hoofed animals that injured the soil. The love she felt for this landscape was, partly, for its endurance.

At the gate closest to the flying ground, she discovered that the hasp on the padlock was still cut. She drove through, parked, and went to the old fence. There was still no sign from Morrie. She glanced at the house on the ridge to make sure nobody was watching from the veranda, then climbed through the strands of barbed wire and, at the tree line, shouted, "Morrie! Are you okay?"

After a couple of minutes, she entered the cool, dim pine forest. She had scrambled no more than ten meters up the slope, when a large rock came rolling down. A smaller one flew through the branches above her head and dropped a couple of meters behind her. "Cut it out!" she yelled. Another rock flew overhead. He'd spent five years in jail for the murder of Doug Pembridge and Louise Williams when Jack Williams walked into the police station one morning and confessed he'd done it. That night, Jack hanged himself. Morrie returned to Kalunga an old man.

Diana ran back down the slope.

In forty-eight hours the improvement in the falcon was breathtaking.

The moment Diana threw him from her hand that morning, he became a blade in the sky. He flashed and cut. His long, tapered wings scythed the air.

A small flock of ganggangs was feeding in the trees on Mount Kalunga. Diana could not see them, but she knew they were there because from the treetops came noises like rusty hinges. The falcon, after flying for only a few seconds, spotted their red crests against the pine foliage and zoomed in close to the canopy to try to flush them out. At first the cockatoos stuck together and swooped to lower branches, but he fluttered down and kept harassing until he panicked two birds into breaking from cover. In desperation, they flew for the open sky, where no bird can outfly a falcon. The chase was fast and magnificent. The peregrine rocked and weaved after the fleeing parrots and dispatched one in midair with a strike on the back of its head. He dropped it at Diana's feet, landed on her fist, and hurriedly swallowed the piece of fresh chicken that was his reward. Then he went up after the second ganggang. It was dead in less than a minute.

The day before, he had stayed away from the lake, as if he were fearful of it after his near drowning, but now, when a black duck flying near the foreshore caught his attention, he headed for the water, stalking it so skillfully, flying underneath and maneuvering in its blind spot, that until he burst on it from behind, the duck did not know he was there. Diana whirled in excitement, yelling "Hooray!"

She rewarded the peregrine with more chicken from the bag on her hip and threw him up for the fourth time, feeling her blood mount in excitement. Sometimes falconing seemed like a shadow falling across her memory, as if all she were doing was remembering how to work a hunting bird, and in the calls and gestures made between herself and the animal, the past connected perfectly to the present. At these times she felt the seamless web of life stretching through her, connecting her to every other living being.

After forty minutes, seven bright, limp corpses lay at her feet.

She glanced furtively toward the house before putting a brace of ducks in her bag. She knew she must set the falcon free today, without keeping him in the hack box. Peregrines could get into the habit of hunting for fun, like humans, and once you had a killer bird, you had to put it down. She imagined him soaring away from her, his horizon growing wider, as she dwindled to a dot below.

The bird was drifting about three hundred meters above her, a fleck in the sky, resting up there on his tapered wings. The Alymeri jesses on his ankles would have to be cut off before he returned to the wild. She gave a blast on the whistle and, squinting up, cried,

"Falco!" In the sheer blue air the soaring fleck paused, then began a wide, slow downward spiral. For every falconer there are three sublime moments, and two of them can happen only once. The first is the moment of taming. The last is the instant of setting free. But the other, the daily glory, was this—to call a hunter from the sky to one's hand.

The spiraling fleck gradually gathered speed. Seventy meters above her, the peregrine folded his wings, squared his shoulders, and stooped. He plummeted like a falling bomb. Twenty meters above her head, he was traveling at more than two hundred kilometers an hour—then he flared his wings and alighted on her fist as delicately as a leaf.

"Remarkable!" Parker said to the company in general. He handed the binoculars to one of the boys.

As a special treat, everyone from U-1 had gathered for morning tea on the upstairs veranda because Steve had turned twenty-three that day. Sonja had prepared a cake and little sandwiches but had to dash back to her office for a meeting. "Lek will look after us," Parker said.

He knelt beside Lek to demonstrate the focusing mechanism on the binoculars. She gasped when suddenly she trapped Diana in the lens. "Lord Buddha says good. Good to let birds fly away."

"I don't think you quite understand," Parker said. "She's not letting him go; she's hunting." Above Lek's head he said to the boys, "Falconing happens to be illegal in Australia. I'll have to raise that at the next Ethics Committee meeting."

They sniggered.

"Fax the minister," Steve suggested.

Lek was intent on the scene being played out near the mountain. "Look! Bird is free!" she said.

Diana had cut the jesses from the falcon's legs and tossed him away again. She was already running for her van.

The van took off, followed by the fluttering bird. Both vanished behind a hillock but a few minutes later reappeared, inside the Research now, the falcon still giving chase. His head was down, and he was screaming so loudly his cries were audible to them on the veranda. He hovered down to the level of the driver's window, as if pleading to be let inside, but the window was closed and through the glass they glimpsed a face staring straight ahead.

"How the hell did she get in here?" Parker muttered. "Those idiots in administration must have given her a key."

"What'll we do, Doc?" Freddie asked.

"Nobody can get into U-1," Parker answered, half to himself.

Their attention remained fixed on the chase. The van had now passed the turnoff to Sonja's house and reached flat ground.

"I calculate she's doing sixty-five K," Steve said. "The bird's lost the race."

Suddenly the falcon beat away with thrashing strokes, banked, turned, flew back, then flashed forward again, easily outdistancing the van. Then he veered into a long U-turn, rose higher and higher, his tail fanned and his white breast glowing. He was heading back toward the lake. As he passed over the house he uttered a sharp, wild cry.

"Too much cry," Lek said. She handed back the binoculars with a puzzled expression.

"What is it?" Parker said.

"Ebery animal has Buddha nature and Buddha sound, isn't it?" She had a vertical crease between her eyebrows.

"Absolutely." Parker smiled in anticipation of the nonsense toward which her mind was working. A glance to the boys alerted them that they should listen.

"Why Sailor and Lucy have no Buddha sound?" Lek asked.

"Hmm," Parker said. "Freddie, can you enlighten us on this conundrum?"

Freddie, who had met a computer on his thirteenth birthday and found true love, screwed up his face, as he always did when Lek asked a question. "I don't understand the problem," he said to Parker.

"Lek asks, Where is the Buddha voice of Sailor and Lucy, and does their not having one mean that their Buddha nature—surely you re-member what Buddha nature is, Freddie?—is somehow diminished?"

Freddie struck himself on the forehead with the flat of his hand. "*Riiiight,*" he said. "Well, Lek, it's like this: we cut their vocal cords." He pointed to his throat.

"Excuse me?"

"We cut their vocal cords so they don't make a nuisance of them-selves." He again pointed to his throat and made a slicing motion. "It doesn't hurt," he added.

Lek felt her soul slip out of her throat like a handkerchief pulled from a magician's sleeve. Her dark bean-shaped eyes blinked for a moment, as if she had not understood, then she collapsed with a thump. The men gazed down at her in amazement.

"Now look what you've done, you great sweaty goon!" Steve said.

They tried maneuvering her so her head was lower than her heart, but she remained a lolling, unconscious lump. "C'mon," Parker ordered. "You take her feet, Freddie." They carried her into the bedroom and laid her on Sonja's bed. Parker stayed watching her, while Freddie got a glass of water.

The boys had tidied up the teacups and were trudging down the veranda steps when Sonja returned.

"Where's John?" she asked.

"In the bedroom with Lek."

Sonja stared.

"She fainted," Freddie called as Sonja bustled past.

Parker was sitting upright on the bed with a glass held to Lek's mouth when his wife burst in. *"What are you doing?"* she said. The tableau before her was more dreadful than anything she had imagined. In her own bed! In broad daylight!

He put a finger to his lips, buying time to collect himself. He had been fondling Lek's breasts to help her regain consciousness and had developed something of an alp in his trousers. "Just coming round," he whispered.

She's pregnant, Sonja thought. He's made her pregnant.

Lek opened her eyes slowly and kept opening them until they were wide with fright. "Excuse me," she said. "Bery sorry. Silly."

Parker had never seen her so meek. Sonja smiled and took her hand. "Will you be able to go back to work?" she asked in a concerned voice.

"Oh, yes. Bery silly. All right now," Lek said.

A round midnight on Friday, Tom and Billy crept out of bed. They had trained themselves to wake in the middle of the night, when they could be certain their grandmother was asleep.

They made their way on foot through cool, silent streets until they reached Fig Tree Gully Road. Tonight would be their first adventure in almost a week, since the rousing they got from Grandma after she had discovered the things in the chookhouse. For four nights she had stayed awake almost all night, watching to make sure they did not go out. But she had fallen into a deep sleep at eight o'clock in front of the television, and they felt sure she would sleep all night.

Outside Diana's house, they stood beneath the bedroom window, listening. "Wish she'd snore, like Grandma," Billy said. There was silence above them. The van was parked on the other side of the house, but although the sound of starting the engine seemed as loud as an earthquake, somehow the stone walls muffled it, and Diana never woke.

Often, they just drove around for a while, but on special nights (when the petrol tank was full), they went on long trips, driving out to the lake or to neighboring towns, not getting back until almost dawn. On these forays they found all kinds of useful things: money, a chain saw (which they had hidden down by the river), a box of canned peaches, and other objects people left lying around. They had a fire extinguisher, a baby bouncer, and Kerry Larnach's bolt cutters. Twice they came home with kittens, but Grandma made them put a note in the news agent's window saying "Lost Kitten," and people took the kittens away. They were not allowed to have a puppy either, because Grandma said they were not responsible enough to look after it, since they forgot to water the hens and one died of thirst. Their most exciting trip now was to go to the Research, where, ten days earlier, they had cut the padlocks off all the gates. They had been back once already but had so far only brushed the surface of possibilities inside the Cyclone-wire fence. The guards with flashlights and nightsticks made going there even more thrilling.

Billy, who was taller and could see better over the top of the steering wheel, drove. As soon as they were safely out of Fig Tree Gully Road, he slowed down to take a look at the fuel gauge.

"Full!" he and Tom cried in unison.

An hour later, they were almost at the lake and saw that lights were burning in the outlying house at the Research.

"Should we use another gate?" Tom asked.

"Why?"

"Because we've used this one twice already. The guards might be watching for us."

"We'll park outside and leave the gate open," Billy said. "If they chase us we'll run for the gate, jump in the van, and drive off. They'll never catch us."

"What if they've got guns?"

"We'll duck." Billy clashed the gears with vigor as he rounded the corner of the fence onto the last stretch of road.

It was a long walk from where they left the van, near the base of the mountain, and by the time they had passed the airfield Tom's legs were tired. "It's too far," he said.

"Just to that house," Billy urged. The house glowed through the dark enticingly, its latticed verandas making a pattern of light like a Chinese lantern. When they reached the garden, they ran forward on tiptoe, looking up at the veranda. There was no sound of voices or smell of cigarettes. "They're all asleep. Let's go up," Billy said.

On a table on the veranda Billy found a pair of binoculars. "Hey, Tom! I can see *everything!*"

"Shh!" his brother whispered. He did not want to go inside the house and was already descending the steps.

Billy swept the binoculars across the landscape. "It's all *green.* I can see a Land Cruiser parked near those buildings where we went before, and three men. . . ."

"Come on!" Tom said.

Downstairs, they spent a few minutes in the cabin of Sonja's Land Cruiser, which was unlocked, examining its sound system and making driving noises.

"Let's look in there," Tom said.

The laundry was boring, but the door next to it was open, and they saw with astonishment the Inclin-ator that ran alongside the stairs.

"You keep watch with the binoculars," Billy said.

Tom found a position in the garden from where he could see the laboratory complex through the night sights.

Lek had gone to sleep after her evening meal but woke a few hours later, her teeth rattling with fright from a dream. For a long while she lay awake in the unfriendly dark, feeling cut off from herself, unable to think clearly and knowing she must try to go back to sleep, but her thoughts whirled obsessively around what Freddie had told her that morning.

"I've been stupid," she reproached herself.

During the afternoon, the boys had asked her, "Have you ever taken an aspirin? Have you had an injection against smallpox? Do you wash your hair with shampoo? Have you ever taken a pill for diarrhea?" When she said yes, they yelled with derision. "All those things were tested on animals to make them safe for *you!*" She felt ashamed of herself for not understanding what sacrifices the animals made for human beings. She had always considered things from the human point of view. When she was kind to animals it was because she wanted to gain merit in heaven for herself, she realized. Now she wanted to thank the animals for what they did for her.

She got up, pulled on a pair of jeans and a sweater, and walked through the hushed, cold garden that separated her cabin from the house. During the day, it was a rule that the upstairs door must be kept locked, but since she intended to spend only a few minutes in there, just long enough to say thank you to Lucy and Sailor, she didn't bother shutting it.

The chimps were curled up asleep in their separate nesting cages, their hands and flat feet tucked in, their heads curled into their chests, so they looked like folded woolly black socks. They woke when she turned on the light. Lucy moved over on haunches and knuckles to talk to her, raising her hand to make the sign that meant "Let's groom each other." Lek said, "Thank you, Lucy." Lucy's eyes yearned at her with a look of wanting to talk back. Her silence made Lek cry again. She rested her head against the wire where Lucy could reach it, and settled down for a grooming session. Big black fingers worked delicately through the roots of her hair, bringing on a drowsy sense of well-being. She was still resting against the cage when Billy walked in.

Lek scrambled to her feet and pressed the emergency button. In the house above, Sonja woke with a leap, while up at the condominiums, the siren hee-hawing in Parker's bedroom roused people in adjoining houses.

By the time Sonja had reached the monitor in the kitchen, all she could see in U-1 was Lek, fully clothed, standing in the Big Lab, her hands held to her mouth in fright. Sonja did not pause to dress but rushed downstairs in her nightgown, an old one she wore only when John was not around.

She grabbed Lek by the arm. "What are you doing here? Why did you set off the alarm?" she yelled.

"I saw a ghost," Lek whispered.

Sonja smacked her across the face. "Tell me the truth! What were you doing?"

Lek held her cheek. "I don't know."

"*Get in there.*" Sonja shoved Lek toward the open door of the Animal Room, but suddenly she had another idea. "You need to be out of sight," she said. "There'll be people wanting to come in here in a minute. You go into Level 2." The girl balked, but Sonja shoved her hard. "It's not dangerous. You're to vanish until the fuss is over."

She pulled down the blind on the inside of the Animal Room so that the chimps could not be seen through the one-way glass. Then she turned on all the lights, adjusted her nightgown and her expression for the security guards, and was ready when two of them came pounding down the stairs, squinting at the white glare of neon.

"It's okay!" she exclaimed. "But thank you. Thank you for coming so quickly."

They darted alert, inquisitive glances in all directions, paying no attention to her.

"I'm afraid it's just a malfunction in the alarm," Sonja said.

One of them looked toward the Animal Room doors.

"I've checked in there. I've looked everywhere, in fact."

"The door hasn't been tampered with?"

"No."

"You unlocked it yourself?"

Sonja nodded.

The guards glanced at each other and shrugged. "Okay. Hope you can get back to sleep."

"Thank you again." She shepherded them out of the Big Lab to the staff room, where a blue plastic tub of ice cream was on the table, with a spoon beside it. It had been there long enough for condensation to form and trickle down its sides. One man raised an eyebrow. "Get hungry, did you?"

Sonja stared at him. She had not noticed the ice cream tub when she rushed in to question Lek.

"Oh—yes. I think the fright I had . . . I had to have something for my blood sugar."

"Know what you mean," the other one said. His gaze rested lovingly on a six-pack of beer on top of the fridge.

"Would you like a beer?"

"Wooden say no."

They cracked the tops off the cans and lifted them thirstily to their lips. The big-bellied one winked. "Don't tell Joe. He's a bit . . . you know." He flicked on his walkie-talkie, but from underground it would not work.

The three of them were sitting at the table, chatting in a desultory way, when Parker came down the steps three at a time, wild-haired, wearing a brown fishing pullover over striped cotton pajama pants.

The cheap pajamas, his unshaven cheeks and disheveled hair, gave him the look of a derelict. "God almighty, woman! What's going on?" he said.

"Malfunction in your alarm, Doc," a guard said.

Parker continued to stare at Sonja, hoping to read from her expression if something was wrong, but her acting defeated him. He turned to glare at the guard. "What are you doing here?"

The men finished their beers and got to their feet.

"It's okay, Doc," the younger one said. "The alarm went off. We weren't far away, so we came and checked it out. No problem." They retreated toward the stairs. "Good night."

"Good night," Sonja called.

Parker followed them upstairs, where the security man who had driven him over from the condos was sitting inside another Land Cruiser. The first pair of guards went to chat with the one who had just arrived. Parker managed to smile as he called good night to them.

In his absence upstairs, Sonja rushed to the washbasin to splash water on her face and try to fluff up her hair. She hated her husband to see her without makeup. In the cabinet she found some toothpaste, which she rubbed around her gums. The splash of water and the fluffing had helped—but I still look a fright, she thought. As she peered at her reflection in the mirror, she felt a wave of hatred for Lek. It's her fault I've been humiliated, Sonja thought; forced to appear in this horrible nightdress in front of John and those louts from security.

"Your little Thai friend set off the alarm," she said when Parker returned. "I hid her in Level 2 before the guards arrived."

"She'll have to go," he muttered. His instincts told him Sonja was in a dangerous mood. Did she see me squeezing Lek's breast yesterday? he wondered.

"If you ask me, what happened to Carolyn Williams should happen to her."

"What? *Murdered?*"

"No. Cut her vocal cords. That'd shut her up."

"How did you find that out?"

"At a confidential briefing for directors." Suddenly she covered her mouth with her hand to suppress a gush of laughter. "Imagine." She tittered. "Imagine a woman whose vocal . . ." She opened her mouth wide, as if screaming, then shut it. The laughter in her chest made a farting noise through her lips. Parker stared, fascinated. She opened her mouth again, this time grabbing at her throat, uttering strangled squeaks. Her face grew red, her eyes shone with merriment. He was enthralled. A moment ago, he had been frightened; now he was laughing with her, and at her, thinking, You'll never know what Carolyn and I used to do. Then he wondered, Can I ask Sonja to let me do it to her? He stepped forward and took her hands, smiling down at her meaningfully.

"Why don't you lock Level 2, and we'll go upstairs," he said.

Tom was standing in the garden, watching everything through the night-sight binoculars, when the alarm went off. We'll be caught, he thought. Moments later, Billy came running along the road through the garden. "Billy!" Tom called. "Here!"

The elder boy paused.

"I'm in here." Tom was behind a banksia tree. Its saw-toothed leaves scraped his arm as he grabbed at his brother. Billy was panting so hard that for a few seconds he could not speak.

Then he whispered hoarsely, "They've got little grillers in there!" Tom's eyes shone.

"There was a lady who looked a bit like mum. She was patting one." Tom gaped. "What did she say?"

Just then all the lights in the house went on, and they heard someone running down the stairs. "Quick!" Billy said. They drew back behind the banksia.

"That's a lady I've seen in the news agent's," Tom said.

They watched her run under the house and disappear.

"We better go," Billy said.

"No! I wanna see the grillers."

They crept back toward the house, but suddenly a beam of light illuminated the branches of a tree in front of them. From the direction of the lab complex, which was on higher ground, headlights were boring through the dark. Without a word, the boys turned and ran back through the garden, dashing across the road and striking out over the paddocks toward the fence.

"What if there's snakes?" Tom whimpered.

When they had gone two hundred meters, they stopped and looked back. Nobody was following them, but another Cruiser was on its way to the house.

"When they leave we can go back," Tom said.

"No!" Billy replied fiercely. "Not tonight. It's too late."

His younger brother started to cry. "It's not fair! I didn't see them."

"Tom!" Billy said. "It's too *late*."

Tom gave a loud sniff and sat down.

"Get up!"

"I'm tired," he sobbed. "It's not fair."

Billy hunkered down beside his brother. "We'll come back another night. I'll stay on watch, and you can go down and see them."

"Was she really like mum?" Tom asked.

"Kind of. But with straight hair."

"She might give us one," Tom said.

"What?"

"A griller."

"She might."

"We'd look after it properly. We would, wouldn't we?"

"You bet! We'd *promise* Grandma. . . ."

They got up and walked toward the fence, planning where they would house the baby gorilla. They were so excited they did not see, even though the moonlight was quite bright, the thin naked man standing not far from the van, observing them as they climbed inside.

Sonja returned to U-1 later that night, holding John's hand, feeling strangely powerful. She could not say she had enjoyed herself physically, but she'd enjoyed what had happened *psychologically*, as it were. By allowing John to indulge his little fantasy, she had felt a control over him that was utterly delicious. To rule, but not to dominate: that's my strategy, she told herself.

For his part, Parker was feeling indulgent toward his wife. A flood of unfamiliar affection for her made him squeeze her small, bony hand as they descended the stairs side by side. Both of them were dressed now, ready to interview Lek. John was wearing his favorite brown corduroy trousers, his fishing pullover, and a pair of sneakers. Sonja had put on linen trousers, a shirt and jacket, and a dash of eau de toilette.

In the corridor outside Level 2, they masked and gowned in silence. Parker unlocked the door, then turned to Sonja. "In case she's done something silly, you wait here," he said.

Above the mask, Sonja's eyes widened until the whites showed above and below her pupils. "What could she do!"

"I don't know. But . . ."

"Take something with you."

"What?"

"The chimp prod!" She turned and dragged open the door out to the Big Lab. A few moments later, she reappeared with the implement they used to control the apes if they became violent. It was half a meter long and gave an electric shock, like a cattle prod.

Holding it in one hand, Parker leaned his shoulder on the door to the high-containment lab, slowly letting his weight overcome the negative air pressure. Sonja stood behind him, alert, ready for Lek to spring out.

The girl was lying on the floor with her eyes closed. "Oh, God!" Parker murmured. "She's injected herself with something!" There was a whole pharmacy in the drug cabinet. Suddenly Lek opened her eyes. "Get up," he said. She scrambled to her feet. "Have you done something to yourself?" he demanded. She shook her head.

Sonja, watching from the doorway, stepped inside. She had checked her appearance in the mirror in the corridor and was delighted at how mysterious she looked, gowned and masked in blue cotton, like a surgeon. Her inscrutable look, on top of her new power over John, gave her a sense of superiority toward Lek. All that time, Sonja realized with surprise, she had felt intimidated by Lek—by her straight gaze (most un-Oriental, one would have thought), by the way she wrinkled her nose in disgust at the sight or smell of non-vegetarian food. Beneath the mask, a smile flickered on Sonja's lips.

"We'll go outside," John said.

"No! Let's stay in here," Sonja interjected.

His shoulders moved impatiently. "I suppose, now we're here . . ."

She did not wait. "Now, Lek: you tell us exactly why you were in the Big Lab at night and why you called the guards," she ordered.

Lek said nothing.

"Go on," Parker urged.

She gave another sullen shake of her head.

"Don't you defy me!" Sonja said. "*Tell us why you were in the lab.*"

"I want back to Thailand," Lek muttered.

"*What were you doing?*" Anger was making Sonja's face turn red.

"Nothing," Lek said. "I doing nothing. Then I see ghost."

"Ghost!" Sonja exclaimed. "You saw a ghost! What ghost?"

Lek shook her head.

"Was it a woman ghost or a man ghost?" Parker asked.

Lek shrugged.

"Was it the ghost of that woman who was murdered three weeks ago?" Sonja put in.

Parker felt a thrill. Now that the question had been asked, it seemed obvious that Lek had imagined she had seen the ghost of Carolyn Williams. He turned to smile at his wife, whose excited glance held his for a moment.

"No woman," Lek said. "Boy."

"*A boy?*"

Lek nodded. "Black-black," she said, and grimaced. "Bery dark. Maybe demon."

Parker gestured to his wife to step aside so they could confer. They skirted the dissection table with its bone saw and plastic tent and strolled toward the back of Level 2, where there was a large negative-airflow cabinet. "I think she's going mad," he whispered.

Sonja nodded.

"We shouldn't try to question her any more. We should calm her down, and I'll phone Otto tomorrow. Why don't you take her back to her cabin and make her a cup of Ovaltine?"

"Whatever you say, my love."

I'll do that to Sonja more often, he thought.

It was three o'clock in the morning by the time they got Lek back to her cabin and into bed. Parker accompanied the women only as far as the cabin's front door before making a diplomatic withdrawal. While Sonja was fussing with the girl, he went upstairs, poured himself a whiskey, and, despite the cold, went to sit on the veranda. It was one of those still inland nights when the air seemed composed of some perfect, subtle substance that, on touching living things, revived them. He breathed in and looked up at the sky. Stars were not as visible as on some nights because of the Easter moon, which would be full in another day or so. Its light was falling on the lake in a long white ramp that wavered slightly along the edges and stretched almost to the foreshore. Suddenly he sat upright. He had heard something and thought he saw a pale-colored vehicle driving without headlights past the northern fence. He reached behind to the shelf where they kept the night-sight binoculars. They were not there. Parker got up and turned on the veranda light. The binoculars had vanished.

He switched the light off again and squinted at the lake foreshore. Sure enough, there *was* a vehicle there. It was driving very slowly—no wonder, without lights—and he recognized it. It was Pembridge's van. He watched from the edge of the veranda as it reached the corner of the fence, turned, and headed toward the highway, then he hurried indoors. At the back of the house he could still hear it, but although he leaned out a window, he could not see it—until suddenly its headlights came on and there was a clash of gears.

Parker felt perplexed as he returned to the veranda. He heard Sonja's footsteps on the stairs below and decided to keep his puzzlement to himself.

• • •

On the highway, Tom and Billy were already planning how to return to the Animal Room and, if possible, remove one of the baby gorillas. Using the van, they knew, was dangerous because its lights could be seen by the people who lived in the house upstairs. Tonight, because of the moon and the special binoculars they had found, Billy had been able to steer without the headlights as long as Tom, looking through the binoculars, corrected his direction from time to time. But they would not be able to do that when the moon began shrinking again—and anyway, they could not risk taking the van too often, or Diana would notice her petrol was disappearing. The difficulty was getting to and from the Research and having some way of bringing home their pet.

"Tell me about the room again," Tom said, and Billy recounted for the fifth time everything he could remember: the lady who reminded him of their mother, the two little gorillas, like Michael Jackson's Bubbles, the cages of white rabbits, the kindergarten-size table and chairs, painted yellow and red, the climbing ropes on one wall, the exercise bicycle—

"Bicycle!" Tom said. "They can ride bicycles! We could ride our bikes out in the daytime. Then we could dink it home."

"We could both dink one," Billy said.

"Yeah, we could take both of them!"

"We'll have to wag school."

"Just one day. Anyway, it's the holidays soon."

They fell silent in the joy of contemplating what lay ahead. Nobody else in the whole of Kalunga had a pet griller.

"Diana's got a book about them," Tom said. "We'll read it and find out what they eat."

When Joe arrived at his office, on the top story of the administration building, on Monday morning, the floor was awash with a fax from Homicide that had come in overnight. It was a report from Perth, where detectives had tracked down and interviewed the two men with whom Carolyn Williams had left the Kalunga Arms on Saturday night three weeks earlier.

He began reading while he was standing up and became so engrossed he forgot to sit down. The report said that the men, both in their early twenties, had not been part of the Victoria and New South

Wales shooters' cohort that camped by the lake. They had been unable to bring camping equipment on the flight from Perth and had
stayed in town, in the motel, economizing by taking a single room
and making their own breakfast. The motel was booked solid with
shooters, all dressed in camouflage gear, all leaving for the lake in
the predawn dark. It had been easy for them to come and go without the manager realizing he had two guests for the price of one.
Smuggling Carolyn Williams in there on Saturday night had presented
no difficulty—except, as they stated in their interviews, for the noise
she made. The three of them went at it hammer and tongs, and by
ten o'clock the men were exhausted. They had been awake since
4:00 A.M. and had not slept much the night before, on the airplane.
Williams had jumped up and said, "Oh, hell! I've got to make a phone
call or I'll miss my lift home." She said that if she telephoned from
the room, the manager, who also operated the switchboard, would
be "sus." "I'll go to the post office, to the phone box there." It was
only a block away. They all got dressed and walked around to High
Street. She emerged from the box exclaiming, "All fixed! I'll be collected in five minutes." The last thing she had said was, "Wow! I stink
of spunk." She laughed and seemed to be looking forward to shock-
ing whoever it was who was driving her home, because she added,
"Wait till I tell my chauffeur there were *two of you!*" and danced
about on the pavement.

In another couple of days, the fax said, there would be a DNA
reading to determine if the shooters' sperm matched the sperm found
in the deceased.

Joe wandered to the window and looked out between the white
blades of his venetian blind. He felt a turmoil of relief and anger. At
least my instincts were right, he congratulated himself. He was picturing the site out near the mountain, how he had thought at the
time that if this was a rape-murder, it was a weird one. But the
thought of her, an educated girl, going off with two blokes . . . It
made him feel odd. When he was courting Sandra—he'd been
twenty, she was eighteen—girls were terrified of getting pregnant.
Now they weren't frightened of anything, except perhaps AIDS.
What's happened in thirty years? he asked himself. Has the world
got worse—or have I turned into a fuddy-duddy?

He felt so dispirited he decided to ring his daughter for a chat. He
dialed Susan's work number first and was told she was signed off,
so he rang her at home.

Susan Miller, whose nickname was Weasel, lived half a kilometer

from Bondi Beach, where she swam each day, and competed annu-
ally in the Iron Maiden contest. Three times a week she worked out
in the police gymnasium, and on the other four days she exercised
with free weights at home. She had never married, and Joe did not
expect she ever would, although she would make some man a wonderful wife, was always the life of the party, a good cook, marvelous
with kids. They had called her Weasel when she was little because
she was so lithe, restless, and full of curiosity. And she looked a bit
like a weasel, these days even more so, with her thin face and green
eyes darting about, seeing everything. One of the best surveillance
officers of all time—could follow a puff of smoke for a hundred K—
youngest sergeant in the squad. Joe stared gloomily at the sliced
landscape on the other side of the venetian blind as her phone rang
and rang. He was about to leave a message on her answering machine when she cut into it, panting.

"Just got in from the surf," she said.

He rambled on while she caught her breath. Suddenly she interjected, "What's wrong?"

Joe hated being put on the defensive. "Nothing, sweetheart.
Thought I'd like a chat."

"C'mon!"

"You remember the murder out here a while ago?"

She looked up at the living room ceiling and saw it needed a coat
of paint.

"Did I mention to you that the crime scene looked odd to me?" he
said.

A thousand times. "I think so."

"Well, sweetheart, the explanation has come through on my fax
this morning. It wasn't a rape-murder. The deceased had sex that
night by consent. One to five hours later, the perpetrator murdered
her—and tried to make it look like rape."

He had even forgotten he had guessed this scenario himself and
discussed it with her weeks ago. "Looks like the Homicide blokes
were right about that bloody vet." His depression sounded worse
than ever.

"Hey!" she interrupted. "Why don't you come to Sydney next weekend and stay with me, and we'll go to the Easter Show on Saturday
afternoon? Go on the Ghost Train, see the champion cows . . . Remember when you took me to the show and I fell into the pigpen?
Ooh, *please*, Dad. I've got five days' leave and I can't afford to go
away."

I could go surfing, he thought. There are probably things around her flat I can fix for her—or I could help her look for a new car. He was whistling when his secretary arrived with a cup of coffee.

"Why are you smiling like that, Daphne?" he asked.

"It's so nice to see *you* smiling, Mr. Miller," she said. He realized, with a shock, that she was sweet on him. I'll buy her a present in Sydney, he thought.

Chapter **Fourteen**

At dusk on Saturday evening, Grace and Diana set off
through the garden side by side, a broad, slow shape moving beside
a tall, fast one. It was a warm evening, ringing with the calls of birds
that had gathered for the food Grace had put out for them earlier. A
small party of bluebonnet parrots, with dark-red patches on their
wings, was still on the grass, straight as soldiers on parade. As the
women approached, they uttered sharp alarm calls and took off with
rapid wingbeats, flying fast and erratically into the trees. They cried,
"jak, jakajak." Grace replied, "jak, jakajak" in the same pitch. "I wish
you'd try 'pseet-you, pseet-you,' " Diana said, giving a poor imitation of a wedgetail eagle's song. She could accurately mimic only
five different birds, but Grace could make the calls of at least thirty.

"That old eagle, she a clever one," Grace, said. "Not fooled by me.
Fifteen year ago, when we still living out at Williams' place, I watch
her hunting. She sees wallaby on the hillside. Flies behind the hill.
Wallaby's eating, not looking. The eagle, she came down slowly from
the sky, behind the hill, hiding, begins flying fast . . . whoosh, she
fly up back o' the hill, over the top, down onto the wallaby. Bash!
Wallaby, he dead." Grace raised her eyebrows at Diana, as if to ask,
So how will you cope?

"I've got this!" Diana waved the leather hood that, in a few minutes, she would try to put over the eagle's head. In her other hand was a pair of pliers. Grace was carrying some unskinned rabbit and the long, green-hide gloves they would need when they entered the eagle's mews. The plan was to hood the bird, which would make it stand still, then remove the steel pin from its wing.

Diana had always taken birds to a vet to unpin broken wings. The procedure was not difficult and not painful enough to justify a general anesthetic, but it did frighten the creature, and Diana was not looking forward to doing it herself, for the first time, on an eagle. In the past fortnight the bird had shown signs of friendliness, and it was several days since she had struck out with her foot. Yesterday, during her shower under the hose, she had whistled as she tossed her mane feathers, flinging a rainbow into the air. Until then, she had been too sulky to show pleasure in anything.

The eagle was perched on a block, staring straight ahead when they arrived. Her head swung, and she glared possessively at the rabbit in Grace's fingers. Diana had given the bird only half-rations of food for the past two days.

"Go on!" Diana said, urging Grace forward. "Just hold it out. But don't throw it."

Grace looked doubtfully at the distance between herself and the eagle. Although the bird could not fly, she could jump, the leash attached to her jesses being a good three meters long. She was already so intent on getting the food that jumping was just what she had in mind, Grace could see. Diana, meanwhile, was tiptoeing behind with the hood. The eagle crouched, preparing to grab the piece of rabbit, but Diana slipped the hood over her eyes. Grace stepped up and held the rabbit to the eagle's beak, while Diana grasped the bent wing in one hand, snapped the pliers onto the metal pin, and as fast and straight as she could, yanked it out. A bit of skin and some filoplumes came away with the pin. The eagle shuddered from head to foot, but blindfolded, she would not strike out. Diana dropped the pliers and flicked open her knife. The leather thongs binding the wings fell to the ground; she plucked off the eagle's hood and stepped back—but too late. The wings flew open and Diana staggered away, holding her eye. The eagle then leaped at Grace, who stumbled back, before turning quickly to confront Diana again.

The tip of a flight feather had caught her eye, making it water profusely. The eagle realized who had the advantage and prepared to push home to victory. With her open wings blocking Diana's exit, she advanced in short jumps, trapping her quarry against the wall at the back of the mews.

"Throw the rabbit!" Diana called to Grace.

Grace aimed for the ground just in front of the bird but managed to hit her on the neck. It was enough of a surprise to dint the eagle's concentration.

"G'arn! Get back!" Diana said, and stamped on the concrete.

The great wings lowered, the flat head turned sideways in a final threat, then the beak seized the food. Diana snatched up the pliers and skirted past.

Last week, she had removed two wooden lattice walls that had divided the big room behind the open mews area into three small rooms. It was now an enclosed space nine meters wide, five meters long, and four meters high. It had a perch close to the back wall, positioned halfway between the concrete floor and the wooden ceiling, and on a side wall another perch, three meters off the ground. Now that the eagle could use her wings again—she would not be able to fly properly for days, maybe weeks—she would want to roost at night on the lower perch. With the power of her tremendous legs and a bit of pumping of open wings, she would be able to jump up to it.

As the pythonlike neck bulged with rabbit, Diana undid the leash from the block perch and jerked it, making the eagle stagger after her into the big, dark room. There were three doors, each with a glass spy hole for viewing the birds. When the eagle was fully inside, Diana darted out through one of the other doors.

"That a clever old eagle," Grace grumbled.

"Have faith," Diana replied. Their eyes met with tenderness. All the years they had known each other, Grace had told Diana: Have faith. Faith, she said, was how her people lived. She chuckled and took a sideways look at Diana. Her colors seemed brighter and clearer today. She would need good colors if she was going to tame the eagle.

But as evening drew on, Diana's confidence weakened. She sat for a long while on her terrace, watching night creep out from the earth, full of doubt that she could tame the wedgetail on her own. She felt a passionate longing to give up before she had taken the first step. It seemed as if she really was, as Grace had cautioned her days ago, attempting something that could fail badly, for herself and the bird. It had been on the tip of her tongue a dozen times to admit to Grace that when she found the eagle she had also discovered Carolyn. There was something urgent in her desire to see the bird flying once more, as if releasing the wedgetail from her crippled state would free Diana too. To fly any hunting bird was difficult. The human had to flow into the animal and raise it to a more conscious state than it had known when it was wild. Training a small, brilliant creature such as a falcon was like opening a succession of gates into another world. But to train an eagle, an animal so much stronger than oneself . . . The actions that lay before Diana seemed beyond her power to visualize; they seemed a rhythm, a dance, a storm that was invisible yet vibrating in the air.

In the morning, she woke from a dream in which she and Grace were seeding wheat. They walked side by side, throwing the seeds from their aprons. As they fell, the seeds turned into little birds and darted away. It seemed auspicious. She was hungry, which was good too, because she knew that once breakfast was over she might not be able to leave the enclosed room for the rest of the day. She was washing up the frying pan when Grace arrived to open the gallery at 9:00 A.M.

"Wish me luck," she said.

She had ready on the kitchen table a dead rabbit and the contraption Raoul had made. It was a wide belt from which two aluminum rods jutted like flying buttresses, supporting a cantilever for her left arm. "Don't s'pose I'll be needing this yet," she added. Her immediate task was to force the eagle to take food from her hand. It was called "manning." Manning was where most falconers failed.

In the shed, she gloved up and tied the food bag on her hip, then peered through a peephole into the dark room. The eagle was asleep. When Diana entered and turned on the lights, everything stank of eagle. On her perch on the back wall, the bird sprang awake, raised her shoulders, and leaned forward. Diana stretched up her gloved fist, on which she held a strip of rabbit. "Come on, Aquila," she said. The bird crouched above her, motionless. She could stand on a high branch and survey the landscape for an hour before swooping on prey. Inside the room, they both stood like statues for twenty minutes. Diana was watching for a sign of the coming onslaught, but there was none. The eagle abruptly launched herself at the food. It took Diana all her will not to duck as the enormous feet slid through the air toward her face. But she stood still and suddenly moved her hand so the feet missed. The bird landed, folded her wings slightly, and jumped away until she had room to half-beat, half-leap to her perch again. Diana realized she had forgotten to whistle. She again held out the food, and this time she whistled. The eagle turned in profile and gave a distant stare. Diana waited. From time to time the bird twirled her face around with an expression of fury. Diana had the feeling that in these moments she was calculating when to jump.

Without warning, she launched herself again, giving Diana such a surprise she almost ran, but at the last moment she stood her ground and pulled the food away. They would do this all day.

There was no rule about when to reward a wild bird with food during its breaking in. The short rations of the past three days, and the sudden increase in mobility, were making the eagle hungry and anxious about eating. Her intention was to grab the food while avoiding touching or being touched by the human. She had to be forced to overcome her instinctive fear and go to her falconer. This could take hours or even days. If Diana miscalculated, she would overheat the bird, sending her into convulsions from which she would die. A hundred lesser mistakes were possible, from broken feathers to injured feet, and any of them could cripple the eagle for good.

Diana's task was to set her own body aside. She had to feel only the bird's hunger, its temperature and heart rate. She crooned softly, "Come on, Aquila, don't be frightened."

On the eagle's fourth attempt to snatch the food, Diana rewarded her when she had landed by tossing a sliver of meat, just enough to stimulate the gastric juices and make her eager for more. When she regained her perch, the torment began again. In the back of Diana's head, a dull voice complained that her arm was aching.

At eleven o'clock, Grace put a note on the front door saying BACK IN FIVE MINUTES and hastened through the dappled shade of the eucalypts down to the aviary. She was trying not to spill a mug of tea. Outside the mews room, she gave the call she and Diana used as a private greeting. Back came the three notes that meant: Wait. She waited, taking a peek inside. Diana had her back to the door and was staring at the eagle, which stared back at her from the wall. Grace left the mug of tea on the concrete.

At two o'clock, Diana lurched into the kitchen. She had bird muck on the navy T-shirt she was wearing, and her face was pale from strain. She licked dry lips, wanting to say something as she leaned against the sink, letting hot water run over her hands.

After she had eaten a plate of sandwiches, she mumbled, "It's going okay."

At six, Grace closed the front door and put her cashbox in the small safe in the cupboard under the stairs. It was time for the ducks to come back from the river.

Overhead, birds streamed into the trees in the garden. A flock of forty or fifty white cockatoos had landed and was feasting on the seed she had put out. They lurched over the grass, broad-shouldered, yellow crests erect, yelling at each other like drunks in party hats. Above them, the branches were full of less belligerent birds, including the party of bluebonnets, too frightened of the cockatoos to come down. "Git off, you!" Grace called as she approached. The cockatoos rose with grating cries, and from all sides small, bright, quick bodies swooped to the ground.

She paused outside the room again and whistled. There was no reply. At first when she peered through the glass, the room was so dark she could not make out what was happening inside. But as her eyes adjusted, she saw Diana standing toward the back of the room, blood oozing down the side of her face. She was as pale as cheese. Her right hand supported her left elbow, and on her bent arm stood the huge, dark eagle.

As Grace watched, Diana let go of her elbow and took from the bag on her hip a long, slim feather. She stroked the eagle's legs and feet with it. The bird fluffed herself up, shook her tail, then resettled her plumage like a hen settling on her nest. Very slowly, Diana walked with her toward the lower perch. The eagle peered forward but showed no inclination to move until Diana jerked her arm lightly. Then the bird hopped off and roused her feathers once more.

Diana backed away, placing one foot quietly behind the other until she reached the door. Grace stood aside. Neither spoke. Diana had a gash on her head and another on her shoulder, which had dribbled blood onto her jeans. She wandered out to the open section of the aviary, where she could see the sky. Her left arm was so painful, she now realized, she wondered if she had damaged a nerve. From where she stood, the big moon was visible, and she felt as if its clear light was a mirror of the light that still filled her, radiance from the moment when, just before dusk, she had stood still and felt through leather and steel a grip twice as strong as that of human hands tighten around her arm. The huge dark wings had rustled above her head, then feather slotted into feather, like giant fans closing, and slowly the folded sails lowered against the eagle's sides. The bird squeezed and rocked slightly to test this strange, human perch. Then she stood still. Diana smiled.

In the distance, the train from Sydney rumbled across the bridge.

"Will you get the ducks, Gracie? I don't think I can move," she said.

Next morning, when Lek had not appeared in U-1 by eight o'clock, Parker sent Phil to her cabin to see where she was. Phil returned with the news that Lek was still in her pajamas, either sick or sulking, he was not sure which, and would not speak to him, he said, but shook her head at all his questions as if she did not understand English today.

Parker stalked upstairs from the lab, through the garden, and rapped on her door. She was still wearing pajamas. "Get dressed and come to work," he said. "The animals need feeding and cleaning." With a defiant glance, she closed the door in his face. He walked slowly back through the cool, still garden, thinking about what he would do to her. After a while he went upstairs and asked Sonja to lend a hand with the animals before she went to work.

In Kalunga, the Research minibus arrived at Fig Tree Gully Road at 8:00 A.M. to take Diana, as an observer, to her first Ethics Committee meeting, and so she did not notice that her van was low on petrol again. By the time she returned home that afternoon, Grace had run some errands in it and had filled the fuel tank.

Only the shell of the old Pembridge homestead remained. Inside, in what had been the warm center of the house, everything she loved had vanished. In place of deep, tatty old chairs, the stone fireplace, milk-glass lamps, and steer hides on the floor, there was nondescript carpet and skinny-legged furniture. On walls where there had been paintings by friends and things found in paddocks—part of a tree that looked like a human torso and thighs, the white backbone of a kangaroo, a cream-colored snakeskin, almost translucent—there were prints from the Heidelberg school. On a long table in what had been the living room, meeting papers and glasses of water were set out in front of eight chairs, seven clustered at one end, one of them at the head, three on each side, while the eighth chair was banished to the far end of the table, two meters away. That was where the observer was to sit, a secretary explained.

The sound of voices on the veranda was followed by the entrance of members of the committee, led by a very tall man Diana had seen in Kalunga. He advanced toward her, smiling, his hand outstretched.

"John Parker," he said. He was English, with a deep, well-modulated voice and the shabby dress of an academic. The color of his eyes was accentuated by a royal-blue cashmere sweater. His hair was a bit too long and needed a wash. "I'm chair of this committee. Delighted to have you here, Miss Pembridge. We're looking forward to your contribution. It's a pity that today you're still an observer." He sighed. "I'm afraid the wheels of bureaucracy grind slowly." His voice dropped a key. "How are your birds?" he added. "The falcon?"

"They're okay," she answered cautiously.

The blue eyes smiled, inviting her to take him into her confidence about birds.

"You saw the falcon?" she added.

"*Did I!*" He chuckled and looked at her intently again. Diana blushed. He's lecherous, she realized. His look seemed to indicate that *she* found *him* attractive. "Well," he said, "we'd better get to work. Let me introduce you . . ."

He was an efficient chairman of a stultified committee. Seated opposite him, Diana tried not to meet his glances or, when she did, to gaze back coolly. He was doing, she knew, what every cunning chairman does with a new member: attempting to win her to his faction. She had decided to resist alliances until the politics that were at work became clear. Once the meeting began, she was quickly lost in a maze of jargon, acronyms, and references to earlier events. It'll take me weeks, she realized, before I know what's going on. Meanwhile, she looked for clues in details of the appearance and behavior of the three women and four men who studied the agenda papers, and grunted from time to time. Parker did almost all the talking, referring to the printed reports they should have read (but evidently had not). Each laboratory team had reported on its use of animals in the preceding two months, giving details of the processes the animals had been put through, the use of anesthetics in the case of surgical procedures, whether animals had been sacrificed, and so forth. Graphs accompanied each report, and each concluded with a request for permission from the committee to carry out further experiments. Most lab teams, Diana noticed, were granted permission without discussion, while others, proposing almost identical work (from the animal point of view), had their submissions queried peevishly, analyzed for small discrepancies, and, in one case, rejected outright. Parker projected the image of a neutral chairman, but as Diana watched the glances that jumped back and forth across the table, she saw that he was orchestrating the votes. When the lab team working on Legionnaires' disease had its proposal knocked back, Parker, she noted, wore a troubled expression, although he had said nothing to support the submission when he had the chance. Instead, he allowed a battle-ax from the New South Wales Health Department to thunder against the proposed work on the grounds that it would duplicate experiments already done at Westmead Hospital. They broke for morning tea.

"Well," Parker said, "do you find it interesting?"

"Hmm," she said.

He bent close to her ear. "Of course, you and I are the only people in this room who're seriously concerned with animals."

Diana murmured, "Yes." She tried to keep her expression composed, to stop her heart from pounding so loudly, for just in front of her nose, on his blue sweater, there was a bunch of dark hairs about ten centimeters long.

He gave her another intimate look. She could smell his unwashed scalp. I'll gag, she thought, but she moved a fraction closer to him and her hand edged toward his sweater. Touching him seemed loathsome. Suddenly he seized her fingers and squeezed them. "See you at lunchtime," he said quietly. She flinched.

The meeting dragged on until twelve-thirty, when a buxom young woman approached the table diffidently and Parker said, "Oh, here's lunch!" making everyone laugh at her. Diana had barely heard a word in almost two hours. She had been trying not to stare at Parker's sweater, trying not to let him realize what she was thinking—that the hair on his sweater looked like the hair on Carolyn's T-shirt.

People shuffled their papers together to make room for the platters of sandwiches, fruit, cheese, and petits fours that began to arrive. There was too much food, Diana thought, but from the veranda other voices could be heard, and she realized that the committee would be joined for lunch by Research staff. They came traipsing in, men in beards, women with hefty shoulder pads, Joe Miller, and the man who had almost broken into a run to escape from Carolyn in High Street one day. For a moment Diana remembered Carolyn's head turning as she jeered across her shoulder at him. Could several of them have been in on the killing? Diana wondered. Her glance darted from one to another, but the rest of her face was as still as a mask. She was introduced to the Gang of Six. She knew most by sight already but had previously spoken only to Joe and the carroty-haired busybody who lived in the house on the ridge and was friendly with Jason.

"Sonja Olfson," she said. "I'm John's wife. Let's go outside."

She tried to remember what gossip she had heard about Sonja Olfson. The only thing that came to mind was Grace's pulling a face at Sonja in the news agent's shop. Diana followed her out onto the veranda, wondering how such a small, hygienic-looking woman could be married to such an unwholesome man. Sonja pointed to two folding canvas chairs beside a table where they could rest their plates.

"I prefer being outdoors," she said, gesturing in a proprietary way toward the well-kept lawn and flower beds. One rosebush still had a blowsy yellow flower on it. Diana's mother, Joan, had grown it from a cutting, but there was no point in mentioning that to the director of personnel, she realized.

As soon as they were seated, Sonja launched into a complaint about how the Research was run on a traditional energy-inefficient model, while she was using solar power and making compost—so why couldn't everyone else? Environmental witch sniffer, Diana thought wearily. She knew the ritual observances of people like Sonja: every time they used a paper bag instead of a plastic bag they congratulated themselves. It was egotism wearing a cloak of green. Sonja had arranged their chairs around the table in such a way that nobody else could sit with them without being intrusive, and was rushing on under a full head of steam, too busy to eat now that she had arrived at the subject of the coming planetary cataclysm owing to the selfishness of human beings. At public meetings on land care, one had to put up with people like Sonja. Diana continued to nod slowly, hoping her face did not betray her boredom. She bit into another of the roast beef sandwiches heaped on her plate. In the doorway, Parker appeared. Diana, mouth full of food, gave him a welcoming glance.

"You're not vegetarian?" Sonja asked, leaning forward, her voice rising in disbelief.

Diana swallowed, shaking her head, then suddenly stared at Sonja's cream linen jacket. Partly hidden by the lapel was a long, dark hair, identical to the one on Parker's sweater. She reached forward and plucked it off with such a quick movement that Sonja did not realize what had happened—but Parker, at their elbow now, hesitated and glanced down at his own clothes. Noticing the hairs on his sweater, he quickly brushed them away.

"Hair falling out," he murmured. "It'll be teeth next." He gave a mournful smile.

Sonja tittered.

Diana wanted to leap to her feet and shout, "You're keeping chimpanzees! You're experimenting illegally on them!" But all she did was give a silly grin and slip her fingers, holding the hair, into her trouser pocket. Sonja had missed it all.

"Darling, I was longing for you to join us," she said.

Parker's presence had caused his wife to become suddenly more vivacious, with a new edge of anxiety in her manner, an attempt to capture his attention entirely, not allow him to speak or look at Diana, as if she imagined Diana was a dangerous flirt.

He gave a mocking bow. "Miss Pembridge, may I invite you to join me for coffee?" he asked. "We'll be starting again in five minutes, and I want you to have a chance to talk to a couple of the committee members. . . ." He raised his eyebrows at his wife in some shared understanding. Diana followed him indoors.

She still felt unsettled when she got home late that afternoon.

Upstairs in her study, the boys were lying on the floor, surrounded by books. Slowly and carefully, Diana pulled the pocket out of her trousers and plucked off the hair.

"What's that?" Tom asked.

"Chimp hair," she said.

The kids gaped.

"Those bastards are using chimpanzees. Illegally. Unquarantined. Killing them however they like."

"*Killing them?*" Tom asked.

Diana nodded. "Up to thirty, so far." She fell silent, thinking, Plus Carolyn. She pictured the mauve corpse again, and its mouthful of flies, and turned away to hide her face from the children. They made you dumb, like an animal, she thought.

Tom's crybaby face was ready to burst. "*Why do they kill them?*" he whined.

F orty kilometers away, on Sonja's balcony, Parker sat brooding over the day's events. Sonja, seated on the other side of the weathered outdoor table, glanced at him, restraining herself from asking what was going through his mind. He had already shouted at her once that afternoon.

"Christ almighty, woman! On a light-colored jacket you *should* have seen it!" he'd muttered when they drove home together in the Land Cruiser. "It isn't as if you never look at yourself in the mirror. You spend half the day primping." Sonja steered on in silence, concentrating on the road ahead. "D'you need glasses?" Parker asked.

She pressed her lips together and kept her foot down.

The silence on the veranda continued. At last he turned to her with a smile. "I forgive you," he said.

Sonja thought, *He* forgives *me!* For shouting at me? For abusing me? When it was he who asked me to help him with the chimps this morning, because we can't trust Lek.

Outrage made her face pasty, but she showed no other sign of anger. "Thank you, darling," she replied.

Parker visibly relaxed. "Bloody girl," he mumbled, and shook his head. According to the boys, Lek had arrived at work as soon as he and Sonja had driven off in the Land Cruiser. "I'm going to ring Otto and tell him Lek must be replaced immediately," he announced.

"What about Joe? Shouldn't we drive up to admin and ring from the pay phone?"

"I'll speak in riddles," Parker said. An amusing thought crossed his mind.

Sonja wanted to ask what riddles, but intuition told her it was something to do with the flesh trade.

In Mae Wong National Park, Michael Romanus shifted his backbone against the tree trunk and resettled his legs across a branch, wide as a child's bed, that he had chosen as his hideaway for the night. Sunset was still an hour away, and from where he was sitting he looked out across an ocean of treetops, all the way to Burma. Beneath him, five meters down, there was a salt lick, which was visited sometimes, the park rangers had told him, by a tiger. He had dragged his equipment up to the branch and already had one camera set up on a tripod. Another, for hand-held shots, had a blimp on it so that shutter sound would be inaudible, even to a tiger's ears.

It was the quiet time of the afternoon, before the evening ruckus when the day shift, as he thought of it, left and the jungle's night shift appeared; he had half an hour, at least, before any night creatures would come to lick the salt. He took his telephone from the pocket of his shirt and pressed the button for Raoul. After a few rings the familiar "*Sí?*" sounded in his ear.

"How's it going, pal?" Romanus asked.

"*Mierda!*" muttered Raoul. "*Idiotas!*" He could not get the fax machine in his room to work and had been obliged to complain to the hotel manager. He was still waiting for another machine to be installed.

"So you haven't sent the stuff yet?" Romanus asked. "The stuff" included his photostats tracing the illegal sale of the baby orangutan, plus documents Raoul had collected from a dealer in Chiang Mai about trade in other protected apes. Up there, protected animals were often taken as payment for heroin.

Yes, he had faxed it all last night, Sabea said, but because he had heard nothing in reply, he was not satisfied the fax had gone through properly, and he wanted to send the material again, tonight. He added something in Spanish, then translated: "The noose around Otto's neck grows tighter."

Romanus was still grinning sardonically after he put the phone away, picturing Grossmann at the moment when he discovered his crimes were known. The thing he hated most about Otto was that he had the power, through his money, to do good.

Otto Grossmann was tête-à-tête at home in Bangkok at two o'clock on Monday afternoon when his butler entered the drawing room to say that Dr. Parker from Australia was on the phone. Grossmann left the room, taking with him the crumpled pages, sent by fax, that he and his visitor had been discussing.

"Put the call through to my study," he told the butler, who acknowledged the order with a faint bow, murmuring the honorific "Khun Otto."

The study was air conditioned, like most of the house, which was one of the remaining teak mansions of Yannawa. Its garden was screened from the noise of the city by a high, whitewashed wall, and to enter it one had to cross a narrow, ornate bridge that spanned a pond with carp glinting in the depths and a cunning, savage turtle. Besides the bridge, the pond was spanned by steppingstones, but when people were leaving Grossmann's parties they were sometimes too drunk to step on them. Guests who fell in the water invariably suffered a bite from the turtle. When this happened, Grossmann would announce he was going to catch the reptile and have it killed, but when everybody had left he would go to his study and laugh until tears ran along the creases near his eyes and into his small, flat ears.

There was an orchid in a pot on his desk, the archetype of the white flower that was Siam Enterprises' logo. Grossmann found its shape mysteriously pleasing. As he lifted the telephone receiver he looked at it intently, hoping for a relaxation of the tension that had built up in him during his interview in the drawing room. He laid the faxed pages on the desk so he could read them again while he talked.

"Hello. Grossmann," he said, his eye running down the report, which was written in Spanish, a language he spoke and read with ease. It was titled "Siam Enterprises: Illegal Exports" and had been sent to CITES in Geneva, with a copy to the Primate Rescue Organization in California. It said that Siam was exporting chimpanzees and other apes to private collectors in Europe, Japan, Australia, and America, in defiance of CITES regulations governing endangered species, to which Thailand was a signatory. It gave details, including some cargo receipts, of ninety-eight apes it claimed had been sent from Thailand illegally. This information was followed by the heading "Background" and several paragraphs of confidential data about the company, including that its board was composed of a number of Thailand's "unusually rich" men. It gave their names and went on to say that two of them were known to be engaged in illegal logging in Burma and Cambodia and were suspected of supplying arms to the Khmer Rouge.

"Shit!" Grossmann muttered. "Spanish shit!" He was more angry than he had been for years. Michael must have known about this, he thought. Why didn't he warn me? A wave of angst rolled through him. He tried to see the Spaniard pointing a gun at Michael, threatening him to keep his mouth shut. The effort to imagine this made Grossmann pant, and the pant turned into an angry laugh. You've played me for a fool, he thought.

Parker's voice continued whining from the telephone. He had used such heavily veiled language—"our friend from the northern guesthouse," meaning Lek—that Grossmann had not understood at first what he was complaining about.

"John," he said, "it's full moon here. All the Buddhists are going to the temple. She's probably upset because she's missing the festival."

Parker continued to complain.

"So what if she saw a ghost?" Grossmann shot back. "A billion Chinese see ghosts. In England, people used to see ghosts—that's what we learned at school anyway: there are ghosts in England, but they can't cross the English Channel." He laughed.

Parker realized he should not have mentioned the ghost episode as evidence that Lek was going mad. He should simply have said she was behaving irresponsibly and he wanted her replaced.

"What I'm trying to say, Otto—"

Before he had finished the sentence, Grossmann made one of the fast imaginative connections between disparate facts that had made him a millionaire. His plan would make Parker happy too.

"John," he interrupted. "Am I right in thinking you don't like this friend of mine and you don't want to entertain her? Listen: I'll invite her to return to Thailand *as soon as possible,* so she doesn't annoy you. But if you wouldn't mind, I have another friend who wants to visit Australia." He fingered his ear, massaging its stiff, curled rim. "We'll talk about the details later."

When the call was finished he pressed the buzzer on his desk. A few moments later, the butler returned.

"Tell Somchai I want to see him when my guest leaves." Grossmann glanced at the title page of the report again. It had been sent from Chiang Mai. How ironic, he thought, that so much that is complex and secret has been uncovered, while simple facts are overlooked: that I own the hotel from which this was sent, for example. Grossmann tapped the phones and faxes of guests in that hotel and was often able to pass on useful information to his friend the minister for internal security. Everyone knew Chiang Mai was a heroin town, and a lot of fascinating dialogue went through the wires. I've always been lucky, he congratulated himself.

He bared his strong, square teeth in triumph when he returned to the drawing room, where the hotel security manager from Chiang Mai awaited him.

In the servants' quarters behind the house, Somchai, the after-hours chauffeur, was lying on his mattress, wearing only Y-front underpants. He had pictures from magazines stuck on his whitewashed walls, including some *Penthouse* pets, Arnold Schwarzenegger and Mike Mentzer. For the past six months, Somchai had been following Mike's magazine advice about using NutraLife products to help build his biceps and brachials.

When the butler poked his head in the door, Somchai made fists and crunched his pectorals, for the fun of seeing the look on the butler's face. "Whaddaya want, Frogshit?" he said.

"Master wants to see you in his study."

"Tell 'im to wait."

As soon as the butler left, Somchai leaped up and began dressing in his white uniform, first strapping his knife to his leg. His calves were so big now the knife was becoming difficult to conceal. He had asked Khun Otto to allow him to wear a pistol, like other night chauffeurs, but the master answered, "My life isn't threatened. I don't need a bodyguard." He had patted Somchai on the shoulder, adding, "Anyway, I don't know if you can shoot." I can shoot, Somchai thought, flushing with the memory of insult.

Diana had work to do quickly on Monday afternoon when she returned from the Research, then she had to turn her mind to the eagle. The bird had been outdoors all day on the block perch, with no food and nothing to do except watch the sky.

As she approached the ti-tree fence, Diana felt her heart rate rise. Will the eagle still be tame? she wondered. She had tamed the bird yesterday, but today the bird could be wild again.

Outside the aviary, she paused and gave her imitation of a wedge-tail's call. There was no reply, except from the ducks, who quacked loudly.

Duck feathers were in a wet mound near the base of the perch, and a few still clung to the eagle's foot. The eagle herself was back on the block, gazing at something on another planet. Diana poked at what was left of a drake: a pair of yellow feet and the wings. None of the raptors had killed the ducks before.

"Well, Aquila," she said, "I brought you some rabbit, but obviously that won't be necessary."

The eagle continued to ignore her, but when Diana turned on the hose she twisted her head to watch and in anticipation began to loosen her plumage. Daily hosing had strengthened her feathers and encouraged her to preen, and she was now as glossy as satin, embellished with a tawny band, like a shawl, on her nape and across her wings. She preferred, Diana had discovered, to be bathed in a cone of fine mist. As the water began falling on her feathers, the bird's expression became less severe. It was remarkable how much emotion she could convey—all in the eyes. Diana had read that the golden eagles in Afghanistan, trained to hunt wolves, became as tame as cats, willing to have their legs stroked not just with a feather but by hand. Some people said that the great birds loved their trainers. Only a fool would believe that, she thought. Love, for an animal, was simply food. Only for humans was it confusing and painful.

At the end of the shower, she approached the bird, her braced arm still sore from the strain of yesterday. Because of the height of the perch, Diana had to bend over, her face level with the huge curved beak. For a moment nothing happened. Then Diana's shoulder jolted as the eagle stepped onto her arm.

That evening, the fax machine in her study began to roll. A transmission from the Fish and Wildlife Lab in Oregon was coming through, a further report on the hair from Carolyn's T-shirt she had sent three weeks earlier. It could now be confirmed, the fax said, that the hair came from a female chimpanzee kept in close confinement. Diana sent back a message saying she had dispatched by special delivery that afternoon one more hair. It, too, was from a chimp, she was sure. Would it be possible to confirm if this hair (which would arrive in three days) was from the same animal? Ten minutes later, the reply came: "We think so."

J oe Miller telephoned his daughter again on Monday evening to ask if she had heard anything at her end about the Williams case.

"I found out something," Weasel said diffidently. "You know my friend Donnelle, from Intelligence?" She paused.

"What about it?" His voice was offhand.

"Nelly's been put onto Nichols's computer."

"That so?"

"You know she can hack any computer."

"Really?"

"I could find out what was in his closed files." Weasel waited a beat. "If you'd like to know."

"Don't go to any bother."

His blindness used to exasperate her. "I could give her a ring. It'd be no trouble."

"If it's just a phone call . . ."

"Yeah—that's all it would be."

"Well, then, it'd be interesting to know what he was up to. I'm going to take you up on staying over Easter, by the way."

As soon as she was off the phone, she began tidying the flat. She gathered up the cassette tapes he would not like and hid them in a drawer in her bedroom, and took some photographs off the refrigerator door, including one of Donnelle in studs and leather and a postcard of Marlene Dietrich that opened with the greeting "Darling Doughnut."

• • •

After speaking to Grossmann on Monday night, Parker took Sonja with him to talk to Lek.

The cabin where the animal keepers stayed was made of weatherboard, like the house, and had its own solar energy panel on the roof. It was one large room with sitting space and a tiny kitchen just inside the front door. At the far end there was a bed and a capsule bathroom. The bed was a double in case, at some time in the future, the cabin could be used for its original purpose as a guest room. It had a window but no back door and no fan, and in summer it was an oven. But as Parker pointed out, the keepers were used to heat.

"What a pong," Sonja said as they approached. When the door opened, a cloud of incense poured out.

Lek's eyes were drowsy from meditation.

"We wanted to see how you are this evening," Parker said. He had to cough. "God almighty! You need a gas mask?"

"I no understand."

"Are you all right?"

"Sank you, all right."

"You're going back to Thailand soon. I've spoken to Khun Otto. You're going home."

"*Home.*" Her face broke into a smile they had never seen before. "I going home!" She reached out and grabbed Parker's hand as if to kiss it. "Sank you. I bery happy. I pray Lord Buddha. Sank you." She pressed her palms together and, turning first to Parker, then to Sonja, bowed.

"Seems to be okay," Parker said as they returned to Sonja's house. His wife made a grating noise in her throat. "You don't agree?" he added.

"Oh, absolutely! Lek's had a trip abroad, she's had a bludger's job for three months, done nothing but play with animals all day, and now she's bored and would like to go home, and that's being arranged for her too. She's a smart little operator, and we're a couple of bunnies."

He knew that this was a moment when he should turn to his wife and soothe her resentment, but he was still angry about the hair. Sometimes he felt as if two enormous shadowy figures were fighting within him—one of them imaginative, rebellious, and proud, the other logical, angry, and destructive. Endlessly they struggled for supremacy, appearing in his mind like two giant boxers punching and grappling each other inside the ropes of his soul. He had to be the referee.

"Why do you sigh?" she asked sharply.

"Just exhaling, dear."

They had agreed in the morning that he would stay at her place that night. During dinner, when their fight seemed to be over, Sonja began looking forward to having sex. But as bedtime approached, Parker's yawns made it seem he had no interest in anything except sleep. Sonja, still hopeful, removed her cream silk pajamas and her bracelet before getting into bed. "Nighty-night," he said as he rolled his back to her. She wondered if she should take half a Valium to help herself off to sleep. After a few moments, she got up, put on her pajamas again, and went into the bathroom. John did not stir when she returned to lie beside him.

She awoke suddenly, knowing instantly that he was gone.

She ran to the kitchen, switched on the lights, and turned the U-1 monitor in every direction, hoping that somewhere down there she would see John. Every room in the laboratory was in darkness.

The boards of the veranda felt cool under her feet. Above and around her, the full moon cast a white, vaporous glow, giving an enchanted look to the trees and bushes of the garden. Many birds were awake, because of the moonlight, and the sound of their calls came to her across the water—the honking of swans, the quacking of ducks, and cries she did not recognize. The whole night was pulsing with vitality and beautiful light.

She made her way through the garden to Lek's cabin, where a candle, placed on the table inside the front door, spread a yellow glow.

He was there, as she knew he would be. After what I let him do to me last night! she thought in fury. But she had been waiting for this to happen, she realized. Now that it was taking place in front of her eyes, she felt a peculiar satisfaction. She was also intensely curious to know what he did with another woman, but the window through which she was looking was placed so that all she could see were his feet.

Sonja returned to bed and closed her eyes. When John crept in about an hour later, she made a few quiet snoring sounds, breathed deeply, then turned over to escape the stink of sex and incense.

Just before dawn, she became conscious of the noise of running water. John needed hours less sleep than she did, which was another reason she had agreed to his proposal that when they married, he should keep his condominium. How naive I was, she thought.

He came into the bedroom and kissed her forehead with a mouth smelling of toothpaste.

"Good morning, my darling," he whispered.

His wet hair dripped on her neck. "Morning," she murmured.

When he went out to the kitchen, she lurched across the bed and plunged her nose into his pillow. The smell of incense from his hair almost made her gag. I didn't dream it, she congratulated herself.

Parker had eaten breakfast, watched the television news, and left for work by the time Sonja felt strong enough to get out of bed. There was a stool in front of her dressing table, which she had decorated with decoupage, using a pattern of cherubs and wreaths. With her bottom pressed onto a cherub, she jacked one foot on the rung of the stool so her thigh was steady while she injected herself. She felt better instantly, and hungry. During those hours lying awake beside John while he snored and farted, happy as a pig, she had done some serious thinking. "My husband," she muttered, twisting her diabetic's bracelet round and round her bony wrist. "He's *my* husband." She glanced at herself in the dressing room mirror. "Hello, Fox," she snarled.

Diana was on the road through the Research on Tuesday morning when she saw John Parker driving a Land Cruiser. In the habit of the bush, she slowed down to talk to him as their vehicles drew abreast.

"Hello. Going falconing again?" He smirked.

"No. I'm going to fly an eagle today."

"Ooh—can I see?"

She got down and opened the back of her van. For a minute they stood side by side in silence, admiring the huge, hooded bird. With covered eyes she had an eerie appearance, seeming to be not quite eagle, but something more.

Parker stepped back so Diana could slide the door shut. "You're quite a gal," he said, his eyes tugging at her.

"Would you like to watch us training?" she asked.

"Love to. But my rabbits, I'm afraid . . ."

"Which *is* your lab? Yesterday I couldn't tell from the papers where you normally work."

"I'm all over the place. There's a small setup under Sonja's house. I work there sometimes. . . . Then, up at the complex. Right now, for example, I'm on my way to the breeding house."

"I'll look out for you tomorrow."

"Tomorrow?"

"I'm being taken on a tour of the Research tomorrow."

"Oh," he said, and looked bored.

Flocks of parrots and choughs were feeding on the ground at the base of Mount Kalunga, but again there was no sign from Morrie waiting for her beside the fence post. Diana went to the edge of the pine forest and called out twice. After a moment she heard a shot from high up on the mountain. She decided that if after another week there was still no request for food, she would climb up to his cave.

Her arm was so sore she had to strap on the cantilever before she could carry the eagle from the van to the fence post, which would be the bird's perch for training today. She checked that the creance attached to the leash was long enough for the eagle to glide three meters safely. Then she removed the hood.

The bird was momentarily stunned by light and the new environment. Blindfolded in a strange place, she suddenly found herself on her own territory once more. She crouched, opened her wings, and jumped. But her muscles were still so weak, she could only flap from the post to the grass below. Diana had deliberately fattened her during convalescence, and she now weighed seven kilos. An eagle at that weight, even with the huge wings that this one had, could never fly fast enough to hunt. She would need to slim down to six kilos before she could be freed, but dieting had to be undertaken carefully, or the flight feathers would develop starvation breaks.

Having eaten the duck yesterday, the eagle was not really hungry enough to be anxious for food again, but now she was used to being fed twice a day, and Diana had given her nothing before leaving the aviary that morning. She let the bird ride on her arm from the ground back onto the post and took up a position three meters away. There she held out a morsel of rabbit. The eagle became instantly alert, stretched her neck, and launched into a glide. As she got within twenty centimeters of Diana's glove, Diana jumped away. The bird landed, offended she had missed. Diana shooed her back toward the post and lifted her up again. Then she repeated the temptation and the trick.

For the next twenty minutes, with rests and occasional food rewards, Diana made the eagle fly toward her hand. In three weeks, she hoped, Aquila would be able to make these short flights for an hour at a stretch, twice a day. Then they would move on to the next stage: Diana would stand on a stepladder, holding out food, while the eagle would stand on the ground. She would have to pump up to Diana's hand, first one, then two, then three meters of vertical flight. This would put immense pressure on her wings, and at first the bird would be able to do the exercise for only one minute, twice a day. But Diana hoped that after three weeks of pumping, plus an hour's gliding and flapping morning and evening in pursuit of a lure, the eagle would be strong enough and tame enough to fly free in pursuit of live game. Diana planned to net some rabbits, keep one in her hip bag, put the eagle on a very long creance, then toss the rabbit onto the ground. It would bolt, and the eagle would try to catch it. After one or two tries—the eagle would almost certainly miss—Diana would let her off her creance. She would be flying free but would be so intent on catching the next rabbit, so convinced rabbits came from Diana's hip, she would not fly away. That was the theory anyway.

If all went well and if they trained six days a week, by the beginning of winter the eagle would be ready to be freed. The thought of her soaring above the mountain again made tears come to Diana's eyes. It would be like that morning on the lake, when the great bird had watched them all from the sky.

She reached into the bag for more food. "One last time," she called.

The eagle adopted a pose of dignified hostility and turned her head to observe the lake. Diana waggled the grub of meat, but the bird remained resolutely uninterested and, after a period of scrutinizing the water, turned her attention to the clouds. I hope another eagle hasn't moved into this territory, Diana thought. She wanted her bird to be able to return to a known hunting ground. If another wedgetail had seized the territory while it was unguarded, her eagle would have to fight to regain her land—and despite her size and strength, there was no guarantee she would defeat a younger, smaller rival.

Diana looked up, trying to see what the eagle could see, her eyelids wincing from the light. *Something* . . . There was a mighty whack on her cantilevered arm, which almost sent her sprawling. Next moment, she felt the strange, convulsive tightening of gigantic hands and the shimmering noise of feathers closing. The wings came down and were folded smooth. The huge, scaled feet under the dark feather trousers were fastened around her arm, and the beak was fifteen centimeters from her left eye. The serpent neck bent, and the food disappeared. Serves me right, Diana thought. Falconers had been killed by eagles.

An hour later that morning, driving on a straight stretch of road on the approach to Kalunga, she saw Billy and Tom riding toward her on their bikes. They slowed down, stopped, and looked as if they wanted to vanish, but on either side there were fenced paddocks and no trees.

"Where are you going?" she called.

They hung their heads. "Nowhere," Billy replied.

Although they were on the road that went to the Research, it was such a long ride out there that it did not occur to Diana that the Research could be their destination. "You're wagging school!"

"Only a bit," Tom said. "It's almost the holidays."

She got down from the van. "C'mon. We'll put the bicycles on the roof, and you can ride home with me." They had baskets on the front of their bikes for schoolbooks. "Where did you get all these bananas?" she asked.

They drove in silence for a while, until she said, "Well? What are you up to?"

Billy glanced at Tom, whose face had turned to a piece of wood. "Nothin'. Don't tell Grandma."

"Why not?"

"She's always cross with us."

"*Please,*" Tom wheedled. "We'll get in trouble."

"You're to promise not to wag again."

"We promise."

When they got out of the van, Billy said to Tom, "We didn't tell a lie." On Thursday, school would let out and people would be arriving for the Easter bird-watching tour: Grandma and Diana would be too busy to notice they were not there. "I'm going to call mine King Kong," he added.

On Tuesday morning, Michael Romanus returned to Bangkok after almost three weeks of taking photographs in Mae Wong National Park, northwest of the capital. The nature reserve was in a mountainous region, watershed for the Mae Wong and Ping rivers, which feed the mighty Chao Phraya of central Thailand. Its waterfalls, rarely seen because of the rough terrain, were considered among the most beautiful in the world. Romanus had photographed two of them on this trip and had a case of undeveloped transparencies showing hornbills, wild elephant, wild dog, wild pig, the waterfalls, and—triumph!—twenty frames of a tiger drinking from a pool. He had spent all night in the hideaway above the salt lick and seen nothing. But the following day, when he was on the ground, the cat had stepped out of the trees just three meters in front of him and trotted on big, soft feet to drink. He had been too excited to be frightened. Hallelujah! The blimp's on! he thought. When it had drunk, it glanced in his direction, as if to say, I know you're there. Then it trotted back into the forest.

From Mae Wong to Bangkok was a drive of almost four hundred kilometers. As he drove, he rehearsed how he would break the news to Raoul about the tiger shots. He had called him a few times that day but only got the message "This telephone is out of range or unattended. . . ."

"I got the big waterfall, a few birds, a few elephants, and a cat," he would say.

"*A cat?* What sort of cat?"

"Stripes on it."

"*Stripes?* Must be spots, Michael. Civet has spots."

"Reckon they're stripes."

Romanus yelled with laughter as he gunned down Highway 1. Sabea had been due in Bangkok from Chiang Mai two days earlier; tonight they would celebrate the end of eighteen months' work. Tomorrow it would be time to disappear. "Mongolia, I think, might be a nice spot," Romanus had said. "How about Bosnia?" Raoul had replied, laughing.

They rented rooms in a Khao Sahn boardinghouse. The place was clean and cheap, and although it was a rough area, full of social-fringe farangs, it suited them. They needed a base in the capital where they could leave extra gear when they went up-country. Grossmann had often pressed Romanus to move into his palace in Yannawa, adding, "Sabea is welcome too." But it was obvious that Grossmann disliked Sabea. In part it was a natural clash of temperaments, but mostly it was jealousy of the friendship between the two younger men.

"The old man feels young and horny when you're around," Raoul said. "You're the son he wishes he had."

"He'll kill me," Romanus muttered.

The boardinghouse was in the alley off Khao Sahn, and he was able to drive right to the front door to unload his gear. The man in the tattoo shop next door came to lend him a hand; the woman on the corner who sold fruit bobbed her head and gave a blessing for his return. I love this town, he thought. Everything today was pure pleasure. As soon as he had showered and shaved and caught up with Raoul, he would visit the Mamba. The thought of her had been exciting him on and off for the past week.

When the photographic gear was all upstairs, he went along the tiled corridor and knocked on Raoul's door. There was no answer.

He clattered down to the kitchen, where the old lady who ran the boardinghouse was grating coconuts. She said she had seen the Spaniard two days ago but had not noticed him around since then. I know what you've been doing, Romanus thought.

An hour later, in fresh clothes, wearing the gold chain with its good luck charm that the Mamba had given him, he climbed the spiral staircase to the No Name Bar. The bar was empty, and he had to drink his beer with nothing for company but the mural of a man divided into a Buddha and a devil holding a skull. The alternative decoration was a wooden carving of a huge face eating a small human.

"Seen the Spaniard?" he asked the barman. Not for weeks, the barman said.

Romanus swallowed his drink and went downstairs thoughtfully. No need to panic, he told himself. In Khao Sahn he hired a tuk-tuk to go to the Mamba's house. It was only a quarter to four, and the Mamba did not start work until four o'clock; he hoped to be her first customer.

The crone who worked as her maid opened the door and cackled with delight at seeing him, cupping her old, bent hands over his. She led him into the small sitting room. "You wait. Mistress not long," she said, and shuffled off to get him a beer. Romanus felt annoyed he had not arrived early enough to be first cab off the rank. At least there were no other men waiting.

A bamboo rack held magazines printed in Thai and Chinese, and on the coffee table there was a copy of the *International Herald Tribune*. He tried to read.

After a few minutes Sabea's favorite girl—Romanus could never remember her name—came into the sitting room. She was holding her hands in front of her like starfish, waiting for the varnish on her nails to dry. She had a big orange bow in her hair, the same color as the varnish.

"Mi-kal!" she said, and flung her arms around his neck.

"Hey, gorgeous, you're looking great."

"You frien' mean to me." She pouted.

He nodded cautiously. "What'd he do?"

"No see me." She sniffed. "Already four week. He promise, I come back Chiang Mai, I come to you house, we all day, all night. I give you two hundred dollar, I buy you silk dress. . . . He no come."

"He no come?" Romanus repeated. "You no see him yesterday?"

The bow flopped from side to side when she shook her head.

"Who's in with the Mamba?" he asked.

"Nobody. Mamba still resting."

Romanus went to the bedroom door and knocked.

The Mamba's husky voice said, "Who?" in an unfriendly tone.

"It's Michael."

"Hey! My man!"

He heard her bound off the bed, and the door opened. He stepped inside and took her hands. "Shh," he said, with a look over his shoulder. She bent to listen, painted eyes wide. He liked to tell her she was the most beautiful creature he'd ever seen. She had a haughty nose, long eyes, broad lips, and skin the color of bronze. She was dressed in a red brassiere and bikini pants. "Mamba," he whispered, "you see the Spaniard?"

She shook her head vigorously. "He man of my frien'!"

"I know. But you're sure you haven't seen him?"

"I no steal her man! I no see him. She ask everyone in Bangkok: Where my man is? You see my man? She sick in her heart. Crying, Why my man no come?" Her red mouth opened, and her long, raspberry-colored tongue licked his ear. "You stay with me now?" she said.

Her gaze softened. She was thinking about a dress she wanted to have made and what she would eat for dinner. He was looking at her red-dyed nipples, visible through the lace cups of her brassiere. She unzipped his fly and slid her hand around his erection.

"How long time you want?" she asked.

"An hour," Romanus said automatically. He felt unexpectedly ill at ease. Why had no one seen Raoul? He watched the Mamba rummage in a drawer crammed with condoms, lubricants, and butt plugs, and felt suddenly bored.

"Do you like animals?" he asked distractedly.

She hesitated before replying, calculating the right response. "Animals?" she hedged. "You mean pussycat?"

"No—tigers, wild pig, gibbons."

The Mamba grimaced. "I no eat such things."

He pulled her toward him and murmured, "I meant, do you like to look at them?"

"What for?" Her eyebrows conveyed disgust.

"Because they're wonderful."

"Wonderful?" Her expression, which was tending toward bad temper, lit with a smile. "Money is wonderful. Gold is wonderful. Food is wonderful." She smiled sweetly. "You is wonderful. Best lover in the world." She made a fist and laughed, trying not to notice he had rezipped his fly.

I've got to find Raoul, Romanus was thinking. He let out a gasp, smacking his hand on his back pocket. "I forgot my wallet!" he said. An expression of contempt crossed her features. Sometimes you can see what she'll look like when she's thirty-five, he thought: angry, and hard, and disgusted with life.

"I'll bring the Spaniard back here, and we'll all go out to dinner. The four of us. We'll go to the Dusit," he said. To himself he added, You're a shit. Neither he nor Raoul would go to the Dusit with a pair of nothing-to-say whores. The Mamba knew he was lying.

"You wonderful lover," she murmured. "You stay with me." She ran a finger across his upper lip.

He could smell her sweetish, alkaline odor. "Back soon," he said.

Protocol was that a customer left by the bedroom's second door, to avoid seeing the next customer in the waiting room. He gave the crone a good tip. She bobbed and chortled as she let him out onto the lane behind the house, where he hailed a taxi. As soon as he was inside, he felt a wave of relief. "Khao Sahn," he said. "When we get there, wait. I might want to go somewhere else."

I n U-1, Parker and his team remained seated around the staff room table after lunch, continuing the planning session that had engrossed them for the past hour. They had a strategy for evasive action in case Diana Pembridge insisted on inspecting U-1 on Wednesday. There would be at least thirty minutes warning before she arrived. The yellow and red kindergarten table and chairs, the toys and the shortened bicycle, were to be taken upstairs, some to Sonja's bedroom, some to Lek's cabin. Sailor and Lucy and the monkey chow would be loaded into the Land Cruiser and be driven around for the duration of the visit.

"There'll be plenty of time," Parker said, to reassure himself as much as the boys. He hated to rush or be rushed. He held open his long-fingered hands, counting off each person's task. "Are we all clear about our jobs?"

The telephone on the wall near the microwave rang. It was Grossmann. Could Parker be in Sydney at seven o'clock next morning to meet "a friend" who was arriving then? he asked. "You'll like him better than the lady who sees ghosts."

"I can't get to Sydney by seven!" Parker almost shouted. There was not only the threat of an inspection tomorrow; he was having difficulty with one of the columns in the HPLC machine, and first thing in the morning, he needed to test its beads.

Grossmann grunted irritably as he listened to Parker's excuses. "My friend doesn't speak much English, John. If nobody meets him he might get lost. You understand?"

"Do I know him?" Parker asked cautiously.

"You've seen him in my car in the evening sometimes."

"Somchai?"

"A good man, eh? He'll fit in well."

Fit in well! Parker thought. Somchai had tattoos, and he grew the nails on his little fingers ten centimeters long. They resembled a crocodile's claws. I won't have him! he wanted to shout. "I'm sure he will, Otto, but the fact is, even if I leave here first thing, I can't get to Sydney until ten-thirty in the morning. Let's think of somewhere to meet."

"I'd like him to see the zoo, John."

Parker groaned to himself. The Taronga Park Zoo was on the other side of the city.

"I'm thinking of bringing a few chimps and orangs down to Bangkok, and I might get Somchai to look after them. I'd like him to see how the apes are housed in Sydney."

"I'll meet him at the chimpanzee enclosure at around one o'clock tomorrow. There's a map inside the entrance, with pictures of animals to show where they are."

"Sounds okay," Grossmann said. "Just a moment." Somchai was standing at a respectful distance from the desk. He nodded as his boss explained the arrangements to him. "He's happy with that. I told him to take a taxi. The taxis in Sydney look like taxis in Bangkok. Is that right?"

"They're even driven by people from Bangkok," Parker said bleakly.

While he was on the telephone, the boys busied themselves with minor chores. None of them, he was sure, knew that Lek had come into U-1 in the middle of the night and set off the alarm; like everyone else, they believed there had been a malfunction. But they would realize he was worried about the girl, he thought. Several times that day he had left his bench, mumbling, "I'll just see how she's getting on," and had entered the Animal Room. She cowered from him. When he tried to grab her, she ran to a corner and turned her face to the wall, whispering, "I scream." After his third attempt, he had given her a hard slap on the bottom and gone back to work.

When he put down the telephone, he tried to look pensive but calm. "Lek is leaving us, and we're getting a male keeper," he announced. "She's needed back in Thailand."

The boys' expressions were disappointed. "I was just getting used to her," Steve said.

"I'll fly to Sydney tomorrow to meet him and bring him back here. We'll have to rethink our anti-Pembridge plan, I'm afraid. I'm not sure what the arrangements for Lek's return to Thailand will be." She had arrived illegally, via Karatha, without a passport, and would probably have to leave the same way. Somchai, however, would be traveling with a passport and ticket.

By five-fifteen that afternoon, Bangkok time, the taxi carrying Michael Romanus was driving slowly along Khao Sahn. Both pavements were crowded with people, food, and goods for sale—fake Gucci, fake Hermès, fake Levi's 501s, pirated cassettes, curries in banana leaves, chunks of pineapple and watermelon kept on ice. Music from the 1960s blasted out of loudspeakers near a shop specializing in snakeskin clothing: boots, jackets, sneakers, a pair of two-tone black-and-tan men's shoes, from the toes of which reared baby cobras. There were stalls where for a hundred dollars you could have the whole of Paradise tattooed on your back. The Thais in this part of town had adopted Western incivility and yelled, "Fuck off!" at tourists who jostled them. Young white men, so stoned they looked like apes, wandered along, batting out of their way child beggars who carried hand-printed cards that said I HAVE A DREAM TO GET AN EDUCATION. On the corner of the alley that led to the guesthouse, there was a secondhand bookshop where Henry James, Ruth Prawer Jhabvala, George Eliot, Flaubert (in English), and Goethe (in German) were for sale. A sign next door said WE BUY EVERYTHING: CAMERAS, RADIOS, SUNGLASSES. The restaurants advertised in English the videos they would be screening that day. *Unforgiven* was a big attraction. As his cab moved slowly toward the alley, Romanus searched the crowd, hoping to see Raoul.

There was no one in the courtyard except for a woman washing clothes in a bucket. Romanus found the landlady in the kitchen again. She slipped on her plastic outdoor sandals and followed him back across the yard, grumbling about letting him have the Spaniard's key.

The rooms were whitewashed, furnished with a double bed, a bedside table, wardrobe, and chest of drawers, and, for five hundred baht extra per month, a ceiling fan, a coffee table, and chairs. At each end of the corridor was a bathroom with klong jars of cold water. People with long leases, like Romanus and Sabea, could decorate their rooms. Raoul had covered his walls with bird photographs. Every time Romanus went in, he would glance at the picture of an eagle flying straight at the camera and think, I wish I'd taken that.

The eagle picture was lying on the floor when he opened the door. A carousel of transparencies had spilled. Otherwise, the room looked a little disheveled, but normal. Somebody had been lying on the bed; the pillows showed the indentations of a body.

Romanus picked up the eagle picture. Underneath it was one of Raoul's shoes. He looked for the other one. Maybe he's getting it fixed, he thought. A camera with a blimp on it lay on the coffee table. The blimp was cracked, and flecks of whitewash clung to it. He pulled it off and had a look at the film. It was slow black-and-white, and there had been eight exposures. Up-country, he and Raoul always took some black-and-white animal pictures to sell to newspapers in Japan.

He was about to leave, when he realized that the collection of photographs of former girlfriends Sabea kept on his bedside table on the far side of the room was missing. There were six of them—a couple white, one black, the other three Asian. Raoul told terrible lies about how the affairs had begun, developed, and ended. "Venus is a cruel goddess," he would say, laughing.

Romanus walked round to the other side of the bed: the photographs were lying on the floor, and underneath them, broken as if stamped on, was the mobile phone. Everything—the phone, the girlfriends, the floor tiles—was sticky and spotted with old blood. He turned and ran downstairs. "Ten more minutes," he said, and pushed fifty baht through the window of the cab.

Five minutes was all he would need to develop negatives from the film in the blimped camera. He pounded up the stairs again and into his room. "C'mon, c'mon," he whispered as he shook the cylinder of chemicals. He could read negatives as easily as a layman reads prints. When he pulled the wet roll out of the shaker, the first two were black. The third was out of focus but showed Raoul's wall, where the eagle picture hung. A short man was standing in front of it, features so blurred Romanus could not make out who he was. On the fifth exposure he recognized the face, and on the sixth he saw the knife. The man, holding a knife with a blade about twenty-five centimeters long, was looking at Raoul, who must have been holding the camera in his lap. The seventh negative was another blur, but Romanus thought he could see a second figure behind Somchai; the eighth was of the ceiling.

"Dry, get dry," Romanus muttered to the strip of celluloid. As soon as it was dry enough, he rolled it up, put it in a film cylinder, and gathered up some clothes. His photographic equipment was still packed. He shoved the clothes into a nylon sports bag.

The cabdriver was looking hot with impatience when Romanus ran downstairs with three bags and a tripod just before six, but he cheered up immediately at the word "airport." At this time of day, it was a two-hour trip.

Sonja left work exactly at the official close of business, nine minutes to five, on Tuesday and cycled home. It was a warm, mild autumn afternoon. The country looked refreshed after the rain of the past couple of weeks, and the air was pleasantly soft with moisture. It was unusual, so far inland, to have the sort of milky air one found in the eastern coastal cities—but there it was filthy, humid air. As she cycled, a sense of well-being enveloped her, the rhythm of her legs pushing down on the pedals, the wheels spinning, her breath flowing easily through her chest. A decision she had made earlier had kept her happy all afternoon.

Before leaving for work that morning, she had cooked the leek, onion, and potato for a vichyssoise that would be the first course of a moonlit dinner that evening. The soup had been too hot to put in the refrigerator before she left for work, but it would have cooled to room temperature by the afternoon. All she needed to do was add cream and chill the whole lot for half an hour. For the second course she planned grilled lamb skewers and a Greek salad. Lamb shish kebab was John's favorite meat, and vichyssoise was his favorite cold soup. Even Hilary acknowledged that Sonja's vichyssoise was good. Hilary was not speaking to her at the moment—not since Sonja had rung her last week after the directors' meeting to tell her what she thought of the way she was running her portfolio. Hilary had replied, "Listen, you pissant, if ever I ask for advice from you, you'll know I've got Alzheimer's. Meanwhile, just shut up and enjoy earning ninety thousand dollars a year, which is *eighty thousand more than you are worth!*" She hung up.

"She'll get over it and say she's sorry," John said.

"I don't want her to," Sonja replied.

All morning she had looked forward to her seduction dinner with

John. He won't go off to that Thai bitch tonight, she told herself, because I will get him first.

But just after lunch that day, John had arrived in her office to say he would not be eating or sleeping at her house tonight but at his condo, because he needed to be up and away early. He had to catch the minibus into Kalunga at seven-thirty next morning, he said, to make Kalair's nine o'clock flight to Sydney to meet the new animal keeper. Sonja had remained calm.

"While Lek's still here, I'm not sure where the new chap will sleep," he continued. "I don't want to put him in the cabin with her."

"Why not?"

"Well—in Thailand, men and women don't . . ." He gestured vaguely.

"Good God! Now we're running a boarding school. I'm sure that for a week, or however long it takes to get rid of her, they can both sleep in the cabin. Lek's not a *nun*."

He was leaning on the edge of her desk, looking out the window at the lake, ready for a nice, leisurely chat, totally unaware of how she was feeling. She wanted to scream: *Last night you got out of my bed and went and had sex with that slut. Tonight I've made you vichyssoise, but you're not even going to eat with me, because your work is more important than I am.*

"What will you do this evening?" he asked.

She gave a radiant smile. "I'll do some decoupage."

He ruffled her hair. "Good girl. See you tomorrow night." At the door, he paused and blew her a kiss.

By a quarter to seven that night, an enormous yellow ball had appeared above the lake. Sonja left the veranda to go to the bedroom for her second daily injection. She put the needle she had just used in the top drawer of her dressing table, beside the bottles of insulin. Then she reached to the back of the drawer.

In the kitchen, she removed the soup tureen from the refrigerator and ladled two servings into attractive blue-and-white stoneware bowls. One she placed on a tray, and laid beside it a silver soup spoon and a miniature salt-and-pepper set. The other bowl she returned to the fridge. She found a blue napkin that matched the blue of the soup bowl and set off the pale-colored soup. I need a napkin ring, she thought. She fumbled around in the napery drawer until she felt one of the silver pair she had bought for herself and John. Hers was round. His was oblong. She thought the round one would make the better fit. And indeed, when she wrapped the napkin around her tools, she could only just push the napkin through the ring.

"Right," she said aloud. She was feeling cheerful as she carried the tray through the garden. It was not heavy, so she could hold it in one hand as she knocked on the cabin door. "Lek," she called. "I've brought you some soup."

That night, Susan Miller rang her father at home. When he heard her voice, his first thought was that she wanted to cancel his invitation for the weekend.

"You always imagine the worst." She laughed.

"That way you never get caught."

"I've talked to Nelly, Dad."

From his armchair in the living room Joe could see the big yellow moon, so full it looked ready to burst. He remembered how when he was a kid they used to look forward to the Easter moon, because it meant the end of Lent was close and they could soon start eating steak and chops and all the good things his mother refused to cook during the fasting season. "Nelly's read Nichols's closed files," Susan was saying. "And guess what? He was running an illegal steroid supply network in Sydney."

"Go on."

"He was supplying all the eastern and inner-city gyms. He's got lists of clients and suppliers going back ten years."

"I'll be buggered."

"There'll be plenty of arrests."

"Well," he said, "I picked him as a closet queen, but a scam fits too. Something must've gone wrong, though, to make him move out here. Anything about the work he did at the Research?"

"All his files from 1990 to 1993 have been erased. Nelly's trying to reconstruct them."

"You heard anything about the postmortem blood tests they did on him?"

"Not yet." She gave a yawn. "Oh—I must go to bed. I've got to be up at five. I'm on first shift at the airport, and I've got this new kid I'm training. . . ."

"How's the Sydney weather?" he asked.

"Hot! Today was the hottest April day for thirty years. Heat wave, plus full moon, plus the beginning of the holidays . . . Listen to this." She held her telephone toward the window. The sound of a police siren came blaring from the street outside.

They made their final arrangements for the weekend: he would arrive at her flat in Ocean Street on Saturday morning, and they would go straight down to the surf. Joe pictured the long, glassy waves with their curled lip of white water. He could remember the exhilaration of leaping into a rolling wheel of seawater and being lifted up.

W̲hen Michael Romanus decided to get out of Bangkok as fast as possible, he did not know exactly what he should do. Between realizing that Grossmann had sent his man to murder Raoul and telling the taxi driver to go to the airport, he had no time to work out a plan.

The cab had smoked-glass windows, but all the same he sat well back in the seat and from time to time took a quick look out the back. How had Otto found out? They had only one more day's work to do on Siam, and then Grossmann's neck would be so far in the noose he would not be able to escape.

His first thought had been to flee to Kalimantan, go up-country, and spend a few months photographing orangutans. But when he reflected on the thousands of hectares of uninhabited jungle and how the law in a place like that was pretty much what people made of it, he changed his mind. If Otto could send Somchai after Raoul in the middle of Bangkok, he could send him to Kalimantan to find me. So where to? Los Angeles and the Primate Rescue Organization people? They had good contacts with the local police. Romanus opened his phone and began to dial, before realizing it was 3:00 A.M. in L.A. His leg jigged with nervous energy. I'll go home, he thought.

At the airport, he went straight to the hotel, booked in, and rang a travel agent on the list in the guest directory. "I want to fly to Australia tonight," he said. The 10:00 P.M. flight was full, with a waiting list. It took almost an hour of fiddling, but by nine o'clock he was booked on a flight from Bangkok via Singapore and Jakarta to Sydney, leaving just before midnight.

He had an hour free before check-in. He took a table in a downstairs restaurant from which he could watch both the entrance and the door to the kitchen. At ten o'clock he pushed his luggage carrier across the walkway to the terminal building, just missing Somchai, who was catching the earlier, direct flight.

S̲omchai had only a backpack for luggage.

"You may carry that on board, sir, if you'd like," a woman at the check-in counter said.

He shook his head. He could not take the backpack inside the airplane, Khun Otto had warned him, because it had his knife in it. And his knife had to be inside the backpack, not on his leg, where it belonged, because people were not allowed to wear knives on airplanes.

"Why not?" Somchai had asked.

A lingering uneasiness affected Grossmann's mood. Early yesterday, when his chauffeur had returned to the house to say he had driven the Spaniard to Saraburi and now he was dead, Grossmann caught sight of a whirling madness in the small, dark eyes. I have the power to raise demons, he thought. Do I have the power to still them? A twinge of fear took hold of him. "It's just a rule," he'd replied.

On Wednesday, when Joe Miller unlocked his door, he saw his computer blinking with the sign that it had a letter for him. He typed in the code word and pressed Enter. Onto the screen came the row of symbols indicating that the letter was from Homicide. "Quick," he said, hitting Next Page.

First came the blood analysis. Nichols had AIDS. Next was the record of interview with his physician. Jason wanted to keep his condition secret, his doctor said, for his parents did not know he was gay. The doctor pointed out that in a country town Jason's illness would easily become known from the batches of AZT sent to the local GP, so Nichols decided to drive to Sydney to collect his medicine from the Saint Vincent's Hospital pharmacy—and to visit the channelers, clairvoyants, and psychic healers who had set up shop around the inner city. By late 1992 he was sweating at night and suffering from low-grade infections. In March 1993, his condition deteriorated suddenly. On the Friday before he was found dead, he had learned that his T cells had dropped from 400 to 250. He became upset during the consultation, hinting that he was being blackmailed by people who had discovered he had AIDS. The doctor guessed that Jason was doping horses for them. He had been urging him for more than a year to drop the pretense of being well and heterosexual and to tell his parents, at least, that he was ill. He had noted an increasing paranoia in Nichols in recent months: he was blaming different people for deliberately infecting him, saying, "They deserve to die."

Chapter Seventeen

Sonja did not usually watch television at breakfast time, but on Wednesday morning she had reasons to do so. She wanted to hear the weather forecast for Sydney, where John would be. The other reason was less clear to her, but it had something to do with Tuesday night. The forecast was appalling: 32 degrees, followed by a thunderstorm. *In April?* Well, that was greenhouse, and it was too late to escape. As John said, the lifeboat was already sinking under the weight of its passengers: "It's time to start throwing some overboard. Either we do it ourselves or the planet will do it for us."

After breakfast she hung out the clothes to dry. It was another beautiful day, warm but not hot, with a tall blue sky that was cloudless now although, later, fluffy cumulus clouds would probably form in the east. She felt so blithe she took credit for the fine weather and almost skipped to the clothesline. That morning, she had put fresh linen on the bed, cold white cotton that smelled of lavender. The sickly incense-ponging sheets and pillow slips from two nights ago were washed. She hung them evenly so they would dry straight and not need ironing. When she had finished, she stepped back to admire them. Everything was under control.

She opened the door to U-1 and went downstairs. The boys were already at work, Phil and Freddie seated side by side in front of a screen where the image of a swollen blue-and-red thing like a black-berry engaged their attention. Steve was writing at his bench.

"Lek's not well," Sonja said. "She wants to stay in bed today. Can you look after the animals until this evening?"

"Yep," Steve answered without looking up from his notebook.

"Does she need anything?" Freddie muttered.

"No. And she told me she doesn't want visitors."

Phil, who had been intent on the blackberry, suddenly tuned in. "That's no good!" he said, frowning and looking first at Freddie, then across the room to Steve. "Lek has to help us move the chimps and stuff, in case that nut from the Ethics Committee wants an inspection."

"I forgot," Freddie said.

"We'll have to reorganize the jobs again."

Steve and Freddie grunted, their attention back on their work. Sonja looked from one to the other in irritation. "Nobody told *me*," she said, "that you needed Lek today."

"No hassle." Freddie squinted at the protein molecule on his screen. "We'll manage without her. Hey, Phil—look at this."

"She's got a sore throat," Sonja persisted. None of them seemed to hear, so she turned and went upstairs.

Diana was in the aviary when she heard the phone ringing in the house and realized she had forgotten to switch on the answering machine.

I hope it's not that kid with the kite, she thought. A schoolboy from a property two hundred kilometers away had found a fork-tailed kite, poisoned by something it had picked up near a slaugh-teryard. While the kite was on the ground, disabled by poison, a cattle dog had mauled it. Diana held telephone and fax conferences with the boy almost every day, but usually later than this. She was teaching him how to imp the bird's broken feathers.

After six or seven rings the noise stopped, and she returned her attention to the eagle.

The bird had seemed sluggish early on, and Diana wondered if she had worked too hard on her first day at the flying ground. But she came to Diana's arm willingly, half jumping, half gliding a cou-ple of meters from her perch. When Diana carried her to the block outdoors, she cast from her crop a felted mass of fur and duck feath-ers, leftovers from the feast of two days ago. After casting she became perky, whistling as she shook out her feathers and waggling her tail. Last week, while her wings were still tied, Diana had imped the damaged tail feather, using a sliver of bamboo to join the broken part to an eagle tail feather she had in her collection of spares. You needed a magnifying glass to spot the mend. Now when the eagle preened, the perfect layering of her plumage was magical. Feather overlapped feather with ingenious artistry. The bird seemed at these moments to be another sort of human, one who came down from behind the sun.

A few moments after the phone stopped ringing, she heard Grace call "It's America!" from a window upstairs.

Diana was panting when she picked up the receiver. A bright American voice said, "Hi, Diana. Hope I haven't interrupted your dinner." They could not come to grips with the idea that Australia was eighteen hours ahead of the West Coast. "A courier has just delivered your latest hair. There's been no time for proper analysis, but we thought you would like to know what we all think, just from comparing the two samples. . . ." Diana held her breath.

"They're from different animals," the bright voice continued. "We're saying that based on a visual comparison of color and length, and after putting the new hair and one of the earlier hairs side by side under the microscope. Even allowing for the variation in hair on different parts of the body, this second sample appears to be from a lighter-colored animal, with a finer coat. Our guess would be that it comes from an animal that has been in a tropical climate and outdoors more recently than the first one, which, as we told you, showed signs of being kept indoors, with no sunlight, in air-conditioning. But the sex and type of food of this animal, that we can't tell yet."

Diana felt a thud of disappointment. Hairs traveled like seeds. She knew that Sonja had dined with Jason on the night he had treated the circus chimp: it was possible that chimp hair on Jason had transferred itself to Sonja's clothing and then to her husband's. "Would you mind putting all that on the fax to me?" she said. I must keep an unprejudiced mind, she told herself. I mustn't suspect people just because they give me the creeps.

She was still thinking about Dr. Parker and his foxy little wife when she returned to the aviary. At lunch at the Ethics Committee meeting, the wife had said, "Animals are so much nicer than humans. Wouldn't it be wonderful if all the humans vanished and the animals could have their planet back?"

"No," Diana said.

Sonja had looked astonished.

"Animals don't want us to leave them."

Sonja gave a nervous laugh. Her ears were turning red from some complex emotion caused by the sudden arrival on the veranda of Dr. Parker.

At Sydney's Kingsford Smith Airport on Wednesday morning, the first jumbo of the day lifted from the runway like a slow arrow. The sky was already hot, although it was barely light. Overnight, the temperature had stayed at 22 degrees. Susan Miller did not mind being on the early shift at the airport in this weather, because by the afternoon, when the heat would be booming like a kettledrum, she would be surfing into the cool green sea. She had swum in the ocean pool just after dawn, and because of that had arrived a few minutes late at the meeting in Customs' Operations Room. She was wearing a navy skirt and preppy striped cotton shirt, to look like airport ground staff. Her short, chemically yellow hair was still damp.

The marks, three of them, all in the heroin trade, were not due to arrive until 0700 hours, but there were some details of coordination between Customs and the Dogs to work out before the aircraft landed. A fact discovered only last night had complicated the operation: the apron controller had allotted Bay 15 to the 7:00 A.M. flight from Bangkok. Number 15 was the only detached bay at the international terminal, and therefore it was possible that in the short distance between the jumbo and the finger walkway, one of the marks could pass his load to an accomplice working on the tarmac. The insecure bay meant that a team would have to drive onto the tarmac, park as close as possible to the aircraft, and keep both lines of disembarking passengers under surveillance. The marks were a Caucasian male aged thirty, a Chinese male aged forty-one, and a Thai female aged twenty-three. The Chinese was the boss. He was flying first class and would not be carrying drugs. The woman was in business class, and the younger male was in economy. As far as Customs could figure from the list of passengers' names, the flight had at least twenty-eight Chinese males aged between thirty and forty-two, eighty Caucasian males aged twenty-five to thirty-five, and seventeen Thai females aged eighteen to twenty-five; picking them by sight would not be easy.

Susan slid into a seat next to her probationer, Debbie Smith.

"What have I missed?" she whispered.

Smith had dimples, a beauty spot at the corner of her top lip, and succulent-looking breasts, which had so disturbed one of the men at the briefing that he had turned his chair at an angle so he could not look at them. Her expression was bewildered. "I don't know," she whispered back.

Sergeant Miller tried to keep a pleasant look on her face. She was sick of being den mother for these thickheaded girls who never lasted out their probationary year, although she had to admit this one was gorgeous.

"I was wondering . . . ," Smith said. She wanted to make a good impression on Sergeant Miller. "I was wondering . . ." A photograph of the Chinese appeared on the screen. Weasel nudged Smith to shut up.

The plan they made that morning was to construct a double filter that would not alert the marks (or whoever might be waiting to meet them) that they, in particular, were under surveillance. First, a sniffer dog would be stationed in the corridor leading to passport control. The dog could find drugs in hand luggage or carried outside the body, but skillful couriers knew how to confuse drug dogs. These marks were expected to get past the dogs while a score of people with foodstuffs and Buddha sticks would be grabbed by the dog. At the immigration barrier, officers would have instructions to put the symbol for a luggage search on the customs card of every Caucasian male aged twenty-five to thirty-five, every Chinese male aged thirty-five to forty-five, and every Thai female aged twenty to twenty-five who disembarked from the first Bangkok flight. The broad net would trawl in all sorts of unexpected contraband. By 8:00 A.M., there would be seven hundred fifty passengers in the arrival hall, all fatigued, all ending long journeys, all anxious to pass through Customs as fast as possible.

Miller and Smith were assigned to the finger walkway. After that they were to change into jeans and T-shirts and take up positions in the luggage collection area, ready to help in arrest. In the case of nothing being found on the marks, they were to keep the woman under surveillance when she left the terminal. They would have a backup team of five, plus two cars.

W hen the aircraft landed, the first thing Somchai noticed was that the weather was not so cold as he had thought it would be. He felt some easing of his fear of being so far from home. Khun Otto had said it would not be for long: just a few months, until any trouble over the Spaniard had passed. Although Khun Otto said it was safer for him to be in Australia, Somchai did not feel safe, and as he followed the other passengers along a corridor of raw tan brick he felt increasingly nervous, especially when he saw the wooden barricade. Beside it were two blue-uniformed men, one of them struggling to hold a panting German shepherd dog. The animal quivered with excitement and yanked her leash. Somchai was frightened of dogs, as were many of the other passengers.

The smiling young handler said, "Don't be afraid of the dog, ladies and gentlemen; she won't bite, and there's no rabies in Australia," but only a few people understood him.

The dog shoved her nose in Somchai's crotch, sniffed the legs of his jeans and his Reeboks, and passed on.

Meanwhile, on the finger walk, Weasel had already observed the Caucasian male hand a plastic carry bag to the Thai woman and alerted the Customs men at the barrier. The dog went into a frenzy of snarling and barking, and the woman was led away.

In the baggage claim area, the hundreds of people milling around the carousels were so intent on their own problems that only a handful realized a young white man had just been surrounded by three others and forced to follow them. The Chinese had gone through, clean, and was standing in a queue outside the terminal, waiting for a taxi. The two men standing behind him in the queue, dressed casually to look like disembarking passengers, were federal police officers. The Chinese stepped into a cab. Seconds later, the officers stepped into a taxi that jumped the line. A burgundy-colored Mazda pulled out from the two-minute standing zone and fell in behind the cabs.

"Well—that's our work for the day," Weasel said. "What would you like to do now?"

Probationer Smith had been hoping for drama and felt disappointed by the speed and quietness of the arrests. She was expecting something more glamorous. "Could we go for coffee?" she asked. There was a coy inflection in her voice.

So young and so flirty, Weasel thought.

Somchai was just emerging from the men's lavatory. He had collected his backpack from the carousel, gone into the lavatory, removed his knife, and strapped it to his calf, so that if he was stopped at Customs (Khun Otto had explained all this) his knife would not be seen.

"Where would you like to go?" Weasel asked Smith, who shrugged and looked open to any suggestion.

Somchai, his blue backpack slung on one shoulder, walked out into the hot Sydney morning and joined the end of the taxi queue.

He registered on Weasel's brain for a moment before she returned her attention to Deborah Smith.

"Let's go back to headquarters and get rid of our gear. Then we'll be fancy free," she said.

"Sounds good to me," Smith replied.

A white Commodore turbo cruised to the curb. Weasel got in the front and Smith in the rear. "Office," Miller said.

"After that?" the driver asked.

Weasel turned for a moment to Smith, who flashed an encouraging smile. "We've earned a cup of coffee. Where do *you* reckon?" Weasel wanted to suggest the Gelato Bar at Bondi. Then she could say, "How about a swim?" and she and Deborah could walk up to her flat. . . . Maybe that was rushing things.

"Mate," the driver said, "you can't do better than what the tourists do: Go down to the quay, sit by the water, watch the ferries, have a beer. I'll drop you there."

When Michael Romanus arrived in the terminal, the congestion of the earlier flights had cleared. Outside the Customs hall, he telephoned his mother, who burst into tears and asked, was he sick? was he dying from a tropical illness?

"No, Mama. I'll be home soon," he said over and over. When she quieted down she began complaining about her sister and her brother-in-law and how the government and the customers were squeezing her to death. After that she listed all the things in the house that needed repair and how, without his father, life was useless. Then she began crying again.

He had to blow his nose when the call was over.

Before booking a flight to Brisbane, he wanted to speak to the woman Raoul had been in contact with about the chimps going to Australia. Since it was still early, he tried her private number first. A recorded message announced that it had been disconnected. He rang the Research, where an android said, "Thank you for calling the Exotic Feral Species and Microbiology Research Centre. If you wish to speak to someone in Administration, press 1. If you wish to speak to someone in Personnel, press 2. If you wish . . ." Eventually a human came on the line.

"Dr. Carolyn Williams has passed away," the human said. "Is there anyone else who can help you?"

Romanus was so taken aback, he did not ask how she had passed away, or when. I'll chance it, he thought. "Dr. John Parker."

After a moment the android came back on the line. "The person you wish to contact is unavailable today. If you wish to speak to someone else, or leave a message, press 9."

He hung up. What would I say to Parker anyway? he wondered. Tell him, You better come clean, pal, while you've still got time?

He knew he had to go to the police as soon as possible. He also knew that the disappearance in Thailand of a Spanish national would not interest the Australian cops, so he would have to convince them that animals were arriving unquarantined in Australia. If they believed that, they would be willing to bring in Interpol, which was the only way of overriding Grossmann's power in Thailand. His plan, worked out on the flight from Bangkok, had depended upon meeting up with Carolyn Williams, discovering what she had found out about the final destination of the chimps sent from Saraburi, then going with her to the police.

In his hand luggage he had the contact numbers of wildlife protection agencies throughout the world. He turned to the index and found the Primate Rescue Organization contact for Australia. Raoul had warned him about the PRO rep: she was La Loca, the Mad One. "I understanding not this woman, although she knows much of birds," Raoul said. She had tried to shoot him once: a jealous woman. "And Carolyn Williams, she, too, is mad. She and La Loca are half-sisters, but nobody talks about that." I'll have to talk to the crazy half-sister, Romanus thought.

The woman who answered said, "She not here now."

Romanus asked, "Do you know what happened to a woman called Carolyn Williams?" There was silence.

"She been murdered."

He collected his wits. "When did it happen?"

"A month ago."

He counted back. A month ago, he and Raoul were in Alor Setar, in Malaysia. Raoul had telephoned Williams with the details they had gathered about a chimp called Lucy, who, according to the staff at Saraburi, had been sent to Dr. Parker in Australia three months earlier. Romanus remembered the date because the next day Raoul was flying to Chiang Mai, and he was driving to Mae Wong, via Saraburi, carrying the decoy baby orangutan to give to Otto. It had a tattoo inside its lip so it could be traced.

At the information desk he found the name of the airline that flew to Kalunga, but it was fully booked for that day and the next. After a long wait he got through to State Rail: he was too late to catch the train, so his only option was to hire a car and drive. A yawn almost stifled him. He had been too tense to sleep more than a couple of hours on the flight from Bangkok, and when he did doze, dreams tumbled him about.

He rang back and explained to the woman who answered La Loca's phone that he wanted to meet Diana, but he could not get to Kalunga until Thursday afternoon.

"You comin' on the bus?" the woman asked. A special bus was leaving from Sydney's Central Railway Station next morning, she said, taking a group of bird-watchers to Kalunga.

He pushed his luggage cart out of the terminal, into the steaming morning, and caught a cab to the Airport Hilton, half asleep before he checked in.

Diana's tour of the Research that morning was in concert with two other members of the Ethics Committee and was conducted by the director of administration. He began by taking them to the rabbit breeding house, where they spent almost an hour. Next was the fox enclosure. The cubs were as playful as puppies and sucked and nipped at their fingers, but the fox stink was almost unbearable. Diana waited a few minutes until her olfactory nerves overloaded and switched off and was then able to spend the next half hour examining their enclosure, unable to smell anything. Administration and the others stood upwind, waiting impatiently. When she rejoined them, Administration said, "It's nice someone takes this committee so seriously." His pink lips inside his beard gave an irritable twitch.

"I'd like to inspect Dr. Parker's laboratory next," Diana said.

"Dr. Parker's laboratory?" His eyes shuttled from side to side, his tone was faintly incredulous, as if the suggestion that Dr. Parker had a laboratory was odd, if not completely bizarre. "I'm not sure . . ."

"U-1," she said.

"*U-1?*"

That morning, Sonja had buttonholed him on the third floor and said that whatever happened, he was not to take people traipsing through John's laboratory today, while John was away. She gave him a note on a memo sheet, saying, "Please ask the director of administration to delay inspection of U-1 until my return. I want to be present to explain to members of the Ethics Committee our animal-keeping practices."

"He phoned this message to my secretary," Sonja said.

"But it's all arranged," Administration had objected. "U-1 is on the list."

"Well, take it off the list," Sonja said. "Take it off."

He inflated his chest. Diana fixed him with steady pale eyes.

Somchai had rehearsed with Grossmann the words he was to say to the taxi driver about going to the zoo. Khun Otto had told him to sit in the front seat, for that was what men did in Australia. He sat in the front and said, "Take to Taroona Park, please."

The driver turned to him, squinting. "Eh?"

"Taroona Park," Somchai said loudly.

"No such place, mate," the driver replied. He glanced at the trademark on Somchai's backpack. "You from Thailand?"

Somchai did not reply.

The driver translated the question: "*Khun pen khon Thai mai. Khrap.*" Somchai smiled and nodded. The driver sympathized. Australia was horrible, and he was dying to go home. He would, as soon as he'd earned enough money to buy a rice field.

Somchai explained that he had to go to the zoo, to meet someone there at lunchtime.

"But it's only nine o'clock," the driver said. "If I take you by the harbor tunnel you'll be there before ten. You'll have to wait for hours."

By the time they reached Oxford Street, the driver had proposed a different and better travel plan. Instead of going by taxi all the way, Somchai should ride to Circular Quay and catch the zoo ferry across Sydney Harbor. "You'll save fifteen dollars," he said, and translated this sum into baht.

Somchai laid his hand on the driver's arm. "I'm in your debt," he said, nodding portentously.

At Circular Quay, the taxi driver parked and accompanied Somchai to the wharf from which ferries to the zoo departed. They arrived just in time to miss one. Green water swung up and down, slapping against the pylons. The cabbie apologized and accompanied Somchai to the ticket kiosk, where he bought a ticket. He explained that the next ferry would leave in forty minutes and showed his compatriot where to wait. He even offered to order him coffee, but Somchai did not want anything to drink. He wanted to stare at the foreigners. "Too many foreigners here," he said, making a face. "They live here," the driver explained.

Weasel noticed Somchai half an hour later, when she and Deborah arrived at the Quay. "Remember him?" she asked. Deborah looked blank. "He got off our flight," Weasel prompted.

"They all look the same to me."

Honey, are you in the wrong job, Weasel thought. She said, "He's got long hair, he's got only one ear, and he looks like he's wearing acrylic fingernails. How can you say . . . ?"

Deborah giggled. "Oh, you know what I mean."

They made their way to a café beside the seawall. This part of Sydney usually felt clean and crisp from the salty air off the harbor, but the wind was already hot and the temperature was climbing through the twenties. Weasel glanced to the west, to the skies over Parramatta.

"Cumulonimbus," she said. "That'll be the thunderstorm this arvo."

Every few minutes, ferries surged against the nearby wharves, unloaded and loaded passengers, and departed on a whirlpool, while overhead, seagulls balanced on the air, screaming to be fed. A few yachts were already out; by noon, there would be scores of them tacking back and forth, since Wednesday was a racing day for people who could afford time off in the middle of the week.

"You notice so much," murmured Smith. "I don't know how you do it."

Weasel felt herself relax. "Don't you?" she said. "Don't you know the basic—"

"I wish you'd teach me," Smith interjected. Sergeant Miller remained outwardly calm. She had already established that Deborah was also on leave until Easter Monday. The way things were going, they could spend Thursday and Friday in bed.

"Have I said something wrong?" Deborah asked.

Weasel had turned to hide her smile and was staring across the water. As she looked at Smith again, she saw a man she recognized coming toward them. She narrowed her eyes, trying to recall where she had seen him before. Was he on a suspect list? Every day, she spent forty minutes memorizing faces, and she reckoned she now had about two thousand mug shots stored in her head. A gust of wind lifted his long hair and made it lash about.

"Tell you what," she said. "How about we decide on a mark—any mark—and spend until lunchtime on a surveillance exercise. Then we can have lunch and . . ."

"Fabulous!" Smith said.

"Okay. Pick someone."

Deborah glanced around. "Him," she said, as Parker strode past.

It was a stupid choice because his height made him so easy to follow, but Sergeant Miller did not mention this. Instead, she leaned across the table and touched Deborah's hand. "Good," she said. "Let's do it." She had remembered he was the one they called Dandruff: a semi-frequent traveler to Thailand, who had had a brass elephant in his sock.

Parker was feeling hot and sticky after his cab ride from the domestic terminal. He sat on a wooden bench and tried to read the *Sydney Morning Herald*, but the wind buffeted the pages and after a few moments he gave up and looked irritably about. He had had a trying morning already. On the flight to Sydney he was seated beside the lunatic director of finance, on his way to the periodontist, who twitted him about the financing of U-1. "You must be onto some good contracts, John. I reckon that lab costs three hundred thousand dollars a year to run." Parker chose to remain silent, but after a few minutes the wretch plucked his sleeve. "Why are you going to Sydney?" he asked.

"I'm giving a lecture at Sydney University."

"I'd like to come to that."

"It's by invitation only, I'm afraid. Had I known you were interested, I'd have arranged a ticket."

A party of adolescent schoolchildren spilled onto the quay, apparently free to spend their last day before the Easter break on a trip to the zoo. A teacher tried to quiet them, but already they had broken into rival gangs and were yelling insults at each other. One pimpled youth was teasing a colossal puppy of a girl, who emitted ear-splitting squeals. Suddenly she leaped up and ran. As she dashed past the bench where Parker was sitting, he darted his foot forward.

"Oh, sorry! Sorry!" she said as she picked herself up. Her palms were grazed.

He gave a nod of acknowledgment for her apology.

The ferry arrived. Parker hung back while mothers pushed strollers on board and the yelling mob of schoolchildren surged forward. He was just about to step onto the end of the gangplank when a woman's voice called, "Hold it!" He looked round. A creature with a face like a rat and peroxide hair was taking a photograph of a friend.

Minutes later, when he was standing at the bow, admiring the harbor, he saw them again. The rat-faced woman was still photographing her friend, who was equipped with a glorious set of mammary glands. Parker did not consider himself a breast man, but hers were so palpable he had an urge to squeeze them with both hands. The one with the camera said, "To the left a bit." He was standing to her left. The voluptuous one simpered at him as she stepped closer. He gave a hesitant smile.

"Sorry," she said.

"I don't mind at all."

For a moment the three of them said nothing. Then the rat piped up, "I'll take both of you."

Parker smiled down at the glorious udders and put his arm around her shoulders. He breathed in deeply. "The sea breeze," he said. "Lovely smell of dilate dimethyl sulfide."

"Beg yours?"

"I'd like to stroke your clitoris," he added quietly.

"*Pardon?*"

He switched on his moth-eaten smile. "Say cheese."

As soon as he heard the click, he disengaged his arm. How much more exciting, he thought, as he moved away from them, to do everything in imagination, instead of groveling about in copulation, with its smells and noises. He had enjoyed thinking about what he would do to Lek much more than actually doing it. One never seemed able to achieve exactly what one fancied.

On the northern shore of the harbor, a bus was waiting to take the ferry passengers to the main gate of the zoo. Weasel wanted to know what the mark had said to Smith.

"I didn't hear," Deborah insisted.

They paid their entrance fees. Ahead of them, Parker was crossing the road, striding toward the information desk, where a vivacious, well-groomed matron wore a badge saying FRIEND OF THE ZOO.

She gave him a map and, leaning over the counter, pointed out where he was now—"near the alligators"—and what to look for in this area: koalas, then the giraffe paddock to the left, and, not far away, the chimps. "So sweet," she said. "They've got lots of babies at the moment, with little white topknots of hair." She pointed with a red-lacquered nail to drawings of an elephant, a tiger, a rhino, hippo, orangutan, camel, crocodile, bears . . . "The insect house, the seal playpen." She wound up with an expansive gesture that knocked a kilo bag of compost off the counter, onto Parker's foot. He picked it up and handed it to her. "I'm so sorry!" she said. "There really isn't enough space for the Zoo Doo here." Her diamond-ringed hands set the bag upright again. "But people love it, you know. If you're a gardener . . ."

"I'll buy some on the way out," Parker said, with a courteous nod.

What an interesting face, she thought. Such appealing eyes.

P arker had almost an hour to spare before the rendezvous at the chimpanzee enclosure. He bought a soft drink from the kiosk and sat in the shade to read his newspaper. It was the usual set of catastrophes: war, famine, and stalled peace talks. Things will be different soon, he reflected. In a few years, a live birth will be page one news.

"He's meeting someone," Weasel said. She had explained to Smith that their aim now was to make themselves invisible to the mark while at all times keeping him in sight. "He's making it easy for us," she added.

Now and again, Parker allowed his attention to drift away from the dreary pap of economic and political woes and linger on his amorous encounter on the ferry. My sex life is undergoing a renaissance, he thought, recalling in detail what he had done with Sonja three nights earlier and then the fun he'd had with Lek. In the months during which he was concentrating on perfecting Vaccine II, Sonja's conjugal demands had been loathsome, but now that he was feeling confident about the progress of V II, he was thinking about sex a great deal. He wondered if he could find the bosomy girl again and say, "Come here and I'll lick between your toes," and watch her squirm.

The gardens were beginning to get crowded. He threw his newspaper in a bin and looked around at the scores of people, white for the most part, although many of these were torturing their natural color to a reddish brown. "Your hobby is growing skin cancers, is it?" he murmured to a blonde who had fried herself the color of teak. She had a cystal dolphin hanging around her neck. Parker particularly disliked dolphinophiles. They were among the worst of the ecomystics, the ones who would close the schools and universities, except for courses in "feeling." In them he detected the signs of the tide of superstition that was sweeping forward, bringing a new Dark Age. He passed a middle-aged woman with art nouveau fairies hanging from her ears. "New Age thought policewoman," he muttered. When he first met Sonja she wore fairy earrings after office hours. He gave a whinny of disgust.

A sign on the low Cyclone-wire fence said PAN TROGLODYTES, beside a map of Africa showing in black the areas where chimpanzees came from. In theory, Parker said to himself. The poor old trogs will be extinct soon, unless something is done about Africa.

Inside the fence there was a moat of khaki water and, behind it, a grassy hillside with bushes, a tall dead tree, rocks, and climbing structures. The chimps, although captive, were untamed. They bounded, loped, and staggered about in boisterous activity, like a game of football, all jinks and dashes, unexpected U-turns and sudden acts of aggression. A big male bared his fangs at a female who was eating an apple, then reached to snatch it from her. "Get it, boy!" Parker called out. But the female turned and offered as a distraction her raw pink behind. "It's a trick," Parker said to no one in particular. A mother pushing a pair of twins in a stroller moved away from him. Above them, the sky was turning purple-gray, and the heat had suddenly increased. Leaves twisted fretfully in the hot breeze. Parker stood close to the wire, shaking his head at the big black male; while he was copulating, she was gobbling up the apple, and as soon as she finished the last bite she stood up, almost knocking her lover off his feet. "Sucker," Parker chortled. He glanced around and noticed Somchai at the far end of the wire, standing near one of the zoo security guards, a uniformed man with a walkie-talkie. Somchai had been watching him, he realized, but when they made eye contact the Thai gave a very small shake of his head.

Somchai had been waiting by the chimpanzee enclosure for almost two hours. The security guard, who did not like the look of him, had finally decided to question him. Somchai thought he was a policeman and was terrified. I should have done exactly what Khun

Otto told me, he rebuked himself. He had never seen so many white people. Their horrible pale eyes would not leave him alone.

On the hillside beyond the moat, the chimps hooted, hugged, bit and caressed each other. Their hands were like those of very old workmen, with black wrinkled skin and nails as thick as curved stones. From time to time they paused to cast yearning, puzzled glances at the humans on the other side of the moat.

After watching them for a few minutes, Parker felt melancholy. One point six percent, he said to himself. There was only 1.6 percent difference between the DNA of Pan troglodytes and Homo sapiens. When he thought about the limitations imposed on man by evolution, what a tiny flame his intellect was, what an ocean of darkness his inheritance from the animal world, was it any wonder an intelligent man despaired?

The air was so hot, it was difficult to breathe.

With an effort, Parker drew back from his reflections on the human race and looked around for Somchai again. The Thai had vanished. Then a movement caught Parker's attention, a flash like a match flaring. He saw Somchai waiting for him about five meters away, on a path leading down toward the harbor. When they made eye contact, the Thai again gave a small shake of his head. Parker knew these Bangkok louts. The climate turned their brains to oil. They throve on drama—and you could add to that Asian shyness, the way they preferred to do things unseen. All the same, he felt faintly alarmed.

The Thai was carrying a blue backpack and kept just ahead of him on the brick path, his shoulder-length hair floating up and down in the hot, gusty wind. At the end of the path there was a cage of orangutans.

Somchai leaned on the outer wire, with his fingers hooked through it, pretending to watch an ape that swung listlessly from an old tire. The policeman, as he thought him, had not bothered to follow Somchai, and there were no other policemen in sight now. A group of people shouted at the orangutan, trying to stimulate it to do something interesting. After a while they drifted away, giving Parker room to stand beside Somchai. As soon as he moved forward, the Thai walked off toward a grove of hakeas.

Parker waited for a moment, then followed. He felt anxious, foolish, and irritable from the heat and the effort of skirting the dry, twisted trees without having his eye poked by their small, tough leaves.

The hakea grove ended in a cliff bisected by a flight of broken steps. Somchai did not really know what he was doing; he just wanted to get away from the hundreds of foreigners.

Parker peered over the edge and saw the Thai already at the bottom of the steps, signaling him to follow. Down there, hidden from public view, the park turned into a wilderness. There was nobody else in sight. Parker moved his feet gingerly, negotiating the crumbling stairs.

Above him, Susan Miller was standing on the edge of the hakea grove, waiting for Smith, who had gone to find a toilet. It had been a boring exercise until a few moments ago. But after Debbie left, Weasel had realized with a jolt that the mark was ticktacking with the long-haired Asian she had seen leaving the flight from Bangkok that morning. The mark was a frequent visitor to Thailand, and now he had a clandestine meeting in the zoo? Christ almighty! This is a handover, she thought. The backpack was luggage from the hold; it had got past the sniffer dog.

Weasel remembered from the zoo map that there was a service road branching off a path about fifty meters away. The road, she recalled, led down to the area where the mark was heading. She began to run.

Down below, it was as hot as a jungle and had the warm stink of rotting vegetation. There were long canes of elephant grass ending in feathery seed heads, lambs'-tongue, purple trumpets of morning glory, spicy-smelling lantana vines, and crofton weed. Ahead of Parker, the Thai ran through the knee-high grass, turning every so often to look back. They came upon an earth path that ended in a curved concrete wall. Somchai disappeared behind it. When Parker followed him around the curve, he realized they had reached the Zoo Doo pit; inside the concrete semicircle was a mountain of garden cuttings, straw, shredded paper, and animal dung. In the dripping heat, he could feel waves of hotter air rising from the compost. Parker wiped sweat from his eyes with his sleeve.

"What's wrong?" he demanded.

"Police following me," Somchai said. He glanced at the clifftop, which was now all they could see of the zoo. The humidity and the storm in the air made Parker feel he could keel over.

"Don't be bloody ridiculous! Why would the police be following you?"

At that moment, Weasel came dashing at full tilt around the side of the compost pit, as astonished at running into them as they were at seeing her. "Police!" she shouted. She reached into her bag for her pass. Somchai bent quickly to the ground. "Stand up!" she yelled.

He had his knife in his fist—and suddenly it flew.

Weasel collapsed like an ox. When he pulled the blade out of her throat, a gout of blood bubbled after it. Somchai grunted and, grasping a handful of yellow hair, cut her from ear to ear.

Parker was hypnotized. He had seen knifings in movies but had never realized how extraordinary the reality would be. Its speed was astonishing. One moment, a human. The next, the human had vanished. "Beautiful," he whispered. It was beauty in the Greek sense, something mysterious, something divine.

Somchai wiped his hands on the grass, stood up, unzipped his fly, and urinated. Parker walked forward as if in a trance, unzipped, and began to piss too, but as his water started to flow he suddenly laughed, and he hosed back and forth, up and down, squirting everywhere—in a nostril, into the ear, into her mouth, shouting with laughter. Somchai turned away from him.

An electric whip lashed the sky. The air beat time for a few seconds before the thunderclap; a drop of rain shattered on the ground, and in less than a minute lightning and thunder crashed together. Raindrops fell so hard they bounced half a meter into the air. Somchai threw back his head, held up his arms, and let red serpents of water leap wriggling from his body to the ground, where they scurried off into the earth. In minutes he was washed clean and Weasel's blood was sluicing off the concrete.

They heaved the corpse into the compost and tossed in her handbag, then shoveled compost on top of her. When she was buried, they stood back to hold up their hands and faces to the waterfall. Parker swung Weasel's Nikon around his neck. "Let's go," he said. He gave Somchai a gentle push.

Parker led the way along a flattened earth path that ran close to the face of the cliff and found, at the end of it, a neglected Cyclone-wire fence. Neither spoke, for their only interest was in escape. After a few meters they came across a section of fence that had been pushed down and trampled. On the ground nearby, there was one small football boot, a pair of socks, and a Latin dictionary. They had discovered, Parker realized, the school children's entrance to the zoo. It came out on the roadway above the wharf.

Half a dozen dripping people were waiting for the ferry, which stood off the wharf, pitching and rolling in the rain-lashed waves. Branches of trees floated past. Parker and Somchai sat apart on wooden benches. From time to time Parker glanced proudly at the Thai and looked away, smiling to himself. Then his expression became grim as he tried to work out why the police bitch had taken his photograph. He dared not question Somchai yet, in case people remembered seeing them together on the zoo wharf.

Abruptly the wind and rain abated. A bus arrived and debouched more wet people. The ferry departed. Halfway to Circular Quay, the sun appeared in a fresh blue sky. It was two-forty-five in the afternoon.

At three o'clock, Deborah Smith realized she had lost Sergeant Miller. Feeling rather offended and something of a failure, she decided to go home. That evening, she caught the train to Albury, to stay with her mum and dad.

Once the ferry had set off, Parker made eye contact with Somchai, then left the warm, diesel-smelling cabin to stand outside at the rail. After a few moments he sensed Somchai standing beside him and, without looking, cupped his large white hand over the pygmy fist. "Thank you, dear boy," he murmured. "Why were the police following you?"

"Bad men," the Thai said. "Bad men make trouble for Khun Otto."

"Who?"

"Photographer. Thin nose. Bad, bad man." He screwed up his face as if he had sucked a lemon.

"What trouble?"

"He tell lies about Khun Otto. Wanting hurt him. Say he doing illegal. Make trouble with animal people."

The Pembridge bitch is involved in this, Parker thought. Sonja had been right about her.

From Circular Quay they caught a train to Town Hall. In Gowing's, Parker bought himself and the Thai tracksuits, socks, underpants, and cheap sports shoes. He also bought a baseball cap to cover Somchai's hair. In their new, dry clothes, they ate in a café in the railway arcade. What an adventure, Parker kept telling himself. He was terrified of being recognized and could hardly swallow his toasted sandwich, but the excitement was fantastic. I've never felt so alive, he thought. By four o'clock they were in a cab, going to the domestic airport.

Kerry Larnach always allowed Parker to wait in the room in the terminal building used by Kalair crew between flights. After a while all the aircrew left, and Parker grabbed the telephone. He rang Grossmann at his office in Bangkok, catching him just before a meeting was due to begin.

"We had a bit of trouble earlier today," he said. "The gendarmes."

"Bad?" Grossmann asked.

"Yes."

"I have a beautiful new lab here, John."

Parker glanced around to reassure himself he was alone except for Somchai. "Otto," he whispered, "I have to get out as soon as possible. So does the boy."

"That's exactly what I've been asking you to do for more than a year, my friend. But the boy needn't return. Could you, ah, leave him in Sydney?"

"No!" Parker exclaimed.

"Too bad. Well, see you soon."

They caught the last flight to Kalunga, which departed at six-fifteen.

Whether Administration said that U-1 had been removed from the list for the day's tour, Diana replied, "Not from my list." She turned to the other new members of the Ethics Committee. One was a middle-aged nun, the other an elderly man who bred Persian cats. The nun, Diana thought, had a resolute air. "What about your list?" she asked.

"It's on my list," the nun replied.

"Seems to be on mine," the breeder said.

"So let's go," Diana said, and moved off toward the Land Cruiser.

Administration found his voice. "You can't," he said, and caught Diana by the sleeve. "You can't go there today because it's a high-containment laboratory and the overseer, Dr. Parker, is away. He specifically asked that no tour is made of U-1 without his presence. So I'm sorry, Miss Pembridge, I can't allow it. It's dangerous."

"*Dangerous?*"

"It's high-containment." He had never been inside U-1 himself.

Diana appealed with a glance to the nun. "We don't want to see the high-containment area. We only want to see the animals. Isn't that so?"

The nun nodded.

"I'm afraid I have no authority for that." His pink lips were pressed together inside their furry retreat.

"Very well," Diana said. "I want to speak to the director of security immediately." Her hand inside her bag was grasping the fax from Oregon about the chimp hair she had found on Sonja's jacket. It could be from the circus chimp; but until that was proved, Diana had a case.

Administration smirked. "That's impossible, I'm afraid. The director of security is attending a personnel development course all day."

"Christ almighty!" Diana blurted. "Bureaucracy! The rule of *Nobody.*"

Administration inflated his chest. "Shall we continue?"

The cat breeder nodded and the nun said, "Yes, please." Diana tagged along behind.

The flight path from Sydney was due west, at first over the gleaming rope of the Nepean River and the dark folds of the mountains. Somchai had a seat aft and had gone to sleep a few minutes after takeoff. Parker was just behind the grubby blue curtain that separated the pilot from the cabin, and he had a magnificent view of the evening light spreading across the countryside below. The storm had cleared the sky of pollution, and now the air sparkled. I've come to love this light, Parker thought, and for a moment felt sorry he was seeing it for perhaps the last time. Then fury with Grossmann returned. Leave the boy in Sydney, eh? he said to himself. Such a brave and loyal boy! Somchai would cut off his right hand for Otto. Parker smiled to himself and settled to the task of working out *how* they could all leave Australia—he, Somchai, Phil, Freddie, and Steve. And Sonja and Lek, of course. It was essential that the boys come to Thailand with him, and he began to think of arguments to convince them to leave willingly, and immediately. He considered how long it would take, with seven of them working, to pack up Sonja's house and U-1. They would have to leave the heavy machines, but they would take the computer and all the parts of V II, and of course the frozen aliquot of White Eye. He considered the type of refrigeration he would need on the flight to Bangkok and how they would transport the chimpanzees. There would be seven passengers, plus two chimps, plus another hundred kilos of equipment, plus some household goods and their clothing. The boys would not have much luggage, Lek and Somchai would have none. An aircraft this size would do it, he thought. But how to fly out of the country undetected?

He plucked at the grimy blue cloth in front of him, pulling it aside far enough to see the copilot's head.

"Excuse me," he called over the engine noise.

"Yes, mate?"

"Do you know where Mr. Larnach will be this evening?"

The copilot consulted a clipboard.

"Kalunga," he said.

Parker settled back to enjoy the rest of the flight.

Out west it stayed light longer than on the coast, so as the aircraft descended and circled the airfield, passengers could see the white crop dusters moored at the perimeter fence and the cars of people waiting to meet them parked behind the terminal. There was no white Land Cruiser there. Where's Sonja? Parker wondered.

By the time the Cessna had landed and taxied to a halt, it was dark on the ground, as he had hoped it would be. He wanted Somchai to go unnoticed, although in the bush, people noticed everything. But with luck, Parker thought, anyone who sees Somchai will take him to be a kitchen hand in the new Chinese restaurant. It was essential that when he got into Sonja's Cruiser, nobody was around. At the base of the steps, Parker gave Somchai a signal to become invisible and wait, while he made his way across the concrete to the Kalair shed. My mind is lucid. I am in command, he told himself. For a moment a delicious spasm shook his insides as he remembered the killing at the zoo.

The Kalair office at the airport was a converted two-bedroom weatherboard house. Spare uniform jackets hung from pegs on the walls, and unwashed coffee cups cluttered the sink. After ten years' hard labor, Kalair was still a shoestring operation, with maintenance done at night and on weekends. Larnach had to hire an aircraft to service his Sydney–Kalunga route during the biannual major check. A big maintenance job was due the week after Easter, but so far nobody would rent him a replacement at a rate he could afford. Bookings were good over Easter; he could pay wages for another ten days, or he could hire an aircraft while the maintenance was being done. He could not afford both.

When Parker arrived at the door on Wednesday night, Larnach was trying to find a solution to his problem. He had pulled up on his computer screen a list, hacked from the Ansett Airlines database, of all the aircraft spare parts in the world.

"How would you like a one-way charter job for seven people and two trogs to Bangkok?" Parker asked.

Larnach leaned back in the swivel chair. Seven? he wondered, counting off Parker, Sonja, the three lab technicians, the Thai girl. Who was the seventh? "Tell me more."

"Leaving tomorrow night."

"Thursday? Thursday's hard, mate."

Parker's jaw clenched. "Friday morning, then? Early."

"Can't think of anything I'd like better." It occurred to Kerry to ask what had happened, but he decided that the less he knew, the better. When you've just won the lottery, you don't ask why.

"Mind if I use your phone?" Parker said.

Cheap bastard should buy a mobile, Kerry thought.

Parker made a quick call to tell Grossmann they were leaving Australia on Friday. Then he rang Sonja's house, although he was not expecting her to be home; he thought she would be on her way to the airfield to collect him and Somchai. But after a few rings the telephone switched automatically from the house to U-1, and she answered it there.

"I'm at the airfield. Why aren't you here?" he said.

She giggled. "Sorry, darling. I'm busy. Is everything okay?"

Idiotic question, he thought: *everything* is never okay. "Of course. Are you coming to collect us or not?"

"Could you possibly get the air taxi? I'm really . . ." She made a simpering noise.

Larnach half listened, sneering to himself in disbelief. Fifteen minutes ago, he was a bankrupt. Now he was a free man. He had the scenario for liberty in his head: Fly the Cessna 421 to Bangkok, sell it, use the cash to buy into a business up there. Why didn't I think of doing that before? he wondered. Selling an aircraft was like selling a motorcar: you changed the registration and filed off the engine number. "No problem, mate," he said to Parker. "I'll fly you home."

"There's someone else."

Somchai was waiting in the dark outside the Kalair office. The seventh man, Larnach thought.

Night had settled by the time the taxi was above the lake. The water gave off a Morse code of silver in the moonlight; in the darkness ahead they could see the lights of the laboratory complex and, beyond, the condominiums. Parker grunted with satisfaction when suddenly the lights on the airfield were illuminated. Headlights were moving toward it. "There's Sonja," he said.

When the Cruiser pulled up on the concrete under her house, Parker stared at his wife. She looked overexcited. Had she been silly and skipped a meal that day? Or binged on coconut fudge? he wondered.

"What happened to your clothes?" she asked gaily.

"There was a storm. We got wet." He rested his hand on Somchai's shoulder and felt with pleasure the strong muscles beneath the fabric of his tracksuit. "Are you warm enough, dear boy?"

Somchai nodded.

Sonja giggled again and glanced down. Suddenly Parker realized what it was that he found disturbing: she had the I've-been-naughty look plastered across her face.

"What have you been up to?" he asked cautiously.

Diana stamped straight down to the aviary when she got home from the Research that day. After her outburst over U-1, the animal house inspection had turned into a disaster. She had been too forthright. "I accept that science and farm animals are slaves," she'd remarked, "and I look forward to the abolition of slavery." "*Slaves?*" the nun said in a scandalized tone. "Well, what else are they?" Diana replied. The cat man had already written her off as an extremist, and the nun, whom Diana had hoped to have as an ally, rejected her for blaspheming.

"It was a fiasco," she told the eagle, who continued to gaze at a cloud twenty kilometers away. Diana was irritated that she had given up the eagle's morning exercise in order to traipse around the Research and learn little more than she already knew, although she had to admit that it seemed none of the lab complex buildings had walled-off sections where animals could be hidden. It was now too late in the day to drive out to the flying hill. No exercise meant no food, for the eagle had to lose a lot of weight in the next two or three months. But the bird was tense, Diana noticed, waiting to be fed.

She approached with the hood, which she always put on before carrying her inside for the night. But as she moved forward, it seemed to dawn on the eagle that after waiting all day, she would be left hungry. A look of outrage fixed in her eyes, and she jumped down to the concrete and flung herself backward on her tail, ready for a fight. She'll break her tail feathers! Diana thought.

For five minutes they glared at each other. Then Diana went back to the kitchen to microwave a mouse from the box in the freezer. When she returned to the aviary, swinging the mouse by its tail, the eagle gave a disdainful sideways glance. A second later, she gulped it down. Then, with dignity, she stepped onto Diana's arm.

When Diana returned to the kitchen, Grace, who was shelling peas and trying to keep the kids from eating them out of the colander, noticed that her colors were in a turmoil. Diana slouched onto a stool beside the kitchen table. "You know what?" she asked after a while.

Grace shook her head.

"I'm sure they've got chimpanzees in that bloody place!"

The boys stared at each other.

"What place?" Tom piped up.

"The Research. I think they've got animals there that they won't admit to. And I think they're keeping them underground in the old dam, out near the lake. Where they've put the house with the solar panels."

Tom's little brown fingers clasped the edge of the table, and his face appeared. Billy scrambled up from the floor.

"You want some fruitcake?" Diana asked. She cut off two hunks and handed them a piece each, but they kept staring at her expectantly. She tickled Billy inside his ear, which he loved. "Eat your cake," she said. She looked from one to the other, puzzled.

Billy said, "Promise you won't be cross?"

"*What have you been doing?*" their grandmother said.

"She's cross," Tom whispered.

For a moment all four were silent. "I won't be cross," Diana said. "Tell me."

Tom yelled, "They've got little grillers down there! Billy saw them!" He jumped with glee. "Little grillers! Just like Bubbles!"

Sonja sauntered off toward the door to U-1.

"Stay here," Parker told Somchai.

She walked straight through the Big Lab to the door that opened onto the corridor outside Level 2. When he followed her through it, she was already putting on a gown. Parker felt his calm dissolve. She's done something to the vaccine! he thought. Or even mucked about with White Eye.

She handed him a pair of latex gloves. While he was pulling them on, she heaved open the next door and disappeared inside.

The high-containment laboratory was in a mess. There was a blanket on the floor, and torn clothing was strewn about. He stooped to pick up a pair of scissors and, as he did so, looked over toward the bone saw. There was a naked bluish-brown foot, sawn off at the base of the fibula. He walked over and picked up the foot. It was frozen solid. He laid it on the table beside what else was left of Lek. Other parts of her were already packed into an autoclave bag standing open in its cart beside the bone saw. The plastic tent that covered the saw was spattered with skin and bone fragments, but there was surprisingly little blood. Sonja had bled her, Parker realized, before freezing her.

"Where's the blood?" he asked.

She pointed to a couple of large ethanol containers standing on the floor near the freezer, filled with dark-red liquid. How did she know how to do it? he wondered, then reflected that she had seen him bleeding a chimp before dissecting it for the autoclave. It wasn't difficult.

"That autoclave bag is too full," he said. From what he could see, it contained a leg, or perhaps two legs (minus one foot), and an arm.

"How will I cut the head?" Sonja asked.

She had positioned Lek's torso, which was all that remained intact, so that it lay straight on the table. The head was covered by the plastic tent. Parker peered through it, intending to take just an analytical look, but he found himself mesmerized, as he had been by the corpse in the zoo.

"Fantastic," he murmured. The small dark-brown eyes were open and stared up at him with an obedient expression, quite flat now, due to postmortem loss of fluid. *I am powerful,* he thought with a thrill. "Would you like me to do it?" he asked. It would take only another ten minutes to get the carcass broken down and packed into four separate autoclave bags. He would call Somchai in to help them clean up at the end.

As he worked, he questioned Sonja. "Where did she die?" he asked.

"In the cabin," his wife replied brightly. "I used my bike to carry her through the garden. What a lump!" She giggled. "Then I dragged her in here on the blanket."

He nodded attentively.

"I bled it, and when it was stiff enough—that was about six o'clock this morning—I came downstairs and put it in the freezer. It was easy to maneuver by then."

Parker was moving his head from side to side in admiration.

The bone saw worked on a foot pedal, which he pressed as he pushed the skull toward the whining blade. He wanted to ask how she had killed Lek, but a certain delicacy silenced him. He concentrated on the head, which fell neatly into two parts like a halved fruit: squishy pale flesh and a complex endocarp of pons, thalamus, cerebellum, and medulla. He turned to smile at Sonja. "You're quite a gal," he said.

She gave him a coy look above the edge of the blue cotton mask. "It's not the first time."

"Carolyn?"

She nodded. "I gave her a lift home from town one night—you were away, and I'd had dinner with Jason. She'd been out drinking and fucking, by the smell of her—seemed in a reckless sort of mood. She said, 'John's got chimps in U-1, hasn't he?' I said, 'Come down and see for yourself.' And she did."

Parker chuckled. "Anyone else?"

"I shouldn't tell." Then she giggled. "Jason. But I forgot he was left-handed!"

"Tsk-tsk," Parker said.

He unzipped the front flap of the plastic tent and lifted it back to remove the sawn fragments. "You'll be pleased to know that in thirty-six hours we're all leaving for Thailand. You, me, the boys, Sailor, and Lucy . . ." He glanced at the autoclave bags. "—And this too."

Sonja sighed. "You've no idea what I've been through in the past four weeks," she said. "But shouldn't we do something about the Pembridge woman before we leave?"

"What do you suggest?" Parker asked.

Chapter Twenty

That night, a message flashed onto the computer screens of domestic airline booking offices around the country, announcing that due to the unserviceability of its aircraft, Kalair would not be able to provide its Good Friday and Easter Saturday flights between Kalunga and Sydney. Passengers were asked to make other arrangements, while being assured that the company's service would return to normal on Sunday. Most Easter holiday travel was on Thursday, so the cancellation affected fewer than sixty people. Some managed to squeeze onto other flights, some hired cars, some booked to go by train, and others decided to stay at home.

Michael Romanus slept for twelve hours at the Airport Hilton and woke early on Thursday, feeling as if he had just alighted on earth. Outside his window, the sky was as blue as a butterfly's wing.

In Kalunga, soon after dawn, Diana took the eagle to the flying ground and for half an hour made her glide from the fence post to her hand. Then she rested the bird while from inside the van she scrutinized Sonja's house with binoculars. People were arriving for work in the underground lab.

She flew the wedgetail for another half hour, feeling all her anxieties loosen as she worked, aware only of the movements of her dark companion. When, finally, she held her arm rigid for the huge feet, the hood in her other hand ready to slip over the eagle's head, she realized that a plan of action had formed in her mind: in the evening, she would return to the flying ground, walk over to Sonja's house, and see if she could get inside the lab, as Billy had, and take photographs of the chimps.

Back in Fig Tree Gully Road, she had to spend the rest of the morning organizing flat-bottomed boats for the lake tour the following day. Grace knew the lake even better than Diana, and although she was no longer agile, they decided they would both go as guides. Diana told Grace her plan for the evening.

"I'll leave the flying ground at dawn at the latest, so I'll be home by six-thirty or seven," she said.

Grace was silent. There was sorrow and alarm in her eyes.

"I've got to, Gracie. I can't turn my back on what they're doing out there. Eh?"

Grace heaved herself to her feet. "Let me come with you."

"No! Absolutely not. Who's going to look after the bird-watching people? They've paid to stay here."

"Tell you what, then," Grace said. "You take Billy and Tom and them night binoculars they stole. You tell 'em to stay back behind the fence and watch. Any trouble, they honk the horn, shoot in the air, make a noise, get them security guards running." She sighed. "Wish I could still run. I'd come with you. Use t' run like a wallaby when I was a girl."

Diana put her arms around Grace. "Ah, you fat old thing," she murmured.

At lunchtime, the boys arrived from school. Grace and Diana told them the plan, then calmed them down so that the van could be packed quickly.

At the flying ground, the sky was still bright but the sun's heat was fading. Diana pulled up behind the low hill that obscured the Research buildings, and while Tom kept watch on Sonja's house, she and Billy knocked over a section of the old fence so the van could be parked closer to the mountain, under the cover of the pines. "We've got to be invisible from the air," Diana said.

They covered the roof and sides with a green tarpaulin to make the van less conspicuous. All through their preparations, Diana hoped Morrie might show himself and give the boys a thrill, but there was no sign of him.

Michael Romanus arrived with all his camera gear in Eddy Avenue, opposite Central Railway Station, at 10:00 A.M., ready to catch the special bus to Kalunga. He was not sure where it would pull up, but he recognized the group waiting for it. There were half a dozen young women with crew cuts and nose jewels, and some older ones carrying thermos flasks and novels. In a group apart, three men with beards were talking to a pair of lithe, tattooed boys. Another man was entertaining them by walking on his hands. I've been too long in Asia, he thought. He felt burdened, worldly, and sharpened—or was it blunted?—by ancient cultures and vices, and too full of anger about Raoul to share the high spirits of his traveling companions. Around the corner came a gaudy vehicle with SABOTAGE! painted along both sides. Underneath, it said SAVE AUSTRALIA'S BIRDS, OUR TREES, ANIMALS, AND GREAT ENVIRONMENT. There were paintings of animals, flowers, and birds around the message.

The driver had a clipboard with a list of names, which he called out in a loud, cheerful voice. When Romanus approached, he said, "Michael, right? Rang yest'dee?"

The bus rattled like a tambourine, jostling passengers against each other. It had no air-conditioning, and as it labored through the traffic on Paramatta Road, gusts of diesel exhaust blew through its open windows. Romanus covered his nose with a handkerchief. A girl came to sit beside him. She had seen the figure on the gold chain around his neck. "Is that your star sign? Are you a Scorpio?" she asked. She had translucent skin, through which, at the temples, a vein pulsed softly. When he said, "No—it's a Thai good-luck charm," she was disappointed. He asked, "Do you know the woman who's taking us out on the lake tomorrow? What's she like?"

The girl glanced behind before answering. "Some people don't like her. She shoots rabbits and foxes."

And blokes, if she can, Romanus thought.

"Do you shoot?" she asked suddenly.

"Only with a camera." She smiled serenely and from time to time touched his arm with long, pale fingers. He began to imagine how she would look naked: too thin, too delicate.

By late afternoon the bus was passing broad fields of green wheat that stretched to the horizon; some were interspersed with paddocks of ewes, their sides bulging with unborn lambs. "See the beautiful curve as she turns," Romanus said to the girl. He got a camera out and focused on a pregnant ewe, but the bus shook too much for him to take a photograph.

When they arrived in Fig Tree Gully Road, the deep blue of the inland sky had faded and orange light was filtering in from farther west.

Romanus wondered how batty Diana Pembridge was and how he should tell her about the Siam chimps and Raoul. He was not sure what to expect. The Spaniard had called her "attractive," but his taste in women was both catholic and bizarre. Romanus imagined a raw-boned country girl with a big voice and heavy thighs.

An old black woman opened the front door. Behind her was a large room with a wooden floor and Aboriginal paintings on its walls.

Everyone but him seemed to have organized an accommodation. Some were sleeping at the house; others were camping, and a few were booked into the motel. There was turmoil for twenty minutes while sleeping bags were unloaded and positions on the gallery floor staked out. The pale girl questioned Romanus with her lovely grave eyes, but he pretended not to notice. Until he had met the PRO rep, there was nothing he could decide. He followed Grace into the kitchen, where rows of scones were cooling on a rack.

"Been baking?" he said.

She gave a glum nod. The change from yesterday, when she had been so chatty on the phone, was strange.

She was shuffling between the refrigerator and the kitchen table with dishes of butter and jars of jam. "Diana and my boys, they go out after school," she said.

"Where'd they go?"

She raised her chin, pointing. "Research."

"Has Diana got a telephone with her?"

Grace shook her head and busied herself with serving the late-afternoon tea. Romanus found the back door and went out onto the terrace.

The sky was as red as fire beyond the tops of the tall trees in the garden. He pulled the phone from his shirt pocket and dialed. The android answered. "Good evening," it said. "You have called the Exotic Feral Species and Microbiology Research Centre. If you wish to speak to someone in the residential complex, please press 1 now." He pressed 1, and when a human voice answered, "Condos," Romanus replied, "Dr. John Parker, please."

At first there was no answer. Then the human returned to say, "I'll try his wife's place." After a longish wait, during which the phone switched automatically from one line to another, a deep, melodious voice said, "Parker here."

Here goes, Romanus thought. "John—Michael Romanus. We met a few weeks ago in Saraburi," he said. "I've come to take some photographs on the lake."

On the other end of the line, Parker's tone changed to surprise.

"Good to hear from you so soon. Where are you?"

They chatted back and forth for a few minutes, until Parker said, "Why don't you come out and stay with us tonight? I'm afraid I can't offer to drive in and pick you up, but there's an air taxi service. The pilot happens to be here with us. Wait a moment." His hand muffled the receiver. "I've just had a word with him. He'll whiz in to the airfield and pick you up. You're in town, are you? It'll only take you ten minutes to drive to the airfield. Then it's another ten minutes to fly out here. No charge for the flight. It's on me."

Romanus returned to the gallery and from his gear removed the negatives of Somchai. He printed a note saying: "These are photographs taken by Raoul Sabea on 6 April showing Sila Somchai, a Thai chauffeur at Siam Enterprises, entering Raoul's room in the New Dawn guesthouse, Khao Sahn, Bangkok. I believe Somchai subsequently murdered Sabea on orders from Otto Grossmann." He signed his name and wrote the date, then scribbled a P.S.: "Going to meet Dr. John Parker at the Research." When no one seemed to be looking, he went up the flight of stairs between the gallery and the kitchen and found a room set up as an office. The desk had a stationery drawer, with envelopes of various sizes. He addressed one "Diana Pembridge, Personal, Confidential, by hand," slipped the negs and the note inside, and left it on the desk.

Downstairs, people were fretting that Diana was not home yet. The plan for the weekend was that they would leave early for the lake, and after spending the morning paddling through the lignum islands in flat-bottomed boats, they would have lunch and rest on the shore, then go on a second bird-watching expedition in the late afternoon. Diana had been organizing lake tours for several years, and some of the people had taken them before. "She'll turn up," they reassured the others. Romanus left quietly, under the reproachful gaze of the pale girl.

For ten dollars the bus driver took him to the airfield, one hand on the wheel while the other fed scones into his mouth. A very small Cessna was standing near the terminal shed, just as Parker had described. "Lotta gear," Kerry Larnach remarked as he heaved a camera bag into the cabin.

A full yellow moon floated above them. Kerry made no effort at conversation, except to shout over the noise of the engine, "That's

The Research," pointing at the lights of a miniature city shining out of the blackness. As the Cessna, bucking and waggling, dropped down toward the airstrip, Romanus saw the headlight of a vehicle coming to meet it.

John Parker was standing in front of a blue perimeter light, his long shadow stretched across the field almost to the wheels of the plane.

Larnach handed out Romanus's bags. "I gotta get goin'. Got a lotta work to do," he said. As soon as Romanus was clear of the propeller, Kerry turned the plane and began to taxi for takeoff. Parker came forward, hand outstretched, his shadow aping his movements. The light had turned one side of his face eerily blue, while the other side was in darkness. "And how's our Bavarian friend?" he asked, taking one of Romanus's bags.

"Ball of muscle, as usual."

Parker opened the front passenger door of the Land Cruiser for Romanus to climb inside.

Three hundred meters away, on the edge of the flying ground, Diana turned to Tom. "Let me look at him," she said. Tom handed her the night-sight binoculars, which she fastened on Parker. "Is he the man who arrived in his pajamas the other night?"

"I think so."

"Billy?"

"Dunno," Billy said. "Why don't we go closer?"

Diana looked back through the dark to where she knew the van was parked. They had left a hurricane lamp burning inside it, turned down low, but its glow was hidden by the tarpaulin. She got her bearings from the dark mass of the mountain, outlined against the sky by moonlight.

"Okay, we'll move forward," she said, "but you tell me first: where's the van?" They looked back, squinting, expecting to be able to see it. "What did I warn you?" she asked. "You've got to remember exactly, from the top of the mountain—"

"I know! I know where it is!" Billy said. He was pointing at the right place.

There was just enough light to walk to the Cyclone-wire fence without using a flashlight. A new lock had been put on the gate, but Diana now had a key. She decided to leave this gate open.

When they came out on the other side of the small hill, they saw Parker and dashed forward, trying to get a closer look at the person he was waiting to meet.

"Quick!" Diana said, handing the binoculars to Tom. "Who is he?"

Tom passed them to Billy, who shrugged. "Let me have another look," she said. The airfield illumination interfered with the night sights, and she had only a blurred image.

Romanus climbed in beside Parker, who seemed to be in an expansive mood. He pointed out that just over there, on the higher ground, was where they were going. His voice and the sound of the engine covered the slippery noise Somchai made when he sat up suddenly behind the front passenger seat. He made two fast, precise movements: his left hand grabbed Romanus by the hair, while his right pushed the point of the knife into his jugular vein.

Chapter Twenty-One

Romanus felt an electric shock of terror, then suddenly he was calm. The knife was pressed so hard against his throat that moving was impossible.

"Great hospitality," he muttered. The words came out half-strangled, but Parker had understood, all the same.

"I spoke to our friend Otto a few minutes ago. He's keen to talk to you about money you owe him, Michael. He wants you to return to Bangkok with us tomorrow."

By pushing air into the top of his lungs, Romanus found he could ease the pressure from his neck a little. He tried to answer, but only a gasp came out.

"Let him speak, dear boy," Parker said to Somchai.

Somchai let go of the strong, dark hair and eased his knife back, but with his left hand he grasped his prisoner on the carotid sheath on either side of his throat. Romanus felt woozy from the diminished flow of blood. He took a deep breath, but as he did so he felt a sharp sting. This time Somchai had cut him deliberately.

"Listen, mate," he panted, "the scam's up. We've got photographs, we've got bills of lading, we've got enough evidence to close down Siam's breeding farm and put Otto in jail. It's all with the police."

"Which police?" Parker asked.

Important point, Romanus thought. "The Australian Federal Police."

Parker seemed to consider this. While he did so, Somchai took the opportunity to press harder on the blood vessels in Romanus's neck. The knife blade felt like a thin, hot wire.

"Don't be crazy," he gasped. "The cops know I'm coming here. I don't owe Otto money—"

"Shut up," Parker said.

The blade moved quickly. Romanus realized he was slipping away, but he was helpless to do anything about it.

"There's somebody else in the Cruiser!" Tom whispered. "Look!" He handed the binoculars to Diana, who could just make out a third figure.

She and the boys continued to walk forward cautiously, one foot in front of the other, over the rough ground. This is how to get bitten by a snake, Diana thought. There were tiger snakes around the lake, and the ground was still warm enough for them to be lying about. Ahead lay Sonja's house, with all its lights on, looking as gay as a party. She stopped and lifted the daytime glasses to her eyes, trying to see inside. "Hey!" she said. "They're packing up!"

Inside the house, several figures were moving in and out of the main room, putting things into cardboard boxes. A long table was set up for dinner close to the glass doors on the veranda.

Diana watched the Land Cruiser disappear among the bushes of Sonja's garden. Parker ran upstairs to the house and downstairs again a few minutes later. Then, after a while, he and another man went inside the house. "There weren't three, there were only two in the Cruiser." Diana frowned. She squinted through the night binoculars again and saw that the man walking behind Parker was not the man who had arrived in the air taxi, nor was he one of the people she had observed arriving at U-1 that morning. His shoulder-length hair was colored green by the night sights. Inside the house, people stopped work and gathered around the dining table. She counted them: Sonja and five men, including Parker and the one with long hair. The others sat at the table while Parker appeared to make a speech, a champagne bottle in his hand. There was a burst of laughter when he finished talking. He poured each person a drink.

"They're going to toast something," Diana said.

"I'd like some toast," Tom murmured.

"There's only sandwiches," Billy said.

Diana smiled. "We'll go back to the van and eat."

She outlined her plan: The boys were to take turns keeping watch with the night binoculars while she went to the house. Every hour, she would come out of the garden and stand just left of the lamp that marked the junction between the spur road to Sonja's house and the road to the airfield, and she'd wave to them. If she did not appear or did not wave, Billy was to drive the van through the gate, across the paddocks, onto the road, and straight up to headquarters. "Honk the horn," she said. "Make a noise. They've got guards up at the labs and around the condos. Say I've broken into U-1."

"I haven't got a driver's license," Billy said. "I'll get in trouble." Diana put her hands around his soft little neck, as if to strangle him.

"If I blow my whistle," she said, "it means I'm in trouble and you're to drive straight to headquarters."

The boys kept watch on the house while she made up a bed in the back of the van. Despite the care she took in hosing it out daily, the sharp smell of bird dung still hung about. As soon as Tom climbed in and lay down, he wailed, "It stinks!" She had to move the bed outside.

It was ten o'clock by the time he was settled. Fifty meters away, Diana set up a second bed, for Billy, on a part of the flying ground from which there was a clear view of Sonja's garden. Diana had brought an alarm clock, which she set at one minute to eleven. When the alarm rang, Billy had to sit up and look through the night sights to see her waving. Then he had to reset the alarm clock for one minute to midnight. At 1:00 A.M., if she was still there and waving, he was to swap places with his younger brother.

Billy had told her that the door to U-1 was standing open the night he went in; he had not bothered to look at its lock. Diana suspected that it was likely to be a pin-number device, which she would have no hope of opening. But in case it was a simpler mechanism, she had brought bush keys: a bit of wire and a strip of plastic. Her other equipment was a small camera with a built-in flash, her pocketknife, the whistle, and a flashlight. If she could get inside the laboratory she would photograph the chimpanzees, the camera's electronic chip recording the date on which each photograph was taken. She knew she couldn't free the chimps: they could be infected with *anything*, and they would be stronger than she and likely to bolt.

It was cold, and the dew was so heavy that the gilgais had formed little ponds. Diana was wearing a padded parka and a woolen scarf, and as she set out across the paddocks she felt warm enough. The moon was high in the sky, yet there was not enough light to see easily, but she did not dare use the flashlight. She could remember, more or less, where the rabbit holes used to be, but had to walk looking down, sometimes stopping and feeling forward with the toe of her riding boot before taking a step. The yellow-lit house seemed a long way off. Whenever she glanced up at it, the people were still around the table. Occasional gusts of laughter rang out.

Parker was entertaining his boys with more stories of life in Thailand.

That morning when Phil, Steve, and Freddie had arrived for work, he announced, "We're moving to Thailand. There's trouble with Australian quarantine." They had known that, sooner or later, this would happen. It had been part of the thrill of working for the Doc: his technique was right on the leading edge, and so were his tactics.

He talked about the better jobs and better pay they'd have in Siam's big new biotech lab. "You'll all be able to afford a housekeeper," he said. "And girls! You've never seen such girls. . . ." He had carried them away into a land of luxury and easy brilliance, while their homes and families and colleagues grew small and dull and simple to leave behind. "I'm afraid, even if you wanted to, none of you would be able to find jobs in science in Australia for a while," Parker said. "Anyway, Asia's the place. Once you've worked in Thailand, you can move on to China. That's where the jobs will be. That's the place for great science, ten years from now."

He gave them the rest of the day to arrange their affairs: get cash, pay their debts if they wanted to, collect their passports, gather some hot-weather clothes, and make any necessary personal phone calls. "Say you've been offered a job in Thailand and you're flying up there over the Easter holidays for an interview," he said. He lent them Sonja's Land Cruiser in case they needed to drive into town.

By three o'clock that afternoon, they were all assembled in the icy whiteness of the Big Lab, where Freddie had hours of work on the computer before it would be ready to move. The others joined Parker in the tedious, fiddly task of packing up the laboratory and the animal house. "We must remove all traces of the chimpanzees," he insisted.

They vacuumed the floors and the walls and mopped the room twice. Then they wrapped the ape cages in clear plastic, making air-holes at the top. Lucy and Sailor poked more holes in the plastic, but the covering kept hair and skin flakes inside the cage. They could not risk burning the kindergarten furniture; local farmers would notice smoke and might even report it. They decided to break up the tables and chairs and dump the pieces, inside biohazard bags, in the giant autoclave up at the lab complex. Autoclave waste was put through a mashing machine and sold as landfill. They also bagged up thirty kilos of monkey chow, and the vacuum cleaner, and drove the lot to the big autoclave.

"By the way, where's Lek?" Freddie asked late in the afternoon. He had everything on backup now, in case something went wrong with the stack.

Parker was sitting at his bench, examining a gel. He hesitated, then laid the dish carefully on the white Formica benchtop. "I wasn't going to tell you," he said. He seemed to be struggling with himself. "You know she was 'sick' yesterday?"

Freddie nodded.

"She wasn't sick. She knew I was going to Sydney to meet the new keeper, so she took the opportunity to go AWOL. She's done a bunk. It seems she's been giving information about our setup here to animal activists in Thailand. We've got her to thank for our speedy departure."

"Sneaky bitch!"

Parker sighed. He was heartily sick of Lek now. While the boys had been out arranging their affairs that morning, he had had to cook her, bit by bit. In his small autoclave it had taken ages. He had two plans for what to do with the bags of sterile material. One was to take them on the aircraft and, at some point over the sea, throw them out. But what would he say was in the bags? Larnach was being officious about how much gear they could take. His second plan was more daring: to send off the bags, as normal, to be tossed in with all the other sterile waste that came from the huge autoclave up at the lab complex. But the image of a split head with its long black hair spilling out of a bag began to torment him. He remembered that Kalair carried mail. He rang Kerry and asked him to bring over a few mailbags. Lek would fit easily into two of them. I'll say it's documents, Parker decided.

When Diana reached Sonja's garden, she checked her watch: she had ten minutes before she had to wave to Billy. She crept quietly up the wooden stairs until she could see the legs of the people seated around the table. One more step, and she saw faces and the backs of heads. Sonja and Parker were seated at opposite ends of the table, while the diners on either side were the young men she had seen coming to work that morning. Up close, none of them looked like the man who had arrived in the air taxi, although it was difficult to be certain. The green of the night sights distorted her ability to match images. Who's the Asian? she wondered. Could Billy have mistaken him for a woman? He had very long hair for a man. His back was to Diana, and all she could tell about him was that he was short, thick-necked, and seemed tense: one bulging calf jigged under the table.

Everybody talked at once, and nobody seemed to be listening to anybody. "But what about extradition?" somebody shouted. "There's no treaty," another replied. "The Doc's right. China's the place. The Chinese are disciplined. We can thank Mao for that." Parker cut in: "The white race is on the way out." A young man laughed uproariously and pointed at the person opposite him. Parker held up his hand. There was a hush. "What about a song?" he said. "What about . . ." But before he could make a suggestion, two of the young men began to sway from side to side, bellowing, " 'If all those young ladies were little white rabbits . . .' " Parker beat out the bass line with his dessert spoon and bellowed along with the others. Diana stared at Sonja: she had a bright spot of color on either cheek but did not look drunk. Abruptly she turned and looked into the dark, as if she had felt Diana watching her.

Diana ran back down the stairs. She skirted the Land Cruiser and a heap of cardboard boxes and went to the door of U-1: it had a combination pad that needed code numbers.

Her watch said three minutes to eleven. She made her way through the cool, still garden to a spot a few meters to the right of the lamp. From the house, sounds of revelry floated out. The hour came. She waved and returned quietly to examine the boxes under the house.

The first box she opened was filled with decorated knick-knacks: a tea tray, a shoe last, a woman's wood-backed hairbrush with a pattern of cherubs and wreaths. The next box had an assortment of household equipment, including an electric whisk, a yogurt maker, and a dough hook. When she opened a box of summer clothes she thought, They're planning a garage sale. The fourth box had a piece of machinery similar to one she had seen during the inspection tour yesterday. None of these boxes was sealed. She eased up the tape on a fifth box with the point of her knife. Inside were two piles of hard-covered, large-format books with lined pages, each with a sticker giving a name and a date on its cover: the lab books of Phil Stephenson, Steve Watson, and John Parker. Are they going to work in a different laboratory? she wondered. Up at the main complex, perhaps?

She counted thirty in the box, stacked chronologically. The volumes on top had all been written up in the last months of 1992, while those immediately below were for earlier in the same year and from the previous year. She lifted out one whole stack and saw that the earliest book was dated June–December 1990. Parker's name seemed to be on more than ten books, as if he had kept the most complete records or had done most of the work. He must have recorded what he does with chimpanzees, she thought. Her hands shook as she opened a Parker book. The page was an impenetrable mass of unknown words, mathematical and chemical symbols, and groups of capital letters. She flipped pages, looking for a sentence she could understand, but the neat lines of cryptograms marched on and on. *Someone* will be able to decipher it for me, she thought. Since he's keeping chimpanzees right now, I'll take a current book. She chose the one he had begun on Christmas Eve, 1992.

By pulling the box hard against her knees, she was able to squeeze it shut again and restick the tape, more or less straight.

The tanbark made dull crunching noises as she returned to the waving spot on the edge of the garden. Out here the bushes hid her from the house, and she could risk using the flashlight. She needed a place to hide the book where she could find it again. She squatted down, pushed the tanbark aside, and made two cuts in the thick black plastic underneath. There was a layer of newspaper below the plastic. She slipped the book under the newspaper, replaced the flap, and spread the tanbark over it. When she stood on the spot, she could feel a bump.

She returned to the parking area, feeling the thrill of a small triumph. The only things she had not examined yet were a couple of lumpy objects lying close to the door to U-1. They turned out to be mailbags, closed with a light chain and small padlocks. She looked around to reassure herself that she could keep her eye on the path that led to the back of the house, then she set to work with her bush keys. Despite probing, the first padlock she tried would not budge. The bag felt heavy. She pushed it on its side, opened her knife, and began sawing at a seam on the bottom of the bag. A stitch popped open, then another and another, but the twine was so tough it blunted her blade, and she had to stop and sharpen it on the edge of the concrete. She was crouched down, grinding it, when overhead there was a thunder of chairs, and moments later footsteps rang on the veranda. She jumped up and ran into the garden.

The branches of the prickly bush where she hid herself were still moving when John Parker strode past, the stocky Asian at his heels.

At the door of U-1, Parker punched in a code and pushed. The door opened, and both men disappeared. Upstairs, there was the sound of people moving around. Diana checked her watch: it was almost midnight.

As silently as she could, she worked her way through the garden, hands in front of her face to protect herself from the bushes. Twigs snapped as she pushed past, and beneath her feet the tanbark crunched as loudly as gravel, it seemed. She hurried on toward the lamp.

When she returned from giving her second signal to Billy, the door to U-1 was still open, and there was no sign of Parker and the Asian man. I could take a quick look, she thought. She ran to the door and stepped inside; there were stairs and an Inclin-ator. She pulled her camera from its case, focused on the stairs, and pressed the button. The momentary blaze of the flash and the hiss of the film spool winding on was like thunder and lightning. She listened for a noise from behind, then ran quickly down the stairs. She had never felt so frightened. With every step, a voice inside her said, Carolyn was murdered down here. At the base of the stairs there was a large, dingy room, furnished only with a table and chairs. She photographed the room from where she was standing, then moved toward the door that Billy had told her led into the laboratory itself. The door was shut. She pushed it open a fraction, her ears straining for any sound from the stairway behind. Then she pushed the door a fraction more. Suddenly it was shoved hard from the inside and Parker's voice shouted, "Bugger it! I've forgotten—" The door closed again as he moved away. Diana turned and leaped up the stairs two at a time, rushing into the bushes, panting and quaking.

She felt around with her hands and feet until she located a spot where she could sit and calm down.

After about ten minutes, Parker and his shadowy companion emerged from the laboratory, carrying something, which they put in the back of the Land Cruiser. Then they loaded in as many of the boxes as would fit. Parker walked to the base of the veranda steps and shouted up, "Hey, Freddie! Steve! Lend a hand."

They came pounding downstairs. "You go with Somchai," Parker said to one of them. "Help him unload. And you come with me." The Land Cruiser set off, driven by the Asian.

It made two trips, but Diana was unwilling to move from her hiding place to watch where it was going. She supposed the boxes of household goods were being moved to the condominiums and that en route, at the lab complex, the mailbags would be off-loaded. But why in the middle of the night? she wondered. She still hoped she would see something that would demonstrate the presence of chimpanzees.

By twenty to one, nothing more had been brought up from U-1. Diana unfolded herself and crept through the garden. When she reached the waving spot, she saw the Land Cruiser returning from the airfield. For a moment she was aghast at the thought that the Asian and the other man had spotted the kids somehow and had driven over to the flying ground. The Cruiser swept past her, back to the house, and soon afterward drove out once more and headed for the airfield, where it stopped. The perimeter lights came on. In the blue-and-white glare she could make out the shapes of people unloading things. They're doing a bunk, she realized. Where are the chimps?

She knew that every time she went to and from the waving spot she risked being seen from the house and that the less she moved, the better. She decided to stay where she was until her 2:00 A.M. signal, then to return and investigate the cabin behind the house. Perhaps the chimps had been moved in there.

At two o'clock, when she turned back to the house, she could barely see it through the trees. Most of the lights were out. At the base of the wooden steps, she halted and listened again. Somewhere in the distance, a mopoke's call caressed the silence.

The strip of neon under the house, which illuminated the parking area, had been turned out, and the only light burning was on the veranda. All the boxes had gone. Parker might still be downstairs, she thought. Suddenly there was a noise on the veranda above her head. A moment later, there was the sound of splashing on leaves and the smell of urine. She kept her eyes screwed tight, feeling small hot drops hit her forehead. The sound of feet on the veranda retreated. She waited to see if anyone was going to come downstairs to sleep in the cabin, but nobody did.

Overhanging trees blocked the moonlight, and no light came from the cabin itself to guide her to it. She longed to use the flashlight, but the memory of the way Sonja had sensed an intruder made her decide she would have to do without it. Grace had taught her the basic tactic for seeing in the dark. She stood with her eyes closed for what she judged was twenty-five minutes. When she opened them she could see everything as if in twilight. The cabin door was dead-bolted. She went round the side to the window and pushed her ear against the cold glass. There was slow, heavy breathing coming from inside. She pulled back and quickly made her way along the path and kept going, out through the garden and onto the road. Her body cast a pale, short shadow, but she felt safe, and when she reached the airfield she shone her light around. There were the boxes that had been under the house, and four suitcases. She looked at each item carefully; none had anything to do with chimpanzees.

It was almost 3:00 A.M., time to wave again, but she was sure Tom and Billy would be smart enough to examine the person with the flashlight through the night sights. Tom was only five hundred meters away. She waved and gave an owl call as well. A few seconds later, a strange sort of owl called back.

Diana used the flashlight every few minutes until she was behind the hill, when she turned it on and chased the beam of light running in front of her feet across the uneven ground.

Both the boys were awake. She explained that the people were going to fly stuff out, probably early in the morning, and maybe at the last moment they would load the chimpanzees. She was still hoping to photograph them. "I want to go back, but I won't be able to wave to you after six o'clock because it'll be getting light." Tom patted her. "You have a sleep," he said.

The sky was still black when the alarm went off at twenty to six. Diana stumbled to her feet, drank coffee from the thermos she'd brought, and set out at a trot. Grace would be awake and getting worried by now—but she could not leave the job half done.

By the time she reached the outskirts of the garden, the first hint of dawn was coming into the sky. Diana was at the base of the veranda steps when the electric light suddenly turned off, making her heart leap. When nothing more happened, she realized that the switch was connected to an automatic timer. She crossed the concrete as fast as she could, to the bushes on the right-hand side of the house. The path to the cabin was on the left, as was the door of U-1. Although she was farther away from the door than on the other side of the house, here she would be able to see somebody coming from the cabin before anyone saw her.

She squatted down to wait, thinking of what to say to the sixteen people who were expecting her to take them bird-watching at 8:00 A.M. If I leave here by seven, she thought, I can drive to headquarters, ring up, and tell them to meet me at the lake in the usual place. On the bus journey from Fig Tree Gully Road to the wetlands, she always gave a talk about the lake and its avian life, explaining how to distinguish species and races, and the basic tricks of birding. She was still thinking about how to reorganize the morning's schedule when, upstairs, an alarm clock rang. Within less than a minute she heard voices, lights were switched on, and the whole house was awake.

Dawn colors were flowing strongly into the sky now, and from the camping ground on the other side of the fence, beyond the house, came the raucous yells of cockatoos and the rich, mellow caroling of magpies. She could hear swans bugling and ducks grunting and quacking. For a moment she closed her eyes and luxuriated in the music of the day.

Almost imperceptibly, she became aware of another sound, interrupting the choir of birds. It was the dull, steady buzz of an aircraft. Diana clenched her fists in irritation, realizing too late that she had chosen a hiding place from which she was unable to see the airfield. The engine sound was so faint that had she not been listening attentively to the dawn song, she would not have heard it at all. She squinted in concentration. It was not the air taxi but something much larger.

It was Kalair's Cessna 421. Overnight, Kerry had painted out his registration number and painted on a different one. He had also sprayed over the Kalair logo on the tail. His plan was to fly up the back way, to Weewaa, staying below 1,500 meters. Flying low chewed up fuel, but under 1,500 meters he could legally fly No Search and Rescue-No Details. After refueling at Weewaa, still flying low, he could just make it to Cooktown on the north Queensland coast. In Cooktown he would refuel and fly straight for Milne Bay in New Guinea, and somewhere over the Coral Sea he would put out a Mayday. He had a stack of stuff—life jackets and Avgas—to throw out of the aircraft to look like a crash. Goodbye, bailiffs. Hello, Bangkok.

There were no Customs in Milne Bay. Kerry planned to have a good sleep there. The rest of the journey to Thailand would be easy. But he intended to be strict about luggage: one small cabin bag each was all they could take.

As he approached the airstrip, he saw the pile of boxes. "Bloody hell," he muttered.

In the house, Diana could hear the sounds of people hurrying about and Parker barking orders. Soon the young men came pounding down the stairs, carrying more bags, talking in excited voices. The Asian trotted after them. They all piled into the Land Cruiser and set off too fast. Not long afterward, the Cruiser returned, with only the Asian driver and one young man, who jumped out and almost ran to the door of U-1. He punched in the code. As the door opened, Diana heard him say, "We'll use the Inclin-ator." Over on the airfield, the plane landed. It was almost 6:00 A.M.

Parker and Sonja came downstairs and stood by the Land Cruiser, their backs to Diana. They talked in low voices, then Parker said, "What the hell are they doing down there?" He strode to the door and yelled down, "Hurry it up, chaps," and disappeared inside. Sonja paced up and down, her open-toe shoes making a scuffing noise on the concrete. She was wearing smart black trousers and a white silk shirt, and carrying a straw hat. She hunched her shoulders against the cold morning air and wrapped her arms around herself. On the middle finger of her left hand, Carolyn's broad gold ring glinted.

Suddenly Parker came hurrying out the U-1 door, calling, "Here's Sailor. You drive, Sonja." She climbed into the driver's seat and turned on the ignition. A moment later, the Asian and one of the young men staggered out of U-1, carrying between them a crush cage with some clear plastic wrapped untidily around it. Inside was a chimpanzee. They were only four meters from Diana. She had her camera ready, but as she was about to shoot she realized there was so little light under the house, the camera would automatically flash. She lowered it and watched. The chimp was squeezed hard against the side of its cage by the crush plate, held so tight it could move only its eyes and mouth. Its mouth opened wide and its lips drew back to scream, but no sound came out. *You bastards!* Diana thought.

Sonja said in a high, plaintive voice, "The petrol tank's empty."

Parker answered, "You can drive forty K on empty."

"It's been on empty for two days." She looked out the window at the young man. "I thought you were going to fill it up yesterday."

"Sorry," he muttered. "Forgot."

"We better take as much as we can on this trip," Parker said. He turned to the Asian. "Dear boy, go and get Lucy."

A few minutes later, the young men carried a second chimpanzee out to the parking area. This animal was not so difficult, apparently, because it was in an ordinary cage and its plastic wrapping was more or less in place. Eventually they were all inside and set off, Sonja driving.

Diana stood up and stretched the cramped muscles in her legs. There was no sound coming from the airfield, which meant that they would not be flying off for a while yet. In the silence, she heard thumping noises from the direction of the shed.

The air was heating up and she wanted to remove her parka, but she had to keep it on to protect herself from the bushes. Banksias grew on this side of the house, and their leaves were like saws.

The cabin had a window on its right side. The thumping stopped as she reached the door. She glanced around and listened for a mo-

ment before looking in. She could see a table and two chairs, a miniature refrigerator, and, just beneath the window, a sink with a dripping tap. She thought something on a shelf opposite was a brass
bell, until she realized it was a Buddha. By going to one edge of the
window and craning her neck, she could look farther inside. There
was a bed, but nobody was lying on it. She pushed her ear to the
glass again but heard nothing. She walked around to the door and
tried the handle; it was still dead-bolted.

Inside the cabin, Michael Romanus lay still, listening for the door
to be opened. During the night, while he struggled to untie his hands
and feet, he had rolled off the bed onto the floor, and he was stuck
there, barely able to move, except to kick with both feet on the wall.
He gave another tremendous kick, but there was no response from
outside. Perhaps it was just the wind, he thought, slumping back
onto the dusty floor. The gag in his mouth made him thirsty, and the
slow drip of the tap over the sink tormented him.

Outside, Diana had heard the Land Cruiser approaching and was
already hurrying along the path. She ducked into the bushes as the
vehicle swept under the house. The Asian was driving. He was alone.

Diana heard him pull on the handbrake and then the sound of
grunting and dull thuds as he unloaded things. She took a look and
saw that he had brought back several of the boxes that had been
moved to the airfield last night. He carried them upstairs, locked the
doors that opened onto the veranda, and returned to the parking
area. Diana edged forward to see what he was up to, but he had disappeared. He's the caretaker, she thought. He's either gone down to
the lab or gone back to the cabin.

From the path behind the house, she heard a voice raised in temper.

"You get in car!" a man said. Then he shouted a command in a
language she did not understand. There was a crash, as if something
had been flung against the chassis of the Land Cruiser. What is it?
she wondered. Another chimp?

"I cut you throat!" he yelled.

A door slammed, and a second door. The Land Cruiser started, reversed, and, accelerating fast, shot out from under the house. Diana
glimpsed a man, gagged, apparently with his hands tied behind his
back, flinging his shoulder against the door of the Land Cruiser, trying to jar it open. A moment later, the Land Cruiser stopped. She
heard the driver try the ignition, but there was no response.

She took out her knife, pulled the blade open, and moved quietly
out of the bushes. Ten meters in front of her, she saw the Asian man-
handling his prisoner out of the Land Cruiser. The prisoner's legs

were tied at the ankles, so he could take only mincing steps. As the Asian pushed him, the man jerked his chin down at his legs, indicating that he could go no faster unless he was untied. The Asian, who was a whole head shorter than the prisoner, was holding him by a nylon rope that tied his wrists behind his back. He jerked it so the man had to stop. Then he bent down to his own left leg and drew a knife from a sheath on his calf. He quickly cut the bonds around the man's legs and, straightening up, jabbed him in the back with the point of the knife. They began walking down the road to the airfield. With one hand the Asian grasped the rope around his prisoner's wrists, while the other held the knife against his back. Diana looked around for something to throw. There was not even a stick or a rock. The camera was all she had. She grasped its cord in her right hand, took a deep breath, and with her left hand reached inside her shirt for the whistle. She started to run. The noise of the aircraft engine muffled her steps. Two meters behind them, she bit the whistle between her teeth and blew as hard as she could. Birds in the camping ground rose shrieking into the air, and both men leaped in shock. The Asian swung round, eyes wide, in time for Diana to bash him across the face with a swing of the camera. He slipped and fell to one knee, pulling the prisoner almost on top of him. As he recovered, she threw the camera straight at his face. Instinctively he tried to protect himself, letting go of the nylon rope. "Run!" Diana shouted. The man, meanwhile, was running, but in the wrong direction, heading up the hill toward the lab complex. The Asian's hand jumped with surprise, and his knife, flung from his hand toward the man's back, landed harmlessly in the grass beside the road. Diana yelled to the man, "Follow me!" and ran onto the rough grass of the paddock. The Asian rushed to retrieve his knife. Diana was sure she and the prisoner could outdistance him, but the prisoner's tied hands were a disastrous handicap. The knife man had picked up his weapon and was pursuing them.

Diana slowed until the prisoner was beside her. "The fence over there," she said. She took a quick look behind and saw that the Asian was only eighty meters away. "There's a rabbit hole just up ahead," she panted. "I'll shout *Now*, and you run on one side and I'll run on the other." He seemed to understand.

"*Now!*" she shouted. They diverged around the rabbit hole, which was invisible until one was on top of it. A few moments later, they heard a shout and, looking back, saw that the Asian had fallen in. Diana grabbed the man's swollen fingers pulled him to a halt and began sawing at the rope around his wrists. The blade was very sharp and sliced through most of the rope. She glanced back. The Asian had picked himself up and was running again. She gave a final, desperate swipe and sliced some of the man's skin. Blood oozed, but his hands were free. "Go!" she yelled. The Asian was only twenty meters behind them now, and he had his knife ready again. For a moment she glanced at the airfield. The propellers on the big Cessna were spinning so fast they had disappeared. At every window there was a face staring out at them. Parker was standing at the top of the steps, and she had the impression that his hands were clenching his hair. She suddenly felt a sting shoot from her ankle up to her knee, and a moment later she landed on her face on the grass. She had fallen into a rabbit hole. Her ankle was on fire as she pulled herself onto all fours. The Asian was thundering toward her, his hair flying behind him, his knife raised. She looked around and saw that the gagged man had stopped and was dancing about from foot to foot, flapping his hands at the Asian like a bird trying to draw a predator away from its chicks. The Asian hesitated, then veered from Diana and ran after the man. They were heading straight for the Cyclone-wire fence. Diana began to stagger after them, yelling, "Go to the left! There's a gate to the left!" She could see what would happen: the man would be trapped by the fence and the Asian would kill him, then come back for her.

On board the aircraft, Kerry Larnach said, "Not long now. Got 'im against the fence . . ."

Steve turned to Freddie. "Fantastic, eh?"

"Amazing!" Freddie breathed.

They were only meters from the wire. When Romanus hit it he began climbing, pulling himself up by his fingers . . . half a meter . . . a meter . . .

Diana limped forward. Who is he? she wondered. She lifted the whistle and gave a long blast and looked up, as if she expected to see a bird come to her hand from the sky, crystal clear all the way to the horizon.

Ahead of her, the Asian had reached the fence. He pulled up, judged his throw, and raised his arm almost lazily. It was an easy shot into the broad, sweating back. Romanus looked behind him. Somchai swayed and seemed to inhale as he fell dead on the grass. The sound of a gunshot rang across the lake.

Tom and Billy, cowering beside the van, saw the old bush black turn and vanish into the mountain.

"We're off," Kerry said. He pulled out the throttle. The Cessna gathered its strength and charged.

Romanus climbed down from the fence and pulled off the gag, flinging it on the ground with a look of disgust. When Diana limped up to him, he was massaging his jaw. For a moment they stood in silence, watching the plane lift into the air. A cloud of ducks that had taken wing circled and, quacking loudly, headed toward the center of the lake.

He turned to her and tried to smile, but his face hurt. "Thanks. You saved my life."

"Back there, you saved mine," she answered. She felt numb, as if her emotions existed outside herself. "*So who in hell are you?*" He looked vaguely familiar.

"Michael—" His face crumpled, and sobbing with relief, he slid to the ground, his back against the Cyclone wire. She hunkered down beside him and laid a hand on his knee, still not certain if he was friend or foe. Suddenly he lunged at her and pulled her to his chest, kissing her neck. Blood from the cuts on his hands and neck smeared her shirt. He sat back and grinned. "I'm so happy, it's ridiculous," he said, and touched her hair, then pressed his parched lips against her ear. "You're so beautiful," he whispered. "I had no idea . . ."

A delicious, diffused awareness was taking hold of her, so that she noticed everything at once, but dreamily, as if she were seeing the world and him from underwater. Floating around down there, she remembered a picture of him from the jacket of one of Raoul's books.

"You're a photographer," she murmured. "You worked with Raoul Sabea."

"He's dead." He looked past her shoulder. "That bastard murdered him."

She turned to see what he was looking at, and at once the spell broke. She scrambled to her feet, wincing, and limped over to the corpse.

Their pursuer was lying on his side with a smallish wound in his chest over his heart and a large exit hole in his back. Diana glanced at the mountain. Tom and Billy were approaching the fence, running a bit, then coming timidly forward. Billy was carrying her slide-action rifle. "No!" she said. "No!"

Romanus came up beside her. "Did the kid shoot him?"

What have I taught them? she asked herself. *Billy has killed a man!* When Michael touched her hand, she snatched it away as if he'd burned her. "He couldn't have, not with that rifle," she said. She nodded toward the twinkle in the sky. "It must have been one of them." She felt panicky and began to hurry toward the fence. It was 7:00 A.M. "I've got to make a phone call."

An alert went out on Friday for Kalair's Cessna 421, but it gave the real registration, not the new one that Kerry had painted on. It also described the Kalair logo, now missing from the aircraft's tail.

Larnach made a refueling stop in Weewaa and flew on to Queensland. Parker and Sonja then moved in on the boys, all of whom were sleepy or asleep. It was easy to inject two of them with Pentothal and Thiobarbital. Freddie, waking as Parker was injecting Steve in the neck, shouted, "What are you doing!" but Sonja was ready with another syringe, and Freddie went down with almost no struggle. "It's for the best," Parker said. "They had no future."

Kerry was frightened when he discovered what had been done. "Y' didn't say you were gonna *murder* them," he whined to Parker.

"Don't be melodramatic," Parker said. "It didn't hurt. Anyway, we're going to ditch them. You've been complaining about the weight."

It was a calm, clear, moonlit night over the Coral Sea; the empty black water glistened peacefully as the plane descended. Kerry carefully depressurized the cabin.

240   **W H I T E   E Y E**

"We'd better slit their stomachs first, or they'll float," Sonja said.

"You think of everything," her husband replied. "But do we want them to sink? Won't it look more like a crash if they float?"

She gave him a knowing smile. "What if they're found quickly and a postmortem reveals they died from cardiac infarction, not trauma? We can't rely on sharks, you know."

"You're right, as usual."

By now the aircraft was flying at two hundred meters. Parker went forward to ask Kerry when he could open the door.

"Another three minutes. Here—take the Avgas and pour it out. And that other stuff—the life jackets and clothes."

Parker returned to the aircraft door, checked his watch, then turned the handle to open it. They were so low, he could see the bright, puckered surface of the sea rushing below them, glowing red, green, and white from the aircraft's navigation lights.

"Here goes," he said to Sonja. "Give me the knife."

He made a fast, deep incision below Steve's breastbone, then shoved him through the open door. The air rushing past made the body rise for a moment before snatching it away into the dark. "Next," he said. Phil went. Then Freddie. "Avgas," he ordered. He had to cling to the doorway as he sloshed it out onto the rushing black air. "Life jackets!" She handed them to him and he flung them through the door. "Mailbags." They took some effort to push out.

"That's that," Sonja said.

Parker edged back from the doorway. "Want to look?" he asked. She peered forward and down into the dark and took a small step, one hand grasping the doorway. The plane began to circle again. Sonja tried to grab the other side of the door with her free hand, but her foot slipped on spilled Avgas as she moved. Suddenly both feet slipped and she lost her balance completely. As the aircraft turned more sharply, her legs flew from under her, out the doorway into the rushing air. Both shoes were ripped off. "John!" she yelled in panic. He reacted so quickly that she did not realize what was happening until she felt the explosion of his fist in her face. His other hand chopped at her fingers. The next moment, she was spread-eagled above the glistening sea. She twisted, trying to fly back to the plane, but it was rising and she was falling, and all the events of her life were rushing in pictures through her mind—terrible pictures, for everything she had done to others was now happening to her. "You murderer!" she screamed. Curses shot like sparks around her head.

From the cockpit came the sound of Kerry shouting, "Mayday! Mayday!"

The Cessna rose to five hundred meters. Parker ducked his head as he entered the cockpit, where he lowered himself into the co-pilot's chair. "We'll enjoy Thailand," he said.

After a while, Kerry asked, "Where's Sonja?"

"She's lying down." Parker yawned and massaged his knuckles; a delicious sense of relaxation spread through his limbs. He luxuriated in daydreams of the future: an outbreak of White Eye, not in a monkey house, as Otto Grossmann had planned, but in a city. Hong Kong, with all its air-conditioned buildings, would be ideal. Thousands would die in the first twenty-four hours—but somebody had to make a sacrifice. Meanwhile, all over the world, pictures of the effects of White Eye would be appearing on television screens. He would go to Grossmann and say, "You must act! If this is traced to Siam we'll be executed. Act! Say we have a vaccine."

The Chinese government—any government—would grab at a vaccine, waiving normal medical safety controls. Every other government would be urged to follow suit. Grossmann, of course, would not know that now only Vaccine II existed. But when the mass vaccinations were under way, Parker would tell him, "You must speak publicly again. You must cite the experience with chimpanzees and warn that vaccination may cause sterility." *Sterility?* The world was stampeding in panic, demanding vaccination. Nine months later, labor rooms from Helsinki to Hobart would be silent. The reign of the monster would have come to an end.

Parker stretched and gave another yawn.

Joe Miller had had to abandon his trip to Sydney because of the security crisis on Good Friday. In the afternoon, he rang Weasel's flat and left a message on her answering machine. When she had not returned his call by Saturday night, he grew impatient. He telephoned her twice on Sunday, but it was not until 6:00 A.M. on Easter Monday, when she did not arrive at work, that alarm bells rang. At midday her body was found, and that afternoon, with a team of thirty Homicide people on the case, Deborah Smith identified Sila Somchai as the man Parker had met in the zoo. His knife was found to be the same size as the knife that had killed Weasel. The attorney general, who had been keeping Senator Olfson informed of legal developments, summoned her to Canberra.

That evening, Hilary Olfson put out a terse but dignified press release announcing her resignation as minister for science, technology, and the environment. She was looking forward, she said, to spending more time in her garden and helping the unemployed. During the media conference on Monday night, a reporter questioned her about her younger sister, Sonja, whose body, along with other wreckage from an aircraft, had been found by Taiwanese fishermen in the Coral Sea. Did the senator believe that her sister was involved in the deaths of Dr. Carolyn Williams and Jason Nichols? the reporter asked. Hilary's principal private secretary said, "Don't answer that, boss." She motioned to him to be quiet. "My sister always expected the worst of life," Hilary said. "And she was an unhappy person. From my observation, unhappy people are often cru—" The senator lifted a large white hand to cover her twitching mouth. Her body shook uncontrollably as she stood and hurried from the room.

In Thailand, the chief executive of Siam Enterprises, Otto Grossmann, announced an inquiry into apparent wrongdoing by Siam staff employed at its primate breeding station north of Bangkok. He promised that if company investigators discovered that primates had been shipped without observing the CITES regulations governing endangered species, those responsible would be handed over to the police. Meanwhile, Siam was donating four million baht to a reforestation program in the northwest, an area damaged by logging. An Italian journalist stationed in Bangkok asked Grossmann about the death of his chauffeur: Was it true the chauffeur had murdered an Australian policewoman in Sydney? And that he had assassinated the wildlife photographer Raoul Sabea? The chief executive of Siam replied in Italian, "Tiziano, you've lived here a long time. How can you ask such irresponsible, crazy questions? I don't understand a mind like yours."

In Australia, it remained unclear how Somchai had been shot. Ballistics experts found the spent cartridge from the bullet that killed him and reported that it did not come from Diana Pembridge's rifle, which had not been fired recently anyway. A detective complained to his inspector, "Getting info out of people in the bush is like throwing eggs at a wall." The investigation team decided to accept, in theory, that someone on the airplane had shot the Thai, perhaps while aiming at Michael Romanus.

For two days following their meeting, Diana and Michael were never alone. At first they were with Research security guards, then it was Kalunga police, then Homicide detectives. Back in Fig Tree Gully Road, Diana's house was a turmoil of bird-watchers and visitors wanting to find out what had happened. Romanus needed medical treatment for his wounds. He was ordered to rest for twenty-four hours, which he did, in the Kalunga Motel. All that time Diana was in his mind, sometimes above, sometimes just below the surface of his thoughts. Sometimes he laughed aloud at the Spaniard's cunning: Raoul had never let on that La Loca was the blonde in a black dress whose photograph he kept most prominently beside the bed.

Diana, meanwhile, had to entertain the bird-watchers. Grace had run the tour by herself on Friday, but on Saturday Diana had to do her share. By nightfall she was so tired she dragged herself into bed. On Monday morning, the bird-watchers departed, and Michael left his motel room and came to the house. His neck and hands were patched with adhesive bandages. Grace watched him as he strolled around the gallery, and noticed the way Diana's blood came and went in her cheeks as she looked at him. The colors around her body throbbed and flowed, rose-red, rose-pink, violet around her shoulders, orange around her head, and around her hands a bright, clear green.

"I must shower the eagle," she said abruptly, hoping he would ask to see it. When he did not try to follow her, she asked, "Would you like to . . . ?"

In the aviary, he stood looking around, impressed. Diana had gloved up and strapped the belt and cantilever around her waist. She carried the eagle out of the mews. "Do you want to give her something to eat?" she asked. She removed the hood. As soon as the eagle saw Michael, she crouched like a snake, her eyes bitter. "She's tame," Diana said. He gave a skeptical laugh, and as if to prove he was right, the bird reared her wings open and jumped toward him.

"I think I'll wait outside," he said.

When Diana came out, her hair sparkling with droplets from the hose, he put his hands on the ti tree on either side of her head. Up close, she felt frightened of him. He appeared almost monstrous, with the bar of black brows across his forehead, the mane of thick hair. She turned her face away, thinking of Raoul, who had opened her up, then tossed her away. Michael bent and kissed her neck.

"I really came to say goodbye for now," he murmured. "I've hired a car, and I'm driving to Queensland. I'll ring you from up north. I need to see my family."

That evening, after she had brought the eagle back from the flying ground, Diana sat in the study, staring at the colored spines of books above her desk. There were scores of volumes on birds, and several on falconry. The words of a troubador song lilted through her head. She searched for the book in which she had read it, whispering lines she remembered: " 'Alas for me, who loved a falcon well. So well I loved him, I was nearly dead. Ever at my low call, he bent his head and ate of mine; not much, but all that fell. Now he has fled, how high I cannot tell. . . .' " She began to cry—for Raoul, and for the man Raoul had sent her. She searched on but couldn't find the book.

Next morning, her mother arrived. "You need a break," she said. "I'll look after the animals and help Grace with the gallery. You take yourself off somewhere. Go to Byron Bay or Queensland. The weather's lovely up there at this time of year."

"No!" Diana said. "I've got to rehabilitate the wedgetail."

"You're more important than a wretched eagle." Her mother frowned and went down to the vegetable garden to talk to Grace. She was gone for a long time. When she returned, she did not refer again to Diana's need for a break. Instead, she hired a man to clean all the windows, while she took everything out of the kitchen and washed the shelves with scouring powder. At the end of a fortnight, she had turned the house upside down and was digging up the garden. Diana made weak protests, which her mother brushed aside with a calm smile. Under this domestic onslaught, life, Diana realized, was being worked back into an ordinary rhythm.

In the mornings, she took the eagle to the flying ground and after an hour's exercise left her there, tethered on a twenty-meter creance. It was good for the bird to be back in her territory, spending hours in observation, becoming reaccustomed to open space. In the evenings, Diana returned and they worked again. Sometimes there was an empty container of tea or sugar near the fence, but no other sign from Morrie.

After a week Michael rang her from Brisbane. At the sound of his voice, her pulse raced. "Good drive?" she asked.

"Not bad. How're things?"

"Fine." There were a thousand interesting things she had been saving to share with him, but they all flew out of her head.

He said he planned to stay three months in Queensland, getting together the photographs for a book on nature parks in Thailand and spending time with his mother. "How about you?"

"I'll be here," she said. "I'm always here."

"You never migrate? You're not like a tern?"

"Not me. I stay put."

"Ah," he commented. "I'll ring you again, soon."

Every day, when she returned from the flying ground, she ran up the stairs to her study, to listen to the answering machine. After a week she stopped running. Her mother returned to her house at Noosa, leaving behind a pantry full of preserves and a linen cupboard full of new towels and sheets. The day she left, she took Diana's hands, her cool gaze searching her daughter's face. "Sometimes we just must forget," she said. "I had to. But you were so young when it happened. It was such a shock. One minute he was taking you everywhere with him, teaching you to shoot foxes and ducks, and ride the motorbike, and mark the lambs. And next minute he was—"

"Blown in two by a shotgun," Diana said evenly.

Her mother's calm, mild eyes turned to the direction of the lake. Diana had been twelve when her father was found lying in trampled bulrushes, with the headless body of Louise Williams nearby. I should have sold up and taken her to live in Europe, Joan Pembridge rebuked herself. But she had stayed on, running the property herself until Diana was old enough to leave school and work on the farm full time. It was a mistake, she thought, as she looked at her daughter, so smooth and polished on the outside, yet so vulnerable.

The eagle was sleeker now, with a shallow crop, her breastbone almost outlined beneath her plumage. Diana weighed each gram of food the bird ate, thinning her down to hunting weight. Every morning, the eagle cast a neat package of feathers and fur, always at 6:00 A.M., twelve hours after her evening meal, and having cast was keen for food and exercise again. Now when Diana went to the flying ground she dressed in a leather jacket to protect her back from a strike, and took with her a rabbit-skin lure to which she tied small pieces of meat. She stood the eagle on a fence post, clipped on the hundred-meter creance, and sprinted away, swinging the lure above her head. As the *whoomp! whoomp! whoomp!* of wings came up behind, she zigzagged and jinked. The wings beat so strongly, their tips almost brushed the ground.

After ten days the bird was flying with such power, Diana could not run fast enough to make chasing the lure worthwhile. The bird was striking on one out of five attempts, which was excellent, for in the wild a hunting eagle missed nine out of ten animals it tried to kill. Rehabilitation had passed the halfway mark.

Her weeks were busy but lonely, for day by day her hope of speaking to Michael faded, turning first to disappointment, then to resignation. When a month had passed, by which time she was ready to start training the eagle in vertical flight, she told herself she had been right to reject him. Yet his memory became a background noise, which she could ignore but not eliminate. She drove back and forth to the flying ground holding angry conversations with him.

When he did phone, her attempt at coolness was shattered by his voice. She clung to the receiver, her heart bumping. His mother had been in hospital. "You step out of life in those places," he said. They spoke for a few minutes about this and that, when suddenly he added, "I've been thinking about you all the time. I'll be there next week." Diana felt her body shimmer and shine.

By the time he arrived, which was not one but three weeks later, because he was detained by the death of his mother, the wedgetail was capable of powerful vertical flight. Diana could stand on the stepladder and hold out her hand, and the eagle would beat straight up with great lashing strokes of her wings. At first she could do this only once or twice in a session, but after a fortnight she could make repeated vertical flights with ease. Her whole body was now hard with muscle, and she was looking like a wild eagle again. Diana had to be careful that she did not let the bird become too hungry. There was no word in English for *yarak*, the hunting frenzy of falcons, and Diana did not know if an eagle could go into *yarak;* but she sensed a lustful violence as the wedgetail went for food. It was time for "entering."

On the day before Michael was due to arrive, Diana went rabbit catching with Tom and Billy on the camping ground by the lake. The boys netted four rabbits in half an hour. Even Grace was impressed.

Michael arrived just after midday. To Diana he seemed relaxed but introspective. He had brought his tripod and a brace of cameras. "Thought I'd shoot some transparencies," he said. After lunch he helped her stow the rabbits and four buckets in the van, and they set out. She was so excited at seeing him again, she could barely talk. "Was your mother . . . ?" She did not know what she was trying to ask.

He shrugged. "I'm sad. But she wasn't. She never let go of my dad when he died. She wanted to die, to be with him." He turned to look at Diana. "Why don't you stop hanging on to all those dead people?"

"*What?*"

"Leave this place," he said. "Leave the ghosts you've collected— your dad, his girlfriend, their daughter. . . . You've got a whole Madame Tussaud's here."

"It's my home."

"It's a graveyard."

She gripped the wheel, too astonished to reply.

When they reached the flying ground, the eagle made a brief flight from the fence post to show her excitement. What if she doesn't come back when I whistle her? Diana thought. What if she doesn't wait on? Today, for the first time, she was going to fly the bird free.

She grabbed a rabbit from the cage and shoved the kicking animal under a bucket, then repeated the operation three times, at intervals of twenty meters along the flying ground. Romanus chose a spot close to the mountain, set up his tripod, and gave her a wave when he was ready.

She did not bother with the cantilever today: if all went well, she would need only her gauntlet and glove until the last moment, when the eagle returned to her arm. The bird had been observing the preparations with interest and was staring at the third bucket.

Diana unclipped the creance from the jesses, offered her arm to the giant feet, and, when they fastened securely, turned her head away and let her arm drop with a jerk. The eagle's wing flew open. Diana dropped her arm again and staggered back from the force of the eagle leaping into the air. She beat up two meters, three, four, ten. Diana turned up her face to watch her rise . . . *and wait*. At fifteen meters, the bird balanced on the air with short, strong wingbeats, looking down for a sign. Diana began to walk away at a leisurely pace, too slow for the eagle to follow her. After a moment, the bird lifted her head and shoulders to the horizontal of flight and began to flap away. Diana's heart was in her mouth. Is she just raking off—or have I lost her? she wondered. She glanced at Michael, who was watching her, nodding, as if he knew what she was going through. A bolt of love for him went through her.

The eagle, meanwhile, had found a small thermal—there were many around at this late time of day—and had risen another twenty meters. She was now a hundred meters away, flying with slow, strong beats, beginning to turn. Diana flashed a tense look at Michael, who had not said a word, not even made a sound with his cameras to distract them. The eagle began to circle. Diana waited while she flew a complete revolution, rising higher on the hot afternoon air, the emarginated primary feathers on her wings making constant delicate movements, adjusting her flying to the air currents, keeping her head and body straight. She was a perfect creation, divine and serene. When she began moving out toward the lake, Diana blew her whistle and ran for the nearest bucket. Instantly, the eagle made a midair swerve. Diana rushed at the bucket and kicked it over. The flushed rabbit took off, with the eagle in pursuit. Five seconds later, the rabbit bolted into a hole, safe and free. Michael shouted, "Come on! Do it again!" grinning encouragement.

The eagle beat up once more, with increasing power this time, and raked off two hundred meters. She missed the second rabbit too. And the third. "She's not judging her descent and sprint properly," Diana called. "I haven't given her any practice going for prey at this height before."

Michael was beaming. "You're fantastic," he said. "I've got shots . . ."

"You ain't seen nothin'!" Diana felt childishly happy as she ran back toward the row of buckets.

On the eagle's fourth flight she flew higher, mounting with grandeur on the hot afternoon. She poised herself in the sky, long wings held in a shallow dihedral, wing tips fingering the air. She seemed enraptured by movement and by the wind in her wings, as if she wanted to fly forever. But when Diana flushed another rabbit, she changed immediately into a hunter. She descended fast until she was little more than a meter above the ground and only just behind the rabbit. Then she began to sprint, her wings flattening the grass and making a rushing wind. She was flying at forty kilometers an hour when suddenly the pale feet came down, the booted legs shot forward. The rabbit swerved—too late. The eagle flung her wings upward and stumbled a little as she came to rest on the earth, her prey impaled on one foot.

Diana ran over to stand beside Romanus again. "I might loose her here," she panted. "She'll want to take the food up to a tree to eat, instead of eating on the ground. Since she's free, and fed, she may not come back." The eagle tore apart the rabbit where she had caught it, but when Diana approached her and gave a whistle, she flapped to the proffered arm. Diana hooded her and carried her to the van.

Sunset was approaching, sending the first pale-orange streamers of light out across the lake. Waterbirds set up their evening ruckus of honking, grunting, and quacking, while frogs in the marshy foreshore began to chirrup. Romanus folded his tripod and took it back to the van.

"What now?" he asked.

"Let's watch the sunset," Diana said.

He was standing with his fingers on his hips, one eyebrow quizzically crooked.

"I've got a rug in the van if you're getting cold."

"A *rug?*" He wished he hadn't grinned. She's so nervous she looks ready to bolt, he thought. He found her magnetically beautiful.

They walked to a place where the ground was more or less even and lay down to watch the fire of the day playing above the water. Michael stroked her face and hair. "Let go, Diana. Let go of the past."

That night, back at the house, she took him shyly into her bedroom. In his urgent embrace she felt years of loneliness dissolve and turn into joy. Toward dawn they put on some music and got out of bed to dance barefoot, circling slowly as light filtered into the bedroom and birds began to sing.

Two weeks later, they set out with the eagle, hooded, in the back of the van. They were both bundled up against the winter cold. The land was an emerald sea of wheat and oats. Paddocks were full of young lambs.

"We used to start marking and castrating the lambs at this time," Diana said. "Tails off, ears marked, inject 'em with 5-in-1. That was against tetanus, pulpy kidney, and blackleg."

"*Blackleg?*" Michael liked playing city slicker, because it made her less shy. She was still only half tame, he felt, still half afraid of him. She could toss her head like a wild mare and bolt.

Today she was going to free the eagle. Instead of driving to the flying ground, they were making a long detour to the other side of Mount Kalunga, where a trail led to the top of the mountain. The eagle had been fed well the night before and again in the morning, so she could survive a couple of days of unsuccessful hunting. Diana was anxious to release the bird today, because yesterday, at the flying ground, they had seen another wedgetail and Diana feared the new eagle had claimed the mountain and lake as its own territory. Her bird would have to drive it out or find a new home for herself.

The mountain path was slow and difficult. On this side, away from the moisture of the lake, vegetation was light, and the trees were predominantly gray box and ironbark, with some mulga. Michael, with the cameras, and Diana, with the hooded eagle, had been climbing for half an hour, when Diana stopped and looked up, then grabbed the binoculars with her free hand.

There, way above the mountaintop, the foreign eagle was soaring on long wings, its broad wedge tail like a rudder. From the color of its plumage, it was a young adult, but whether male or female, and how large, she could not tell.

She was filled with foreboding.

At the top of the mountain there was rocky ground and a stand of gray box. She perched the eagle on a broken-off branch near the ground; Michael put down his gear, and they rested for a while. The foreign eagle was directly above them, but so high it was only a dot.

"This is it," Diana said at last.

She felt shaky. In minutes, all her months of effort could be ruined, her eagle a fugitive, or crippled. She gloved and gauntleted her arm and, holding it straight, squeezed her fist shut in the strange falconer's gesture that Michael watched, each time he saw it, with fascination. She did not bother with the cantilever, for the eagle would ride for only a moment on her arm.

She went to the branch and with ceremony cut the jesses from the bird's ankles, then plucked off the hood. "C'mon, Aquila," she murmured. The bird stepped solemnly, one unbound foot, then the other, onto the gauntlet. But in a fraction of a second she had looked up and seen the other wedgetail. Her feet grabbed and pushed down. Thrashing wings overshadowed Diana as the eagle mounted the air. In seconds, she had found a thermal and was rising in a soaring spiral, pausing, rising again, weaving a pattern against the sky. The other bird was descending and had turned from a dot to a large dark spot, which assumed eagle shape.

"No!" Diana wailed. She turned her face away.

The strange eagle had folded its wings to stoop while Aquila hovered in midair. The other wedgetail was now traveling like a torpedo and in moments would smash into Aquila. "Fly!" Diana yelled. She lifted the whistle to her mouth, then hesitated: something extraordinary was taking place. The strange eagle suddenly pulled out of its dive, swung up like a pendulum, and rolled and somersaulted through the sky. Diana and Michael were openmouthed.

"What's it doing?" he asked.

"I'm not sure if it's attacking her or . . ."

Again the young bird stooped, falling on closed wings like a crashing airplane. Then it flared, made a vertical climb, and stalled, wings open, pinned to the sky like the eagles that stand for empires. Once more it swooped and rolled and turned a cartwheel in the air. They had never seen anything like it: an eagle dancing.

All this time, Aquila had been flying in a leisurely circle. But when the strange bird stooped at her for the third time, she abruptly began to fly at the spot where it would begin an upward climb.

"Here she goes," Diana whispered. "She'll either fight or . . ."

Swooping up toward each other, the two great birds flung themselves backward, their legs outstretched. Their feet locked like acrobats' hands, and one above, one below, they whirled through the sky—and whirled, and broke, and leaped apart, and seized each other again to spin, tumbling and twirling, in the nuptial dance.

* * *

Almost a year later, Michael and Diana were at work together in a bird sanctuary on the far northwest coast, outside the town of Broome. They arrived in September to record the numbers and races of half a million migratory wading birds. The birds lived part of each year in the sanctuary before returning to their breeding grounds in Siberia. The water off the coast was famous for its milky turquoise color, and the earth, too, was strange in this part of the world: redder than rust. According to local Aborigines, it was the place where divine spirits had first set foot on the planet and begun to sing.

Sometimes tourists came to see the birds, but mostly Diana and Michael were alone on a long, pale crescent of beach. Their love had deepened in the year they had known each other. Diana no longer feared that he would reduce her to something less than she had been before they met. He had made her happy, more able, more filled with hope. To him it seemed as if his life before he met her had been off-center and all his restlessness was a search to find his point of rest, which was in this woman's love.

When they went into town they bought the newspapers, days old, flown in from the south. Otherwise, they were cut off from the world except for a radio, on which they listened to the BBC news. It was from a shortwave signal that faded in and out like a nervous voice that they learned Otto Grossmann was dead. He had died just before Christmas, in his house in Bangkok, from what was believed to be a leak of poisonous chemicals. Four of his household servants perished at the same time. Police in Bangkok evacuated other houses in the area, including some diplomatic residences, in case the poison spread.

When Michael heard the news he telephoned friends in Thailand for details, but nobody knew any more than the media reported. Police had called medical experts to Grossmann's house, he learned. Some foreign journalists claimed that the eyes of the corpses were covered in a film of thick white matter, unlike anything ever seen.

He and Diana talked for hours about Grossmann's empire, the rumors Michael had heard about a disease that struck its monkey house in the 1980s, and how John Parker had been brought in to help. But when there was no more news from Thailand, their interest waned. Each day there were thousands of beautiful birds to occupy their attention: redshanks, broad-billed sandpipers, Asian dowitchers, yellow wagtails—all growing plump from feasting on the bounty of the milky blue water. By March the birds were brilliant with breeding plumage and ready for the journey north.

One morning in autumn, Michael was alone at the hut above the beach, writing up notes from the day before and listening with half an ear to the radio news: *The city of Calgary is in panic tonight following the deaths of three thousand office* . . . The signal faded. . . . *died in the* . . . *one of the tallest buildings in the world. Poisonous gas spread by* . . . *Islamic fundamentalists are suspected* . . . He was still half listening when the next sentence made him jump. *The same symptoms as those of the industrialist Otto Grossmann, who died along with household servants in Bangkok last year.*

Down on the beach, the wind, a thousand meters up, had begun blowing from the southeast. This was the monsoon the birds needed for their northern flight, and they started to rise from the sand, a few at a time at first, then by the hundred, crying and calling for the others to follow. Michael scrambled up. "Diana! Diana!" he shouted. But she had heard the cries of the birds and had gone down to the beach, where a flock now circled. If the wind kept blowing for twenty-four hours, the birds would leave in their thousands, until not one was left.

Diana gazed in wonder at the wheeling sky, but when she saw Michael running toward her, awe turned to alarm. "*What is it?*"

"The news on the radio," he panted. "The same thing that killed Otto Grossmann has been used on a whole building full of people in Canada."

All day and all night the wind blew from the southeast, shaking the thin walls of their hut. Diana lay in Michael's arms as they talked into the night. "But how could the disease Parker was working on at the Research be involved?" she wondered. "He died in the plane crash." Michael cocked his head to listen. In the pitch dark, above the sound of the wind, they could hear the birds crying as they took wing.

At dawn he began photographing them. Birds rose from the shallow water, joining the huge flock that cried with twenty thousand voices. Suddenly they turned, as if at a signal, and headed for the open sea. When Diana came down to the beach, the sun shone on her face, turning her skin the color of wet sand. "Do you remember the day we met?" she asked.

Michael lowered his camera. "Is this a trick question?"

She shook her head. "I was thinking about those people at the Research, and out of the blue I remembered that a few hours before I saw you, I stole a lab book and hid it in the garden. I know exactly where I put it." Her eyes said, I want to go home.

Michael took her hand. "Wherever you are, I am," he said.

"Let's get packed," and she smiled.

I thank the Literary Arts Board of the Australia Council for a two-year fellowship, which enabled me to work on this novel.

Many people gave generously of their time and knowledge to help me with research. In the scientific and medical field, I wish to thank: Dr. C. H. Tyndale-Biscoe and Dr. Mark P. Bradley of the CSIRO; Dr. Peter Stewart of the Faculty of Science, ANU; Mr. Robert Chiew of the Microbiology Unit, West Mead Hospital; Dr. David McGavin, Webster's Vaccines; Dr. David Handelsman, Royal Prince Alfred Hospital; Dr. Ian Clarke, Prince Henry's Institute for Medical Research; Dr. Gerry Both, CSIRO; Allison Imrie, St. Vincent's Hospital AIDS research; Dr. Marcus Sacks; Mr. David Woods, for a fascinating afternoon on anesthetics; Stan Wesley of the Public Works Department for information about air-conditioning; and finally and especially Dr. Andrea Nicholson, of the Garvan Institute, for the hours she spent explaining and demonstrating the processes of genetic engineering.

In the animal field, I am in the debt of Fred Spiteri, Steve Wilson, and Judith Chapman for information about raptors and for eyeball-to-eyeball experience with eagles and falcons; and vets Mike Cannon and David Bell. Paul Davies, chimp keeper at Taronga Park Zoo, was very helpful, as was Tim Childs of Animal Liberation.

On illegal matters, I was greatly assisted by Commander Ray Philips of the Australian Federal Police and Detective Superintendent Bill Harrigan; at Sydney Airport, Chief Inspector Ian Taylor of the Australian Customs Service was most generous, as was Mike Shannon of the Civil Aviation Authority.

Nancy Knudson helped me understand running a small airline; Audrey Raymond explained decoupage, and Jon Lewis talked to me about photography.

Trevor and Jackie Bolte of West Wyalong were most generous with their time and hospitality while I was doing research in and around the town.

For reading the manuscript and making suggestions, I wish to thank friends John Lonie, Sandra Hall, Carl Harrison-Ford, and Rose Creswell, and for her editing, Bryony Cosgrove of Penguin Books. At a late stage, Bob Asahina of Simon & Schuster, New York, made some excellent suggestions. My agent, Tony Williams, was, as ever, encouraging and cheerful.

On page 42, the reference to seeing one's reflection in a black piano lid is from the poem "A Mirror We Face All the Time," by Jaan Kaplinski of Estonia. I thank my dear friend for his permission to use it.

Blanche d'Alpuget's first book, *Mediator* (1977), a biography of Sir Richard Kirby, arose from the interest she shared with him in Indonesian affairs. Like *Monkeys in the Dark*, her novel set in Indonesia and published in 1980, it received critical acclaim. *Turtle Beach*, her second novel, set in Malaysia, was published in 1981, and won the Sydney PEN Golden Jubilee Award, the the South Australian Government's Bicentennial Award for Literature, and the Braille Book of the Year Award.

Her biography *Robert J. Hawke*, published in 1982, broke new ground for writing about living political figures. It won both the NSW Premier's Award and the Braille Book of the Year Award in 1983.

Her third novel, *Winter in Jerusalem*, published in 1985, explored aspects of the Lebanese war and was awarded the Australian prize in the Commonwealth Literature Award of 1987.